HARMO

MW00715095

- BY -

Nicholas Ifkovits

Also by Nicholas Ifkovits

Cloud Drops .... Nov. 1998
Other Dreams .... Nov. 1999
Harmony's Angel ...... July 2001
Strange Change .... July 2002

Counter-Force Press

Mesa, Colorado

Counter-Force Press
POB 138
Mesa, CO 81643

Library of Congress Control Number: 00-090398

Title: HARMONY'S ANGEL

ISBN: 0-9651700-4-7

Manufactured in the United States of America.
  10   9   8   7   6   5   4   3   2   1

Cover art by Debra Ann Alire.

Dedicated to my wife and best friend in all the world, Debra Ann Alire.

Go to the ant, thou sluggard; consider her ways, and be wise....
— Proverbs 6:6

HARMONY'S ANGEL

1

DEMONS AND DARKNESS

Sixteen-year-old Harmony Hammerschmidt had fantasized several different ways of killing Uncle Bob in the three years since being abandoned by her mother on his doorstep, the top floor of a three-flat on Chicago's far west side. In fact she entertained three murderous fantasies specifically.

The first involved killing only Uncle Bob. She would simply wait for some Saturday afternoon when Aunt Rosie was gone with the kids, Melissa, 12, and Jerry, 13, and with Uncle Bob passed out drunk on the couch, beat him to death with Jerry's baseball bat and flee.

The second fantasy entailed the exact same scenario with the difference that Harmony would hide in the hall with the bat until Aunt Rosie returned with the two monsters. In the moment of stunned surprise when the three found the hideously beaten Uncle Bob, she'd sneak up from behind and with a series of quick wacks crush their skulls as well.

The third fantasy involved locking the two brats in their bedrooms with wedges under their doors, then dousing Uncle Bob and Aunt Rosie with gasoline as they slept, flipping a lighted match on them and bolting out the backdoor.

With a sigh Harmony finished peeling the last potato, cut it up into the water in the pan on the stove and turned on the heat before Aunt Rosie's squawk popped the bubble of her dark dream. "You'd better check that roast again. You know how your Uncle Bob gets when you overcook the meat," she warned from the couch where she lay sprawled like a beached whale 16

5

hours a day puffing cigarette after cigarette while watching an endless stream of soap operas and TV talk shows.

"Yes, Aunt Rosie," Harmony sighed. Turning to the oven, she opened it and peered inside. Like she could tell anything from *looking* at the damn roast! Like she had x-ray vision and could see through to the center to see if it was properly pink! She had followed the directions in the cookbook and if Uncle Bob or Aunt Rosie didn't like the way it came out Aunt Rosie could start making dinner herself for a change. And breakfast, too. And Melissa's and Jerry's school lunches as well.

"How's it look?" Aunt Rosie asked the moment Harmony closed the oven and turned to the pile of dirty dishes in the sink.

"Like a roast in an oven," Harmony wearily replied, turned on the water and squirted dish washing liquid into the sink.

"Don't get smart with me, young lady, or you can go find somewhere else to live. We were nice enough to take you in when your mother dumped you, now you just shut your mouth and earn your keep. Understand?"

"Yes, Aunt Rosie." Auntie and Uncle weren't looking out for the abandoned child, they were using her. And sadistically abusing her. In fact the whole family was. And enjoying it immensely.

It had been a chilly, wet, late September afternoon a month before her thirteenth birthday when her mother had told her to go up to Uncle Bob's and wait, assuring Harmony she'd only be a few minutes. The "few minutes" turned out to be forever. Harmony identified her from a police photograph a week later. Her mother had died in a car wreck somewhere in Texas.

Harmony never really knew her father, but had the vague memory of him that a three-year-old might, like the time he rapped her across the mouth for spilling her milk. Perhaps it was her most vivid childhood memory because that was the morning he left and never came back.

That had been 13 years ago. But now, at 16, Harmony Hammerschmidt was a "looker" with large, blue-green eyes, even white teeth, full sensuous lips and a dimpled smile that melted the heart of every boy at school. A slender, blossoming figure and long golden locks the color and texture of young corn silk were her crowning features.

Harmony heard the door open and turned just as Jerry, Melissa and Uncle Bob burst into the kitchen, the two kids jabbering excitedly about their day at Great America Amusement Park. "You should've been there, Harmony," Jerry breathlessly exclaimed, "the corkscrew roller coaster was awesome!"

"Unbelievable!" Melissa put in.

Forcing a smile, Harmony nodded, inadvertently catching the familiar wicked gleam suddenly alight in Uncle Bob's eye. Damn. She shouldn't have smiled. It seemed to incite him. Harmony studiously turned back to the dirty dishes heaped in the sink but it was too late. In three quick strides Uncle Bob crossed the linoleum-tiled floor and with an open-handed slap, smacked Harmony hard, her head bonking off the corner of the kitchen cabinet. Bursting into tears and clutching the side of her head, Harmony turned away sobbing, "What was that for?"

Snotnosed smirks on their faces, Melissa and Jerry giggled while Uncle Bob shrilly bellowed, "That's for whatever you did today that I don't know about! Now quit your ballin' and finish your chores or I'll really give you something to cry about!"

"As a matter of fact the little smartass was getting sassy with me just before you came in," Aunt Rosie squawked from the couch, "so she had *that* one coming and she knows it!" To her children she said, "Jerry, Melissa, you've got some time before dinner so let's hit the books."

With a last cruel giggle for Harmony, both kids said, "Okay, ma," and scampered off to get their schoolbooks. Returning to the living room, they plopped down at the coffee table in front of the TV.

Fixing himself a tall whiskey and soda, Uncle Bob called from the kitchen, "Wanna drink, Rosie?"

"Sure," she called back. "Heavy on the ice."

Harmony finished with the dishes, set the table, opened a can of cat food and plopped it on a saucer, set it on the floor near the door by the water dish and kitty litter box, tossed a salad, whipped up mashed potatoes, put it on the table with the gravy and peas and called out none too loudly, "Dinner's ready."

Taking their places at the table, the family was quiet, tense, every anxious eye on the master of the house as he sliced roast beef. Four slices later Uncle Bob laid the carving knife and fork down and glared at Harmony for one long, silent moment.

"Yes?" Harmony's whimper was barely above a whisper.

"The meat is overcooked again. It's supposed to be pink in the middle," he informed her evenly.

With head bowed and tears welling up, Harmony replied in a voice that trembled, "I'm sorry, Uncle Bob. I cooked it three minutes less than last time."

"Well, Harmony, I'm sorry, too. But until you can learn to make a decent roast I don't think you deserve any."

There was an almost audible sigh of relief around the table. There would be no violence tonight. No plates of food breaking off Harmony's head or the roast flying across the room. Uncle Bob apparently hadn't enough whiskey in him tonight.

"Okay," Harmony replied gratefully. The bastard. He knew roast beef was one of her favorites. But at least he hadn't thrown it at her. Nor was she being sent to her room. At least she could still have some of the mashed potatoes and gravy, peas and salad, thank you. She was hungry.

After dinner the rest of the family gathered before the TV while Harmony cleared the table and washed, dried, and put away the dishes. Then, from the edge of the living room she timidly asked, "Is it all right if I take a shower, Uncle Bob?"

Sprawled in his favorite easy chair, Uncle Bob looked up. Slurping his fourth whiskey and soda, he had to think about that one. "Okay," he grunted, "but don't take too long. You're always wasting water."

"I won't," Harmony promised and immediately headed

down the hall to the bathroom.

She carefully chose the times when she requested a shower. With the bathroom doorknob broken off and not even a hook on the inside, her cousin Jerry, and sometimes her uncle, had a habit of coming in while she was showering and under the flimsiest of pretexts drawing the shower curtain aside with a sudden need to talk to her. One time her uncle even grabbed her arm and told her to turn around and look at him. Now with everyone gathered in front of the TV maybe they would leave her alone.

But it was not to be. The sadistic games the entire family played on her were beginning to develop sexual overtones. God only knew where these games would end. Thirteen-year-old Jerry had his own ideas about that. So did Uncle Bob. Stumbling into the kitchen to fix his fifth whiskey and soda, he noticed the dirty cat food saucer on the floor. Immediately enraged and cursing, he slammed his empty highball glass on the counter.

Everyone looked up from the TV, his wife asking with a frown, "What's wrong?"

"Harmony didn't finish washing the dishes."

"Well get her butt out here and make her finish! She knows better than that!"

"Ya damn right I will!" Uncle Bob huffed indignantly and stormed down the hall. Kicking the bathroom door open with a bang, he stomped into the room, snatched the shower curtain aside, grabbed Harmony by the hair and yanked her dripping-wet-naked from the shower. Marching her down the hall and through the living room to the kitchen, he stopped in the doorway, pointed at the dirty saucer and screamed, "What's that!?"

"What?" Harmony cried, burning with humiliation, the giggles of Jerry and Melissa in her ears as the two scrambled to their feet to watch.

"The cat dish!" Uncle Bob shouted, "you left the dirty cat dish on the floor!"

Naked, wet, shivering, Harmony tearfully explained, "But

it still had cat food in it when I left."

"Well it doesn't now! Wash it, and when you're done with that mop up this water you dripped all over the floor." Roughly shoving her, he ordered, "Now get to it!"

Tearful, humiliated, resentment burning in her soul, the whole smirking family watching, a naked Harmony snatched up the saucer, washed it, crossed to the closet, retrieved a mop and mopped up the water, then fled wailing down the hall to the bedroom she shared with Melissa. Diving beneath the covers, she pulled a pillow over her head and lay their sobbing.

                    *   *   *

Tossing and turning, Harmony groaned. With quickened breath she managed to stifle a shriek and sat bolt-upright in bed, the sheets damp, her face hot. The nightmare of Uncle Bob and Jerry taking turns at her while Aunt Rosie and Melissa egged them on was too close for comfort. Suddenly Harmony knew what she had to do.

It was dark. Quiet. After a moment she rubbed the sleep from her eyes and looked at the bedside clock glowing amber. Eleven-thirty-five. In the shadowy gloom three feet away she could just make out the lump of covers that was Melissa in the other twin bed.

Soundlessly slipping from the blankets, Harmony quickly dressed in the dark, finishing with jeans, rust-colored sweatshirt, and sneakers. Being careful not to rattle the coat hangers, she took her denim jacket from the closet, spread it open on the floor, tossed an extra change of clothes on it, her hairbrush and Bible, folded the jacket into a neat little bundle and tied it off with the sleeves.

Quiet as a church mouse Harmony picked up the bundle, crept to the door, opened it a crack and peeked out. Aside from the steady ticking of the grandfather clock all was dark and still. With a glance at Melissa she stepped out, eased the door closed and slipped down the hall to the kitchen.

Setting her bundle on the table, Harmony tiptoed to the utensils drawer, slowly pulled it open and in the faint glow of the street lamp outside the window, withdrew a 15-inch butcher knife. The same knife Uncle Bob had used that evening to carve the roast. Smiling with the thought, Harmony turned to the kitchen door, unlocked and opened it a crack, then turned and crept back down the hall clutching the carving knife.

At Uncle and Auntie's bedroom door she hesitated momentarily, listening, took a deep breath and gently eased it open. The darkened room was filled with the snarfling snore of Uncle Bob and the labored breathing of fat Aunt Rosie. The smell in the warm, closed-up room was revolting like rotting butter. But that didn't matter now. Nor would it ever matter again.

Barely breathing, Harmony tiptoed to the mirrored dresser where Uncle Bob always laid his keys, change, and wallet. Keeping her eyes on Uncle Bob, Harmony snagged the wallet, retreated to the hall, eased the door closed and crept back to the kitchen. Setting the knife on the table, she stuck the wallet in her back pocket, grabbed her bundle, and gently closing the door behind her, slipped out into the balmy May night.

She hurried through the backyard to the garage to the alley where she paused long enough to dig through the wallet. Finding $43 dollars, Harmony pocketed the cash, tossed the wallet in a dumpster and set off at a brisk pace down the alley.

At Grand Avenue she turned west. Without a specific destination in mind all Harmony knew was that she was going to put as much distance as fast as possible between herself and Uncle Bob. And she damn well might not stop until she felt the Pacific Ocean lapping at her toes.

Harmony had been hoofing it at a steady, determined pace for nearly an hour and it was well after midnight when she made River Grove, the first suburb west of the city proper. There, a seedy-looking, unshaven man with long, greasy hair and a dirty gray trench coat suddenly reversed direction, crossed Grand Avenue and started following her.

He probably forgot something, just remembered, and is going back to get it, Harmony silently assured herself. *But then, why had he crossed the street?* She picked up the pace a little. When Harmony checked again, her increased speed had not increased the distance between her and the man. In fact the distance between them had *decreased.* Okay, Harmony said to herself, fake him out. At the next corner she turned right onto a residential street. If the man followed she was going to walk up to a house like it was hers. That would put him off for sure.

Walking quickly, in fact just short of a run, the next time Harmony looked back she was shocked. Not only had he followed her, but he must have run to catch up the moment she had been out of sight around the corner. With fear-borne adrenaline pounding through her veins Harmony looked back again and her heart leapt to her throat. Only some 20 feet away, the dirty, unshaven man was *running straight for her!*

Tucking her bundle under one arm like a football, Harmony bolted across the street, jumped a picket fence, ran between two houses and cut across to the next block with nary a look back.

HARMONY'S ANGEL

2

SCREWED AND TATTOOED

As the prosecutor droned on Quentin caught himself dozing for the third time. He struggled with a wide yawn and made a halfhearted attempt to straighten out of his slouch, the admonishment of his mother to sit up straighter in court echoing through his mind like a song that wouldn't quit. "It might help," she had said over and over again during the past two weeks of the trial. And she really believed it. That was the funny part. Quentin smiled with the thought.

* * *

The world called him black but he was actually the color of hammered bronze. He had a wide, friendly smile that revealed two rows of even white teeth, a prominent nose with large, flared nostrils and deep brown eyes set close together. His jet-black hair was close-cropped with twin lightening bolts that looked more like Nazi "SS" insignia carved to the scalp on the left side just above the ear. Despite his mother's pleas he had refused to alter his hair style for the court sessions. "My haircut don't matter!" he had stubbornly insisted. He was dressed neatly if simply in a tan suit, pumpkin-colored dress shirt open at the neck, black loafers and dark brown socks. He didn't like ties.

Having recently completed a three-year stint in the army 21-year-old Quentin was already registered to attend college in the fall. Although football-player-size with a chest like a beer

13

barrel and biceps that could break a rusty chain, he wouldn't be going out for football. Or basketball either. He was an artist. He sculpted in clay and was good at his art because he loved it. Because, in a way, it was something only he could do. Something that he conceived in his mind and shaped with his hands, lovingly, carefully, until it was just right....

*   *   *

Quentin felt an elbow nudging his side. Snapping awake, blinking against the harsh light, he suddenly sat up straighter. "Quentin," his lawyer whispered, "the judge is addressing you. Answer him!"

"Huh?"

"I said," the judge repeated tediously, "have you anything to say for yourself before I read the verdict?"

The verdict? Oh yes, he had plenty to say. But what good would it do? Would it change anything? The judge was white, the jurors were white, his lawyer was white, and the prosecutor was white. Quentin felt very black in a white world. He locked eyes with the judge and slowly shook his head.

"Very well, then," the judge responded, looking down at Quentin over the tops of his bifocals. He picked up some papers and began reading in a tired monotone....

*   *   *

The bar was packed, wall to wall people. A good, hard rockin' band was kickin' out some heavy, foot-stompin' jams. Although Quentin was the only black in the place he didn't feel conspicuous. Having grown up in Wheaton, a predominantly white, upper-class suburb of Chicago, he was quite comfortable around large groups of whites. In fact most of his friends were white. And other than a few racial slurs and fistfights years ago when a child in grade school, Quentin rarely had any trouble. Tonight would be the exception. The exception that would change his life forever.

Wendel Globstuel, assistant manager of a Cicero super-market, mentioned to a friend that the nigger was looking for trouble just by being in the place. Wendel looked tubby in his bright-yellow *Shazamm!* T-shirt, and his black horn-rimmed glasses and mustache were comical. He drove an SUV that bogged in second and hadn't had an oil change in 38,000 miles. And Wendel thought he was hot stuff. He didn't know his foxy looking, just a pinch overweight wife cheated on him Friday nights when he worked late. And he didn't know she was about to goad him into a fight he would lose.

Being 6' 2" and well-built, Quentin moved among the ta-bles and people like a friendly giant, nodding and waving to friends as he made his way through the crowd. He stopped to talk to some friends and didn't hear Wendel call him a nigger, nor did he see Wendel's wife dip her napkin in her scotch and soda, wad it up, and whip it at him, catching him splat on the left cheek.

Quentin turned to see who the culprit was, immediately dis-missing Wendel and his group. They were much too old for such nonsense. But right next to them were three guys and their dates, all looking barely old enough to be in the place, all swig-ging beer, their table littered with numerous empty bottles. Dragging a hand across his cheek confirming the assault, he asked in a knowing voice, "Okay, so who the wise guy?"

They shook their heads, motioning to the neighboring table. Just then another wet, wadded-up napkin bounced off his other cheek. Quentin whirled around and stared at Wendel and his group. Six middle-aged adults. Drunk, laughing, Wendel's wife in the act of wetting another napkin in her drink. Catching Quentin's eye, Wendel snarled loudly, "What're *you* lookin' at, boy!?"

For a moment Quentin was confused. He hadn't asked for it. "Someone threw somethin' at me," he said in a low, embar-rassed voice.

"What, *boy!?* " Wendel yelled, angrily shoving his chair

back and standing up.

Pointing at Wendel's wife, Quentin firmly replied, "The chick threw somethin' at me."

"Don't talk to my wife like that, nigger!" Wendel bellowed for the audience that was quickly developing.

"I didn't say nothin' 'bout your wife." Quentin retorted.

Figuring he had the kid on the run, Wendel made a move towards him, fists clenched. "Apologize to my wife, *boy!*" he screamed hoarsely.

Quentin glowered. Surprising some and bringing satisfied smiles to all, he looked the man dead in the eye and said evenly, "I ain't your boy. Your boy's at home."

"Don't smart-mouth me, nigger," Wendel snapped, "or I'll knock you right on your ass so help me God!" Then he quickly returned to his seat.

Glaring down at the man, Quentin stood with hands on hips, legs apart, "Then step outside, bitch," he said tightly.

"You wanna fight?" Wendel asked, his voice rising with the sudden realization that he was in this alone. Then he got a bright idea. "Okay," he said with renewed confidence, "I'll go outside and fight with you."

"Fine," Quentin replied, then turned on his heel and made his way through the crowd for the exit.

A grinning Wendel took a moment to look around his little entourage. They smiled back at him. With a half-shake of his head he rose from the table and sighed, "Ah well, guess I'll just have to teach this nigger a lesson." With that he turned and shoved his way through the crowd.

Wendel was a 43-year-old wimp. He went to the toilet and combed his hair. He returned a little less aggressively, dusting his hands together and saying proudly, "I guess that takes care of him."

"Oh Wendel!" his wife blubbered, slurping at her scotch.

Wendel chuckled. "What the heck, it was nothing."

Yes it was. It was cold outside. Quentin gave the man three

minutes and when he didn't show, yanked the door open and went back inside muttering, "I ain't puttin' up with this bull!" He made his way straight to Wendel's table and ordered, "Get yo' ass outside, bitch!"

Knowing a fight in the bar would be broken up in a matter of seconds, without warning Wendel leapt from his chair and lunged at Quentin. They toppled backwards across a table and crashed to the floor, scattering drinks and guests in all directions. The band played on.

Wendel came out on top astride Quentin. Punching him square in the face with his right, he was winding up for the second punch when Quentin managed to give him the heave-ho. Struggling to regain his dominance, Wendel slipped in the mud and the blood and the beer spilt on the floor, planting his fat face square on the jagged edges of a broken glass bottom. Trying to get up, blood spewing from the ghastly wound, he slipped yet again and landed on his butt where he sat shrieking like a woman, "My eye! God help me, I lost my eye!"

Slipping and sliding in the puddles of disgust and broken glass, a blood-splattered Quentin just managed to regain his footing when four cops came through the door like gangbusters, two of which immediately grabbed Quentin from behind, slammed him face-down across a table and snapped the cuffs on. The third helped Wendel to a chair while the fourth called for an ambulance on his portable. And before you could say Jack Splat it was all over.

"Hey, officer!" one onlooker called, "the black kid didn't start it, the other guy did."

"Yeah," someone else volunteered indignantly.

Ignoring them, the officer who called for the ambulance shouted, "Okay, everybody clear the way, I've got an injured man here!" He moved forward clearing a path through the crowd while his partner followed, guiding a stunned and blubbering Wendel by the elbow.

The other two cops yanked Quentin to his feet and shoved

him roughly towards the door with a terse, "Okay, man, let's go."

*   *   *

Quentin suddenly sat up straighter in his chair. "What?" he whispered hoarsely.

"Ten years," his attorney said drily. "You've got ten years in Stateville for assault with a deadly weapon. You're going to Joliet. You shouldn't have taken his eye out with that broken glass bottom. If it hadn't been for that maybe I could've gotten you off." The young court-appointed attorney looked down at his hands. "I'm sorry, kid, I did my best."

Quentin was frightened, his eyes wide with disbelief. "How long do an appeal take?" he asked as he wiped his sweaty hands on his trousers.

His attorney was already packing up. "We've exhausted all our appeals, Quentin," he said heavily, truly sad he had lost because he sensed Quentin had been telling the truth all along. "Unless new evidence comes up," he paused, hating to say it, "there's nothing more I can do."

This was it? Prison? Quentin could hear his mother crying somewhere. "But I didn't *do* nothin'!" he cried, throwing his hands up in exasperation. "I told ya, the man *fell* on the broken glass bottom, I didn't stick 'em with it!"

The judge immediately rapped his gavel, declaring loudly, "Quiet, son, this court is adjourned."

Then, as if caught in a nightmare, his heart sinking like a stone, officers were leading Quentin from the courtroom to a waiting van.

HARMONY'S ANGEL

3

WILD CHILD

As he ambled down the sidewalk Christopher Robin could tell from three doors away that no one was home at his house. His parents always left a single light burning in the kitchen to ward off burglars. Silly people. Any burglar who watched the house for more than a day would catch onto that trick. And who'd wanna ripoff their place, anyway? Though it wasn't the worst looking house in that working class neighborhood of Franklin Park, just west of Chicago, it wasn't one of the better ones either. Besides, there hadn't been a burglary in their neighborhood in years.

Christopher was glad his parents weren't home. He left the sidewalk and cut across the neighbor's front lawn to the side door near the back that led into the kitchen. He was always glad when his parents weren't home. A single clay flower pot with a couple of crusty dead petunia plants sat on the window sill. The boy stuck his hand into the pot and retrieved a key with which he let himself in.

Kicking the door shut with one foot, he turned to the small kitchen table and the note that was under the salt shaker. The boy snatched up the note, knocking the shaker on its side and scattering salt across the table. There it would remain until his mother returned. "Dear Chris," the note began, "your father and I have gone up to Uncle Harry's for the weekend. We wanted you to come along but you didn't show up for dinner or call so we assumed you weren't coming home tonight. Love, mom."

At 5' 9" Christopher Robin was unusually tall and broad-

19

shouldered for a 16-year-old. Otherwise he looked like any other street punk; black leather jacket decorated with a gaudy array of zippers and chrome trinkets, jeans, T-shirt, and scuffed black army boots.

Long, straw-colored hair fell from the top of his head almost to his shoulders. And although big for his age his large blue eyes and round, ruddy cheeks gave him a little-boy face. Sometimes when in trouble that seemed to work to his advantage. But when he got angry it was hard for anyone, especially adults, to take him seriously. They just laughed as if he were a little kid, and that only made him angrier.

Christopher threw the note down. Good. He hadn't wanted to go to Uncle Harry's anyway. The only thing to do there was watch the adults get drunk, and that had lost its thrill years ago. Worse yet, every time the old man got smashed he'd take it out on him. Christopher didn't mind the abuse so much when they were home alone, but around others the boy found it intolerable. So, of late, he avoided the family as much as possible.

He was surprised to find his parents didn't seem to mind. In a way they sort of grew to like it. It was a lot easier not having him underfoot. It gave his parents a freedom they hadn't experienced since before he was born and they felt quite at ease going out for the evening, or even the weekend, and leaving only a note of explanation.

Given the situation the boy had more freedom than he knew what to do with. And increasingly he found himself faced with a dilemma. Most of the kids his age had to be in at a certain time, particularly on school nights. Thus would he find himself alone on, say, a Saturday night at 10:00 o'clock with nothing to do and nowhere to go except home. And who wanted to go home to a dark, empty house? That was all right though. He was learning to like it. He didn't seem to have much choice.

But Christopher Robin had no doubt about what his choices were tonight. Tonight he was going to have fun. Tonight he was going to do something he had never even dreamed of doing before. The boy was so excited by the prospect of the night's adventures he was barely hungry. But he suspected it might turn out to be a long one so he hastily threw together two bologna sandwiches and wolfed them down with a tall glass of milk.

One of the older guys who hung out at the strip mall on Grand Avenue had given him the idea. Told him about sneaking out his old man's car at night—until he'd gotten caught. "What kind of car was it?" Christopher asked skeptically, thinking how impossible it would be to sneak out *his* dad's car at night. The deep-throated rumble of the big V-8 would wake even the dead, let alone the sleeping. Anyway, the kid replied that the car had barely been a year old. A brand new midsize Ford. Then he went on to tell how he'd gotten caught, but Christopher wasn't listening. The conversation had started his brain-gears turning. The kid was pretty dumb in the first place to take the car out with his parents home. *Why not wait until they were gone?*

His father had made one mistake. When his son reached 14 years of age he started taking him out for rides in the country and on back roads allowing the boy to drive, all the while coaching him. By age 16 Christopher was pretty good behind the wheel and knew more than a few tricks.

Christopher finished the last of his sandwiches, guzzled his milk and set the glass down with a bang. Then he was out of his seat and rummaging through his parent's room for the keys. He found them in the sock drawer. His father always kept the keys in the dresser, but fearing burglars, altered which drawer he put them in when he went away. Duh.

Once Christopher had the keys he stopped for a moment and looked down at them in his open palm. Now it was time to slow down and start savoring every moment, every sensation. At 16 driving automobiles was about the only thing the kid couldn't get enough of besides sex. Letting loose a spontaneous shout of elation, Christopher tossed the keys into the air, caught them in one hand behind his back and headed for the garage.

As he raised the overhead door and flicked on the lights the smell of gasoline, oil and automobile made his heart quicken. He stood in the doorway gazing at the machine. It was the most beautiful car Christopher had ever seen; a gleaming, 1969 candy-apple-red Mustang. It was the 428 Cobra-Jet model, its hood painted flat-black, a shaker scoop rising up through its center. Of course it was equipped with four-on-the-floor, high-performance clutch, heavy duty shocks and Ford's version of mag wheels. And of course this almost 40-year-old collector's dream, a mere 40,000 original miles on the odometer, would stand up on its rear wheels and howl when it was floored.

But his father never beat the car. In fact it was in showroom condition and totally original. With the foresight of a prophet, in 1969 he had perceived that 30 or 40 years later there wouldn't be many 428 Cobra-jets left in the world. If a man were to buy one, keep it original, in the garage, and only drive it once a month to keep all the parts lubed, somewhere down the road he'd be able to sell it to a collector for big bucks.

It had taken every spare dime he'd had at the time to make the payments but some 40 years later he'd been proved right. Through an agent he had recently put the car on the market and received an offer of $50,000 from a collector in England. But Mr. Robin decided to hold out for $75,000. Then he'd retire from his job at the box factory, sell the house and move to Florida with plenty enough left over for his son to attend community college if he wanted, although at this point it didn't look like Christopher was college-bound.

Full-coverage insurance on such a vehicle had always been expensive, naturally. But he didn't need full coverage, his father had reasoned, because the car was only out of the garage on Sundays. Dry, sunny Sundays. Thus he felt minimal insurance was enough.

Of course the car was almost an obsession with his father and he tinkered with it endlessly, always adjusting and perfecting or waxing and polishing. And of course Christopher was never allowed to touch the car—except on that rare sunny

Sunday when he and his father were alone on the back roads. It was the only thing they ever did together.

Christopher's hand shook a little as he unlocked the car, his stomach queasy as he slid into the cockpit behind the wheel. And not just from excitement, either. He was scared. His old man would have a coronary if he suspected Christopher was even sitting in the car, let alone contemplating *driving* it. That his father was involved in big-bucks negotiations to sell the car Christopher hadn't a clue.

For a moment he considered saying the heck with it, but then thought, why not? His parents had left him all alone and were out having fun. Didn't he have a right to have some fun once in awhile? Besides, what could possibly happen? He was going to be careful. Maybe he'd just take it once around the block and come home. Take it real easy, too. He couldn't afford to get stopped by the cops. He didn't have a driver's license. But then what did a driver's license matter, he reasoned, as long as he knew how to drive? Besides, next fall he'd be getting his learner's permit so what would a little advance practice matter? What would once around the block hurt?

All his rationalizing hadn't quelled the queasiness in his stomach as he reached for the ignition switch. He turned the key and the engine wheezed, coughed once, sputtered and rumbled to life. Though the engine was tuned to a "T" it hadn't been started in weeks and needed a moment to warm up. The deep-throated burbling of the exhaust sounded strong and healthy, though. And if ever the song of the mockingbird was music to a man's ear the sound of this machine was a symphony to the ears of the 16-year-old boy. It was intoxicating, Christopher already thinking that twice around the block wouldn't hurt.

The engine sufficiently warmed, he put the car in gear, eased the clutch out and nudged her carefully through the narrow garage door. He glanced back to make sure he had cleared the doorway, slipped the trans into neutral, set the parking brake and went back to close the garage door. As it came down with a bang he excitedly hurried back to the car and jumped in.

He sat there for a moment gripping the wheel tightly in both hands, arms straight out, then reached for the gear shift... As he made a right turn out of the driveway and onto the street he wondered if any of the guys were hanging out at the strip mall. Wouldn't they drop a load if they saw him in this!

Once around the block to get reacquainted with the idiosyncrasies of the machine and he felt confident enough to head up to Grand Avenue and the strip mall. So much for once around the block. His confidence was growing with every passing minute. Anxious to impress his new found friends with his dad's butt-kicking car, he was disappointed when he got to the strip mall and found it deserted.

He sat at the corner for a moment, the engine idling easy. The L-shaped strip mall across Grand Avenue consisted of a supermarket, music store, Italian beef stand, laundromat and liquor store.

Quickly revising his plans, Christopher revved the engine. Almost forgetting to look, he gunned it across the four-lane Grand Avenue into the nearly deserted parking lot. Afraid of being scraped by some careless driver he was careful to take up two parking spaces out front of Melvin's Liquors.

He'd bought beer at Melvin's once before and was hoping to do it again. The plan: cruise around awhile, drink a few beers and return to the mall later, which would give the guys time to show up. And then he'd really impress them. Not just with the car but with the beer too. It was funny, though. He hardly knew the guys he was striving to impress. And when they got in their cars to go somewhere they never invited him along. But if he could win their approval, Christopher was sure, he'd have a crowd of his own. As it was now he stood alone.

As soon as the kid came through the door Melvin, of Melvin's Liquors, let out a silent groan and thought to himself, *oh no, the kid probably carries a gun and smokes pot!* Melvin watched as the boy walked to the back of the store and took a six-pack of beer from the cooler. He was big enough, but certainly didn't look old enough, to be in a liquor store. Christopher stopped across from Melvin and set the six-pack on the counter. He looked the older man right between the eyes with deadly seriousness and tossed ten bucks down. Melvin took a deep breath before asking, "Are you old enough?" Crazy, hopped-up gun-toting kids. What was he supposed to do?

"It's for my old man," Christopher answered evenly, his gaze unwavering.

"Yeah," Melvin said, dropping his eyes as he snapped open a bag and slipped the six in. He rang up the sale, snatched the ten bucks and slammed the drawer shut. Now it was Melvin's turn to stare. The youngster knew he was getting away with something and wouldn't dare ask for his change. Melvin knew that. And it wasn't stealing because the kid knew. Everyone else short-changed customers but not Melvin. Short-changing customers was one thing he would not do except with the weird-haired teenagers. They were scary. Besides, they didn't count. They weren't supposed to be buying beer in the first place.

The six-pack securely under his arm, Christopher could scarcely contain his elation. He'd done it! Twice now! Without a word he turned on his heel and left the store. After getting in the car the first thing he did was pull a beer from the bag. He set the rest on the passenger seat, stuck the key in the ignition and snapped open his first beer of the evening. Taking a timid sip, he was surprised anew at how bitter-tasting the stuff was. Christopher took a second small drink and grimaced again, then set the can on the passenger seat and reached for the ignition switch. This time the engine, oiled up and hot, started instantly with a deep-throated rumble.

Christopher tromped the throttle and the car snarled menacingly. With a little chirp from the fat tires he let the clutch out, swung the gleaming red 428 Cobra-Jet around in a tight arc and rumbled across the parking lot. Neglecting to look right or left he pulled out onto the avenue. Providence was with him and the powerful car surged ahead without mishap.

Without a destination in mind he was just driving. East. Towards the city. Gripping the wheel tightly in both hands, head tilted back, he peered over the top of the steering wheel while repeatedly glancing at the speedometer to keep the car within the 35-mile-per-hour speed limit.

Unknown to the boy the first few sips of beer had already affected him ever so slightly, numbing his mouth and tongue. As a result the next few sips he took, cautiously while driving, didn't taste quite as bitter and he congratulated himself on so quickly acquiring a taste for beer. Proof that he was just as adult as anyone.

After awhile he grew tired of Grand Avenue and decided to explore the unfamiliar neighborhoods he was passing through. Flipping on the left turn signal, he peeled off Grand Avenue and onto a dark residential street. He drove a half block up the quiet street, stopped in the middle of the road and drained his first beer. Crushing the aluminum can with a squeeze, he tossed it out the window.

One beer down, five to go. Christopher reached for another. There was a pop and hiss as he snapped open the can, a fine mist spraying the windshield. The boy cursed. His old man would sure notice that. He set the beer on the console and reached under the seat for a rag his father kept there. As he came back up he knocked the can off its precarious perch. It was only on the floor for a split-second before he snatched it up but the beer foamed over the sides, dripping on the carpet, seats and everywhere else he frantically held it until it finally stopped foaming.

Now he'd have to do a major cleanup job on the inside of the car. Cursing a blue streak, Christopher tucked the beer between his legs, slammed the gear shift into first, let the clutch out fast and gunned the powerful high-compression V-8. The squalling tires left hot rubber smoldering on the pavement as the Mustang roared up the street with an accelerating whine.

But Christopher had picked the wrong time and place to

become angry. Before he hit second gear a girl dashed blindly from between a row of parked cars directly into his path, and although his reflexes leapt it was with seemingly dream-like slow-motion that his right foot plunged down on the brake. All four wheels locked up, the tires streaming blue smoke as the car screeched to a howling stop. But not before the girl's body thumped off the hood and went down before the front of the car.

Immediately a frantic little voice whispered in his ear, urging him to run for it and hauntingly reminding him of the time his father jokingly remarked to a neighbor that it would be better to back up over someone you hit rather than leave them alive to sue you. Besides, she was probably dead anyway and what good would him getting in trouble do? Would it bring her back?

The panic-stop had killed the engine. With a trembling hand he reached for the ignition switch, but before he could turn it another force seemed to invade his being, filling him with the nauseating horror of what he was about to do. Shaking uncontrollably he struggled with the door handle, all the while fervently praying to dear God that the girl wasn't dead. The door finally swung open. On legs almost too weak to support him Christopher got out, the stench of burnt rubber thick in the air. With a sick stomach and a pounding heart he went around to the front of the car.

Either he was very lucky or there really was a God who answered prayers. There was no blood. No anguished cries. Instead he found a stunned Harmony sitting on the pavement looking dazed but apparently unhurt. "Are you all right?"

"I think so," Harmony answered, looking up at him dully and trying to focus her striking blue-green eyes. "Did you see the guy that was chasing me?"

"Uh-uh," Christopher shook his head. "Wanna go to the hospital?"

"No," came the quick reply. That was all she needed.

"Then c'mon, I'll take you wherever you're going," he said, anxious to get away before the cops showed up. Surely someone had heard the squealing tires and called by now.

"Okay," she said amiably. Yet she remained on the ground looking around for something.

"What're you looking for?" Christopher asked impatiently.

"My bundle."

The boy frowned, his eyes scanning the area. "There," he pointed, "behind the front left tire."

Harmony turned and grabbed her precious few possessions and got to her feet. "Thanks."

"Forget it. My name's Christopher Robin," he said, eyeing her with interest as she dusted herself off, "what's yours?"

"Harmony."

"Harmony what?"

"Hammerschmidt."

"What!?" Christopher burst out laughing. "That's a funny name!"

"With a name like Christopher Robin I wouldn't talk!" Harmony snapped indignantly. "Where's Winnie the Pooh?"

"I've heard that joke a million times. Doesn't bother me a bit."

"Well I've never heard anyone say my name was funny," she said as she finished dusting herself off.

Looking up, she actually saw him for the first time and was immediately drawn to him by some unknown stirring deep within her adolescent body. Noticing the black leather jacket she was about to ask if he thought he was tough when he spoke first, awkwardly trying to make up for the name-laughing blunder. "Where'd you get a name like that?"

"I got the last name from my old lady's second husband," Harmony answered, "'cause supposedly he adopted me or something. He's dead now, though. Got run over by a big green bus when I was ten. I think he was drunk at the time."

The starry-eyed lad was feeling his own somewhat more prominent stirrings and shifted uncomfortably, totally overlooking the part about Harmony's second father and saying, "A big green one, huh?"

Harmony nodded, adding, "Don't you think we'd better get out of here before the cops show up?"

"Yeah, let's," Christopher agreed, suddenly snapping out of his dream world. Getting into the car, he paused, muttering curses.

"What's wrong?" Harmony asked, tossing her bundle in back and ignoring the seat belt as she got in and closed the door.

"When I stopped my beer went flying and now it's all over the car." He found the can and tossed it out. It bounced off the pavement with a *clink* and rolled into the gutter. Ignoring his own seat belt Christopher turned the key and the big V-8 rumbled to life. Easing the clutch out, he started up the street. Slowly.

"Want a beer?" he asked as soon as they were under way.

Harmony shook her head. "No." Then, cynically, "Do you always drink when you drive?"

He nodded, snagging a beer from the bag and snapping it open. "Always. How do you like my car?"

Not knowing a thing about cars Harmony gave the interior the once over. "Nice."

He simply drove around the block, returned to Grand Avenue and stopped at the intersection. "Which way?"

"Right," Harmony replied.

Christopher made the turn and accelerated up to speed. After several minutes of silence he asked, "So, where were you going in such a hurry when you ran out in front of me?"

"Where were *you* going so fast?" Harmony retorted.

"Just cruising around."

"Do you always cruise around at a hundred miles an hour?"

"Do you always run out in front of speeding cars? You a suicide case or what?"

She looked at him, "No, I'm not a suicide case you moron, I just didn't know there was a maniac on the road when I decided to go for a walk."

"That's some walk." Before she could reply he quickly added, "Look, skip it." Then, "It was an accident. But if I'm going to take you home I have to know where you live." A long silence followed. "Well?" He changed lanes and speeded up.

After a moment Harmony answered simply, "West."

"West?"

"Yeah. Out west."

"But where out west? What town?"

"I... I'm not sure," Harmony stammered.

Then it dawned on him. "Ohhh. I get it, you're running away."

Harmony nodded. "Yeah."

"From what?"

Harmony shrugged. "My aunt and uncle and cousins. They treat me like dirt. Like, they're doing the Cinderella routine on me. I get to do all the housework." Harmony had to stifle the onrush of a sudden sob as the events of only a few hours ago assaulted her memory.

"Hey, take it easy," Christopher said, glancing at her with concern. "Was it that bad living with them?"

Heaving a tired sigh, Harmony turned and stared out the window. "You wouldn't believe me if I told you."

"I don't know about that," Christopher said, "but it sounds like you don't want to talk about it."

Still staring out the window, Harmony answered, "You're right, I don't."

A long silence followed, broken when Christopher brightened with an idea for getting himself a little tail. "Hey!" he exclaimed, "I know! Why don't you come home with me?"

Turning to him, Harmony laughed. "Sure. I bet your parents would just let me move right in, huh? No thanks. I'm hitting the road, pal."

He looked at her and chuckled. It had been a long shot.

Harmony was counting every minute and every mile the car carried her away from her angry uncle. And then she had an idea for getting a free ride across the country. Trying to sound seductive but lacking experience in luring people, she inquired shyly, "Why don't you come with me?"

Now Christopher laughed. "Wish I could but my old man would kill me." Silence followed as he wistfully reflected on the possibility. Although their friendship spanned less than an hour he had developed strong feelings for her even if the feelings were nothing more than the pressure he felt in the crotch of his jeans. Reaching down the front of them he straightened himself and said, "Look, I'll take you as far west as I can but I have to be home by morning. Ten a.m. at the latest."

Harmony flashed him a smile. "Thanks." The steel and glass towers of glowing light were receding into the yellow haze that hung over the city. They were out of the concrete jungle now, distancing themselves from the windy cement canyons and hurrying faceless crowds.

The suburbs went almost unnoticed, the endless rows of tract homes, Quick-Shop stores and strip malls flashing by and left behind before they knew it. And just beyond was rural Illinois with its fields, barns and silos rising against the glowing sky.

Aware of Christopher's eyes on her, Harmony turned to him and was about to ask where they were when something in the darkness up ahead caught her attention. Funny, she could almost *feel* it. Then the realization struck as they approached the railroad grade. Although a fast moving freight train pounded towards the crossing, the black-and-white-striped gates stood in silent attention, the warning lights dark, no bells ringing. "Stop!" she shrieked and grabbed Christopher's arm.

With lightening-quick reflexes Christopher slammed on the brakes. The car skidded sideways, tires smoking as it screeched to a stop only a few feet from the tracks, but not before Harmony's head thumped soundly off the windshield.

She didn't even feel it. She just sat there watching in horror as the oncoming police van neither she nor Christopher had a chance of warning rolled up onto the tracks. Fiddling with the radio, the driver was caught completely unaware as hundreds of tons of cold, unforgiving steel roared down upon him.

The windshield exploded as the train slammed into the van, an ear-splitting screech ripping the night as the crumpled, twisted hulk was pushed 40 yards along the rails where it trundled to the side and plowed up the earth before coming to rest. The panting steel monster, sparks flying from its wheels, thundered to an abrupt halt far beyond the wreckage and all at once it was quieter than the night before Christmas. "My God," Harmony whispered as she stared in disbelief at the crushed blue and white van that had once been a police paddy wagon. Then she noticed a tiny movement near the wreckage. "What's that?"

"What's what?" Christopher asked, quietly cursing under his breath as he moved around in the dark.

"There," she pointed. "I saw something move over there. Let's go check it out." She opened the door and was about to get out when she stopped and looked at him. "What on earth are you doing?"

"That's the second beer I spilled tonight," he fretted. "Now the seat of my pants is all wet!"

"Well there's nothing you can do about it now. Come on."

"All right," Christopher fumed, got out of the car and slammed the door. Things just weren't working out tonight. As they headed for the wreckage he tossed the empty can. It bounced off the pavement with a *clink* and rolled into the gutter.

HARMONY'S ANGEL

4

SICKENED AND SHAKEN

Maybe it was a miracle that saved Quentin. Maybe it was circumstance. A jumble of senseless thoughts flickered through his mind and he rolled over onto his back, an agonized groan escaping from between clenched teeth, eyes squeezed shut, chest heaving, hands clutching at the throbbing pain in his head.

When the big black kid moved Christopher instinctively took a step back, a sense of guilt pervading his mind that he didn't entirely understand nor was capable of acknowledging. Disregarding her own unreasonable fears Harmony dropped to her knees beside Quentin. "Easy," she said softly, laying a gentle hand on his forehead.

Her hand felt wonderfully cool on his pounding head and Quentin's eyes fluttered open. The hellish thoughts trampling his mind were instantly swept away as he regained consciousness. Blinking, he started to sit up. "Easy," Harmony cautioned again, gently restraining him. "Is there anyone else in the van?"

"Yes," Quentin answered tightly, almost breaking into tears, "but I wouldn't go lookin' if I was you. There ain't nothin' you gonna do for him."

Christopher promptly turned on his heel and made straight for the van. It was so thoroughly destroyed he had trouble telling which end was which but finally found a place to stick his head in. After a moment his eyes adjusted to the darkness. What he saw was what a human would look like after being caught in a giant metal-stamping machine. Broken raw ends of gray-white bones protruded through the tattered cloth of a blue uniform, quivering pinkish flesh bulging gelatinous through the numerous rips as the squashed human reinflated in a grotesque, almost cartoon-like fashion. The horrid smell of guts and warm, sticky blood splattered everywhere was overpowering. Gagging, Christopher immediately pulled his head out. Struggling not to vomit-up his dinner of bologna sandwiches and milk, he turned and ran from the scene.

Sickened and shaken, Christopher returned to the others. He found the black kid sitting up now, Harmony on her knees beside him. "And this is Christopher," she was saying.

At the moment Quentin didn't much care. "Where am I?" he asked, a confusion of shrieking sirens beginning to fill the distant night.

Harmony could sense the older black kid's growing alarm. "I don't know, maybe 50, 60 miles west of Chicago," she answered.

Quentin squinted in surprise. "Sixty miles west of Chicago?"

Harmony nodded. "Something like that. Where're you going?"

"I've got a better question," Christopher cut in crisply, staring down at Quentin with hands on hips. "What were you doing in that police wagon? You don't look like no cop to me."

Quentin was still in the brown suit he'd worn to court. Prison garb would be issued upon arrival at the state penitentiary. He hesitated before answering simply, "I was in jail."

"For what?"

"It's a long story," Quentin replied with the slightest irritation, his muddled mind not fully aware of the conversation or Christopher's belligerent attitude. He was floating with his thoughts, trying to focus his eyes.

Dissatisfied with that answer Christopher decided to needle him a bit and sneered, "What're *you* lookin' at, *boy!?*"

That did it. With a disbelieving shake of his head Quentin looked up at him. It was Wendel Globstuel all over again, and although every fiber in his body ached he was on his feet like lightening and had Christopher by the front of his jacket, drawing it tight around the boy's throat in one large, strong fist. Breathing hard, Quentin said through clenched teeth, "If you think a leather jacket with trinkets hangin' on it makes you bad you is in for a surprise, *boy!*"

Christopher's mouth went dry, his stomach fluttering as his macho stance withered and his legs involuntarily drew in to protect his manhood. Out of the corner of his eye he caught Harmony watching with rapt attention. Burning with humiliation he stammered, "I—I just wanted to make sure you were okay before giving you a ride in my car."

Being a sensitive artist, Quentin felt sort of sorry for the kid regardless of his offense. And in an odd way because of it as well. How could a young man with everything going for him (white, anyway) be so ignorant? So blind? So dumb? With quiet contempt he inquired, "So, who asked you for a ride?"

Christopher's shame was complete as he lowered his eyes. It was the longest silence he had ever endured. When Quentin finally spoke the heat of his anger had cooled somewhat but his words had not. "It's practically my duty to whup yo' ass up an' down this street. Do you realize that?"

Christopher nodded glumly.

"And I wouldn't blame you if you did!" an incensed Harmony interjected.

Quentin's eyes shifted to her momentarily, then he released Christopher. But he wasn't finished. "Any brother with any sense would beat you senseless. Maybe break an arm or two. You owe me an apology, *boy!*"

Christopher looked up at the man and solemnly stuck his hand out. "I really am sorry. I don't even know why I said it."

Quentin hesitated, pondering a faint sense of dissatisfaction, a feeling that blood should be let, revenge taken. Still, he'd seen enough blood lately to last a lifetime. And besides, he hated fighting even when he could easily win because he hated hurting people. And the thought of seriously injuring someone accidentally as in the case of Wendel Globstuel made fighting repulsive to him whether he was in the right or not.

"If you need a ride someplace my car's right over there," Christopher offered meekly, feeling foolish with his unaccepted hand still extended but afraid to withdraw it.

Quentin's mind was made up for him as he heard sirens drawing near. There was no time to lose. "Thanks," he said and slapped Christopher's hand, "let's go." Christopher breathed a sigh of relief as the three of them turned to his father's beloved car and hurried off. Halfway into the backseat Quentin paused, let out a long, low whistle and remarked with a grin, "This car's so macho it's probably got hair in the wheel wells!"

Christopher chuckled nervously and said, "Yeah," then they all got in and shut the doors. The panic-stop had killed the engine and it took a moment before it popped-off and rumbled to life. Turning the car around in a tight circle, Christopher maneuvered along several side roads until he found a detour around the stalled train. "Anyone want a beer?" he asked as soon as they were back on the highway and cruising at a steady 60 miles an hour. He held up three beers clinging to a plastic ringer and dangled them before Harmony like a bunch of grapes.

She shook her head.

His headache receding, Quentin said, "Thanks," reached forward and plucked one for himself. There was a pop and hiss as he snapped open the can.

Christopher was still trying to get Harmony to have one. "You sure?" he asked.

"Yes I'm sure," she replied, unable to hide a note of irritation in her voice.

"Well open one for me," Christopher ordered. He had already forgotten his most recent emasculation.

Harmony felt like telling him to open his own beer but not wanting to jeopardize her ride popped the top on one and handed it to him.

"Thanks," he said as he took the can. Experiencing a slight headache of his own he wondered if the beer wasn't responsible and took a swig of the bitter, foamy liquid. Glancing in the rearview mirror at Quentin, he asked, "What'd you say your name was?"

"Quentin."

"Mine's Christopher and this is Harmony."

"We already met," Quentin said with an approving grin.

Glancing back, Harmony shot him a smile.

Christopher just said, "Oh." Then, "Where're you from?"

"Wheaton."

"I'm from Franklin Park."

Turning in her seat, Harmony asked, "What'd you do?"

Quentin looked at her questioningly.

"I mean to get in jail?"

"Nothin'," he replied curtly.

"Oh come on!" Harmony scoffed, "They don't put people in jail for nothing. Not even black people."

"The hell they don't! *I* got put in jail for nothin', little sister. For a fight the other guy started. Maybe the worst of it be I never even managed to hit him. He hurt himself when he slipped and fell. An' *I'm* goin' to jail for it!"

"Not anymore," Christopher smiled big in the rearview mirror. "What kind was the other guy?"

"White!" Quentin spat the word with disgust. There the conversation died and they rode in silence. It was Quentin who broke it. "How far you goin'?"

Christopher caught Quentin's eye in the mirror as he spoke, "I have to be home by morning but I'll take you as far as I can before then."

"Sound good to me," Quentin replied, settling back in the seat, silence prevailing as each turned to their own thoughts.

Unconsciously Christopher was speeding up, his mind distracted by thoughts of how to get Harmony to give up her pants and her plans of running away and coming home with him instead—if only for the weekend.

Quentin finished his beer and crumpled the can. "Where we puttin' the empties?"

"Out the window," Christopher answered without taking his eyes off the road.

Harmony turned and offered to take the can when a disturbing sight caught her eye. "Uh-oh," she muttered.

Following her gaze Quentin twisted around in his seat and looked back. He had only one word to say. "Damn!"

"What's going on?" Christopher asked, glancing at Harmony, but she was on her knees now and turned completely around.

"There's a police car comin' up fast from behind," Quentin answered.

But Christopher was already watching the flashing red lights in his mirror when it dawned on Quentin; every cop within 50 miles probably heard about the train wreck on their radios. By now they might even know it hit a police paddy wagon carrying a prisoner. Maybe they were even aware that he was missing from the wreckage. If this cop pulled them over he'd be sure to see him sitting in back and put two-and-two together. All at once Quentin knew what he had to do. Get out of the car and make a run for it. Fast. Hide someplace and lay low until the heat died down and he could figure out what to do next. "Stop an' let me out," he ordered.

Tensely gripping the wheel, Christopher replied, "I can't."

"Why not?" Quentin shot back. Time was running out.

"Because I don't have a driver's license and if my dad finds out I'm driving his car he'll kill me!"

"If I get caught I'm gonna be doin' ten years. Stop an' let me out." Slamming a fist to the back of Christopher's seat, he shouted, "NOW!"

"But I'll get caught!" Christopher cried, his eyes darting between the road and the mirror.

"You think you gonna outrun the cops, stupid?" Quentin demanded.

"Yeah!" Christopher retorted defiantly. "This is the fastest car in three counties!"

"Let me out first," Quentin replied evenly. This white boy was crazy.

"I can't stop now!" Christopher cried. And with that he pushed the accelerator to the floor. The steady drone of the quadra-jet rose three octaves and the front of the car lifted slightly as it exploded down the highway with an accelerating whine that pressed everyone into their seats.

"Crazy honky," Quentin spat with disgust. If he wasn't killed in the ensuing chase he'd be going back to jail. For sure. With nothing left but prayer he asked for deliverance and closed his eyes. Damn! Freedom had been so close!

The car dipped low into a right-hand curve and came out of it with smoking tires and a snarling surge of power, the flashing red lights of the squad car dropping from view. Then Christopher saw it go by on his left, a dirt road disappearing straight into the woods. Up ahead the highway curved again. Just maybe....

"Hold on!" he shouted, suddenly slamming on the brakes and whipping the wheel hard to the left. Harmony's head thumped off the windshield for the second time that evening as the car careened sideways with a howling screech, skidded around a full 180 degrees and came to an abrupt halt in the middle of the highway. The stench of burnt rubber stung their nostrils as blue smoke swirled around the car and spiraled into the air. Without waiting to catch his breath Christopher hit first gear, floored the accelerator and popped the clutch. The tortured rear tires bit hard and with a howling whine the stubby little Mustang screamed up the highway back the way it had come.

"You gonna play chicken with a cop!?" Quentin shouted. Harmony was down on the floor now, lips moving in whispered prayer, the double black-and-blue knot on her forehead swelling painfully.

"I'm going to take a chance on the only chance we got," Christopher said grimly, his eyes narrowed with concentration. Once again he shouted, "Hold on!" and slapped on the binders, the tires howling as the car started to careen. At the last moment he released the brakes, whipped the wheel hard to the right and found the dirt road just where he expected. Moments later gravel was rattling and pinging off the sides of the car as they churned yellow dust down the narrow, tree-lined lane. Christopher switched off the lights, the rusty DEAD END sign hidden in the overgrowth of shrubbery going unnoticed.

Sensing victory he cried, "We made it!" He was glancing over his shoulder at Quentin and boasting about his superior driving skills when the road suddenly disappeared, replaced by a pond shimmering silvery beneath a quarter moon. He never even had time to take his foot off the accelerator let alone hit the brakes. With his own boastful words still ringing in his ears and a shriek from the suddenly over-revved engine as the wheels left the ground, the little Mustang sailed off the end of the road and splashed down in the middle of the pond in a great explosion of water.

Above their terror-stricken cries for God's help was the crinkling, crackling sizzle of hot steel hitting cold water. The car sank fast, black water rushing over the windshield and casting them into pitch darkness. Everywhere were fountains of water. It jetted in through the vents and burst up in hissing streams through the floor where the clutch and brake pedals were.

Everyone was yelling and pounding at the doors and windows. Christopher frantically pulled at the door handle, pushed against the door and then slammed his body against it but the door wouldn't budge. The water pressure outside was keeping it tightly closed. And then Quentin was crawling over the front seat and yelling at Christopher to get out of the way and let him try. Christopher, terrified and irrational, fought back viciously, yelling at Quentin that it was his door and he could do what he wanted with it. At that point Quentin had enough. Forearming Christopher in the face, he lunged over the front seat and grabbed the door handle so hard it snapped off in his hand. The car hit bottom with a soft bump.... Already the water was up to their knees and rising fast.

While Christopher cursed, Quentin was on his back pounding at the rear glass with both feet and making mumbled vows to God. In the meantime Harmony had made a discovery. "I got it!" she shouted. When no one took notice she shouted again but couldn't make herself heard over Christopher's cursing and Quentin's vowing so she just did it. Taking a deep breath, she began cranking the window down as hard and fast as she could. Immediately a cascade of water exploded into the car and Christopher's last words were lost in a gurgle.

Harmony swam straight for the top and broke the surface gasping for air. Coughing and spluttering, Quentin and Christopher popped up one after the other. Treading water, catching their breath, blind panic subsided into frightened confusion. Then Harmony began to swim off towards the farthest side but Quentin hollered for her to come back. She had only just started out and turned around. "The road's this way," he gestured. Immediately they all started swimming for shore.

Quentin reached it first. Out of breath and shivering in his wet clothes he trudged out of the water and sank down wearily on the grass, stretched out on his stomach and folded an arm under his head. He heard the others coming up from behind but was mildly surprised when Harmony, Christopher at her side, lay down next to him, the full length of their bodies touching. The closeness eased their shivering. Then they scrunched even closer together and were warm. For a long time they lay very still, the chirrup of crickets the only sound until one small, worried voice broke the peace. "What am I going to do about my hair?"

"Your hair?" the boys asked in unison, lifting their heads.

"It's going to look just awful in the morning," Harmony

wailed, "and my brush is at the bottom of the lake!"

At first no one said anything, then the boys burst out laughing, Christopher exclaiming, "I just totaled my dad's trophy car. A car he has carefully preserved for almost 40 years as an investment for his retirement, and you're worried about your hair?" Suddenly Christopher wasn't laughing anymore and his speech started breaking up.

Quentin could tell he was about to start crying and quickly reached across Harmony to put one huge, warm hand on the boy's shoulder. "Take it easy, kid," he gently urged, "just be glad nobody dead."

After a few seconds of rapid breathing Christopher relaxed. Face buried in the crook of his arm he offered a muffled, "Thanks, Quentin, whoever you are."

"Forget it," Quentin replied. Funny how it made a person feel good to have compassion. Then, forgetting that he didn't believe in God, figured it was just one of the many positive aspects of being created in his image.

Harmony was exploring the painful double-knot on her forehead when they all heard the crunch of tires on gravel coming up the road fast, bright headlight beams piercing the darkness. There was no time to move but the grassy shore sloped up steeply to the road 20 feet away. Barring an on-foot search it was Quentin's bet this would hide them. "Lay flat as you can and don't move a muscle!" he whispered harshly.

No one hesitated to comply. Holding hands, Christopher and Harmony lay as flat as possible. Seconds later a squad car skidded to a stop at the very edge of the road, its headlights cutting a sharp swath through the darkness several feet above their heads. A spotlight flashed on and swept the area. It tilted down and played on the water briefly, the beam only inches above them. The entire search took less than a minute, then the spotlight was snapped off. Tires spitting gravel, the car backed around and tore off down the dusty road at high speed. For a moment no one moved nor scarcely breathed. Then Quentin got to his knees. Craning his neck to see up the road, he got to his feet and said, "It's okay."

Relieved, Christopher and Harmony stood up. "Well, what'll we do now?" Harmony asked.

Christopher didn't hear her. He was looking out over the water for some sign of the car, but there was none. It was gone. He turned back to his friends.

"Might as well stay here," Quentin was saying. "Those cops gone now an' won't be back."

Christopher shrugged, "We got nowhere else to go."

"Wish I had me some black-eyed peas, collard greens, ham hocks and corn bread," Quentin grinned.

"I wish I had my dad's car back," Christopher was not grinning.

"Let's lie down again," Harmony said, "I'm freezing."

So were the boys. They lay down as before. When they were curled up and settled in like a litter of kittens Christopher said in a quiet, flat voice, "I can't go back." Both Harmony and Quentin withheld comment. "I can't ever go back," he continued. But there was only silence and the chirruping of crickets in the still night air. Maybe he'll feel differently in the morning, Quentin was thinking as his mind began floating on the edge of sleep.

Harmony was starting to drift off too. "Come with me, then," she mumbled, her head resting on Christopher's shoulder, her face warm by his neck.

I'd love to, Christopher thought drowsily, saying aloud, "Maybe Quentin, too." But neither of his companions had anything further to say on the matter. They were sound asleep.

5

ANTS AND ANGELS

Even before Harmony was awake she knew Christopher wasn't beside her. She opened her eyes and lay there staring up at the clear, opulent blue sky and wondering where on earth she was. All at once she remembered and sat bolt upright, turning every which way and calling softly, "Chris?" Quentin was gone too. She called a little louder, "Christopher? Quentin?"

Getting only silence for a reply, she stood up and began brushing leaves and bits of grass from her damp, wrinkled clothing. They'd be back. Probably just out scouting around and decided to let her sleep in. It was a little after eight and as fine a spring morning as Harmony could remember, though she hadn't seen too many out in the country. Warm sunshine streamed over the treetops into the clearing, and the air, filled with the chatter and chirping of birds, smelled fresh and clean like just after a summer rain.

Harmony finished straightening up and with a wide yawn, stretched luxuriously. She liked where she was. It reminded her of a postcard she had seen from somewhere down south, the yellow dirt road disappearing into the trees being the proverbial "lover's lane," and the pond the "old swimmin' hole." The only thing missing was the ancient cottonwood on the bank with a knotted rope hanging from it.

With a jerk of her head she tossed her blonde hair back. Raking her fingers through the tangled mass in a futile attempt at combing it, Harmony strolled down to the edge of the pond thinking she might catch a glimpse of the car now that it was daylight, but there was no sign of it. She turned her back on the water and scanned the area. For the first time a tiny twinge of apprehension mottled her thoughts as she wondered if the boys had abandoned her. It was then she spotted the gnarled old stump some 30 feet off to her left. Curiosity drew her to it, but once there she decided it would be a good place to sit and wait for the boys. She turned and was about to sit down when she froze. The stump was covered with thousands of ants. Red ants. Harmony immediately leapt clear, backed off a safe distance and examined the stump with discerning eyes.

The sides of the stump were perforated with hundreds of holes all in neat little rows with busy ants scurrying in and out. And stretching from its crumbling top to its very base were two long caravans of ants that moved ceaselessly in opposite directions, crossed the diggings piled at the foot of the stump and disappeared into the grass.

Harmony felt a stinging bite under her jeans and impulsively slapped her right leg. One of the little critters curled up and tumbled out, dead. Staring in amazement, the girl backed still farther away. It was a mammoth ant colony. By far the biggest she'd ever seen. And, oddly, there was something sinister and frightening about it. Later she would reflect it was either getting bitten by the ant or the gnawing hunger in the pit of her stomach that caused her to call out in a loud voice, "Breakfast time!"

As if they had heard her say it hundreds of ants instantly and collectively froze. Harmony's mouth dropped open. She could hardly believe her eyes. "Did you guys freeze up like that because I said, 'Breakfast time'?" she asked in a quiet voice.

In the space of two seconds and much scurrying all the ants changed places, then stood absolutely still. Harmony's eyes grew wide with astonishment. Overcoming a growing fear, she inched closer and closer to the gigantic ant colony. Getting down on her hands and knees, she brought her face to within a foot of the stump and studied the ants minutely. To her utter amazement they seemed to be STARING BACK!

Unable to suppress a tiny, self-conscious laugh, she looked around once to make sure she was alone, then, feeling like a fool, asked skeptically, "If you've said 'yes' once how do you say 'no'?" Again there was a flurry of activity as the ants changed places and stopped, only this time they went through their whole song-and-dance routine not once but twice. Harmony slapped her forehead. "It can't be!" she exclaimed aloud.

"Who're you talking to?" The voice shot through her like electricity. "I thought I heard you talking to someone," Christopher said as he and Quentin walked up from behind.

"Uh, no," Harmony stammered and got to her feet. "But look at this," she pointed to the stump. "Have you ever seen hundreds of...."

"Hundreds of what?" Christopher asked, stepping closer to examine the ant colony. The ants were busily scurrying about their domain. "What about it?"

Her face suddenly brightened with an idea. "Ask the ants."

"Ask the ants?" Christopher looked at her dubiously.

"Yes," Harmony replied, "just go ahead and talk to them."

Quentin gave Christopher a bemused smile. Shaking his head, Christopher peered closely at her. "Are you on something?"

"Of course not!" she replied indignantly.

"Okay," Christopher gestured at the stump, approaching the matter anew, "what should I ask them?"

Harmony shrugged. "Ask them anything you like."

Rolling his eyes, Christopher scoffed, "C'mon, Harmony!"

"No!" she insisted, stamping her foot, "I'm serious!"

"Okay, okay," Christopher relented. Turning to the stump, he asked, "Ants, what time is it?" Looking at her with a long face, he paused. "They aren't saying anything, Harmony."

Harmony looked crestfallen. Then she started giggling. "Silly!" she exclaimed, "how're they supposed to know what time it is? You think they got little wristwatches on their left legs? It's gotta be a 'yes' or 'no' question."

Christopher was fed up. Turning from the stump, he said, "Let's go."

Quentin elbowed him gently. "Let me ask a question."

"It's gotta be a 'yes' or 'no' question," Harmony repeated.

Quentin nodded and leaned closer to the stump. "Is today Sunday?" he asked softly. Waiting for the expected response, Harmony also leaned closer. When nothing happened Quentin straightened up and caught Harmony's eye. "I don't get it. What's the joke?"

"Joke?" Harmony looked at him curiously, some kind of odd spell falling away from her.

At that point Christopher threw his hands up in disgust and loudly exclaimed, "Okay, Harmony, that's very funny, now c'mon. We've found the perfect spot to hop a freight train."

Still feeling weirdly disoriented she turned to Christopher. "You have?"

"Yeah. That's how we're getting to Texas."

"Texas? On a freight train? Is it safe?"

Christopher wasn't quite sure what she meant by that but replied, "Sure it's safe. I wouldn't do it if it wasn't."

"Are you coming with us?" she asked Quentin.

He nodded. "Might as well, but I don't believe I'll be goin' all the way to Texas."

"We'd better get going," Christopher interrupted, taking Harmony's hand, "or we'll miss the train. And there's probably only one that comes by all day, too."

Quentin took the lead, Christopher and Harmony hand in hand as they made their way through the dappled sunlight of a small grove. The woods brought them to a meadow abuzz with bees and hummingbirds, the sun warm on their backs as they tromped through the wet, waist-deep grass, their clothes collecting burs. Two minutes later they were standing on a blacktop road. The walk through the meadow had Harmony's tennis shoes just as soaked as the previous night and they squished when she walked. "So where's the tracks?" she asked, picking a bur off her sock.

"'Bout a quarter mile up this road there's a little bridge over the tracks," Quentin answered. "We can hop a train from there."

"From a bridge?" Harmony questioned.

"Why not?" came Quentin's quick reply, "bet it's been done before."

Harmony shrugged. "Let's go."

They walked fast and in no time were standing at the concrete sides of a narrow, one-lane bridge. Looking down on the shiny steel rails below, Christopher said, "I hope we didn't miss the train."

Shading his eyes with a hand, Quentin looked up the tracks to the east until the rails became one thin line to the shimmering horizon. When he saw the feeble yellowish light of an approaching train he cried jubilantly, "There's one comin' now!"

They waited for ten silent minutes. At long last Harmony turned to Quentin. "I don't think it's moving."

Absently biting his lower lip, Quentin stared up the rails. "I think," he started slowly, "you absolutely right."

"Why would it be sitting there all this time?" Christopher asked.

"I don't know," Quentin shrugged, "maybe there's been an accident."

"We know that happens, don't we?" Christopher grinned.

"That's for sure," he agreed, "but at least we know there's a train comin' our way. That should be counted as good luck."

"As far as luck's concerned we've got something going for us," Harmony intimated, planting the heels of her hands on the rough concrete bridge abutment and hoisting herself to a seat on it. "And do you guys know why?"

"No. Why?" Christopher was wary after the ant episode.

"Because my angel's been watching out for us," Harmony answered confidently, bouncing the heels of her shoes off the concrete.

"Your angel?" Christopher gave her a sidelong glance. Quentin silently looked on. Shaking his head, he turned away wondering if maybe he wouldn't be better off ditching these two half-witted youngsters.

"Yes, my angel," Harmony said firmly. "Who do you think's been getting us out of all this trouble? We could've been killed several times last night. But look, we got away every time."

"Chris sure outran them cops!" Quentin cut in with a grin.

Christopher stopped and looked at him blankly, then continued, admonishing with a chuckle, "Harmony, everything that happened to us last night, both good and bad, was just luck and didn't have anything to do with angels. Where'd you get a crazy idea like that?"

Harmony looked perplexed. "From the Bible," she answered. "All throughout the Bible it talks about angels. Didn't you ever read the Bible?" Her glance shifted to Quentin. "Either of you?"

"I went to church," Christopher said proudly, "when I was little."

"You still little," Quentin quipped with a smirk.

Christopher opened his mouth in rebuttal but Harmony quashed Quentin's diversionary tactic by interjecting, "Then you must know there are angels."

"Harmony," Quentin began tediously, feeling like a grade-school teacher, "the Bible is a storybook written by men long ago. It's a fairy tale an' not meant to be taken literally. Everybody know there ain't no such thing as angels."

Christopher started laughing derisively and calling heavenward, "Hey angel, come on down here and give us a lift to the train!"

Joining in the fun, Quentin snickered, "Do your angel talk to you when you're lonely?"

Then Christopher turned serious. "God, Harmony, I can't

believe you're so dumb. You're like a little kid. Do you believe in Santa Claus and the Tooth Fairy, too?"

"All right," Harmony said with hurt defiance, "go ahead and make fun of me. See if I care. But look who was crying to God for help last night. You and Quentin *both* were!"

"Oh c'mon!" Christopher scoffed, revealing a trace of concern for the girl. "There's no such thing as angels or God and you damn well know it!"

"He be right, Harmony," Quentin put in. "Originally God, he a creation of ancient man's mind to explain things he couldn't understan'. Even in modern times it be comforting to believe there's a super being who's goin' to make everything all right and bring justice to an unjust world. But that's all just a fantasy started long ago. It's not real. If you want to live in the real world you gotta learn to deal with reality, girl," Quentin finished, satisfied he had convinced her.

Harmony was flabbergasted. "But Quentin!" she exclaimed, "last night you were pleading with God to help you. PLEADING WITH GOD! And now you stand there and deny he exists!" She shook her head. "I just don't understand it."

"Last night a different matter," Quentin said defensively. "I was in a blind panic, afraid I was goin' to die."

"But in those moments when you were pleading with God to save you, you believed. For that moment you automatically and without question accepted God. Don't you see what I'm getting at?"

Quentin numbly shook his head. "No. I was in a panic last night. Irrational. Everybody get that way when they about to die. It's natural to fear dyin'."

"Yes, but is it natural to plead with a being that doesn't exist? Even within your own imagination?"

A thick silence hung in the air for several seconds. Then Christopher spat disgustedly, "Everybody knows there's no God and you know it too!"

"No I don't know it!" Harmony stubbornly insisted, adding,

"used to be some people thought the world was flat, too. They *knew* it. Hah!"

"That just shows how stupid you are!" Christopher heatedly retorted, the insults flying back and forth as the argument grew more fierce by the moment.

Quentin put an end to their bickering by loudly proclaiming, "It's movin'!"

Harmony and Christopher instantly ceased arguing and turned to peer up the tracks. "I see it!" Christopher shouted excitedly.

"Me too," Harmony said half to herself, fear gnawing at the pit of her stomach with the thought of actually jumping from the bridge onto a moving train. "Why don't you go first?" She turned to Quentin. "In case the train's going too fast."

"Thanks, you make me feel real indispensable." After a moment he added seriously, "I think it'll be pretty easy to tell how fast the train's goin' just from lookin'. If it's goin' too fast we don't jump, that's all."

"Who'll go first?"

"I will," Christopher volunteered.

"Harmony'll go second," Quentin put in.

Christopher nodded. "Sounds good to me. How about you, Harmony?"

"Sounds good to me."

"Okay," Quentin went on, "when the train reaches us everybody wave so the engineer don't get suspicious or nothin'."

Several minutes later Christopher let out a long, low whistle at the sight of the three-engine train. "It must be over a hundred cars long!"

In response to their waves the engineer gave a short, double-blast on his twin air horns, then they were feeling the throbbing thunder of the massive diesels as the train rumbled under the bridge. As soon as the third engine cleared the bridge Christopher zipped up his jacket and hoisted himself onto the concrete and sat on the edge, feet dangling in space, waiting for just the right moment to jump.

After several tense seconds he leapt, landing square on the catwalk of a boxcar, arms outstretched, knees flexed as he struggled to maintain his balance on the swaying roof. Once secure he turned around, giving the thumbs-up signal, and was surprised to see how faraway his two friends already were. The train was picking up speed.

"Okay," Quentin said, "anytime you're ready I'm right behind you."

Harmony nodded and climbed into position. With a pounding heart she watched as one boxcar after another passed beneath her feet.

"Hurry," Quentin urged, "there ain't much time."

Within her heart crying out for God's help, she leapt. Her left foot hit the catwalk but her right missed and skidded out from under her on the dew-slick sheet steel. As she went down the boxcar lurched. The roof wasn't where she expected and she hit hard, getting the wind knocked out of her. Grappling frantically for the catwalk, Harmony grabbed on, the sharp teeth of the grate biting painfully into her flesh as she bounced to the edge of the roof. With tears streaming across her face and gasping for breath, she hung on for dear life, her feet hanging precariously over the edge.

Christopher saw what happened and in his frantic haste to reach her, tripped and fell, almost rolling off the roof himself.

Quentin immediately vaulted into position, hesitated for just a moment, then jumped. Both feet hit squarely in the center of the catwalk, the grate biting into the soles of his shoes. He teetered, caught his balance, and then with the poise and grace of a seasoned sailor, sprinted up the jolting catwalk and leapt from car to car until he reached Harmony.

Gripping her tightly at the wrists, Quentin easily pulled the 95-pound girl to safety. Terrified, she clung to him tightly, her tangled mass of blonde hair streaming in the wind as they stood upon the swaying roof of the boxcar that rushed towards the western horizon with ever increasing speed. A moment later Christopher was beside them. "Are you all right?" he asked breathlessly.

Harmony nodded, broke away from Quentin and turned to him. He took her securely in his arms and the three stood close, lightly holding onto each other and rocking with the motion of the train. "What'll we do now?" Harmony asked, her trembling voice revealing the fear she still felt. "We can't just sit up here on the roof."

"We got to find a car with an open door," Quentin offered rather loudly to be heard above the rush of the wind and the clatter of the jouncing car.

Christopher looked doubtful. "How'll we get inside from up here?"

After a moment Quentin conceded, "Yeah, I guess you're right. Got any ideas?"

"Yeah. Ya know how hopper cars slant inward on both ends?"

Quentin nodded.

"Well right on the end, under the slanted part and just over the wheels, is a little flat area. We could ride there. When we're going through a town we lay flat and hope no one sees us."

"Sound good to me," Quentin said agreeably. "If there's a hopper car like you talkin' 'bout on this train."

Christopher looked towards the front, then towards the rear. "There is!" he exclaimed. "I think. It's kind of hard to tell for sure from this far away."

Quentin shrugged. "All we can do is try. Let's go." And with that he turned and led the way towards the rear of the train. Harmony followed right behind him, holding onto his thin black belt. Christopher brought up the rear.

When they reached the end of the car it took them a good three minutes to talk Harmony into jumping across the gap. At first she wanted to climb down the ladder and cross over on the coupling, then climb up the other side. But they managed to convince her that it would be too much work and far more dangerous. After a lot of coaxing she finally agreed.

Quentin jumped first, then turned and waited for her with open arms. Hesitating for just a moment, she backed up and took a flying leap over the chasm.

After that they ceased stopping to size up every jump and would just leap in turn, one after the other, and continue on their way. Once Harmony had confidence it was easy.

When they reached the hopper car they stood looking across at it. "That the car you had in mind, Chris?" Quentin asked.

"Yeah. See how it slants inward from the top? Right below that is a little platform over the wheels." They all leaned over for a better look.

"We'd even be protected from the rain some," Quentin observed.

"It looks excellent, Chris," Harmony chimed in.

Quentin was about to jump across to the hopper car but paused while the train clattered through a crossing, then he leapt. Because the hopper car had five large, square hatches in the roof it lacked a catwalk. "Be careful!" Quentin shouted across to them, "it's kind of slippery."

Harmony went next, jumping into Quentin's waiting arms without incident. After Christopher made it safely across, Quentin went straight for the ladder that disappeared over the side and climbed down to the platform below. When Harmony started to follow, Christopher nudged her. She stopped and turned. It was the look on his face and the clumsy way he reached for her that told her what was coming next. When their awkward, inexperienced lips met, what had been forced inexplicably became natural as she folded into his strong, secure arms. They held the embrace for a long moment, tenderly exploring each other's faces with gentle kisses.

When Christopher and Harmony finally climbed down the ladder and swung around to the platform, they found Quentin leaning against a steel strut and gazing out over the endless, rolling farmland. He didn't turn around but kept his eyes on a distant tractor creeping across a field. To Quentin the rhythmic click-clack of the wheels was sad music. He wouldn't be going home for a long time, if ever. At last he turned around. "What took you guys so long?"

"Nothing," Christopher smiled, giving him a sly wink Harmony didn't see.

Quentin nodded and quipped, "Glad to see you two found each other. I thought last night you was goin' to get it on in the front seat at a hundred miles an hour while tryin' to outrun the cops."

"Wasn't that incredible!" Harmony burst out as if she had enjoyed it.

"What's incredible is Chris droppin' that car into the pond. If he hadn't we wouldn't be here right now. We'd be in jail."

"Well believe me, I didn't do it on purpose," Christopher intoned. "I'd give anything to have that car back right now. That was my old man's pride and joy and a retirement investment. With one dumb move I wiped him out."

"Well they ain't nothin' you can do about it now," Quentin said, "'cept forget it." With that he went to the edge of the platform, held onto a crossbeam and leaned out to see ahead. Pulling himself back in he announced, "There's a town comin' up. We better take cover."

Without hesitation Christopher and Harmony lay flat on their stomachs. After a moment Quentin did likewise, the three lying side by side across the width of the platform, Harmony in the middle. "Do you think anyone will see us?" she whispered.

"Ain't no need to whisper," Quentin said loudly, "nobody gonna hear us. An' nobody gonna see us, neither."

"What makes you so sure?" Harmony asked.

"Because no one gonna be lookin' for someone hidin' on the train, and not expectin' it, they won't see it."

As they approached the road they could hear the warning

bells growing louder, then the train rumbled through the crossing, the clanging bells quickly fading. The train rolled through two more crossings as cars, shops, buildings and people flashed by. In a matter of moments the small community was far behind and they were once again racing across the countryside, the high-stressed steel of the hopper car creaking and groaning to the steady clatter of the wheels. "I think it's safe to say we're not gonna be spotted," Quentin said and sat up.

Christopher and Harmony both nodded and also sat up, Harmony asking, "What're we going to do about eating? I don't know about you guys but I'm starving."

"Starve," Quentin said glumly, "for now, anyways."

"When we get off this train the first thing we're gonna do is buy some food," Christopher assured his friends.

"You got money?" Quentin asked.

"Of course. Never leave home without it," he grinned.

"How much?"

"Twenty U.S. government-issue green stamps!" Christopher proudly proclaimed.

"Wow," Harmony said sarcastically, "that's a lot of money, Chris."

"Well how much dough do you got, miss smartass?"

Smiling primly, she replied, "Forty-three bucks."

"Well at least we not gonna go hungry," Quentin interjected, "but let's stick with this ride for awhile and get our selfs a safe distance from Chicago. What'd you guys say?"

"I'm all for it," Harmony quickly agreed.

Stretching out on his back and folding his hands behind his head, Christopher said amiably, "Whatever you guys want." Harmony kicked back beside him and Quentin took his station at the edge of the platform to keep an eye on things.

The sun was high and hot now, shining down warmly on the two young bodies lying close together. In time the gentle swaying and rhythmic clatter of the wheels rocked them into a blissful sleep in which time ceased to exist.

For Quentin each minute was 30, each hour eternity. He was acutely aware of his empty, grumbling stomach and his heart thumping in his chest. Struggling to hold back tears, he faced a cold reality. A reality so bleak and unsettling it could make even the loveliest of spring days appear gray. Home would have to be wherever he found it. Maybe for several years. Maybe forever. Who knew? His chest swelled and he swallowed hard. He was glad his companions were asleep when the tears finally spilled hotly down his cheeks.

6

CHICKENS AND NEGROES

In a dream Christopher was in that final race, sweeping around that last curve with a triumphant blast of power. The police car flashed by, and then the explosion of water as they crashed into the pond and sank into the murky depths. Through it all his father's face surrounded him, as if Christopher were in a fishbowl, his father looking in from every side.

A rumbling bang rippled the length of the train and Christopher snapped to an instant sitting position. Wet with sweat and disoriented, he stared wide-eyed into the blackness. Quentin, too, leapt awake. Harmony was a little slower. "What's going on?" she asked through a yawn. She was jolted to full awareness when, coming to a dead stop, the train shuddered and banged for the last time.

"We'd better get off this train," Christopher whispered, "there might be someone walking around out there checking for riders."

Quentin couldn't have agreed more. Getting to his knees, he crawled to the edge of the platform and peered out into the darkness. First towards the front, then the back. "Don't see nothin' from here," he said softly.

Christopher followed his example at the opposite side of the platform. "Me neither," he whispered over his shoulder.

"Why do you suppose it stopped?" Harmony asked in a normal voice.

"Shhh!" Both boys admonished her with a forefinger to their lips. In answer to her question, Quentin whispered, "Probably to drop a car."

"Or pick one up," Christopher put in.

"Whatever." Quentin didn't want to banter about trains. "Let's move while we still got the chance." They climbed down from the platform and stood absolutely still, ears straining, eyes searching, but all they could hear was the distant, low rumble of the powerful diesels idling up front. Just beyond the rear of the train were the lights of a small town.

As they started off, Harmony startled both boys by breathlessly exclaiming, "Look!"

Hearts pounding, they spun on their heels. "What!?"

"Isn't it beautiful?" she sighed, pointing to the horizon. The last light of day was a blood-red river that snaked its way across a darkening western sky scattered with shimmering stars, where it flowed between cloud-puffs and out of sight somewhere between the heavens and the earth.

Momentarily captivated by the sight, the boys gawked for a moment, then Quentin abruptly turned away. "Let's go," he said, starting towards town at a fast clip, his footsteps crunching in the gravel.

Christopher and Harmony almost had to run to catch up. The pace slowed, though, as they approached the tail-end of the train, both boys becoming wary and sharp-eyed for railroad workers. With none to be found they continued on. "Well, the sky was certainly worth stopping to take a look at," Harmony said once they were safely past the train. They walked beneath a huge grain elevator, its four massive silos lined up in a row along the tracks. "I mean, how many perfect sunsets do you get to see in a lifetime?" she continued chattily.

Neither of her companions said anything. They were almost to town now and Quentin and Christopher were still all business. No sense getting busted at this point. Leaving the tracks, they crossed a strip of dew-wet grass for a sidewalk, its broken slabs tipping up and down, weeds pushing up through the cracks.

The outer edges of town were littered with a few

dilapidated buildings, broken beer bottles, and the stench of organic fertilizer. An old soda can tinkled across the street, blown by the wind. A candy wrapper scraped by. Even in springtime it was a dusty place.

Coming upon a wind-battered corrugated steel warehouse, its sides bowed and folding in on themselves, Quentin stopped. Above a large sliding door was a weather-beaten wooden sign over which a single light bulb glowed weakly. Digging at a grain of dust in the corner of one eye, he was just able to make out its faded blue lettering; "Greensprings, Iowa, Warehouse and Storage Company," he read aloud.

"Well now we know where we are," Christopher quipped sarcastically.

The sarcasm was lost on Quentin as he replied, "Not really. Iowa a big state. Could be we way south or way north, or even east or west. God only knows."

"Don't start talking about God," Christopher warned, "or you'll get Harmony started again."

"If you want to go to hell that's your business," Harmony snapped, "I don't care."

"And if you want to go to jail," Quentin interjected, "just keep standin' here talkin' till the cops come."

The three were a motley-looking crew as they walked into town. Harmony's rust-colored sweatshirt was wrinkled, her tangled hair a mess. On the end of her nose a spot of black soot on her otherwise dirt-smudged face was cute in a childlike way.

Christopher looked pretty road-weary, too. His hair hung in greasy little ringlets around his face, his T-shirt dirty and shriveled from the previous night's dunking. His black leather jacket seemed to have fared well, though.

By far Quentin looked the worst. His dress clothes were the least resistant to dirt. His trousers were so shrunken and wrinkled they were up around his ankles, and his tan suit was covered with black grime from the platform of the hopper car. While the others could dust a lot off their jeans, jacket, and sweatshirt, it was hopeless trying to dust it out of Quentin's wrinkled tan suit. It left him feeling very uncomfortable, for he was a very clean, neat person, but there was simply nothing to be done. Not for the moment, anyway.

Downtown Greensprings Iowa was nothing more than a bar and grill, a *Cold Beer* sign glowing neon-blue in the window, and across from that, a little grocery with a laundromat on one side and a hardware store on the other. The town's motoring needs were served by a single gas station just up the street. "The place looks pretty dead," Christopher commented. Aside from a car and two dusty pickups nosed to the curb out front of the bar, the town was deserted.

"I see a light on in the grocery store," Harmony said hopefully.

"Might be worth a try," Quentin shrugged and started across the street. He reached the door and twisted the handle. Turning to the others, he shook his head. "Closed."

"No it's not," Christopher pointed, "look, there's someone behind the counter."

"Yes it is," Quentin insisted, rattling the door, "See?"

At the sound of the door the clerk looked up from counting the day's take and saw the three kids peering in through the glass. He shook his head and pointed to the clock on the wall. It read 7:30 p.m. Completely absorbed in his work, the man resumed counting.

Stepping up to the door, Christopher hammered on it, causing the clerk to look up with a frown.

Laying a restraining hand on Christopher's arm, Quentin urged, "Let's hit the bar an' grill an' get somethin' there."

Christopher irritably shook off Quentin's hand. "No. Just leave me alone a minute." He pulled a crumpled $20 from his pocket and smoothed it out against the glass so the man could see it.

With a huff the slight, middle-aged clerk threw down what he was doing and came around the counter. He still wore his white apron splotched with beef stains. Thick, wire frame glasses were perched on a beaklike nose and the crown of his head had a large bald spot. "We're closed," he shouted through the door, "can't you see the sign?"

"I know," Christopher shouted back, his voice echoing off the dingy brick buildings and empty streets. "But look, I've got $20 bucks here and we just want to pick up something real quick."

The clerk looked as though he were thinking about it.

"C'mon," Christopher begged, "It won't take ten minutes, and you could use the money."

Finally giving in, the clerk unlocked the door and let them in. "Okay, but make it quick," he said, critically eyeing Quentin, the "ss" insignia carved into the side of his head, and the filthy suit. "You kids fall into a coal bin or what?" he asked.

Quentin smiled weakly and bobbed his head once.

Charging up the aisle, Christopher was already gone. Harmony grabbed a shopping cart and ran after him. Keeping a low profile, Quentin sidestepped the man and hurried after his friends. The clerk watched silently as the three kids hustled up the aisles grabbing everything in sight.

"Here!" Quentin called, grabbing a loaf of bread and tossing it to Christopher, who deflected it into the shopping cart.

"Basket!" Christopher cried jubilantly.

They grabbed cans of soup, sardines, pork and beans. In the meat section they took bacon, hot dogs, bologna. Quentin snagged a half-gallon of milk and Harmony a quart of orange juice. Christopher grabbed a 12-pack of soda.

Halfway through the store Quentin held up a hand, suddenly calling a halt to their hysteria. "Hold it! Just hold it!" The other two turned to him with questioning faces. "I got a suggestion," he stated flatly.

"What?" Christopher and Harmony asked in unison.

"Why go an' spend all our money here? Why not just spend what we need for a meal tonight an' hang onto the rest? We got a long way to go. Besides," he added, "all this stuff, it's gonna be heavy to lug around, and some won't keep long."

After a thoughtful moment Harmony turned to Christopher. "He's right."

Christopher cast a reluctant eye on the heavily-laden grocery cart. "What'll we put back?"

By way of answering, Quentin stepped up to the cart and withdrew the 12-pack of soda. "We don't need this."

Christopher snatched it back. "Why not?"

"'Cause it's too heavy, for one thing. We might have to walk a ways. We'd be better off buyin' three single cans."

That made sense. Christopher set the 12-pack on the floor. "Okay, what else?"

"We don't need this," Harmony leaned into the cart and withdrew the half-gallon of milk.

Quentin was about to take out the quart of orange juice when Christopher stopped him. "Hold it. You both took something out, now it's my turn."

Quentin shrugged and set the juice back. "Okay." Christopher's eyes roamed over the array of goods and settled on two cans of black-eyed peas. He pulled them.

"My turn next!" Quentin called, reaching into the cart, the pile of groceries on the floor growing larger and larger as they gradually emptied the basket.

The mild mannered store clerk watched it all in silence, then came storming up the aisle. "Say, what's going on here?" he demanded, standing with hands on hips.

All at once aware of how moronic they were acting, Quentin grew warm with embarrassment. He stooped and began gathering up groceries. After watching a moment, Christopher and Harmony joined in. When they were done all that was left was a package of hot dogs, some bologna, a can of pork and beans, a large can of fruit cocktail, a loaf of bread and two quarts of soda.

The grocer rang it up. After Christopher paid, he stuffed the change in his pocket and without so much as a howdy-do or a thank you, grabbed the bag of groceries and headed for the door. But he didn't get far. The door was locked. "Hey," he said, turning back, "we can't get out. The door's locked."

His two companions were still standing by the counter with the grocer. "You sure you have everything you need?" the store owner asked with feigned politeness.

"Yeah, yeah," Christopher answered impatiently. He had never been so hungry in his entire life and if he couldn't actually smell the bologna through the plastic package, with the help of his eyes he was doing a darn good job of imagining it.

"In that case I'll let you out," the clerk said and came around the counter, keys jingling. Quentin and Harmony met him at the door. As the man let them out Quentin turned and thanked him. The grocer managed a smile, then closed the door securely and locked it.

Walking up the deserted street towards the tracks, they instinctively returned the way they had come. "What'll we do now?" Harmony asked.

"Head out of town and find a good place to camp," Christopher answered and shifted the groceries to his other arm. When there was no dissension they walked on without speaking, past the silent, towering grain elevator, and westbound out of town. The train they had come in on was already gone.

Taking wide strides, Harmony tried stepping on every other tie, but it was too hard and she quit. Christopher challenged Quentin to see who could walk the farthest on a rail without falling off, but gave up when Quentin never did.

By now the dense Iowa darkness was upon them, the sky scattered with billions of glittering stars that had Harmony exclaiming with awe-struck wonder, "Look at them all! I didn't know there were so many! Why can't you see them in the city?"

"Because there's so much artificial light in the city," Christopher answered.

"There's so much artificial everything in the city," Quentin put in, "it seems even the people are artificial."

Harmony wasn't listening. "Wow!" she rambled on in fascination, her voice reduced to a reverent whisper. "It's amazing! Eternal! Look how it just goes on forever!"

Quentin nodded. "You keep lookin' up like that an' you gonna get a stiff neck."

"I don't care," she said, "I just want to look!"

Christopher was growing weary of the walk. "Where should we camp?"

"Somewhere we can build a fire an' not be bothered," Quentin answered. They were all painfully hungry and ready to stop just about any place.

The wind, gusting from out of the west, was snapping off the plains in powerful blasts that scattered the tall prairie grass and had tree branches waving frantically. Suddenly Christopher froze. "Look!" He stood pointing. Off in the distant ocean of blackness was the flickering light of a campfire. Quentin settled down on his haunches to take a more leisurely look.

Christopher wasn't interested in looking from afar. He handed Harmony the groceries and wandered off into the damp, waist-deep grass, heedless of Quentin's hushed calls to wait a minute. The night air was chilly and after a short time he returned, wet, shivering, and miserable. He sat down on the tracks beside his two friends.

"What is it?" Quentin asked.

Christopher shook his head. "Don't know. Looks like a couple of people camping to me. A little ways up the tracks there's a trail you come to that goes straight to the campfire."

Quentin nodded, his thoughts turning.

"Maybe we can join them," Harmony suggested.

Christopher liked her idea. "Yeah, we got our own food."

"Well," Quentin was somewhat reserved, "since we went an' got our own food, what can they say?"

"Nothing." It was Christopher. He stood up, took the groceries from Harmony, and with determination set off down the tracks for the trail. It was clear he was going with or without them. And he had the food.

The distance to the fire had been deceiving. Christopher stopped 20 yards from the campers. Now he could clearly see two younger men. They had pitched at the edge of a large grove of oak and sycamore trees. Christopher was about to move on when he felt a hand on his shoulder. "Wait!" Quentin whispered and pulled his two friends down to a squatting position in the middle of the trail. "I thought I heard somethin'. Let's listen a minute an' see just what we gettin' into." Christopher frowned but agreed to wait.

As they sat on their heels listening with barely a breath there was a sudden outburst from what sounded like a complaining old woman; "Raise the window! Lower the window!" the old wench screeched in a falsetto voice. After a moment's silence, and with a complete change of heart, she called sweetly, "Peter?" Then her voice rose angrily as she demanded, "Where are you going?"

Harmony looked at Quentin and he at her but neither had an inkling and they both turned back to listening.

"You didn't think I was going to let you get away without finishing your supper did you?" the old hag threatened.

For the first time since they'd been listening, Peter (whoever he was) spoke up. "I don't want no more!" he insisted, the voice of a mature young man but sounding oddly more like a spoiled child.

"You will not leave the table until you've finished your dinner!" the old woman held firm.

"But Alan, there is no table!" the other protested.

"Alan?" Quentin looked at Harmony.

She nodded. "That's what he called her." Then, "Should we intrude?"

"No," Quentin replied, "let's listen a little longer."

"Don't start playing your evil little tricks on me!" the old woman bellowed, "or I'll get a switch and blister your bottom!"

At that Peter laughed, daring him, "Go ahead and try!" Christopher had only seen two youngish men. Where was the old woman? He raised his head a little higher, craning his neck for a better view. What he saw stunned and repulsed him. The words of the nagging old woman were pouring forth from the lips of a rotund young man daintily bending over the fire carefully stirring something in a pot. "Oh your mouth is just filthy!" he cried shrilly, "it might need a washing with soap!"

"Fat chance mamma Alan," the other heckled from where he was comfortably sprawled beside the fire. He was eating from an official aluminum boy scout dish, his back to a tree.

"Oh dear, oh dear!" Alan exclaimed, his hands flat to the sides of his face, "Whatever am I going to do with you?"

Mystified, Christopher wanted to see more. He stood up.

"Who's there?" Alan asked fearfully, immediately sensing Christopher's presence and dropping the falsetto voice. Blinded by the light of his own fire his eyes were big and round as he peered into the wall of blackness surrounding the camp. Aside from the crackling fire and the chirrup of crickets there was only silence.

"Hey!" Quentin blurted in a strained whisper and reached for Christopher's arm to pull him down.

As he did so Harmony stood up and spoke in a loud voice. "There are three of us," she said woodenly, her own words sounding somehow odd and disembodied to her, as if some unseen spirit were speaking through her mouth. "We're travelers from the east and we come in peace," she continued mechanically, wondering what would come out of her mouth next. And feeling strange. Very strange. By now Quentin just sat there, mouth agape, watching Harmony perform.

"What do you want?" Alan whined.

"We are seeking a place to camp," Harmony answered without hesitation. Then she started forward. Weirdos or no weirdos she was going into that camp. With Christopher in her wake, Quentin sighed defeatedly and got to his feet.

When the three "travelers from the east" stepped into the circle of firelight the one who'd been nagging like an old woman backed around the fire, cowering beside his companion, who remained comfortably seated propped against a tree, legs stretched out and crossed at the ankles.

For a moment the new arrivals and their hosts silently eyed one another. Finally, with a nudge from the one on the ground the other one edged hesitantly forward. "Hi," he began nervously, "I'm Alan Bolten." He held forth a damp, limp hand.

Christopher happened to be standing closest. Instead of shaking hands he asked accusingly, "How come you were talking like an old lady before?"

"We're actors," the one seated quickly replied. "Just practicing."

"Actors?" Quentin brightened. He loved the theater. In fact he loved art and artists of any kind.

"Yes," Alan took up where his friend by the tree left off. "And one day we're going to New York to put on a big show!"

"Well congratulations," Quentin beamed and stepped up and shook Alan's soft, damp hand.

The ice broken, Alan Bolten was not at all shy. He stepped closer to Christopher and introduced himself again, commenting, "I just *love* your jacket!"

Eyeing him warily, Christopher nodded.

When he didn't say anything Alan asked, "What's your name?"

"Christopher."

"Christopher what?"

"Robin."

"Oh." He stepped around Christopher and made his acquaintance with Harmony.

"Hi. I'm Harmony Hammerschmidt," the girl offered, still a little bewildered by her earlier performance.

When Alan finished making the rounds, his friend by the tree called out, "I'm Peter Perish." Motioning with his head towards Alan, he added, "You can call him 'flaky' for short."

Everyone laughed, Christopher just a little nervously. He wasn't sure he liked who they had taken up with, although Quentin seemed completely at ease.

"Come, join us," Perish continued cheerfully, "we're glad to have the company."

"And we're just having dinner," Alan bubbled exuberantly, insisting he was *simply thrilled* to have the chance to try out his new recipe for chicken and noodles on someone who wasn't used to his cooking.

"We got food," Christopher quickly broke in.

Alan waved him off. "We've got plenty, save your stuff."

Christopher suddenly realized he was still holding the groceries and set them down.

"Nice spot you got here," Quentin commented, eyeing the camp and surrounding area. "Like an oasis out in the middle of the Great Plains. Must be water nearby."

The very rotund Alan Bolten nodded. "Oh yes, there is. A little creek runs through these trees. Nothing more than a dry gulch really. But just the other side of this grove down around towards the south end the farmer has a pipe coming up out of the ground where we draw water. It's a low spot where the rain collects and he just adds a little to it now and then for irrigation or to water cattle."

"That's cool havin' drinkin' water so close," Quentin said. "Real convenient."

"Oh yes," Alan beamed, "and you can bathe there, too."

Wondering if that wasn't a gibe at his appearance, out of the corner of his eye Quentin caught Perish staring at him.

Christopher wasn't paying any attention to the small talk. He was more interested in food. Finding the "kitchen" area of the camp, he moved the groceries there, set the bag on the ground and unloaded the beans, hot dogs and other items.

Harmony dropped to her knees beside him. "Want me to help?" she asked.

Christopher stopped and stared at her. "No," he stated flatly, "I want you to fix it."

"Aren't you going to try some of my chicken and noodles?" Alan pleaded.

"You can go an' count me in," Quentin volunteered, dropping to his haunches beside the fire and poking at it with a stick.

Alan smiled and clapped his hands together. "Oh good!" he said, clucking away like an old mother hen, "I'm sure you'll enjoy it. You people... uh, I mean, chickens love Negroes, don't they?" Realizing he'd gotten it backwards he stammered, "Uh, what I mean is, Negroes love... well, you know what I mean. It must be one of your favorites."

"Not especially," Quentin answered, keeping his eyes on the fire.

Alan dished chicken and noodles from a saucepan into a tin plate. "I thought all Negroes liked chicken," he chattered on, handing the plate and a fork to Quentin—and then standing over him anxiously. "Is it good?" he asked eagerly after only one bite.

"Oh, great!" Quentin answered with a full mouth. "Best chicken this here niggra ever tasted!"

"Oh, good, good!" Alan exclaimed excitedly and clapped his hands together again. "I just knew it. My father always used to say, 'Throw a chicken bone into a crowd of nig...' uh, I mean Negroes, an' they'd uh... Well, what my daddy meant was that Negro people love chicken is all."

Quentin stopped eating and stared at the disheveled, pear-shaped 26-year-old man. Holding his hands apart in an illustration of length, he said with a straight face, "An' we got huge dongs, too!"

"Don't pay any attention to him," Perish said easily, "the kid's a complete moron. Babbles endlessly." Then he held up his plate and demanded, "More."

Alan bustled around the fire to Perish and stopped at his feet, took the plate, hurried back to the cook pot, filled the plate and brought it back to him. "There now," he fussed, "is everything all right?"

"No," Perish said between mouthfuls, "I need a can of pop." At 27, Peter Perish was skinny as a rail and at least as tall as Christopher. With stringy black hair that fell down past narrow, sloping shoulders his gaunt, hollow-cheeked face with its thin, bony nose could have been a halloween mask.

"You drink too much pop," Alan said worriedly as he went to fetch it. "It's going to ruin your teeth and make you fat." Contrary to his companion, Alan Bolten was the epitome of short and corpulent. With light brown hair on an oval head, a nose that stuck straight out like Pinocchio's, two dots for eyes and full rubbery lips that quivered over big yellow horse teeth, he was less than attractive.

While Alan was off getting the pop Perish raised his eyes and grinned at Quentin. Quentin avoided the man's gaze and continued eating.

In the meantime Christopher had wandered off to find some roasting sticks for hot dogs. No telling what was in that chicken stuff. Still, it would be best to play it cool. After all, they were guests. And he didn't want one of these jokers sticking a knife in him or something during the night. He came back with four sticks. "Want one?" he asked, offering Alan a stick.

"Oh yes, I just love hot dogs!" he exclaimed enthusiastically.

Christopher gave him a stick and turned to Perish. "How about you?"

"I'm full, thanks," he said with an appreciative smile.

"I'll take one," Quentin interjected.

Christopher nodded. "Okay." Without asking if she wanted one or not he handed Harmony a stick, took two hot dogs, crossed to the fire and sat down beside Quentin.

"Thanks," Quentin said when Christopher handed him a hot dog and a stick. Spearing his own hot dog, Christopher held it over the flames.

Piqued at Christopher's brusque manner with her ever since they had arrived, Harmony took a seat on the opposite side of the fire and began roasting her hot dog with serious intent. Alan watched a moment, then sat down beside her and held his own hot dog over the flames. "I just love hot dogs!" he said for the fourth time. Keeping her eyes on her dinner, Harmony sighed. Trying to think of something else to say, Alan frowned, finally settling on, "I'm from Detroit. Where're you from?"

Harmony cocked her head and bluntly asked, "Who cares?"

Stung, Alan glowered, his eyes intent upon the fire.

Turning back to the task at hand, Harmony caught the faintest hint of a smile cross Perish's lips. An evil smile that chilled her to the bone. She looked across the fire in an attempt to catch Christopher's attention but he and Quentin were sitting knee-to-knee involved in some long discussion she couldn't quite hear. She glanced back at Perish. He met her gaze and their eyes locked. Somehow she couldn't look away. A dark light seemed to sparkle and dance in his eyes and she caught her breath, startled. Where had she seen *that* before? She seemed to remember that look from somewhere....

And then the stunning revelation hit so hard it sent her mind reeling and her heart thumping wildly. It wasn't something she had seen. Rather, it had been a feeling. A presence. The *ants!* Her head spinning with confusion, she tried to sort out what on earth it was about this man that she associated with the unusual ants she had encountered only that morning. His *weirdness?*

Flashing a broad smile then, Perish held her gaze. Suddenly it dawned on her, *he knows what I'm thinking!* Her stomach churning with fear, she lowered her eyes and looked at her hot dog. It was blackened and shriveled, smoke pouring from it. "Damn!" she cursed, flicking the hot dog off the stick.

Eyeing her questioningly at the outburst, Quentin and Christopher looked up. "What's wrong?" Christopher asked, taking a huge bite of his own hot dog.

Flustered (she didn't know what was wrong), Harmony

asked irritably, "Will you come over here?"

Christopher frowned. "Me and Quentin are talking about something. What's the problem?"

"I just want to talk to you," she almost pleaded, feeling an overwhelming desire to be close to him but not knowing how to express it.

"What you so upset about?" Quentin looked at her.

"Just stay out of it, Quentin!" she snapped, "who's talking to you?"

"Now wait a minute, you!" Christopher cut in, stabbing at the air with his half-eaten hot dog. "You're startin' to act like a flamin' rag! Now get this, when I feel like coming over there I will. Until then, shut up!" With that he finished his hot dog in one bite and turned to preparing another.

Exhausted, hungry and confused, Harmony threw down her stick, leapt to her feet and stalked out of the circle of firelight. The others watched her go in silence. "Maybe you was a little hard on her," Quentin said in a low voice.

Christopher shrugged. "What'd I do? What'd anyone do?"

Quentin shook his head. "I Don't know, but why not go on after her. She probably just needin' to eat is all."

Christopher looked at him for a moment, then set his stick down. "Save my place," he said and got to his feet.

In the darkness among the tall, windblown trees hot tears spilled down Harmony's cheeks. Weakness from lack of food more than anything caused her to sink to her knees, her mind a jumble of confusion and fear. Raising her eyes to the glittering, star-filled sky, she whispered, "Dear Lord, please be by me now. Just be by me."

Where's your angel now? a tiny voice seemed to snicker from within the depths of her mind. But *was* it from within? Or *without?* Distracted with this consideration, she suddenly found herself wondering what she was so upset about. This is ridiculous, she thought, the tears already drying on her face when she stood up, turned around, and almost stumbled into Christopher.

"Oh!" she cried, startled.

"I was looking for you," he said, taking both her hands in his. "And I'm sorry for how I acted."

"So am I," she quickly said.

Christopher looked doubtful.

"Really," she added.

"No kidding?"

"No kidding."

He swept her up in a bear hug and kissed her gently. She returned his kiss with one that was neither short nor gentle.

"Whew!" he grinned. "We'd better get you back to camp and get some food in you."

As he took her hand and started for camp she asked with forced casualness, "Do you believe it's possible for evil spirits to get inside of ants and things?"

He stopped and looked at her closely. After a long pause he said, "You mean like in the Bible when those demons got inside that herd of pigs?"

"Exactly," she declared, drawing up short. "I thought you never read the Bible."

"I saw it on television."

"Oh." Then, "Do you think that could really happen?"

"C'mon," he said, ignoring the question and starting for camp with her in tow.

"Well do you?" she persisted.

"No," he said shortly, "religion is just a lot of crap."

"Well you don't have to get angry about it."

He stopped and turned and slipped his arms around her waist. "I'm not angry," he smiled, "just starved. Okay?"

She returned his smile. "Okay." With a short kiss for the road they headed back to camp.

*   *   *

"More chicken and noodles, madam?" Alan Bolten asked with an exaggeratedly straight face. Having run the gamut of roles from nagging old woman to gambler to buccaneer, he was now playing the dignified English Butler.

"No, thank you," Harmony answered, handing him the dish, "I'm full."

"Very well, madam." He turned to Christopher. "And you, sir?"

Upon returning to camp Christopher had been too hungry to resist the chicken dish he had earlier refused. Scraping up the last of the gravy with his fork, he handed the plate and utensil to Alan. "No more for me, thanks. If I eat another bite I'll explode." With a shallow bow Alan took the plate and withdrew.

With a satisfied sigh Christopher settled down against the knapsack Alan had let he and Harmony use as a backrest. Harmony eased down too, resting her head on Christopher's shoulder, both their feet toasty warm by the fire.

With Quentin on the opposite side of the fire sitting cross-legged next to Peter Perish, and Alan Bolten bustling about with his seemingly endless kitchen chores, Harmony and Christopher were effectively alone. And something was gnawing at her that she didn't know how to bring up without raising Christopher's ire. "Do you suppose," she began hesitantly, "a person could come under the influence of an evil spirit without actually becoming possessed?"

Christopher's eyelids were drooping. "Uh-hum," he said, not really listening. He shifted, tucking closer and closing his eyes.

"Maybe that's what's wrong with these two," she whispered.

"I don't know," Christopher mumbled. "I just live for today. Try to have a good time. Let everyone do their own thing."

Heaving a sigh, Harmony gave up. He wasn't listening. Within five minutes they were both sound asleep.

Quentin sat up for more than an hour talking with Perish—out of politeness rather than desire. He was exhausted. Sometimes he felt as though he were being interrogated the way

Perish fired off question after question. Wanting only to close his eyes and go to sleep, he just sat there half-dazed and answering automatically.

At long last the questioning did come to an end. Quentin scarcely noticed. He fell sound asleep where he was, curled up cozily by the fire like a lazy hound dog.

7

ROLLING IN THE DIRT

Peter Perish watched as Alan, Christopher, and Quentin filed up the footpath and disappeared into the grove. Then he got down on his knees beside Harmony and reached for her shoulder.

When Harmony felt the hand resting on her shoulder she naturally assumed it was Christopher's. But when she moved to snuggle closer and felt only the cool morning air at her back her eyes popped open and she sat up, accidentally hitting Perish in the nose with the top of her head. Perish toppled backwards, eyes watering as he cupped his smarting nose.

Not yet awake, Harmony sat there squinting into the 9:00 a.m. sunshine and for the second morning in a row wondering where in the heck Christopher was. Then she looked at Perish. He was sitting on the ground holding his nose and blinking back tears. "What on earth are you crying about?" she asked.

With furrowed brow Perish was about to give her a tongue lashing but stopped short, saying instead, "Because you make me sad."

"What?" Harmony wasn't sure she had heard right.

"Well it's true."

"What happened to everybody else?" she asked, ignoring the remark.

Getting to his feet and dusting off his pants, eyes dry now, Perish answered, "They went for water."

It was another perfect, sunshiny spring day filled with blue sky and chattering birds. Rested and feeling chipper, the previous evening seemed like a bad dream now. In morning's light Peter Perish didn't look so evil or frightening. In fact she felt foolish for what she had been thinking and saying to Christopher the night before. It was like she'd been out of it or something. "How long ago did they leave?" she asked, wondering if she should apologize for last night. Then it occurred to her how silly she was being. How does one apologize for one's thoughts?

"Oh, about ten minutes ago," he lied. Actually it had been about one minute ago. "They'll be back shortly."

There was definitely something odd about Peter Perish, Harmony concluded with a luxuriant stretch. She could sense it. He just wasn't normal. And the odd thing about it was, although Alan Bolten acted the weirdest it was Perish who struck her as somehow different from "normal" people. As she tried to put her finger on what that difference was it came to her all over again. The ants. Unlike last night though this revelation came without fear or dread. Rather, she greeted it with mild curiosity. *What was it about this man she equated with those darn ants?* She felt his eyes on her and looked up.

"You were wondering about ants?" he asked with a broad smile, his hands folded in front of him like a guru as he took a seat on the ground and sat cross-legged facing her.

"A-Ants?" she stammered. It was as if he had read her mind. She looked down at her wrinkled sweatshirt and lamely tried smoothing it out. After a moment she stopped and looked up at him. "What makes you say that?"

He shrugged. "I just thought I could answer some of your questions about the ants."

She looked down at her sweatshirt again. *How could he know what I'm thinking?* When she looked up her mind was set. She would just call his bluff. "Why do you keep talking about ants?"

He shrugged, a silly grin on his face. "Why do you keep playing mind games?"

"I think you owe me an explanation," she firmly replied.

His grin faded. "The only thing I owe you, the one and only thing I can never deny you," he paused dramatically, "is the truth."

Harmony looked at him steadily. That's fair enough, she thought. What more can one ask for than the truth? Before she could open her mouth to thank him for his candid attitude he presented her with another question. "What must man give back to God if he wants to dwell in the light of the Lord?"

When he used the term "man" in this sense Harmony understood that he was referring to both the man with the womb as well as the one without. In answer to his question she shrugged. "What?"

"His free will," Perish answered. "And how does one give up his free will?"

"How?"

"Simply ask God to take it back."

Harmony looked at him dubiously.

"In other words," he added, "live by the will of God."

"How does a person know what the will of God is?"

"Simple. Ask God to take away your will, that you might live by his will alone, and he shall enlighten you." Perish sat back expectantly.

When it dawned on Harmony that he was waiting for some sort of verbal commitment she was taken aback. "Right now?" she asked in surprise.

"Today is the first day of the rest of your life!" Perish quoted the worn cliché as if he'd just made it up at that very moment.

Harmony pondered that one a bit before confessing, "But I'd feel so silly talking to God in front of you."

"Listen," Perish said confidentially and leaned closer, "everyone thinks there are only two kinds of people; believers and unbelievers. But there is a third; the seekers. And in a sense the seekers are even better off than the believers because their faith is active. They not only believe but seek that which they have accepted. Do you understand?"

Harmony nodded, the information slowly seeping in. It certainly makes a lot of sense, she thought. Then she looked at the man who had said the words. *He is special. A prophet?*

"I'm a servant of God," Perish said as if to answer her thought.

"Which is another way of saying 'prophet'!" Harmony exclaimed, startled. Staring hard at Perish, a feeling of exhilaration washed over her. *He can tell what I'm thinking!* At last she stammered, "H-How can you read my mind?"

Perish smiled broadly. "Listen; things that are relative apply to man. Things that are not relative apply to God. You will know that you are standing in his light when things are no longer relative in your life. Then God's law will apply and man's law will be irrelevant. But the key to everything, the most important secret of life, is truth. Seek the truth and the truth shall set you free!" He concluded his speech with much bravado, again as if he had just uttered the last sentence for the first time in human history.

Harmony gaped at him, filled with wonder at his brilliance. Everything he said made so much sense. "I... I feel so dumb about last night," she muttered red-faced.

Waving her off, Perish laughed. "Forget it," he said easily, "that's what forgiveness is for. Error. Besides," he went on, "always remember; every adversity is but yet another chance to prove one's worthiness to his or her maker."

Harmony was quickly reaching the point where she was thrilled by his every word. He had an answer for everything! "H-How do you know so much about God?" she stammered, her face shining with expectation.

"The Lord provides for his own, Harmony. Plus, I am a little special. And I know everything about you."

She squinted at him. "Everything?"

"Everything. Even the night you discovered the pleasures

of your womanly body." At first she didn't comprehend what he was saying, then it dawned on her and she looked down in shame, her face glowing warm with embarrassment. "It's all right," he assured her, "you're not the first nor will you be the last."

Harmony looked up at him in wide-eyed wonder, her shame receding. "What else do you know about me?" she asked in fascination.

Again Perish's words came immediately and without forethought. "I know you're from Chicago. And I know you ran away from a foster home." Harmony nodded in amazement. "And I know Chris and Quentin don't believe in angels. And you met Quentin when he got in a train wreck. And you almost ran into the same train when the gates didn't go down but Chris stopped just in time."

"Wait a minute!" Harmony interrupted, momentarily forgetting that he could 'read' her mind. "Quentin and Chris could have easily told you all of that this morning while I was still asleep."

"That's true," Perish amiably agreed. He had overplayed his hand. But he was already formulating his recovery when he said, "They could have. But I don't know too many girls that meet up with talking ants. And they couldn't have told me about your conversation with the ants because they don't know about that, now do they?"

That was the clincher. Harmony's mouth fell open and she stared at him in speechless wonder, this last tidbit of information just too much. "T-That's incredible," she stammered, "I can hardly believe it!" Neither Christopher nor Quentin could have told him about her communicating with the ants because neither knew. (She entirely forgot about trying to get *them* to talk to the ants.)

She kept her eyes on his through a long silence broken only by Perish asking softly, "Do you really want to know how I know all about you?"

Harmony nodded numbly.

"My power comes from heaven."

"From God?"

He nodded.

"Who are you?"

With a wide smile he asked, "Who do you think I am?"

"Y-You seem to know everything about everything."

"Well who do you think I am?"

"I don't know," she began nervously, finally asking in a tiny voice, "God?"

Perish burst out laughing. "No, silly. I'm your angel."

When he said it she reeled like a drunkard and felt a spark of electricity jump the gap between them and course through her veins like liquid-hot fire. And suddenly it was alive in her and Harmony was dazzled by its brilliance. It was *real!*

Perish was still rambling on, his thin body emanating power, his words drifting into her mind one by one and lodging in her subconscious like particles. "You see, *I* caused the ants to behave the way they did," he was saying. "I was trying to signal you. The truth is I didn't know how to approach you. I mean, it's not every day you tell a mortal you're an angel. I was afraid of scaring you away."

Harmony nodded vacantly. There really were angels weren't there? She had always known that. The Bible said so. But what about last night? Her inner soul kept hammering at her. What about that? But that had been her own dark imaginings. And old Diablo with all his power of illusion. Trickery regurgitated from the bottomless pit of hell... and she had almost been fooled.

Didn't she believe anything was possible with God? All right then! Hadn't Peter Perish proved himself? Besides, couldn't she *feel* the power of him in her? Couldn't she see with her own eyes his unearthly beauty? If he wasn't an angel how could he know all he knew? For a moment she made an awkward, fumbley attempt to pray on the matter, but the power upon her drowned out everything save its own intent. The moment passed and she fell back breathing hard, a flu-like weakness sweeping over her. "Angel?" she whispered, her voice cracking.

"*Your* angel," Perish stated flatly. "Your guardian angel."

Hadn't she heard that *everyone* had a guardian angel? Suddenly she felt as though in a vacuum. Time ground to a halt as they sat staring at each other for an eternity. Forever came and went in a flash and she could hear Perish shouting that it was all true but his mouth was not opening. Still, his voice cried aloud in her head, "Believe! Believe!" And with her two hands she covered her ears but his voice was not diminished by a single decibel.

"Okay, I believe!" she cried aloud, feeling a pure love of the heart, unpossessive and unconnected to the flesh. And it was such a noble, such a *powerful* feeling! She looked at Perish, her eyes growing wide with astonishment. He seemed to glow with a pulsating white light and she found herself uncontrollably drawn to him. Before she knew what was happening she got to her feet and flung herself on him. Laughing, they toppled backwards and found themselves rolling in the dirt.

*   *   *

When the others returned from getting water they found Harmony and Peter Perish sitting cross-legged on the ground enjoying a breakfast of canned fruit and campfire-roasted bacon. "I feel so awful about last night," Harmony was saying emphatically, "just awful."

Perish shrugged. "Don't worry about it, Harmony. There's no way you could have known who I was. But beware!" he added, "just goes to show how easily Satan can trick you. Remember, the closer you are to God the more diligently Satan will pursue you. So watch out. Stay close to me and learn and you'll be safe."

Harmony nodded gravely. "I will," she promised.

Christopher dropped the canteen he carried beside its owner's pack and plopped down next to Harmony. "Morning, sleepyhead," he said cheerily, "what's going on?"

"Nothing," Harmony's reply was clipped.

Taken aback, Christopher asked meekly, "Did I do something wrong?"

Ignoring the question, Harmony confided to Perish, "He doesn't believe in angels or God or anything."

"Oh?" Perish replied with a cautious glance Christopher's way. For a moment no one said anything.

Christopher could sense something was wrong, but what? "Hey Harmony," he finally said, breaking the long silence.

"What?" she asked without turning.

"You never did answer my question."

"Then it must not have been very important."

"Harmony," Christopher stated flatly.

"What?"

"That's what you're supposed to say when *you* forget something. Not when I've asked you an important question."

"What question?"

"I asked if I did anything wrong. You know, why are you mad at me?"

"Oh. Well, I'm not mad at you," she replied curtly, a decided silence settling over the two of them.

Christopher was about to ask why she was suddenly being so cold to him when Quentin cut in. Looking up from something he and Alan were working on in the "kitchen," he called, "Hey Chris! Got your pocketknife handy?"

"Yeah," he said over his shoulder. Giving Harmony a last look, he got to his feet and joined Quentin and Alan.

Left alone, Perish turned to Harmony and quietly commented, "So, you've known Chris only two days, huh?"

Harmony nodded.

"Probably tells lies," he suggested. When she didn't respond Perish asked, "Did he ever lie to you?"

Suddenly remembering, Harmony answered, "Once. About his dad's car. Said it was his."

"See?"

"Yeah, I know what you mean. Unbeliever. Dishonest." Harmony was hanging fresh slices of bacon on a stick for cooking. "Want some more?"

He nodded, saying in his exaggeratedly polite way, "Yes, please." She draped two more slices over the stick for him, then squatted beside the heap of glowing coals and threw a few sticks on. After a moment the tinder burst into flame and she held the raw bacon over them. Licking his lips reptilian-like, Perish watched her every move. What he didn't know was that Christopher was watching *him.*

"This knife got a good can opener," Quentin said as he folded the tool closed and handed it back. Christopher reached for it without looking and slipped it into his pocket. Seeing the expression on his face Quentin asked, "What went an' got into you?"

Christopher didn't even hear him as he pushed off on the balls of his feet and made straight for Perish. Without warning he slapped him hard upside the head. "What're you lookin' at my chick like that for?" he demanded.

At the first slap Perish cowered, holding his hands out in front of his face in a lame gesture of self-defense and whining, "I wasn't looking at her."

"The hell you weren't!" Christopher snapped, then turned to Quentin for support. "Wasn't he staring at her?"

But before an embarrassed Quentin could answer, an outraged Harmony cried, "How dare you! Just leave him alone! It's my body and he can look at me anytime he wants to. And I'm not *your* chick!" she added defiantly.

Utterly bewildered, Christopher looked from Harmony to Perish to Quentin and back again, his mind spinning with confusion. What the heck had happened when they'd gone for water? In any case he couldn't defend a girl that didn't want defending so he backed off. Perish immediately breathed easier and said with downcast eyes, "I thought you were my friend."

"Some friend," Christopher muttered.

"Well I didn't do anything," Perish protested innocently.

"All right, shut up!" Christopher ordered threateningly, "I've heard enough out of you for one day!"

"Well do something," an indignant Harmony urged Perish. "Don't let him talk to you that way."

Perish solemnly shook his head. "No, dear. That is not our way. Forgiveness," he gently instructed. "You must learn the power of forgiveness."

"Oh all right," Harmony said sullenly and sat down beside him with her bacon-on-a-stick. "Here, Peter."

Wiping his sweaty palms on his jeans, he said, "No. You go ahead and have my share. I'm not hungry anymore."

"Okay," Harmony happily obliged him.

Christopher paced back and forth with downcast eyes, his mind whirling. That Harmony had gone through some dramatic changes in the short time he'd been gone he had no doubt. Her whole personality seemed changed. But what could possibly have caused such changes in her? Perish? He stopped pacing and with a last, bewildered look around, stalked out of camp and up the trail towards the tracks.

Quentin and Alan were busily spooning fruit cocktail from a large can. Quentin too, could sense something weird going on but hadn't the faintest idea what and frankly, didn't care. He was happy. It was the perfect setup for the time being. Food, water, a place to rest. And highly unlikely they'd be running into any cops. Furthermore, traveling with an amiable group of white people was good cover for a supposedly lone black man on the run. They finished up the can of fruit and Quentin graciously offered to wash the spoons.

"No," Alan declined and snatched Quentin's spoon, "that's my job."

Quentin wasn't about to argue. "Thanks," he smiled. Without another word he turned and headed up the footpath for the tracks. It was time to have a talk with Christopher and find out what was going on.

With Quentin gone Perish commented, "At least the black man seems good and honest. Maybe we can use him."

"He seems like a good person to me," Harmony agreed.

"Everyone seems like a good person to you," Perish smiled and fondly touched her cheek.

Harmony beamed at him, but the odd coldness to his touch she ignored. Then she got to her feet and started gathering the breakfast things. Peter Perish smiled approvingly. Alan Bolten felt threatened. Harmony felt high.

When everything was in order Perish got to his feet and held out a hand for Harmony. "What a beautiful spring day," he said in sing-song, "let's go for a walk!"

"Okay," Harmony said, "let's."

Childlike, Alan asked, "Can I come?"

"Why sure!" Perish cheerfully replied. Turning to Harmony he said, "A little family should always take walks together. It's good for the spirit."

Harmony nodded, her eyes searching his. He seemed so deep. And it gave her a funny feeling of being very tiny beside this man, or angel as it were, of towering wisdom.

Perish was leading as they walked through the dappled sunlight of the grove and made their way around fallen logs and brush. Harmony breathed in deeply the fresh country air, her spirits soaring. The wind rushing through the branches high overhead sounded so much like a distant waterfall that she asked if there was one somewhere nearby. But Perish never even heard the question as he rambled on about one thing or another, sometimes waving a hand or jabbing a finger to make his point. "You've got to be brave!" he declared, raising a clenched fist, "maybe even willing to risk your life or die for the cause!"

Coming down from a dream, Harmony innocently asked, "Why? What do we have to do?"

With a wicked smile, Peter Perish answered, "Stamp out evil and the forces that empower it!"

"How'll we do that?" Alan wanted to know.

"How do you fight fire?" Perish retorted.

"With fire!" Harmony declared triumphantly.

Perish smiled knowingly. "That's right, Harmony," he assured her. "We must utterly destroy every vestige of evil we come upon. It's our duty as servants of the Lord!"

"And because we're good Christians!" Harmony chirped.

"And because we're good Americans!" Alan declared patriotically.

When Harmony suddenly stopped, Alan stumbled into her. Unaware, Perish kept walking and talking. "Hey!" she called.

Embarrassed that he'd been talking to himself, Perish stopped abruptly and turned on his heel. "What?" he asked irritably.

"What about Chris? Will we be able to convert him?"

Perish slowly shook his head. "I don't know, Harmony. That's solely up to him. As you know, choosing the way of the Lord is a very personal decision. It's strictly up to the individual."

"Well isn't there anything we can do to help him?" she worriedly asked.

Heaving a sigh of exasperation, Perish answered, "We can certainly try, but the ultimate decision is his alone." How many times would he have to tell her?

Harmony nodded. "I understand."

After a pause to make certain she was finished Perish said, "Good," and they continued on their way.

Minutes later they came out on the other side of the grove and found themselves standing at the edge of a seemingly endless field of young corn plants only two or three inches high. "Where did they go for water this morning?" Harmony asked.

Perish pointed to his left. "Round the southeast side of this grove there's a low spot where the runoff gathers. The farmer turned it into a reservoir. Would you like to see it?"

Harmony nodded. "Sure."

"Okay," Perish said, "follow me." As they walked Perish continued with his 'lessons.' "See, according to God there is no limit on the number of people you can love and how intimately you can love them. That's a personal choice. Yours. But this I can tell you, the more you love—in truth—the more God will love you. And," he paused (this was the important part) "sex is one of the most important and positive aspects of love. Since it is a positive element of a good thing why not exploit it to the fullest extent? Just as Satan exploits the desires of men's hearts?"

Alan Bolten clapped his hands gleefully and exclaimed in his moronic way, "Oh I just *love* the Lord!"

Perish elbowed him one in the ribs. "Understand, Harmony?" She nodded slowly, not quite sure if she understood or not.

At the water's edge, their backs to the wind, Harmony asked in surprise, "That's clean enough to drink?"

"We get drinking water off the tap, Harmony," Perish said, pointing to a pipe with a twist-valve sticking up out of the ground several feet away. "It's clean," he assured her.

"Good. I could go for a drink right now."

"Come on, then."

After quenching her thirst Harmony straightened up and felt her greasy, stringy hair. "Wish I had some shampoo so I could wash my hair, but I guess rinsing is better than nothing." Splashing her face with the cold, clear water, she thoroughly soaked her hair. When she raised her dripping head from under the faucet Perish was standing at her side, a big grin on his face as he held out a bar of soap. "Thank you!" Harmony grinned. Taking the bar from him, she soaped her hair down. It wasn't shampoo but it was better than nothing.

"Why don't you take a proper bath?" Perish urged. "The road-dirt piles up fast when you're traveling."

"What," Harmony asked dubiously, peering out from under her lathered hair, "is a proper bath?"

"Wash your whole body. Especially under the armpits. And rinse out your clothes and let them dry in the sun."

Harmony smiled shyly, "Oh, I couldn't do that."

Peter Perish laughed, trying to sound casual as he assured her, "We no longer have to hide from each other, Harmony. We're beyond that stage now. I'm an angel, remember? I can see right through your clothes just as if they weren't there."

Her face turning red, Harmony asked on a high note, "You can?"

Perish nodded. "I'll turn around if you wish," he added politely. "I didn't mean to embarrass you." Dumbfounded, Harmony stood there blinking. "God doesn't wear clothes," Perish added, anxiously building his case. "And neither do angels except when they're in the bodies of men."

Harmony nodded. "Makes sense. Or else you'd get arrested."

"Yeah," Alan giggled, "we'd get arrested."

For a moment there was silence. Then, quite spontaneously, they all burst out laughing, Harmony drawing up short. "Uh, wait a minute fellas. I still don't think I'm ready for this. Do you mind if I just skip my bath for today?"

Perish shrugged. "I don't care what you smell like," he said, peeling off his shirt, "just as long as you're not sleeping next to me." He dropped to one knee and started untying his shoelace.

Harmony found his body, with its concave chest and ribs showing through, repulsive. And when the blubbery, pear-shaped Alan began to disrobe right in front of her she had to keep reminding herself over and over again that heaven was not concerned with the physical body but with the spiritual.

HARMONY'S ANGEL

8

NAKED ANGELS

Quentin found Christopher sitting on the first rail of the track, chin in hand and staring dejectedly into space. When Quentin took a seat next to him Christopher didn't move a muscle. After a respectful moment's silence Quentin asked, "What's goin' on between you an' Harmony?"

"I don't know," Christopher sighed despondently, "but I think that guy Peter whoever-he-is did some pretty fast talking while we were gone this morning."

"Why you say that?"

"Because they turned Harmony against me somehow."

"Now, now, my man," Quentin admonished, "you just havin' a little lover's squabble is all. Don't go blamin' it on those guys." Not in the mood to argue, Christopher didn't reply. They sat in silence until the late spring sun, warm on their backs, gave Quentin an idea. "Feel like goin' swimmin'?"

Christopher shrugged. "It's sure getting warm enough."

"Then we goin' for sure!" Quentin declared and got to his feet. "C'mon."

"What about Harmony?" Christopher asked as they followed the footpath back to camp. "Should I ask her?"

"I'll go an' ask if you want," Quentin offered.

"Thanks."

When they got back to camp they found it deserted. "I wonder where everyone is?" Christopher asked with a begrudging trace of concern.

Quentin shrugged. "I Don't know, but I'm sure Harmony's safe with our new friends."

"*Our* new friends?" Christopher intoned. "They may be *your* friends, but I'm splitting from those two weirdos as soon as possible."

Quentin sighed wearily. "That's up to you, but for now let's go swimmin'."

Christopher agreed and together they started up the path and into the timber. "What do you suppose made her start acting so weird?"

"Don't know what you talkin' about."

"You know," Christopher insisted. "Like last night when she started babbling about demons and stuff."

"Demons? I don't remember her sayin' nothin' about no demons."

"That's right," Christopher frowned, "you weren't with us then. Anyway, she started talking goofy again the way she was on the bridge when she was saying all that stuff about God and angels saving us. Remember? Only this time it was demons."

"She just jokin' an' you didn't know it," Quentin assured him.

Christopher adamantly shook his head. "No. She was *not* joking."

Quentin stared at him. "You both beginnin' to worry me."

"Get off it!" Christopher said disgustedly. "You know as well as I do there's something weird about those two guys."

Quentin looked thoughtful. "That's true," he finally agreed. "An' you think they talked Harmony into somethin'?"

Christopher nodded grimly.

At the other side of the grove they stepped out of the trees and made their way around the curve of timber and up over a rise in the land. At the bottom of the slope were the distant figures of Harmony and her two "angels" gathered around the water spigot. Shading his eyes with a hand to his forehead, Christopher stopped. "I think they're naked!" he exclaimed.

Squinting to see, Quentin asked in surprise, "Harmony, too?"

"No, just those two weirdos. C'mon, let's get down there."

Just then Harmony spotted the boys and pointed them out. Grabbing his jeans, Perish hastily struggled into them, unconcerned with the globs of mud clinging to his bare feet. A panicky Alan followed suit.

Peter Perish was down on one knee tying his shoelace when Christopher stopped before him, legs apart, hands on hips. "Goin' somewhere?" he asked, a dangerous lilt to his voice.

"No," Perish replied, watching Christopher warily as he got to his feet, his gaunt, bony face twitching nervously.

"Then maybe you'd like to go for a little swim with us," Christopher asked persuasively, taking a step closer, "or did you forget your swimsuit?"

Silently watching this exchange, Harmony suddenly stepped up, gave Christopher a hard, two-handed shove and said scornfully, "What's wrong, haven't you ever heard of someone bathing before? Try it some time, maybe you won't attract so many flies!"

Christopher couldn't believe his ears. She was actually making fun of him! For trying to protect her! His first impulse was to backhand her across the face. Instead he pleaded with her, "Harmony, why are you acting this way?"

"What way?" she snapped.

"It's like you're turning against me. Why?"

"Turning against you!" Harmony exclaimed. "On the contrary, Chris, I love you. I want to help you find the truth."

"What truth?" he stormed in exasperation.

"The truth about a lot of things," she answered evasively.

"You're not making much sense anymore, Harmony," he said evenly. "And I'm a little surprised you would come down here and do this with these guys."

"Do what!?" she exploded, "bathe? That's a real big deal to you, isn't it? That just goes to show what's on *your* mind. Well the rest of us aren't like that. But the trouble with you is you're jealous!"

"I am *not* jealous!" Christopher hotly retorted, "I just care about you is all."

"Yeah, sure," Harmony said sullenly. "If you really did you wouldn't always be fighting with my friends." She paused a moment, not sure if she should continue in her present vein of thought. Against her better judgment she blurted, "If I told you who these guys *really* were it would blow your mind."

"What in the world are you babbling about?" Christopher cried in frustration.

"Forget it," she said, turning on her heel and starting back to camp, "you wouldn't understand." On second thought she called over her shoulder, "I'll tell you about it when you're ready." Taking the cue, Peter Perish and Alan Bolten scurried after her.

Christopher turned to Quentin with a look of utter disgust. Quentin calmly gazed back. "Let's go swimmin' an' think a minute 'bout what's goin' on." Without waiting for a reply he peeled off his jacket and shirt, dumped his shoes and socks, pulled off his trousers and shorts and ran for the cool, greenish water. With a shallow dive he sliced below the surface and remained underwater for one long minute before bursting up at the center of the pond. It was at least 15 feet deep and about as good a swimming hole as Quentin could remember besides the one they'd plunged the car into.

Within 30 seconds Christopher was out of his clothes and splashing into the water, too. He swam out to Quentin where they engaged in a brief, frantic splash fight, then both backed off several feet, settling for carefully aimed shots as they drifted to the far side of the pond. When they were shoulder-deep they gradually moved closer together, still shooting water in various ways but no longer at each other. Christopher spoke first. "What do you suppose she meant when she made that crack about, 'if I told you who these guys really were it would blow your mind'?"

Shooting a fistful of water into the air, Quentin replied, "You got me."

"I think they got her conned into something pretty wild."

"You sure it's not just somethin' you did that went an' got her all mad?"

Christopher shook his head. "No."

"Think careful, now," Quentin urged, "it must'a been somethin' you did just since last night. An' remember," he cautioned, "it may be somethin' you not even aware of."

"Well she won't tell me anything!" Christopher wailed.

"Take it easy," Quentin said, playfully bouncing a massive fist off his shoulder. "We're not goin' nowhere without her."

"Promise?"

"Promise."

Relieved, Christopher stuck a hand out. "Thanks." They shook on it. Then, "Let's get back and see what's going on."

"Okay." Quentin immediately cut into the water and with quick, powerful strokes, swam across the pond. Christopher dived after him, swimming furiously in an effort to catch up. Breathing heavily, he trudged out of the water, the soft mushy bottom squishing up between his toes.

Quentin was already heading to the spigot with his shirt, where he washed the dust and sweat out of it. Afterwards the wind and sunshine would quickly dry it. Christopher decided he had better do the same before his shirt began to smell. Once they were dressed Quentin suggested that, just for fun, they should take the long route around the stand of timber and see how close they could sneak up to camp before getting spotted. "I like that idea," Christopher grinned, "and just maybe we'll find out what's going on, too."

Tossing his jacket over his shoulder as they started off, Quentin said, "We sure not goin' to find out nothin' by askin'." Following the curve of the timber, they ambled along talking in low overtones. With the trees to their immediate left blocking the wind, it was quiet and still, the sun warm. In no time they had the camp in sight but couldn't see anyone. Christopher correctly surmised that the others were sitting and thus hidden from view.

He and Quentin stealthily moved into the cool shadows of the trees. If someone at camp should suddenly stand, all he and Quentin would have to do is freeze and they probably wouldn't be spotted. Provided, of course, that the someone hadn't heard something and was specifically looking for them.

Soon they were close enough to hear voices and got down on their hands and knees and crawled in as close as they dared, then settled back to listen. "I don't know, Harmony." It was Peter Perish. "We'll just have to think of some way to help them see the truth."

"But what if we fail?" Harmony worriedly asked. "What if they never see the truth?"

Perish responded with a weary sigh and replied, "Then we'll just have to go on without them. Remember, it's each person's own choice. We can't *make* someone come with us. You do see that don't you?"

Harmony must have nodded her answer because a long silence followed. Alan broke it by getting to his feet and clucking like an old woman, "Why don't I make us a little snack after our lovely bath?" And then he was bustling about the "kitchen."

With Alan occupied Perish started singing softly. It sounded to Christopher like some religious song and he made a face like he wanted to puke. "They're trying to talk her into splitting from us. From *me!*" he whispered harshly. Quentin nodded that he understood, but Christopher heatedly went on, "Let's beat the crap out of those two, snatch Harmony and head for the rails." Quentin started to reply but Christopher continued breathlessly, "And if they come after us...."

Putting a hand over his young friend's mouth, Quentin whispered in his ear, "Peter's strongest argument be our best reason not to do that."

"Huh?" Christopher said, irritably pulling his face away from Quentin's hand.

"In other words," Quentin went on decisively, "if they conned her into somethin' the only thing we can do is un-con her. Won't do no good to go an' kidnap her. We can't *make* her come with us if she don't want to."

Christopher's eyes narrowed momentarily, then he sighed with defeat and nodded. "Okay." After all, it made sense. They couldn't *force* her to come with them. Suddenly Christopher found himself facing the awful truth. He might indeed lose her.

"Let's get back to camp," Quentin whispered. He turned and crawled into the timber. Christopher followed. Once safely hidden by the trees they stood up and made for the trail. When they walked into camp no one even looked up. Quentin and Christopher both headed for the "kitchen" and began nosing around for something to eat.

Then Christopher got an idea. "Hey, Harmony!" he called hopefully, "why don't you and I hike into town and get a few things from the store?"

Stretched out on Perish's sleeping bag with her hands folded behind her head, Harmony turned to her "angel" for approval. A faint smile crept across Perish's face as he nodded his assent. Getting to her feet, she said, "All right, Chris."

Christopher crossed the camp in three strides, put an arm around her shoulders and steered her for the trail to the tracks and town. They walked in silence, their footsteps crunching in the gravel. At last Christopher spoke. "I don't know what to say, Harmony, except that ever since this morning there's been something between us. Now, if I've done something wrong I want you to know it wasn't on purpose. And if you'll just tell me what I did I promise I won't do it anymore." Harmony didn't reply. "Well?"

"It's not that I'm angry with you," she began, "it's just that you've turned your back on me."

"Turned my back on *you!?*" Christopher was incredulous.

"I thought it was the other way around!"

"See?" Harmony retorted.

"See what?" As much as he tried Christopher couldn't help getting heated up.

"You just refuse to understand," she said, then mechanically quoted Jesus in a flat monotone, "he that is not for me is against me."

Christopher hadn't the slightest idea what she was talking about but could tell something was wrong with her. He could tell by her tone of voice and her eyes. Like she was hypnotized or something. At last he said, "Harmony, what in the world *are* you talking about?"

Harmony looked at him scornfully. "You don't have the slightest idea, do you?"

Christopher nodded. "You got that right, chick."

"Well, you want to know?"

"Yes!" Christopher was emphatic. "Please tell me!"

"God."

"God?"

"That's what I just said isn't it?"

Christopher was thoroughly confused. Had he missed part of the conversation? Finally he let out a long stream of air. "Okay," he began, regaining his composure, "so you're talking about God. That still doesn't tell me why you're mad at me."

"I'm not mad at you," Harmony insisted, "but it's like I've been trying to tell you, we're on two separate roads. I'm on the road to heaven. To God. You're on the road to hell. What you perceive as me being mad at you is only the widening gulf between the two different roads we're on. And the farther along these two separate roads we travel the farther apart we'll grow. You see, there aren't three roads, only two, and nobody can travel up the middle. Nobody. Now do you understand?"

Quite honestly Christopher did not. "Did Peter put these ideas in your head about 'two roads' and all of that?"

For a minute Harmony didn't say anything. Then, a little

defensively, "Peter is very intelligent, Chris. He's the smartest man I've ever talked to. He knows all about the Bible and God and everything."

Not sure how to respond, Christopher looked up at the sky and scratched his head. "Look," he began slowly, trying to formulate his ideas, "I don't know anything about religion or God. Never read the Bible. But I sense something odd going on. I can almost feel it but I can't put my finger on it. Know what I mean?"

"Of course," Harmony replied in clipped tones, "the presence of God is strong upon me right now. That's what you sense believe it or not."

"No, No," Christopher frowned, struggling with his thoughts, "what I'm trying to say is, I think you're being conned." She looked at him sharply but he quickly went on. "These two guys have you believing something pretty wild. I can tell. But whatever it is, why don't you just tell me?"

"If I told you straight out what I know to be true you'd never believe it, Chris. You don't even believe in God. How would you ever believe this?"

His frustration mounting, Christopher took a deep breath and tried again. "Look, Harmony, I want to understand, I really do. Just give me a chance."

Harmony made up her mind. The only fair thing was to present her evidence and let him make up his own mind. She at least owed him that much. "All right," she began, "but you're never going to believe this, and I don't expect you to."

"Okay. Go ahead. I'm listening."

"All right. Remember yesterday morning when you and Quentin first returned from your hike and I tried to get you to check out the gigantic ant nest in the tree stump?"

Christopher nodded. "Yeah. I remember. You tried getting me to talk to the ants. You were acting really weird then, too."

"I know, but I had a good reason to be acting weird."

"Why?"

Harmony took a deep breath and declared, "Because those ants were talking to me!"

"Talking to you?" Christopher looked at her gravely.

"Okay, they weren't actually *talking* to me. Communicating would be a better word."

"How?" Christopher asked sarcastically, "by tapping their feet?"

"Well..." Harmony wasn't sure how to answer. Then she remembered. "They did a little dance routine, sort of."

Christopher burst out laughing. "Yeah. Sure, Harmony. Who taught them to dance, Fred Astaire?"

"They were trying to communicate with me!" Harmony insisted.

"How do you know that?"

"Because I asked them questions and by God they answered me!"

"How?" Christopher demanded, glad no one could hear their conversation.

"Through their little song-and-dance routine, like I told you."

"Give me a break!" Christopher exploded."

Harmony shrugged. "See. I knew you wouldn't believe it."

"Well do you expect me to?"

"I already told you the answer to that, too. Of course not." A long silence followed. Then, oddly, her blustery confidence faltered as she hesitantly asked, "Do you think I'm going crazy?"

They stopped walking. Taking her by the shoulders, Christopher studied her closely for a moment, then asked softly, "Do *you* think you're going crazy?"

She sniffed and rubbed her eyes. "I don't know. I—I'm beginning to wonder."

"Maybe you just imagined it. I mean about the ants tapping their feet to send messages."

"They were *not* tapping their feet!" Harmony cried in

exasperation, "and I did not imagine any of it! And even if I did," she added quietly, "the point is, Peter Perish knew all about it."

They started walking again, a deep frown marring Christopher's face. "He knew you talked to the ants?"

"That's right!" Harmony proclaimed, "and I didn't say a word about it to him. He just brought it up all on his own. He told *me* about it!"

"Well what in the world does that have to do with anything, anyway?"

"Chris," Harmony began emphatically, "it has everything to do with everything. That's what I've been trying to tell you. If you didn't tell him about the ants, which you didn't because you didn't know about it, and if Quentin didn't tell him about the ants, which we also know he couldn't have, and if I didn't tell him about the ants, how did he know about it?"

Christopher was growing weary of the conversation. The whole thing was ridiculous. "I don't know," he said vacantly, "you tell me."

"Okay," Harmony said, feeling that at last she was getting somewhere, "Peter knew about the ants communicating with me because *he* caused it to happen. That was his first attempt at contacting me. He told me so."

Christopher looked at her in utter disbelief. "What!?"

"That's right. He didn't want to scare me off. And he wasn't sure how to contact me so he first tried through the ants, and probably would have succeeded too, if you and Quentin hadn't come along just when you did."

"Wait a minute," Christopher said, holding up his hands. "First of all, he hadn't even met you before last night. Second, you're telling me he can make ants do what he wants. Just who do you think Peter Perish is?"

"I know who he is. The question is, do *you* want to know?"

Christopher sighed. "Yeah. Sure. Lay it on me."

"Peter Perish is my guardian angel," she firmly stated.

"Your what!?" Christopher cried. "I really think you are
going crazy, Harmony. I mean, think about it. You're standing
there telling me Peter Perish is an angel! Literally!"

Harmony didn't reply. What was there to say? She had presented her evidence. There was nothing more she could do. Had
she expected him to believe her in the first place?

Silence prevailed as they walked through the chilly shadow
of the grain elevator. The sun was on the far side of the sky
again and Christopher realized the day was wearing on. Somehow the thought of spending another night with Peter Perish and
Alan Bolten was disconcerting. That they had done something
to Harmony he had no doubt. It seemed they had complete control over her. With a sinking feeling he realized he was actually
becoming afraid of Perish and Bolten. What if they could do to
him whatever it was they had done to Harmony?

They left the tracks for the broken, tilted sidewalk and
made their way to Main Street. Somehow the town looked different in the afternoon sunshine. A little more inviting anyway,
and not nearly so deserted as the night before. There were cars
and trucks, farmers and merchants going about their business.
Everything seemed so normal. For Christopher it was like stepping out of a bad dream. The reality was refreshing.

At the little grocery store Harmony stopped and said, "I'm
going down to the laundromat. When you get done I'll be waiting by the tracks."

Watching her go, Christopher frowned. Somehow he had to
straighten her out. Whatever Perish and Bolten had done to her
could be undone. Hopefully. He turned into the market, his
mind on everything but shopping.

It only took a few minutes and he was back on the dusty
street, a brown paper bag under his arm containing a salami,
Colby cheese, and french bread. In his hip pocket was a pack of
Marlboros and a lighter he had swiped.

He looked around, but Harmony was nowhere to be seen.
Figuring she was still in the laundromat, he turned his back to

the store's rough brick wall and leaned against it to wait. Maybe the ladies room was crowded this time of day.

It wasn't long before he found himself eyeing the bar and grill. Wondering if they wouldn't sell him a six-pack, he pushed off the wall and with a glance at the laundromat, started across the street. When he opened the door and stepped in four men turned on their stools and stared at him. It was dark inside and he paused a moment while his eyes adjusted, then went up to the bar and set his groceries down. The men turned back to their business as the aproned bartender approached. "What'll it be, sonny?"

"Six-pack of Bud, please," Christopher said politely. This wasn't the city.

The bartender pointed to the cooler at the rear of the room. "Back there."

"Thanks." Leaving the groceries, Christopher walked into the depths of the dark, nearly empty room, his footsteps echoing with a hollow sound. He helped himself to a six and returned to the center of the long, polished bar where the bartender rang up his purchase. Elated, Christopher laid the money down as the man snapped open a bag and slipped the six in.

By the time he got out of the tavern Harmony, sitting cross-legged on the strip of grass between the sidewalk and the tracks, was waiting patiently for him. He made a beeline for the girl and sat down beside her. "Guess what I got?" he said proudly.

"What?"

"Beer!"

"Beer?" Harmony looked at him in surprise. "You're not old enough to buy beer."

"I guess in this town I am," Christopher grinned.

"I never had beer before," Harmony said, sounding every bit like a little kid to him.

"It'll go good with the salami and cheese."

"I don't like beer."

"How do you know?" Christopher countered, "you never

had it before."

Harmony shrugged, "I guess I don't know."

Getting to his feet, he said, "Well let's go." Then he remembered the cigarettes. "Wait a minute." He set the bags down and pulled the pack from his pocket. With Harmony looking on incredulously he stripped off the cellophane as casually as possible, opened the box and with an awkwardness that revealed his inexperience, clumsily removed a single cigarette. Digging out the lighter, he fit the smoke between tight lips and cupped it in a perfect emulation of the Marlboro Man. Determined that he wouldn't cough like the last time he tried to smoke, he struck a flame on the lighter and puffed. Certain she would be impressed, he looked at Harmony as he blew out a stream of smoke.

"Cigarettes?" she scowled. "You smoke, too?" Christopher's grin faded. "Some girls might like a guy that smells like a dirty ashtray and an empty can of beer but I don't. It doesn't impress me at all."

Stung by her remark, Christopher took a deep drag on the cigarette and blew a cloud of smoke in her face. "You'll get used to it," he said coldly. Throwing the cigarette down, he grabbed the bags and brushed past her. When she didn't immediately follow he stopped, turned around and loudly demanded, "C'mon!"

She stared at him for a moment, then got to her feet. Somehow she was going to make him see the light of day. Somehow.

They walked steadily, neither speaking. When they reached the grain elevator Christopher noticed a small, grassy knoll just beyond, complete with a wooden picnic table. Apparently where the workers ate their lunch in nice weather. Hoping for one last chance to get to the bottom of whatever was going on between Harmony and their two most recent acquaintances (it would be hopeless once back at camp and she was under their influence), he suggested a little picnic. "It's such a perfect spot, and we'd have it all to ourselves," he said, looking at her sincerely with his big baby blues. "Please?"

"Why?" She asked suspiciously, "Can't you wait until we get back to camp to eat?"

"I'm too hungry," Christopher insisted. "I feel like if I don't eat right now I'm gonna die. Besides, when's the last time you had a picnic?"

Harmony's face went blank momentarily. Her lips tightened with the sudden realization that in fact she had never been on a picnic before. Ever. "I don't know," she lied, adding with a shrug, "I don't remember."

"Well, how about it then?" Christopher pleaded. "Please?"

With a sigh Harmony gave in. "Okay." This might be her last chance to straighten him out.

Christopher smiled. "Thanks." Then, taking her completely by surprise he pecked her a light kiss on the cheek and left her standing there as he descended upon the table and laid out the cheese, salami, french bread and beer.

Harmony watched him, the sweetness of his kiss still warm on her cheek, her feelings for him welling up inside. And although she would have loved to run to him and throw her arms around him and hug him and kiss him until they both tumbled to the soft green grass, it was with dignified self-control that she joined him at the table. At this point she wanted to maintain a respectful distance because if she couldn't convert him it would be much too painful when the time came to say goodbye.

He was already slicing salami with his pocketknife, an open beer at his side, when she sat down opposite him. He stopped slicing and laid the knife down. "You want to try a beer?" he asked, "it's really good with salami sandwiches." Secretly he was hoping a little beer would loosen her tongue and maybe help break the "spell" or whatever it was Perish and Bolten had her under.

Harmony shrugged. "Well, I guess one wouldn't hurt."

"Nah," Christopher agreed and reached for a beer. "In fact

everyone should drink at least one beer a day. They say it's good for you."

"They do?"

"Yep." He snapped open the can and set it before her, took a drink of his own beer and went back to slicing salami.

Harmony took a tiny sip and made a face. "It's so bitter!"

"You get used to it," Christopher assured her, not quite used to it himself. He put a sandwich together and placed it before her. "Try this," he urged.

Harmony took a small bite of the sandwich and her face brightened with satisfaction. "Hey, this *is* good."

"After you've had a few bites take a drink of beer," Christopher advised, "and you'll see what I mean about how they go together."

Harmony hesitated, cautiously taking a tiny sip. She looked up and smiled. "Not bad. Not bad at all."

"See," Christopher said as he chomped down on his own sandwich, "I don't tell you no B.S."

Taking increasingly frequent sips of the cold beer, halfway through her first can Harmony's mouth went slightly numb and her sense of taste dulled. Then she began to get lightheaded as her cautious sips turned into full-fledged gulps. Christopher smiled knowingly.

Two sandwiches and three beers later Christopher was feeling pretty good himself. Harmony was just starting her second beer. She turned down another sandwich. Christopher popped open his fourth and final beer and took a long swig. He set the can down and broke out his cigarettes.

Feeling very manly as he puffed his smoke, he tried to think of some way to free Harmony of her crazy ideas. Then again, maybe she wasn't crazy at all. Maybe the bit about Perish being an angel was just a front to throw him and Quentin off. To get rid of them. What could they possibly have offered her? Surely she didn't *really* believe Perish was an angel. Although he hadn't known her for very long he knew her well enough to know she wasn't mentally disturbed. At last he decided the only thing to do was plunge right in. He looked up. "Hey Harmony?"

"What?"

"Tell me straight-up what kind of deal Peter has you talked into. Maybe I'll go for it."

Harmony looked at him oddly. "What do you mean?"

"I mean just tell me whatever it is he's talked you into and maybe I'll join up with you guys. Because I know you got something cookin' with them. Did they tell you they got a house somewhere? Or maybe they got money in New York and they're going to make you a star?"

"What on earth are you talking about?"

Christopher smiled. "Okay, I get it. You're not going to tell me."

"Tell you what?" Harmony was truly puzzled.

"Is Alan in on it too?" he snapped, offended by what he perceived to be her feigned ignorance of what he was talking about.

Harmony frowned. "Uh, I—I'm not sure."

"Not sure about what?"

"Not sure if Alan is an angel or not. I never asked."

Christopher almost exploded with frustration. *How did they get on this subject again?* For the first time he seriously began to doubt her sanity. Swilling more beer, he implored incredulously, "You're not sure if Alan is an angel but you are sure Peter is?"

Harmony nodded. Christopher wanted to grab her by the throat and throttle her. Struggling to maintain his composure, he said, "You seem pretty sure about all of this."

"Well Chris," Harmony started defensively, "I told you all about the evidence. He knew all about me. That I ran away from a foster home, about the ants and how they talked to me and everything else." Then she hesitated, asking in a tiny voice, "Don't you believe me?"

"What? About the talking ants or about Peter being an angel? Don't you see?" he cried, "one thing's just as crazy as another! And none of it makes sense. I mean, do you *really* expect me to believe this weirdo Peter is an angel?" He laughed, shaking his head as if to clear it and chugged the rest of his beer.

"You don't believe me," Harmony said numbly.

"What do you expect?" he spat, crumpling the empty can and flinging it. "You think I'm an idiot?" But the sadness written on her downcast face touched him. After a moment he reached out and took her hand. "Look, Harmony," he started with renewed resolve, "I'm going to tell you this because I love you and want to help you." With gentle firmness he stated, "There's no such thing as angels. They only exist in story books and cartoons and stuff."

"There are so angels!" Harmony sharply retorted, "the Bible says so. If there weren't angels the Bible wouldn't say there were. But I wouldn't expect you to believe that," she went on heatedly, "why should you? You don't even believe in God."

"I do so!" Christopher angrily denied the charge.

"That's not what you told me last night!" she shot back.

"I didn't mean that I didn't believe in God, just that I didn't think about it much one way or the other because I don't know. But when you come right down to it I suppose I do believe in God. I mean, there's definitely some sort of 'Supreme Being' or nature or whatever you want to call it that started the ball rolling. But it's not as if you can look up at the sky and say, 'Lord, my toe hurts make it go away' and presto! It's going to go away."

"Yes you can!" Harmony shot back, "it's called praying."

"Is that so?" Christopher asked, in his heart giving up. The chick was definitely lost. "Okay," he went on, "in that case I'm gonna try a little test-prayer just to make sure it works. Okay?"

Harmony nodded, her soul filling with faith and hope. Now if only God would do *his* stuff.

"Let me see," Christopher pondered and looked up at the sky. First he thought of asking for a lemon meringue pie, but before he uttered the words his face brightened with an idea, and maybe just a twinge of hope as well. "Sir God," he started, "I like Harmony a lot and if you don't use some of your magic power or whatever it is to make her start thinking straight about the two maggots she's taken up with I'm gonna lose her. And you, sir," he added as an afterthought, "are gonna lose one of your best fans to a couple of no good creeps. I've tried talking sense to her, sir, but it don't do any good, so I'm leaving it up to you."

Looking at him with contempt, Harmony said scornfully, "Ha! Ha! Very funny! Now what'll you do for an encore?" Christopher just looked at her steadily. "That's no prayer," she went on, "you're just making fun."

"No I'm not!" Christopher shot back, "I meant every word I said and I sincerely hope God answers my prayer—for your sake."

Harmony looked at him with disgust. How could he be so deceived?

The sun was distant and low now and it was getting a little chilly, the wind picking up some. Leaving the rest of her second beer, Harmony started gathering up the garbage. Christopher bagged the leftovers. Without a word they rose from the table and started back. "One thing," Harmony said as they walked along in the gathering dusk, "if your prayer doesn't work will you come with me?"

"If my prayer doesn't work," Christopher intoned, "it means there ain't no God, which means those two jerks ain't angels and you're coming with me."

"Yeah, but if it does work, then...."

"Right," Christopher interjected with a smile, "I win both ways."

Harmony immediately began a heated protest, offering an in-depth explanation of how unfair he was being, but Christopher didn't argue, he just nodded from time to time and pretended to listen. He wasn't. The chick was good-looking but nuts. He was through. Tomorrow he was leaving and she could have her angels and eat them too if she wanted

*   *   *

That evening Quentin and Christopher sat on one side of the fire while Harmony, Peter Perish, and Alan Bolten huddled on the other. The three of them spoke in low overtones and from time to time would cast a suspicious eye on the two "outcasts."

As the night wore on and the devil failed to make his appearance (quite possibly expected from both sides of the camp) they all settled back for a night's rest and one by one dropped off to sleep until, alone, Christopher found himself gazing at the few remaining flames that danced across the heap of glowing red coals.

His mind had seemingly recorded every second of the last two days with Harmony, and now in vivid detail it relentlessly recalled them; Their first wild ride with the police in pursuit, and their narrow escape with death. Sleeping in her arms on the grass by the pond where he had dunked the car. How warm they had kept each other on that wet, chilly night. Their first kiss on the roof of the swaying boxcar in the warm spring sunshine....

In time though his eyelids grew heavy and he too floated through regressing levels of consciousness until sound asleep.

*   *   *

Harmony's eyes popped open and she lay perfectly still, staring up at the star-filled sky, her heart pounding. If she had been dreaming she couldn't recall, but being sound asleep one moment and wide awake the next left her with an eery feeling. There was none of the early morning lethargy one usually experiences upon first awakening. On the contrary, she was alert, her hearing and vision sharp. And the first thing she noticed were the crickets. They were silent. A vague fear crept into her subconscious. What had so thoroughly awakened her yet left the others so soundly sleeping? What had silenced the crickets?

The slow, deep breathing of Perish and Bolten on either side of her was somehow reassuring. But when she glanced over at Perish he was so pale and still as to appear dead. A resurgent fear rippled the length of her spine and grew into a tight knot in the pit of her stomach. For a moment she considered waking him, but not wanting to appear foolish, decided against it. Instead a fervent prayer seeking the Lord's protection vanquished her jitters and she prepared to roll over and bury her head beneath the blankets when what she saw made her sit up.

A pale, cold, oblong-shaped light rose up out of the soundly sleeping Perish and hovered several feet above him. Strangely enough, Harmony felt no fear, only curiosity. There was something vaguely familiar about it in the same way Perish had reminded her of the ants, although events of the moment kept such speculation at the furthest reaches of her mind.

And then from her left came a sound like that of a gas furnace being ignited and she turned just in time to see another oblong-shaped light forming. It grew from top to bottom, a brilliant, searing, perfectly formed three-foot-by-five-foot rectangle of white-hot light that pulsed and moved within itself.

Its blazing radiance was so intense Harmony at first covered her eyes. But when she looked again it too floated several feet in the air, diametrically opposed to the cooler, paler light hovering over Perish. This new light seemed to burn with fire, but it was not fire and gave off no heat nor flames. And despite its incredible brilliance it shed no light upon the camp nor even upon the blackness immediately surrounding its perfect borders.

An astonished Harmony returned her gaze to the smaller, colder light. It struck her as odd but it somehow seemed dead. Silent. As if a cheap imitation of the vibrant, "living" light that pulsed and sizzled to her left.

Her gaze shifted back to the more powerful figure of light. To her trembling amazement it began to wax larger, its awesome radiance growing ever more intense. As the "living" light increased the "dead" light shrank by a like amount, finally vanishing altogether as it was apparently consumed by the brighter, hotter light.

Paralyzed with fear, Harmony watched the vibrant "living" light slowly advance towards her. It stopped, seemingly stooping over and peering closely at her.

But Harmony wasn't watching any longer. Terrified, she turned away, pulled the blanket over her head and hugged herself as she silently prayed to dear Jesus for the morning time to come.

HARMONY'S ANGEL

9

FOR CHRIST'S SAKE

It was a cold, blustery morning, angry gray clouds hanging close to the earth, the scent of rain in the air. Christopher stood over a still slumbering Harmony, hands buried deep in his jacket pockets, the gusting wind scattering his long, straw-colored hair. He wanted to say goodbye. He wanted to stoop and kiss her one last time. He wanted to recall to Quentin the black man's promise that they would never leave her. But then, that had been more his decision than Quentin's. With a heavy heart he whispered his farewell, turned and walked quickly out of camp.

Quentin was waiting for him on the footpath. Without a word the two friends started up the trail. Making a stab at conversation to lighten the mood, Quentin said, "Maybe we'll get lucky this mornin' an' catch a train right away."

Christopher grunted unintelligibly. He was dwelling on the memory of Harmony's silky blonde hair and blue eyes. Of holding her warm and close while they slept on that first night. Their first kiss. It all seemed so long ago....

They reached the tracks, crunched through gravel and stopped between the double set of gleaming steel rails. Quentin put a hand to his forehead in search of the telltale glimmer of yellowish light that would signal an approaching train. They were in luck. "Let it rain, let it pour," he cheered, "I see a train!" He turned to Christopher with a hand out, palm up. "Gimme five, bro!"

A less enthusiastic Christopher slapped him five. "I sure

113

hate leaving Harmony this way," he sighed.

"Ah, forget the chick, Chris, there's other crabs in the ocean," Quentin grinned. When it became obvious humor wasn't going to work he added seriously, "Besides, somethin' tell me hangin' around here would only mean trouble."

"Why shouldn't we just kidnap her?" Christopher asked, suddenly reviving an old idea.

Quentin shook his head. "We already been through that. What you gonna do, tie her up? She has a right to stay with those guys if she wants to. An' if you wanna know the truth of the matter," he added confidentially, "be glad you rid of her. She seemed pretty goofy. Maybe she escaped from a nut house or somethin'." In reality Quentin didn't feel quite so strongly about the girl as he was coming off (he missed her too), but he was trying to minimize Christopher's feelings of loss.

To some extent it worked, though it didn't stop Christopher talking about her. "She sure seemed normal to me," he went on with a sharp gesture towards camp, "until we met up with those two guys. Maybe they brainwashed her like those religious cults do."

"Maybe," Quentin said absently, examining the sky for rain. The train would be along in minutes and with any luck at all they'd find themselves on it. "Let's hide in the brush so the engineer don't see us."

*   *   *

It was Peter Perish's repeated gagging followed by explosions of lumpy yellowish vomit that awakened Harmony. The disheveled girl sat up half expecting to see the two oblong shapes of glowing light still floating in the air. Her eyes traveled to Perish. Silhouetted against the trees, he appeared paper-thin as he stood with legs apart, doubled over and letting go with gut-wrenching heaves. A worried Alan Bolten hovered nearby. As his breathing gradually returned to normal a pale, watery-eyed Perish straightened up.

The chilly, overcast day was immediately depressing. So was the sinking feeling when Harmony noticed that Christopher and Quentin were gone. She sensed it was for good. But something else was different as well. Something had changed—no—was missing. Something she had no words for. Perplexed but feeling more clearheaded than she had in days, Harmony threw off her blanket and stood up. Tossing her blonde hair back, she raked her fingers through it as she approached the boys.

When she came up from behind both turned around, Perish eyeing her cynically as he wiped flecks of yellowish vomit from his mouth with his sleeve. "What'a *you* want?" he asked sourly.

"Nothing," Harmony replied, taken aback at his sudden nasty disposition.

"Well what're you looking at?" he frowned. "Haven't you ever seen someone be sick before?"

Becoming more confused by the minute, Harmony whimpered, "I... don't understand, Peter, what did I do wrong?"

"Nothing," Perish said, turning on her viciously, "I'm just sick of you hanging around me. I don't even *like* you!"

Totally lost, Harmony turned to Alan with pleading eyes but he just snickered, seemingly filled with glee at this turn of events. Returning her gaze to Perish, she locked eyes with him and insisted, "But you said you loved me, and, and...."

"Loved you?" Perish eyed her skeptically. "I may have said I wanted to *lay* you, but I certainly don't love you."

Harmony was aghast. "B-B-But you told me... I... we..." Watching Alan for a reaction, she blurted, "You said you were my angel!"

"What!?" Perish burst out laughing. "Did you hear that, Al?" he exclaimed, slapping his friend's back. "She thinks I'm her angel!"

"You? Harmony's angel?" Alan giggled.

Perish turned to Harmony and leaned so close the stink of his breath made her draw back. Pointing to his shoulders in

mock seriousness he said, "But I don't have wings!" Roaring
with laughter, he pounded Alan's back again.

Suddenly reality came crashing in, crumbling Harmony's
dream world like a biscuit. All that remained were the cold, unforgiving facts. She had been a fool. Tricked. Tricked by this
disgusting beanpole of a man and his fat, dimwitted friend.

Angels? Ha! The very idea! How could she have been so
stupid? And then all of Christopher's words came flooding back
in a torrent. Panicky, turning every which way, she demanded,
"Where's Christopher and Quentin?"

"Who and who?" Perish squinted at her.

"Oh, just forget it!" she snapped, turned on her heel and
broke into a full run for the tracks. Maybe she could still catch
up to them.

She heard the train even as she saw it, felt the earth shudder
beneath the pounding steel wheels. When she reached the right-
of-way the swaying freight cars were clattering by one after the
other. Fervently praying that she wasn't too late, Harmony
looked up and down the tracks, but Christopher and Quentin
were gone. "No! No! No!" she cried, crumpling to her knees,
the memory of her foolish behavior of the last few days flipping
through her mind in static bursts.

In her grief and despair she found herself cursing God. Why
had he done this to her? What wrong had she done? She had
played the fool *for Christ's sake!* And now she was all alone.
Now she would never see Christopher again.

"Please God, please!" she whispered, "help me. Don't let
me lose my friends!" And it was with an unbearable aching in
her heart that she longed to be near Christopher again. To feel
his warmth. To gaze into his sincere blue eyes.

Sniffling and wiping away tears with the back of her hand,
she looked up and saw as if in a dream a fleeting opportunity to
catch up with her friends. A boxcar, its massive steel door yawning wide, was rushing down on her only 13 cars from the end.
This was her last chance—if Quentin and Christopher had even

gotten on the train.

In a flash she jumped to her feet and started running as hard as she could. Within seconds she was sprinting beside the open door. In one swift motion she grabbed for the edge of the dusty wooden floor and heaved herself in. A lot of agile young men who try what she did end up under the wheels. But maybe she was just lucky.... Harmony got up off the floor feeling mighty pleased with herself. While dusting herself off she peered around the dark, cavernous boxcar. Except for a pile of old rags in the far corner it was empty.

Minutes later thunder crackled and boomed and flashes of lightning flitted across an angry gray sky as heavy black clouds released torrents of rain. Feeling a certain contentment, Harmony took a seat just inside the door to watch the storm. At least she was warm and dry. And now there was no danger of Peter Perish or Alan Bolten getting their grubby hands on her. Thank God for that. Even so, deep inside she was fearful. What if Quentin and Christopher hadn't hopped the train she was on? What if they had caught one hours ago? One that was going in the other direction? Or what if they had decided to hike back into town? Or had walked into the grove of trees on the other side of the tracks and were now hoofing it across some farmer's field in God-only-knew what direction?

What if? What if? What if? Worried sick right down to the pit of her stomach, she lay back, clasping her hands behind her head, and stared up at the ribbed ceiling of the rattling old boxcar as the train gradually gathered speed, the events of the last few days riffling through her mind like flashcards.

Due to her middle of the night experience with the "Beings of Light" or whatever they were she hadn't slept well. Now at least she felt safe, even if frightened and alone, and with the steady drumming of rain on the roof and the gentle swaying of the boxcar she started drifting off.

Realizing it was time for her to show a little faith, and silently praying to God to fill her with it, she was reminded of the old joke about the man asking God to grant him patience and to hurry up, and fell asleep with a smile on her face.

But it was a fitful sleep. In a dream she saw herself standing in the midst of a magnificent mansion waiting with much apprehension for someone very important to appear. Then the splendid mansion began to quake and heave, the plaster on the walls crackling as the house began crumbling around her....

The train rolled around a long, sweeping curve, clattered through a road crossing, past flashing red lights and clanging bells that quickly faded. Now rain blew in the door and lightly spattered the girl's clothes.

It was the noisy grade crossing that caused the lump of rags in the far corner to stir. Quivering with a hacking cough, an old black man sat up, his tattered woolen army blanket falling away. Conjuring up phlegm from the back of his throat, he spat. The yellowish blob hit the opposite wall with a splat, the snot and phlegm clinging momentarily before drooling to the floor.

He was darker than the ancient dirt on the boxcar walls and although 69 years old, didn't look a day over 50. His leathery face, covered with five day's growth of gray stubble, was etched with the creases of a man who had worked long years under a hot sun. Deep, clear brown eyes were set wide on either side of a broad, flat nose. His scraggly, gray-tinged hair grew in clumps all over his head with bare spots in between.

Having worked as a construction laborer for 53 of his 69 years, he had huge calloused hands and dry, wrinkled skin draped like old sackcloth over sinewy, taut muscles. He was dressed simply in a threadbare aqua-blue sweatshirt and bib coveralls that had seen better days. His white socks and orange work boots were spattered with mortar stains.

The old man started to his feet but fell as the car lurched. On his second try he made it and with a wide yawn, stretched and started for the light of the open door when his eye fell upon the young girl asleep on the floor. Leaving his blanket and battered brown suitcase where they lay, he weaved a drunken-like path toward her.

He stooped over and peered closely at her, a saw-toothed grin splitting his wrinkled face, his roving eyes taking in every inch of the blossoming white girl, delicate as a rose petal and surely as sweet as the honeysuckle. Noticing her rain-spattered clothes, the old codger went for his blanket. Taking care not to awaken the girl, he gently covered her against the cold and damp. Coughing up phlegm, he turned and spat out the door. Still struggling in her dreams, Harmony groaned and shifted to her side.

An hour drifted by. The heart of the storm passed and the rain became intermittent, then stopped altogether. Gradually the steel-gray sky began breaking up into patches of blue, the golden rays of a still hidden sun slanting to earth as the light of heaven played upon the rolling green hills with all the colors of the rainbow, blessing the young, frail plants as they pushed up from the soil. The fresh scent of rain-washed air lightened the old man's heart, flooding his memory with all the springtimes of his youth.

The train rumbled through an old section of track, causing an abrupt jolt and earsplitting screech, then the rhythmic click-clack song of its wheels resumed. But not before awakening Harmony. "Chris?" she called out and suddenly sat up. But even as his name left her lips she remembered and her spirits sank. But before she had time to get depressed she noticed the old black man sitting in the doorway and her heart leapt, fluttering with new fear. "H-Hi," she stammered, trying to sound casual but unable to hide the nervousness in her voice. "You just hop on?"

A faint smile crossed the old man's face and he shook his head. "No, child. The train be goin' much too fast."

"Oh," Harmony nodded. *So that had been the pile of rags in the far corner.*

"How 'bout yourself, missy?" the old man asked, "when you get on?"

Harmony shrugged, "Early this morning some time."

"Well it still be mornin'," the old man informed her, scrutinizing the sky. "'Bout an hour of it left, I 'spect."

Noticing the blanket lying across her legs, Harmony looked down. "This your blanket?"

"Yes'm. I loansed it to ya 'cause ya looked cold."

"Thanks." She put the blanket aside in a heap.

He eyed her momentarily before asking bluntly, "What a little baby girl like you runnin' from?"

"I'm not running from anything," Harmony lied to avoid explaining. To do so would have been embarrassing. Insulting. "Just thought it was time to give up the sheltered life and set out on my own. See if the world really looks the way they show on TV."

"Mmmm," the old man nodded. But he wasn't satisfied. "Why a purty little child like you wants to run away from your very own family for?"

"I don't have a family." Harmony's curt reply was edged with bitterness.

"Come now, child," the old man scoffed, "everbody gots a family. 'Specially a little bitty girl like you."

"Uh-uh," she shook her head. "Never knew my dad. Ma died when I was 13, and I've been livin' with my cousins for the last three years."

"Well, that be family."

"Hah!" Harmony's laugh was an angry bark as she spat resentfully, "Then why don't *you* go live with them?"

The old man dropped his eyes. Absently plucking a loose thread off his coveralls he asked rather self-consciously, "You gots a name?"

"Harmony," she replied, the heat of her resentment fading.

"Mr. Henry Rathbone," he said with a shallow little bow, "at your service."

"You don't have to serve me," Harmony promptly replied, "You're an old man."

He chuckled. "How old you think I is, child?"

She shrugged. "I don't know."

"Guess."

"Okay. But I'm not very good at guessing people's ages," she warned.

"Go ahead, child," he urged, "try."

"All right. I'll say 43."

Ol' Henry laughed delightedly. "Forty-three! Well I'll be blessed. Does I look that old?"

"I told you I wasn't very good at guessing ages."

"You best believes it, child," he chuckled again. "Now you wants to know how old I really is?"

"How old?"

"Sixty-nine."

"No way!"

"Yep. Sixty-nine just 'bout three months ago."

"Well you sure don't look it. You're the youngest looking 69-year-old man I've ever seen."

"Well it be the Lord's truth, child. It surely is. Scouts honor." He held up two fingers. Then, "Now that we gots my age down, how old you be?"

"Guess," she said with a smirk.

"Ohhh, I gots to say 'bout 16."

Harmony's face lit up. "That's it! You hit the nail right on the head! How'd you do it?"

"Don't know," he replied with a shrug. "Guess I's just lucky."

All that remained of the storm were cotton-puff clouds in a turquoise-blue sky. Feeling safe with the old man now, Harmony moved into the sunshine streaming through the door and took a seat beside him. From the jouncing, rattling boxcar they watched the morning blossom into a sunshiny afternoon.

Harmony was thinking how refreshed the world seemed after a rain when the old man brought up another subject lingering on his mind ever since he first discovered the girl. "You ought'n be travelin' all alone, child. The world is full a bad peoples that'd just loves to get they grimy hands on the likes a you."

"I know," Harmony admitted, "I already met some creeps like that. But I can take care of myself."

"Shoo-fire, girl," Ol' Henry chortled, "what you gonna do against a big strong man?"

"Kick 'em in the balls," Harmony brazenly declared.

"That be so?" the old man challenged, "let's see!" With that he pushed her flat on her back and with a massive left hand, pinned both her skinny wrists to the floor above her head in a vise-like grip. With his right he grabbed a fistful of her sweatshirt and twisted it so tightly at the throat that she choked.

For a moment Harmony struggled feebly, but without air she became faint, floating, passing out. At that instant Ol' Henry released her, leaned back against the wall and folded his arms across his chest with satisfaction. Harmony's consciousness returned almost immediately. "That's not fair!" she exploded and sat up, chest heaving as she gasped for air.

"That be right, child," the black man said seriously. "An' they ain't no rapist gonna be fair, neither."

As her breathing gradually stabilized Harmony looked at him with narrowed, angry eyes. But after a moment she admitted the truth and her anger passed.

"All I be sayin' child, if you gots to be on the road travel with somebody. Anybody. Just so you gots help in case ya needs it."

"I was traveling with two guys," Harmony replied. "One was my boyfriend, sort of. But I lost them. That's why I'm on this train right now. I'm trying to find them."

"How you know they be goin' this way?"

"Because we're all running away from Chicago. And when we started out together we decided to head west. They certainly don't have any reason to head back east."

"What your two friends be runnin' from?"

"Christopher, that's my boyfriend sort of, he's running away because he totaled his dad's car. Quentin is running away from jail. He's black."

"What he do ta gets himself in jail?"

"Don't know," Harmony shrugged. "He never really said, except that he got in a fight with some white guy and felt the whole thing was really unfair."

"Probably was."

"You're just prejudice!"

"Ho-ho! Looky who's talkin'!"

"Well it's true," Harmony declared. "It's just as easy for a black person to be prejudice as it is for a white person."

"Okay, child," Ol' Henry nodded, giving in. "I admit it be possible for black peoples to be prejudice, too. So what?"

"So buttons on your underwear." Harmony quipped.

"Buttons on my underdrawers would be downright uncomfortable, missy," Ol' Henry chuckled. "Anyways, I hopes you'll travel with me till ya finds your friends or decides ta go back home."

"I'm not ever going back home. I don't have a home to go back to," she stressed, "and you can bet the family farm on that." After a silent moment she added, "Do you think I have much chance of finding my friends?"

"Could be they on this very train."

"You really think so?" Harmony asked hopefully.

Ol' Henry smiled, admitting, "I don't know, darlin'."

"Oh, I hope they are!" Harmony cried. "I'd give anything to catch up with them!"

"Well I be an ol' man, child, so I speaks from experience, be preparin' yo'self for the worst."

Harmony's shining hope faded.

"It don't matter none, child. I mean, you is welcome to come with me."

"I've got to find Christopher." She was adamant, then curious. "Where're you going?"

"Down south to the lands a my birth."

"If you want to go down south you're headed the wrong way," Harmony informed him.

"I am?" the old man asked in surprise. "Well I'll be blessed!" he exclaimed, slapping his knee. "Been havin' a wee-bit a trouble with my geography. Been tryin' to get my body down to Mississippi for goin' on two weeks now. One time I ends up in Ohio. Then Saint Paul. This body gonna be dead an' gone off to the great beyond fo' it ever gonna finds its way."

"Why are you always blessing yourself?" Harmony asked curiously, "that's twice now I heard you."

"'Cause, child, all my life I been listenin' to peoples damnin' themselves, an' I was too till I caught on. I mean, why go 'round damnin' yo'self when it be just as easy an' twice as fun ta be blessin' yo'self?"

Harmony stared at him. For one frightening moment she was beginning to wonder if he wasn't another Peter Perish. "Where'd you say you were going?" she finally asked, dismissing the notion.

"Mississippi. Jackson, Mississippi."

"What's down there?"

"What's down there? They be a heap o' money down there, child. An' it's hid an' I be the only one to know where."

Harmony's eyes lit up. "How much money?"

The old man pondered a moment, the wrinkles in his face shifting. "Ohhh, I has ta say 'bout fifty o' a hun'ert thousand dollars."

"A hundred thousand dollars!" Harmony exclaimed.

The old man could almost see the dollar signs ringing up in her eyes. "Maybe," he warned solemnly. Then, "You knows the way to Mississippi?"

Harmony nodded.

"Would you be willin' to help an ol' man finds his way fo' a share a the money?"

"So you get there before you're dead?" Harmony asked

pleasantly.

"That be right, missy," the old man answered, his deeply-lined face crinkling into a saw-toothed grin, "'cause it just won't do if'n I gets there an' I's dead." He paused a moment, scratching his bristly jaw. "So if'n you shows me the way," he said slowly, "I be willin' to gives you 25 percent."

Harmony was no fool. She laughed. "If you can't get to Mississippi without me," she began slyly, "and I can't get to the money without you, then I think it should be a 50–50 deal."

The old man was taken aback. "Ho-ho," he exclaimed, "listen to this! You surely do drives a hard bargain, little missy."

"It's fair."

Ol' Henry looked at her for a long moment, his face passive. "Only if they's no way to get there without you," he said softly.

Harmony stared at him, suddenly getting the distinct impression that his offer was not so much out of need as out of a desire to do her a favor. "All right," she conceded, "you win. Twenty-five percent to me, 75 to you. It's a deal. On one condition."

"What?"

"Before we head for Mississippi we try to find my friends."

The old man nodded once and extended his hand. "It be a deal, child." They shook on it. Then, "How'd you get yo'self separated from yo' friends, anyways?"

Harmony looked uncomfortable at the question. When she didn't answer he raised his eyes to hers and repeated it. Finally, in a halting voice she asked, "Do you believe there's... such a thing as angels?"

He looked at her curiously, then nodded. "I surely do, child. The Bible don't make no bones 'bout that."

"You believe in the Bible?" she asked in surprise.

Again the old man nodded. "Years ago my mamma done taught me 'bout it, child, an' I never heard no story that made more sense. But you ain't yet begun to tell me how you come to be separated from yo' friends."

"It's kind of hard to explain," Harmony replied, still look-ing uncomfortable. "But suppose an angel were to come down here right now. What do you think it would look like?" As she spoke her thoughts were on the two oblong shapes of glowing light she had seen the night before. Like burning energy.

"Don't know," Ol' Henry shrugged. "Ain't never seen one."

"Well what would you *imagine* an angel to look like?"

He thought for a moment before answering, "Don't know, child, I guess like a man." He stopped short, eyeing her suspi-ciously. "Say, what you askin' all these questions 'bout angels for?"

Harmony was peeling a shred of wood from the floor with intense concentration. "Because last night I think I might've seen one," she answered without looking up.

"Shoo-fire!" the old man scoffed. "An angel? I ain't never heard a nobody seein' an angel before." He looked at her closely. "You ain't funnin' with me are you, child?"

Harmony raised her eyes to his and shook her head. "No. To tell you the truth I think I saw two angels."

"*Two* angels!"

"Or maybe one was a demon," she said on sudden thought.

"A demon!"

Harmony nodded. "And I'm not lying, either," she added, describing the oblong shapes of glowing light. And then she went on at great length, explaining in detail exactly how one had seemed "dead" or "cold," as if an imitation of the one she described as a "living" or "hot" light. She concluded by asking, "Is there really such a thing as angels and demons?"

"I believes so," Ol' Henry replied seriously. "My mamma used to tell me stories 'bout that sort a stuff, too."

"Well how come I've never heard of anyone else seeing such a thing? Am I the only one in the whole wide world who's ever seen an angel?"

"Maybe you was dreamin'," he suggested.

She adamantly shook her head. "No. I wasn't dreaming. I was wide awake. And I hid under the covers till it went away. It was no dream."

The old man looked her in the eye and said conclusively, "I believes you."

"You do?"

"Yes, ma'am," he said, slowly nodding, "I surely do."

"But why did all this happen to me?" she implored.

Ol' Henry shrugged. "Why do the sun shine each an' every mornin'? Lord only knows, child. But you gots to remember, other peoples might'a seen angels an' such too but don't believe in no God or nothin' so they 'splains it away as dreams or illusions or somethin' an forgets all about it by the very next day."

"Then you believe I really saw what I really saw?"

"I believes so," Ol' Henry grinned.

"God, you don't know how good that makes me feel!" Harmony exclaimed with an ear to ear grin. It was a great relief that at least one other person besides herself didn't think she was completely bonkers. "Do you think I'll ever see another angel?"

The old man's face crinkled into a smile. "I couldn't rightly say, child, but you a pretty special little girl if'n you did see an angel. Not too many people gets that chance."

Lying back on the floor and folding her hands behind her head, Harmony said with a sigh, "I'll always wonder why it happened to me."

"Surely you will, child," Ol' Henry said, shifting around with his back to the wall, legs stretched out and crossed at the ankles. "Surely you will."

*   *   *

With a rumbling bang the train came to a stop. Framed in the boxcar door was a narrow, patched and bumpy asphalt street lined with crumbling red brick factories. The telephone poles anchored in the broken sidewalk leaned at crazy angles and cast tall shadows, and everything was bathed in the pale, golden light of late afternoon. Surprised that the noisy stop hadn't roused her elderly companion, Harmony got to her knees wondering if she shouldn't awaken him. Snoring away contentedly, he was slumped against the wall. After a moment of indecision she hesitantly reached for his shoulder. It was then she heard footsteps crunching in the gravel and felt the presence of a man stop at the open door.

10

THE LIVING DEAD

He was 50-ish with graying hair peeking from beneath a blue cap perched on his head. A brass insignia inscribed with *Security* was affixed above the shiny black visor. On his right hip was a semiautomatic pistol, on his left a two-way radio crackling with static. He had tired eyes and a round, deeply grained face with a day's growth of gray stubble.

Frightened, Harmony shook Ol' Henry, coaxing him with urgent whispers. "Wake up, Henry! We're in trouble! A man from the train is here!"

Ol' Henry sat up snorting and wheezing and spitting. "What be goin' on, child?" he asked, squinting at the daylight and the man just beyond the door.

"All right you two," the security officer interrupted, "come on out of there. And if you're thinking of giving me any trouble," he warned, "you'd better think again."

Suddenly wide awake, Ol' Henry said in his most humble manner, "Oh, no siree! We don't wants no kind'a trouble with nobody. We be gettin' down right now, Mr. Sir. I just gots to get my luggage." And lickity-split he was on his feet and scurrying after his suitcase in the far corner.

While Ol' Henry was off getting his suitcase the officer beckoned to Harmony. "Come on little girl, let's go."

Getting to her feet, Harmony asked nervously, "What's going to happen to us?"

"That depends on you," the man answered, holding his hand out to her, "come on."

When Harmony stepped up to the door and looked out she froze in her tracks, mouth agape. A prayer had been answered. Waiting obediently off to one side as instructed in hopes of getting the break the security officer had promised, Christopher and Quentin stood with downcast eyes.

The look of utter astonishment was so vividly written on her face that the officer quickly turned to see what the boys were up to. At that moment she shrieked, "Christopher!" and from where she stood, literally leapt for the boys, the startled officer ducking and shielding his head with his arms.

Equally startled, both boys' heads snapped up in shocked surprise. Setting upon them like a whirlwind, Harmony hugged and kissed them both repeatedly until Christopher swept her into his arms and brought her under control with a bear hug and a passionate kiss.

The baffled officer stood surveying the scene with critical regard. "You kids know each other?"

The three youngsters nodded.

"All right," he motioned with a wave of his hand, "come over here." Keeping their expressions somber, the kids gathered before him. In the meantime Ol' Henry stepped up to the door with his battered brown suitcase under one arm. Turning to the old man, the officer graciously offered, "Here, let me help you with that."

"Why thank you, Mr. Sir," Ol' Henry said and handed down the suitcase. Then he gingerly climbed down from the boxcar, took his suitcase with a little bow of gratitude and joined Harmony and her two friends.

Having three of his own the security officer had a soft spot in his heart for the youngsters. Looking at Harmony, he asked, "Just what're you kids doing on this train?"

"Trying to get home," Christopher quickly interjected.

The officer peered closely at him. "Trying to get home, eh? From where?"

Christopher shrugged and was about to go into a lengthy

explanation when the officer nodded with disinterest, said, "Uh-huh," then turned to Quentin and asked, referring to Henry Rathbone, "Do any of you kids know this fellow here?"

"No," they answered in unison, Harmony volunteering, "he was already on the train when I hopped it."

"I see." With furrowed brow he sighed. Trying his best to appear stern, he added, "Okay, I'm going to let you off with a warning, and this is the warning," he wagged a finger at them. "There's serial killers out there ridin' the rails and preying on kids just like you and if I ever catch you on another train again I'm gonna kick your asses all the way to the police station, understand?"

All three nodded.

"Listen, I'm serious. We found a dead kid out there three weeks ago," the officer pointed to the east, "and the bum, or bums, who did it still haven't been caught. Understand?"

Again the three nodded.

"Good." He turned to Ol' Henry. "Gettin' a bit on in years to be ridin' the rails, aren't you? Where're you going?"

"To the lands a my birth," Ol' Henry answered, eyes bright with determination.

The shadow of a smile crossed the officer's face before he gently admonished, "Well, be careful old timer. Things have changed quite a bit since your day, I'm sorry to say."

Ol' Henry, his suitcase with its broken handle secure under his left arm, bowed deeply to his benefactor and said, "Why thank you, Mr. Sir."

Quentin sighed with relief. A black brother was a black brother. Any trouble and he surely would have been caught up in it. Ol' Henry was never even worried. In 69 years he'd learned a thing or two about the human heart. Or the lack of one. He knew that in some people the spirit burned like a torch, while in others it merely flickered like a candle flame. And in still others there was no light at all. The living dead.

The security officer acknowledged Ol' Henry's courtesy

with a short nod, touched the brim of his cap, and without another word turned and started off towards the front of the train. He was looking for thieves, vandals, and murderers, not destitute old men and hitchhiking kids.

The four vagabonds didn't waste any time getting off the right-of-way. They made the first block and rounded the corner. Safely out of sight of any railroad workers that might be lurking about they stopped for a quick pow-wow to decide their next move. Sensing the closeness of Harmony's and Ol' Henry's friendship Christopher started things off by asking bluntly, "Are you coming with us or going on with the old man?"

Harmony looked at him sharply. She felt like giving him a swift kick in the shins and was about to when a better idea occurred to her. "The question is," she intoned confidentially, "are you coming with us or going on alone?" Blinking, Christopher just looked at her for several stunned moments. Here she was turning against him again! "Well?" Harmony asked.

Suddenly Christopher was acutely aware of the three pairs of eyes staring at him. "Well we can't drag an old man around with us, Harmony," he said defensively. "He won't be able to keep up."

There was a moment's silence before Ol' Henry said, "He be right. You don't wants an old man like me taggin' along. I'd just be gettin' in the way an' slowin' you young'ns down."

"Hold on a minute," Quentin interrupted, grabbing the old man's sleeve as he started to turn away. "Any friend of Harmony's is a friend of mine. If you want to travel with us you is more than welcome." Then he stuck his hand out and introduced himself. "I'm Quentin Carter The Third." With a chuckle he added, "Distant relative to Jimmy Carter, former president of the United States!"

Ol' Henry stuck a hand out, his face crinkling into a saw-toothed grin. "I's Mr. Henry Rathbone," he replied, clearly pleased as he added, "close relative to Mr. Roland Rathbone, former cotton picker from Mississippi!"

With a laugh Quentin grabbed the man's hand and pumped his arm. "Glad to meet you, Mr. Henry Rathbone."

"Just calls me 'Henry,' all my friends do."

At this point Christopher was feeling increasingly left out. And he felt ashamed. He thought Quentin would side with him on dumping the old man. Harmony wanted to say something about Mississippi and the money but hesitated, figuring if Ol' Henry wanted to bring it up he would have. And then Christopher did the only reasonable thing he could. Following Quentin's example he stuck his hand out. "I'm Christopher Robin," he said, but his eyes never met the old man's. Rather, his gaze fell somewhere between the man's nose and chin.

When Ol' Henry extended his hand the sullen youngster grudgingly touched it briefly and withdrew. Pulling a rumpled pack of Marlboros from his jacket pocket he stuck a cigarette between tight lips and flicked the lighter, but the wind snatched the flame away. With the others watching he tried several more times. For a moment the frustrated youth looked as though he were going to throw it all away, then remembered the way the cowboy in the magazine did it. Assuming the proper, cocked stance, he cupped the smoke against the wind and lit it. Confident he looked tough he blew a stream of smoke out through his nostrils.

"Well," Quentin began, somewhat embarrassed for Christopher, "what'll we do now?"

"Get something to eat," Harmony cried, "I'm so hungry I could eat a horse!"

"Sound like a good idea to me," Quentin agreed.

"I've still got a few bucks left," Christopher shyly volunteered, wanting to be included but afraid his desire showed. Harmony kept quiet about the money still tucked in her jeans. That way when Christopher finished squandering his on beer and cigarettes and whatnot she'd have something left to feed them with.

"Well, let's go an' spend 'em!" Quentin exclaimed,

slapping his hands together and rubbing them briskly. "I's game for anything so long as it don't squeal when I bite into it!"

Everyone laughed, Quentin grabbing the old man's suitcase as the four of them started up the narrow, broken street in the fading light of late afternoon, Quentin ignoring Ol' Henry's protests that he "weren't no kind'a cripple" and could carry his own suitcase.

It was good to be walking beside Harmony again, Christopher thought, flicking the cigarette away. Yet he still wasn't over the stupefying experience of her sudden reappearance in his life. It was uncanny. Peering at her through narrowed eyes he abruptly asked, "How'd you get here?"

Harmony gave him a wary, sidelong glance. "On the same train as you," she declared, "you just saw me get kicked off!"

"But it was only this morning that I left you sleeping by the campfire," he retorted. And then it dawned on him with startling clarity. God had answered his prayer! Christopher's sense of wonder was short-lived, though. Without a foundation of faith it was easy to decide that the only intercession had been plain old ordinary coincidence. It had to be.

When the same thing dawned on Harmony, that Christopher's prayer had indeed been answered, she had to wonder, was it a miracle? An answered prayer from God? Or ordinary coincidence? *Please, Lord, increase my faith,* she silently prayed.

*   *   *

By the time they found their way downtown to the local grocery store the sun was below the trees and it was noticeably cooler. Evening was coming on fast.

It only took a few minutes in the store. Christopher spent his last few dollars on a large loaf of bread, a pound of bologna and three cans of bean with bacon soup. Then they all walked to the corner service station where Ol' Henry filled his two-quart canteen.

When they turned from the service station the sun was poised on the horizon, the sky a fiery amber. And flowing from the heart of the sunset were streaks of deep red and flaming orange that melted into soft pink and greenish-blue. For a long time they all stood staring at the sky.

The streets of the small town were fairly quiet now as most families were gathered at home for the evening meal. Two blocks away a dog's lone barking echoed. And somewhere someone's backyard barbecue sent the tantalizing aroma of sizzling burgers wafting through the air. With poignant memories of his own childhood backyard-barbecue-summers, family and friends gathered around, Christopher broke the spell by quietly asking, "Well, where to?"

"We gots to find someplace where we won't gets in no trouble with the police," Ol' Henry put in.

Quentin snapped his fingers. "I know a place." He turned to Christopher. "Remember just before we rolled into town we crossed a little creek with trees all around an' I said what a cool spot it'd be to camp?"

"Yeah!" Christopher exclaimed, "that'd be a perfect spot!"

"How far back is it?" Harmony asked. "Isn't that back where the cop said they found the dead kid?"

"Ah, he was just trying to scare us."

"An' even if he weren't," Quentin put in, "the killers is probably long gone by now. Wouldn't you be if you murdered someone around here?"

"That do make sense," Ol' Henry chimed in, "so let's make do fo' it gets too dark to finds our way."

Everyone agreed and with their backs to the sunset they started up the street. Once out of town they would turn north, pick up the tracks and follow them east to the creek.

After a solid half hour of steady walking they came to a small wooden trestle that ran through a tunnel of cottonwood, willow, and sycamore trees clustered along the banks of a creek. Or rather, Ol' Henry, Christopher and Harmony came to it.

Quentin had fallen behind. With Ol' Henry leading the charge and Christopher and Harmony in their own little world no one had noticed. But no one was especially worried, either. They were curious. From the track bed raised 15 feet on an earthen embankment they could see a small campfire flickering through the trees on the creek bank. "Look," Harmony pointed, "someone's there."

"Damn," Christopher muttered. "Someone's already got our spot."

"Maybe iffin' we asks we can join them," Ol' Henry suggested.

Christopher and Harmony looked at one another. Finally Christopher shrugged, "Just because we had one bad experience doesn't mean everyone out there's a weirdo. C'mon."

Christopher led the way off the embankment, down a footpath and into the trees. A light breeze moved through the branches like a whisper and afar off a bird chittered and chirped its last song of the day. In the hazy orange glow of dusk reflected in the gently flowing waters of the creek it was the perfect picture of God-blessed serenity.

Preparing to greet someone when he stepped into the circle of the deserted camp, Christopher never saw what hit him. One moment he was standing there, Harmony beside him, and Ol' Henry beside her, the next there was the thud of a blunt object bonking off the back of his head and the earth rushing up to meet him. Out.

The scream wasn't out of her mouth before the big one swatted Harmony an open-handed blow to the head that knocked her to the ground. In the meantime the little one kicked Ol' Henry in the balls, punched him square in the nose, punched him a second time, and as the old man staggered back and fell to his knees, pulled a small pistol from his back pocket and trained it on him. "Give me any crap and I'll blow holes through your head, nigger."

Things were not going well for Harmony, either. After

knocking her down the big one grabbed both her legs up under one arm, put a foot on her chest, yanked off her sneakers, flung them aside, then undid her jeans, yanked them and her panties off and tossed them, roughly pulled Harmony to her feet, pulled her sweatshirt off, marched her over to the fire and sat her there naked in the dirt. "Now you can sit here where it's warm," he warned, "or I can tie you to a tree over there where it's dark and cold. Which you want?"

Trembling in stark terror, eyes downcast, Harmony nodded slightly, her throat tight and dry when she croaked, "I'll stay here."

"Okay, then," the big one said. "But if you try an' run I'm gonna catch you and beat hell outta ya, okay?"

Again Harmony moved her head slightly and croaked, "Yes." Then she turned to silent prayer.

By the time the big one returned to his little companion the little one was wearing Christopher's jacket, jeans and boots, had stripped the boy naked and bound him hand and foot to a tree. Through it all a groggy Christopher feebly tried to resist once and was again bonked on the head with the little one's heavy oak walking stick, which was really more like a staff. Maybe like Moses had.

But these were no prophets. No Godly men. They were skinheads with swastika tattoos, shaved heads, guns, knives and hatred. Perverts. Rapists. Murdering thieves, they had elected to devote their lives to Satan. They were hopeful about hell because all their friends would be there. Hitler.

"We might as well shoot the nigger right now," the little one said softly, fingering his small .22 caliber pocket pistol, "I don't wanna screw 'em. Do you?"

The big one chuckled. "No. But if the kids see us blow the old man away they're gonna know what's coming and fight. But if we don't shoot him—yet—they just might be a whole lot more cooperative, which will be more fun for us."

"Okay," the little one said, tucking the revolver away,

"which one first?"

"I'll do the girl, you do the boy, and then we'll switch."

"Okay," the little one said agreeably, "go tie-up the old man." Then he started slapping Christopher to consciousness while loudly crowing, "Okay, let me tell you what's gonna happen, kid. First we're gonna rape your girlfriend and *you* get to watch. Then we're gonna rape you and let *her* watch. Is that cool or what?"

Cool or not, with the big one distracted tying up Ol' Henry Quentin saw his chance and moved fast. Having earlier fashioned his belt into a garrote with a slipknot, he quietly crept out of the underbrush and before the little one knew what was happening had it tight around his throat. In a flash Quentin had the gun in hand and the little one on his knees before him twisting this way and that as he choked on the end of the garrote Quentin held tightly in one fist.

The big one hadn't heard a sound. On his knees, his back to them, drooling with anticipation, his eyes fastened on the naked Harmony, he was busy tying up Ol' Henry. But when he heard Quentin's black voice calmly telling him to lie down on his stomach with his hands out and he wouldn't get shot his blood ran cold. Turning around, he was staring point-blank down the bore of the little .22, Quentin towering over him, the little one choking in the dirt on the end of his leash.

"If you look at me again I'm gonna go an' blow a hole through your head," Quentin said with deadly quietude and fired off a round which whistled past the man's ear and thudded into the ground nearby. "Now lay down on your white belly, put your face in the dirt and your hands out above your head or prepare to meet Satan."

The big one did as he was told. Of course by this time Harmony was on her feet and dressed and loosening Ol' Henry's bonds. Then she took those lengths of clothesline, put her knee in the middle of the big one's back, drew his hands together and tightly tied them behind him. Next she turned to Christopher.

Christopher came around fast. With Quentin holding both men at bay with the pistol, he didn't waste any time getting his wardrobe back. And now the little skinhead was naked in the dirt. And crying. Begging. Pleading. "Are you gonna kill us?"

*   *   *

With the darkness came a stiff breeze that put a nip in the air and set the trees to groaning and rattling their branches. After driving off their attackers they had built up the fire to a crackling inferno. As the flames rose higher the four vagabonds drew close around it, casting huge, forbidding shadows. Now they silently stared at their creation of heat and light. Now they felt secure. Those devils, those "living dead," wouldn't be coming back any time soon.

Quentin had left them dangling on the issue of what to do with them for a good long time. They were escaping execution by a cat's whisker Quentin let them know when he turned them lose. For sure. And if they should dare to come back he *would* kill them both and bury them on the bank of the creek right where they were standing. Without clubs, knives, or guns, in fact stripped of everything but the shirts on their backs they were vulnerable. Naked. Fearful. Cowards. They were gone. Long gone. And they wouldn't be back.

"I'm glad you showed up when you did but where were you earlier?" It was Christopher who broke the silence. So enthralled by the fire and the events of the evening, everyone had almost forgotten they were hungry. As if someone had flipped a switch they all stirred at once—and with the same idea in mind.

With Harmony slapping bologna sandwiches together and Christopher opening soup cans Quentin told his story. He had stopped to get a rock out of his shoe when he saw something move in the brush. On investigation it turned out to be a little brown and white dog. It was the damnedest thing, Quentin went on. It seemed like the little dog, with a peculiar movement of his head, was beckoning to him, but every time he got close it scampered away. This went on for some time before he gave up and returned to the railroad tracks. "By then you guys were way gone," Quentin concluded, "an' the rest, as they say, is history."

"Lucky for us because if you would've walked into that camp with us...." Harmony trembled with her next thought.

"I know," Quentin interjected.

"Maybe it was my angel," Harmony concluded.

"Maybe it be God," Ol' Henry said.

"And maybe we just got lucky," Christopher intoned, "but I've got a question for you, Quentin. How come you didn't just shoot 'em when you had the chance? They would've done the same thing to you."

"To all of us," Harmony corrected.

"It would've been self-defense," Christopher put in.

"Well, I know, but then I would'a had to go an' bury 'em and I didn't wanna have to dig the holes," Quentin grinned. With a shrug he added, "Seriously, if I would of shot 'em I'd be lowerin' myself to their level, an' I don't *ever* wanna be counted among the soulless predators of this world."

"Amen to that," Ol' Henry sighed, adding, "you a good man, Quentin Carter The Third. A good'n."

"Well why'd you have to throw the gun in the creek afterwards?" Christopher heatedly asked. "Maybe we could've used it."

"For what?" Quentin calmly replied. "I don't have no one I wanna go an' shoot. Do you?"

"No, but...."

"No buts about it, now nobody gonna end up shot with some gun *I* handled."

"But what if they were the ones that killed that kid a few weeks ago?" Harmony asked.

"I'm not a cop, Harmony. It's not up to me to be roundin' up suspects for the police. An' besides, I seriously doubt the killer, or killers, are still hangin' around here."

"I gots somethin' we can cook the soup in," Ol' Henry

interrupted. "An' I gots a new knife out of the deal, too," he declared with a big smile and held it up. "An' I also gots a big spoon, a fork, an' my own pocketknife."

"You only have one spoon?" Christopher asked.

The old man nodded. "That be it, child. Guess we just gots to pass the pot around."

"And eat off the same spoon?" Christopher asked incredulously, fitting the opener to the top of the can. "Yuk! That'd be disgusting!"

With a bemused smile Ol' Henry replied, "Disgustin'? Maybe, child. But you gots to look at it philosophically. I mean, you'd swap spit with one a those ladies in the picture magazines in a minute, so what be the big deal 'bout sharin' a spoon?"

Christopher was struck speechless. He looked at Quentin, then Harmony, then the soup can he was working on. "Well you can count me out," he said with furrowed brow as he bore down on the can opener, "that spoon ain't no lady."

The others burst out laughing, Quentin commenting, "Well, the man do have a point you know." Ignoring the remark, Christopher peeled back the lid and dumped the contents into the pot, then went to work on another can.

Ol' Henry warmed the soup on the fire. Afterwards, with his suitcase serving as a table, they all gathered around and sat cross-legged on the ground. Everyone was ravenous and didn't pretend otherwise, the pot passed around and soup slurped up between bites of sandwich.

At first Christopher tried to sip right off the pot but burned his lips, which brought a round of laughter from his three friends. Then, his hunger pangs stronger than his fear of germs or whatever, he gave in and used the spoon, sipping off the very edge up near the handle where he hoped no one had touched it.

Having finished two sandwiches apiece and all the soup, the canteen was passed around, everyone drinking deeply to sat isfy a burning thirst that 15 minutes of nonstop eating had brought on. Then, with sighs of satisfaction they comfortably settled in. Except for Ol' Henry. With pot and spoon in hand he prepared to go down to the creek and wash them.

Anxious to talk to him about the agreement they had made earlier in the boxcar, Harmony offered to help. With a nod of approval from the old man she got to her feet.

"What about our plan of going to Mississippi?" she asked as Ol' Henry sat on his heels at water's edge scouring the vessel and spoon with creek-bed grit.

"What about it, Child?" he asked, keeping his eyes on his work.

"Can Christopher and Quentin come too?"

Ol' Henry thought on it a moment, carefully rinsing the pot, then looked up at her. "It don't matter none to me long as you be willin' to share your take with them." He handed her the pot and began scouring the spoon.

"Okay," Harmony answered carefully. "But since there's more of us, how about half for you and half for the three of us?"

He stopped what he was doing and looked up at her again. After a moment he said with a grin and a shake of his head, "You shore drives a hard bargain, little missy."

"Well, what'd you say?" Harmony asked hopefully. "Please?"

Ol' Henry rinsed the spoon and handed it to her. "Okay," he agreed and got to his feet with a groan and a stretch. "Shoo-fire, I probably ain't gonna lives long enough to spends all a my share anyhow."

Returning to camp, they found Christopher and Quentin hard at work busting up branches and feeding them to the fire. Harmony and Ol' Henry sat down at a comfortable distance to watch. With the fire crackling briskly the boys sprawled out on the ground beside their two friends.

For awhile Harmony waited expectantly for Ol' Henry to bring up the matter of the money, but when Quentin asked where he was headed she interjected, "How would you guys like to change our plans?"

Stretched out on his side by the fire and leaning on one elbow, Christopher asked, "What'd you have in mind?"

"How about if we go to Mississippi?"

Quentin and Christopher exchanged glances. "Mississippi?"

"Yeah, Mississippi. You guys act like I said China or something."

"This must be Henry's idea," Christopher said, his gaze shifting to the old man briefly before returning to Harmony. "Why would you want to go to Mississippi?"

"Money." It was Ol' Henry who spoke.

"Money?" Both boys sat up, their attention directed at the old man.

Ol' Henry nodded. "That be right. I gots a money-makin' proposition, if'n you be interested. I told Harmony 'bout it earlier."

"How much money are we talking about?" Christopher asked, his face aglow with orange firelight.

Ol' Henry's eyes rolled back in his head as he pondered momentarily. "Ohhh, I gots to say 'bout a hunert thousand dollars or so."

Quentin's eyes grew big. "A hundred thousand dollars!"

Ol' Henry nodded. "That be right, Mr. Quentin. At least."

"What you goin' to do, rob a bank?"

The old man's face crinkled up with a chuckle. "No sir. I may be this an' I may be that, but I's no bank robber."

"Why let us in on the deal?" Christopher asked skeptically.

"'Cause I needs help gettin' to it. At first I just asked Harmony, but she said you guys gots to be included too so I says okay."

"What kind of help do you need?" The ever skeptical Christopher asked.

"You kids just gets me down to Mississippi an' I'll do the rest."

A decided silence settled over everyone as the boys thought

about it. Quentin broke the peace. "All we gotta do is get you down to Mississippi?"

Ol' Henry nodded. "Jackson, Mississippi."

Eyeing him closely, Quentin inquired, "Mind tellin' us the whole story, from A to Z?"

"Yeah," Christopher put in, "let's hear the whole story before we decide."

"Okay," Ol' Henry began slowly, "that be a fair enough request. This here story goes back a long ways. Back to when I's just a little fellar 'bout knee-high to a grasshopper." He held a hand up palm-down to illustrate.

"Okay, okay," Christopher interrupted, "we got the idea."

Ol' Henry cleared his throat and continued. "Ya see, we used to live just a few blocks from this kind'a well-to-do white neighborhood, if'n ya knows what I mean. An' the white folks used to hire us kids to tend their lawns an' such. An' I used to work for these folks by the name a Douglas J. Donnelly, his wife's name bein' Miss Kate. Now they both dead and gone. Funny how time moves along, ain't it?"

Harmony nodded solemnly, thinking of her own finiteness. Not so Quentin and Christopher. They were all business. "So who cares?" Christopher interjected, "keep going."

"Okay," Ol' Henry began once again, his pace agonizingly slow. "The Donnellys owned a hardware store in town an' they was pretty well off. But a terrible thing happened to them when I was 'bout nine. They had a little boy, 'bout three at the time if'n I remember correct, an' he gots himself kicked in the head by a horse that year an' it kilt him dead. Mr. Donnelly, he had a fallin' out with his wife over it 'cause she blamed him that the young'n got kilt. After that he got a bad cough or somethin' 'cause I was always goin' to town to get his coughin' syrup. Least ways he always *said* he had a cough. Used to put away at least a bottle or so ever couple a days!" Ol' Henry giggled and slapped his knee.

"Anyways, he was rich. All the white folks is, ain't they?

An' we spent lots a time together in them days, me an' him. Well, he'd get to drinkin' that coughin' syrup and talkin' 'bout how lonely it was livin' with a woman gone cold. Got so's he'd even pay me just to carry his fishin' pole down to the creek for him. 'Course I didn't mind. I'd carry my own too, ya see. An' as we'd be a walkin' he'd be rattlin' away 'bout this an' that. Always used ta tell me, 'boy, don't go puttin' your money in them banks in town 'cause it ain't no good.' Then one day when he was goin' on about the banks he had himself just a wee-bit too much coughin' syrup an' starts tellin' me 'bout how he kept most a his money in the house, hid under the floor an' in the walls of the attic an' such. Now these folks was rich, mind you. Had lan' out in the country an' ever'thing.

"So after he goes an spills the beans to me, an' even shows me some a the loot he had hid away, he come to realize the mistake he done made by tellin' someone an' he got mad, mostly at himself than me I 'spect, an swore if'n I told anyone he'd hang me from a rafter in the basement an' skin me alive.

"Now you gots to remember, I was just a little kid, only 'bout nine at the time an' scared to death a white folks 'cause I heard ever since I could remember 'bout what they done to black folks that gets outta line, ya see, so I never told a soul. No, not one person. Not even my best friend. I just made up my mind to forgets all 'bout it then an' there.

"Well, couple a years later when I was 'bout 12 our whole family packs up an' moves north seekin' work. 'Course I never thought 'bout it again an' that was that, till 'bout three weeks ago." Ol' Henry coughed and spit into the fire, asked for the canteen and took a short drink.

"Okay, okay, so what happened?" It was Christopher again, impatient as ever.

"Well, long 'bout three months ago I lost my job. Company done folded up. So there I was. Didn't have nothin' neither 'cause I'd gambled off most a my money playin' numbers games an' such, an' soon couldn't pay the rent an' ends up livin'

in my car. Then that thing busts down an' I gots hardly nothin'
to eat an' the next thing I know I'm kickin' down the street
sleepin' in subways an' such in Chicago an' who do you think I
should meet?"

"Your best friend from when you were a little kid!"
Harmony blurted.

Ol' Henry's face brightened with a chuckle. "That be it,
child. An' all these years he been livin' in Hammond, Indiana,
an' I never even knowed it!

"So we got to talkin' an' presently he tells me 'bout a letter
he got from his sister still livin' down in Jackson. An' she told
him 'bout how the ol' Donnelly woman just passed away. Said
the old man been dead for years, but the old woman just hung
on, livin' in that same ol' house. But the thing that struck my
friend funny, he told me, was that everbody thought these folks
was rich, but the papers said she died penniless.

"Well I'll be blessed, I says to my old friend, I bet that
woman didn't do nothin' with all that money. Just left it right
where it be, hidden all over the house. Anyways, my friend sure
enough agreed with me, so all we gots to do is go on down there
an' gets inside that house an' look around an' I bet we can find
all kinds a money. But we gots to hurry 'cause the house, it be
real old an' fallin' down an' ya never know but the city just
might go an' tear 'er down. So if'n you kids help me I figure
you be good for a share."

"What happened to your friend?" Christopher asked. "Why
didn't you get him to help you?"

"I did, child, but he gots himself kilt just a couple a days
ago. Squished by a boxcar door."

"How'd that happen?" Quentin asked softly.

"Well, me an' my friend was ridin' a boxcar an' he was
standin' in the door havin' a smoke. I was just about to join him
when the train stopped real sudden. Done hit a car on the tracks
I figure. Anyway, that slidin' door must'a weighed more'n a
hunert pounds an' it slammed shut an' squished my friend.

Squished him so bad as to make me sick."

Quentin and his two young friends exchanged grim, knowing glances. A small world indeed. After the moment passed, Ol' Henry quietly continued, "Now, I might'a lost a friend but I gained some sense. An' I'm tellin' ya this lest you should get squished your very own selfs."

"Thanks for the tip," Quentin said drily, adding, "sorry 'bout your friend. That must be a terrible thing to see your friend get squished like that."

Ol' Henry shrugged. "He gone an' in heaven now."

Quentin nodded, suddenly all business again. "Good, glad you not takin' it too hard. Now, let's get down to it. I like the sound a this. Could be one a those 'once in a lifetime' things you hear about. The question is, how we gonna divvy up the loot?"

"I think four ways even-steven would be fair," Christopher offered.

Ol' Henry looked from one to the other, then answered evenly, "I be figurin' half for me an' half for the three a you."

"How 'bout one-third for you an' two-thirds for us?" Quentin bargained.

Christopher adamantly refused. "No. Four ways even-steven. We're all in this together. Fair is fair." The three kids watched Ol' Henry anxiously but his face remained passive. "It's fair," Christopher repeated.

The old man shook his head. "This be how I see it. I really only needs one to help me. I asked Harmony first an' told her she could have 25 percent. Then she wants you guys along an' bargains me up to half 'cause there be more of you, an' I says fine. She agreed an' that be the way it be. Takes it or leaves it."

For a long time no one said anything. Harmony broke the impasse by siding with Ol' Henry. "He's right. That's what we agreed on."

"That may be what you and Henry agreed on," Christopher intoned, "but me and Quentin didn't."

Harmony shrugged. "I think it's fair."

Quentin was suddenly quick to agree. "So do I."

All eyes were on Christopher. When he hesitated Harmony said evenly, "If you don't want to come with us that's fine, it'll just mean more for Quentin and me."

Christopher threw his hands up in defeat. "All right. I guess I don't have much choice."

Eyeing him, the old man said, "You gots a choice."

Christopher stared at him. "I'm in."

"All right," Ol' Henry said with quiet finality. "But I be the boss. We gots to do it my way or no way."

When the three kids agreed Ol' Henry broke into a wide, saw-toothed grin, everyone shaking hands to seal the deal. "I's glad that be settled," he said. "First thing tomorrow morning you boys gots to get into town an' finds out exactly where we be an' how we can get on down to Mississippi."

"Sounds good to me," Quentin said, "'cept for one thing."

"What that be?"

"I don't need to go an' be seen around too much. Maybe it'd be better if Harmony went with Chris."

"What you worried 'bout bein' seen around for?" Ol' Henry asked, remembering what Harmony had told him about Quentin escaping from jail.

"Sometime I just might tell you about it," Quentin replied.

Harmony understood immediately. "He's right. I'll go with Christopher tomorrow." Christopher liked the idea too.

"Okay," Ol' Henry shrugged, "suits me."

Getting to his feet and feeding a couple of hefty branches to the crackling fire, Christopher casually asked, "What's the address of the house in Jackson where the money is? Just in case you get killed on the way or something."

Ol' Henry thought about it for a moment. "Yeah, but if'n I tells, you could go off an' get all the money for yourselfs."

"Wouldn't do it," Quentin said, shaking his head. "No way."

"And if they even thought about leaving you behind I'd wack 'em in the head with a big stick!" Harmony adamantly assured him.

The old timer just shrugged. "I don't know anyways. Ain't ever knowed. Just know where it is. You gots to remember, I was just a little kid. Didn't know where things was by number an' such, just by the way things looked, if'n you know what I mean."

All three youngsters nodded. They knew exactly what he meant. It wasn't so long ago that they'd been little kids.

When no one challenged his explanation Ol' Henry reached for his suitcase. "Now let's get some sleep," he said, "'cause to-morrow mornin's gonna come early." He unbuckled the straps and pulled out two blankets. He handed one to Christopher. "I only gots two so we hast to share."

"Thanks," Christopher said appreciatively and took the brown woolen army blanket.

"I guess me an' you hast to share the other one," he said to Quentin.

Quentin nodded. "Thanks. Go on ahead an' sleep. I can crawl in later."

"Feel like settin' up awhile, huh?" Ol' Henry put the blanket aside. He could tell the young man was troubled.

Christopher was tired and made no bones about it. Using a small log for a pillow, he and Harmony settled on the other side of the fire against the rise of land. With a contented sigh he took Harmony in his arms and they snuggled under the tattered blanket.

Ol' Henry and Quentin sat in silence for a long time, star-ing at the fire, listening to the soft murmurings of Christopher and Harmony on the other side. When the old man finally spoke the two 16-year-olds were sound asleep, the stars shining brightly in a clear sky, the quarter moon high "What be eatin' at you, Mr. Quentin? An' don't tell me nothin'," he quickly added, "'cause I can plainly see that somethin' is."

Pretending he hadn't heard, Quentin inquired, "What?" got to his feet and threw more sticks on the hissing fire. He had a case of repressed anger big-time and the recent ugly events of the evening had only added to it.

"I said what be eatin' at you?" Ol' Henry's voice went off like a cannon.

"Nothin'," Quentin winced, tossed a handful of sticks on the fire and sat down.

"Don't tell me nothin'," Ol' Henry insisted, "'cause I can see quite plainly that somethin' is."

"Then why don't you tell me?" Quentin snapped, the bitterness he carried sharp, every memory salt in a healing wound that had just been ripped open by two dirty white boys. Child-killers, perhaps. Definitely soulless predators.

Ol' Henry was watching Quentin transform before his very eyes and it was scary, the hate he saw in Quentin's dark eyes. Powerful, ugly stuff, hate. And dangerous to the life, limb and soul of every man, woman, and child under God. Ol' Henry knew he'd better do something and fast before the Lord lost another good man. "Let it go," he said quietly.

"What?" Quentin looked up from a hangnail he was picking at.

"I says let it go."

"Let what go?"

"The bitterness. The hate that's inflamin' your very own soul."

Quentin averted his eyes. "I can't," he almost whispered and choked back a sudden rush of emotion.

"Yes you can."

"No." Quentin shook his head. "An' I don't want to."

After a long pause Ol' Henry said gently, "Tell me what happened."

"You wouldn't understan'."

"Yes I would," Ol' Henry confided softly. "You gots to remember, I'm black too."

"What makes you think it's got somethin' to do with bein' black?" Quentin angrily retorted.

"'Cause," the old man answered with the self-assurance of his years, "I can see when you feelin' it deep down in yo' gut. I can see you a hurtin'. Bad. 'Cause a some white man."

Quentin looked at him with renewed appreciation.

"If'n you talks about it you'll feel better," Ol' Henry urged. "Always makes you feel better if'n you talks about it."

Touched by the old man's concern, and maybe hoping for a little widening of his own understanding of the world, Quentin haltingly began to tell his story. He told about the fight with Wendel. How the cops came bustin' in. And how Wendel lost an eye. He told about the trial and the ten-year jail sentence. About what a joke the truth was. Had they behaved that way because he was black or because they really didn't care what the truth was? He finished his story with beads of sweat on his forehead and clenched fists, his anger coming on like hot flashes as he swore vengeance on Wendel and any whitey that ever got in his way again.

After a moment Ol' Henry said sympathetically, "Don't let that ugly, evil man cause you no more pain. Forget 'bout him an' go on from here. Don't go worryin' none 'bout no revenge. Leave that to God."

"God?" Quentin looked at him with knitted brow. "There ain't no God! If there's a God how come all the crooks is gettin' rich and the simple honest folks are sufferin'? If there's a God why don't he do somethin' 'bout all the monsters runnin' around eatin' children, huh? If there's a God where the hell is he, on vacation?"

Ol' Henry shook his head. "No. Look who lost an eye an' is forever scarred. An' they never got you to jail. An' in that wreck you never got a scratch. Now ain't that justice?"

"Justice!" Quentin scoffed, "you call *that* justice? Just 'cause I luck-out on a freak accident? Now I'm a fugitive of the law. An' what about the college education I'm goin' to miss out on, huh? What about the girlfriend I may never see again? An' what about my good name? An' what about my mother and father? What about all that?" He stopped to catch his breath, adding fiercely, "If that's God's idea of justice then he'd better retire!" Breathing hard, Quentin lay back and stared with unseeing eyes at the star-filled sky.

Ol' Henry paused a moment to collect his thoughts, and then he remembered something his mother had told him many years before when he was dealing with the bitterness of a bad experience, and what came out of his mouth was a little of the Bible, a little of C. S. Lewis, and a little of his own thoughts and memories. "In the end justice gonna win, Mr. Quentin. When the Lord come back justice gonna be measured an' handed out. But when that time come don't matter none, for what do the existence of time matter to an eternal being? To one who been livin' forever there ain't no past. There ain't no future. There be only the present. There be only now.

"An' if'n you wants God to have a hand in the affairs of your own life you gots to ask. 'Cause the only way this God can rule in your life is if'n you seek after his will. But it be all up to you. You gots to choose, then act. There ain't no other way. For the essence of will, Mr. Quentin, is havin' the power to choose. The Lord can't force himself on you 'cause that would violate your free will. Then it wouldn't be your choice, an' you gots to *choose.*

"As for revenge, bury that with your hate. Cast it from your very own heart. For the Lord says, 'Vengeance is Mine.' An' that be the very truth, too. God's got it covered, an' you gonna see it one day, too, along with everybody else when the day of the Lord come.

"But while you be here on this earth you is bound by the physical laws of nature an' the laws of powerful men, whether they be of good or evil. As for the injustice in the world, don't be blamin' the Lord none, but blame The Destroyer."

When Ol' Henry finished he looked across at Quentin, but

the artist was sound asleep, curled up on his side by the fire. With a sigh he reached for the blanket. Coughing, he spit into the fire, then covered himself and his young friend and lay down.

"What be the use?" he whispered to the sky. How does one describe a symphony to the deaf? Muttering a prayer for Quentin, the old man closed his eyes and went to sleep.

11

AN AFFAIR OF THE HEART

For the first time since they began traveling together Harmony awoke to find Christopher beside her. With a wide yawn she sat up and stretched luxuriously. The wind was still, shafts of sunlight streaming through the tall, stately trees, the creek murmuring gently. It was going to be a warm day.

"Mornin', child," Ol' Henry said as he and Quentin walked up from the creek. Both were clean-shaven and had water dripping from their hair. In one hand Ol' Henry carried a shaving kit, in the other a bar of soap in a green plastic container.

"Morning," Harmony said with a sunny smile.

The conversation woke Christopher. Rolling over onto his back, he asked through a yawn, "What time is it?"

"Time for you to get up," Harmony answered, giving him a kiss on the cheek. "You're missing a beautiful morning."

For a moment it looked as though he were going to roll over and go back to sleep, but in a sudden burst of energy he threw off the blanket and sat up. Rubbing the sleep from his eyes, he said, "Let's go get that money."

"Well I'll be blessed," Ol' Henry chuckled, "but that boy just rarin' to go this mornin'!" Then, "If'n you young'ns wants you can take my soap down to the creek 'fore we get started."

Getting to her feet, Harmony said, "I'd love to. I feel like I'll have to wash twice just to get the first layer of dirt off!"

Everyone laughed. Handing her the soap, Ol Henry said, "Just helps yourself to whatever you needs." With a wink he added, "An' see that Christopher get a little bit on him, too."

Harmony giggled. "Thanks, Henry." Then she and Christopher turned and headed for the creek.

After they left Quentin looked at the old man. They started laughing again as Ol' Henry stooped to pick up the kids' blanket to fold and put away. With a last chuckle Quentin sat on a log, his fingers absently working a bit of clay he'd brought up from the creek. "Feel good to be clean."

"That it do," Ol' Henry agreed and got on his knees before the battered suitcase.

From the creek they could hear Christopher's laughter, splashing water, and squeals and shrieks from Harmony. "Sound like they havin' fun," Quentin said dejectedly, thinking of the love he'd left behind as he carefully worked the bit of clay into a tiny, three-inch figurine. "I'd give anything in the world just to hold my girl again."

"Don't worry," Ol' Henry assured him, "you will someday."

"I'll believe that when she in my arms and not a moment sooner. Got your knife on you?"

"Sure," Ol' Henry dug it out, opened the blade and handed it to him.

Quentin took the knife and added buxom curves and breasts to the figure. With the very tip of the blade he went to work on the face. All the while Ol' Henry watched in silent fascination at his speed and skill.

Oblivious to the old man's eyes upon him, Quentin worked on, cutting away the tiniest slivers of clay with the skill of a surgeon as he formed tight curls of hair about the head. Finally he stopped and held the figure out at arm's length. After a moment he turned to Ol' Henry and held it up. "What's wrong with it?"

The old timer shrugged. "Nothin'. It look beautiful to me."

Dissatisfied, turning it this way and that, Quentin looked again more closely. "The legs, they all out of proportion," he said half to himself. With a frown he went back to work, shaving a little here, adding a little there until it was just right. "There," he said at long last and held it up again, "perfect!"

Scarcely able to detect any difference, Ol' Henry nodded approvingly. "It be beautiful, Quentin. You really good at that."

Quentin smiled. "Thanks. I was goin' to study sculpting at college but they say it's almost impossible to make a livin' at it." With a sigh he added, "Guess I'll just head south an' pick cotton for the rest a my life." He laughed. But it was forced. Home seemed so distant. So unreachable... How would he ever get his life back to normal?

"Oh, don't go worryin' none 'bout that," Ol' Henry said encouragingly, "in the end everything gonna work out jist fine."

"Wish I was as confident 'bout that as you," Quentin said, still examining his work. Satisfied, he stood it up against a rock near the ashes of the previous night's fire.

Dripping water, Harmony came up from the creek, bra and panties in one hand and soap in the other. Having nothing else to wear, she'd gone swimming in her undies and kept her sweatshirt and jeans dry. Now she was glad she had for it was quite cool once out of the water. Hanging her undergarments on a tree branch to dry, she tossed Henry the soap and plopped down beside him. After a moment she turned to him with serious eyes. "Is it a sin to have a man before you marry him?"

Ol' Henry looked doubtful. "Why, you thinkin' 'bout it?"

Harmony shrugged. "Just wondering."

Crossing his legs, Ol' Henry cleared his throat and settled back. "Ya see, havin' sex with someone *is* marryin' him."

"Huh?" Harmony cocked her head.

"Well, it be like, when you have sex with a man you be marryin' him right then and there. That be what gettin' married is—lettin' a man have all of you. See, child, back in the olden days they weren't no license or nothin', no kind'a piece a paper from the state. But if'n you took a man in you, you was marryin' him an' that be that."

"Yeah, but what if we haven't been before the preacher yet?"

Ol' Henry shook his head. "Don't matter none. Marriage be

an affair of the heart between two peoples an' God. The preacher man, o' the government man, he just there to make it legal an' keep count a who married an' who ain't."

"So if me and Chris... uh, I mean, if I have uh..." Harmony's face turned crimson. "If we do it without being married it isn't a sin?"

The old man smiled. "What I be tryin' to say is, that *is* becomin' married. When you do it you is. The sin is doin' it with all different men, 'cause you allowed to have only just one husband. But if'n you takin' a man inside you, then you be marryin' him right then an' there."

Puzzled, Harmony frowned.

"Look," he said, trying to clarify himself, "if'n you wants to have a man for the rest a yo' life an' he wants you in the same way, have him and you'll be married. But 'fore you join him physically it be best if'n you joins him in spirit first, 'cause then yo' chances of bein' successful will most surely be greater. Course you gots to be careful you don't get fooled by some guy just playin' witch ya. But if'n you don't want him forever why have him fo' just one night? If'n you be that hot just...."

"Henry!" Quentin exclaimed as his head jerked up.

Growing warm with embarrassment, flustered, Ol' Henry stammered, "Look, this be somethin' you ought'a be talkin' 'bout with yo' mamma."

"I don't have a mother."

"Well then with yo'...."

"I don't have one of those either," she cut him off. "But I think I understand what you're saying. Marriage is really more in the heart than in the church."

"You gots it, child," Ol' Henry said with relief.

"Don't go an' let the Pope catch you sayin' that," Quentin grinned.

But Harmony was satisfied. Leaping to her feet, she said, "Thanks, Henry," and ran back to the creek. She found Christopher still splashing around. "How can you stand to be in that cold water for so long?"

"It's not cold if you keep moving," he called back. "Look, I'm naked and it's not too cold for me."

The girl hesitated. "I can't do it with you."

"Why not?"

"Because then we'd be married and I don't think you're ready for marriage yet."

"Marriage?" Christopher looked at her like she was nuts.

"Yes, marriage."

"But I'm only 16," he chuckled, "My ma probably wouldn't let me. Too young."

"Then you're too young to have me!" she declared triumphantly. Turning on her heel, she started back to camp heedless of his demands to come back.

Three minutes later, hair dripping wet, Christopher strolled into camp stuffing his T-shirt into his jeans. Ol' Henry looked at him. "You two young'ns ready to go into town an' finds out what we needs to know to get ourselfs down south?"

Christopher nodded. "I think we can handle that."

"Good. An' don't waste no time, neither, 'cause we gots to get there 'fore the city go an tear that ol' house down. Know what I mean?"

"Don't worry," Christopher assured him, "we'll get the job done and get back here just as quick as we can." Tossing his trinketed black leather jacket beside Ol' Henry's suitcase, he turned to Harmony, "You ready, hon'?" The jacket he wouldn't be wearing today partly because it was rather warm and partly because he didn't want to stand out.

Harmony nodded. "Yeah. Let's do it."

"See you in a few hours, then," Christopher called as he and Harmony started off through the tall weeds, jumped the ditch and climbed the embankment for the tracks and town.

*   *   *

"That's not true!" Christopher insisted, their footsteps

crunching in the gravel as they trudged along the tracks. "Ninety-seven percent of all pregnancies could easily be prevented if the people doing it just cared a little. If you're careful and watch what you're doing there's no danger."

"Yeah, as long as you know what you're doing," Harmony retorted. "And I wouldn't. I've never done it before."

"Are you trying to say you don't know how?"

"That's right," Harmony answered, "I don't know how. And I have no intention of learning with you any time soon. My ma might not have taught me much else but the one thing she constantly drummed into my head was, any hanky-panky and bingo! I'd be pregnant. Like it or not. And I would *not* like to get pregnant right now, thank you. I have other things I want to do with my life besides bum around aimlessly with you smoking pot and drinking beer."

"Ah, what does anyone's old lady know about it, anyway?" Christopher said in disgust.

"Well my ma knew, believe me. That's all she used to talk about. And right now that's all we're talking about so drop it, will ya? Besides, that's not something you do with someone unless you plan on spending the rest of your life with them, and you already said you weren't ready for marriage. And you don't even believe in God," she added, "so you can't be that smart."

"All right!" Christopher snapped. She was right. It *was* all they had talked about since leaving camp. But at least she was her old self again. He was thankful for that, even if still a little apprehensive, which brought to mind something else bugging him ever since they'd reunited. "Hey Harmony?"

"What?"

"You were just putting me on when you told me Peter Perish was an angel, weren't you?"

Harmony's ears burned with embarrassment as she stammered, "Y-Yeah, I guess so."

"You guess so? What's that supposed to mean?"

"Just what I said. I guess so," she answered, her voice

firmer now.

"Well if you *were* putting me on, why?"

"I don't really have an answer."

"Look, speaking of being smart, you don't blame me for trying to understand what was going on back there, do you?"

Harmony shook her head. "No. It's just that... that... *I'm* not even sure what was going on back there."

Christopher looked at her for a long moment. "Well you didn't waste any time getting out of there after we left. What happened?"

"I finally realized they weren't angels," she answered, then caught her breath.

"So! You really *did* believe they were angels!" Christopher crowed accusingly.

At first Harmony hotly denied it, then abruptly changed tack. She couldn't lie. Not like this. "Yes, it's true," she sighed defeatedly, "I did believe they were angels."

For a long time Christopher didn't say anything. He wanted to ask what could possibly make her believe such a stupid thing but realized he probably wouldn't get much of an answer. Most likely she didn't know herself. Maybe she was a retard... "How did you finally figure out they weren't angels?"

Harmony was burning with humiliation. She felt like a fool. And telling him about the "Beings of Light" or whatever they were was out of the question. It would only make things worse. "I just figured it out," she answered.

"How?"

"Wellll..." Suddenly speaking rapidly, Harmony threw caution to the wind and plunged into the story of the "Beings of Light" appearing during the night, describing everything in vivid detail, Christopher listening closely, eyes growing wide with wonder as he watched her and realized she was not making it up as she went along—it had really happened—at least within her mind. Dreamed it all. Probably. She finished her story asking breathlessly, "Do you believe me?"

One thing he could say for Harmony, she sure had a good imagination. "Of course I believe you," he lied. That's how girls were, he figured. They dreamed so vividly that sometimes they woke up thinking their dreams had really happened. At least she wasn't a retard, thank God, just not real smart.

At the outskirts of town they left the tracks, wandering up one street and down another until they found themselves downtown. "What now?" Harmony asked as they stood on the curb watching traffic go by.

Christopher shrugged. "I don't know. How're we supposed to find out where the southbound tracks are, anyway?"

"We've got to ask someone."

"What about this guy here?"

As he said it Harmony looked up to see a boy several years older than either of them coming out of a bank counting a roll of money. He wore black jeans, cowboy boots, a red button-down shirt, denim jacket and a black cowboy hat to match pulled low over his deep brown eyes. Dark-complected, he had the facial features and shiny black hair of a Latino. As he approached, Christopher whispered, "Ask him."

"You ask him."

"No," Christopher refused.

With a sigh Harmony gave in. "Uh, excuse me," she said as he passed.

Folding the money and tucking it into his jacket breast-pocket, he stopped and turned to them, "Yes?"

"Could you tell me where the southbound tracks are?"

"Train station's just two blocks north, sweetheart," he answered with a southwestern drawl and a friendly grin.

Harmony shook her head. "No, what we need to know is where the southbound tracks are."

He looked at her for a long, thoughtful moment. "Am I to understand y'all want to hop a freight train?"

Harmony nodded.

His eyes shifted to Christopher momentarily. "Where

'bouts down south y'all headin'?"

"Oklahoma," Christopher quickly answered, afraid Harmony was going to tell everything and somehow get still another person involved in their little scheme. She looked at him sharply but said nothing.

"I'm a headin' on down to Oklahoma City myself in just a bit," the young cowboy said.

"You are?" It was Christopher.

"Yep," he gave a short nod. "Hoppin' freights is kind'a dangerous," he went on. "A kid was killed out by the tracks east of here a couple of weeks ago and the killer's still out there. What y'all runnin' from?"

"Nothin." Again Christopher was quick with his words, "We just want to visit her sick dad in Oklahoma City."

"Oklahoma City, huh?"

Christopher nodded. "Before he dies."

Harmony rolled her eyes. He lied so effortlessly!

Pushing his hat back for a thoughtful moment, the cowboy shrugged, "Whyn't y'all ride down with me? To tell you the truth I wouldn't mind the company at all."

This was turning out to be even better than finding the tracks. Holding his excitement in check, Christopher said, "That'd be great."

"What's y'all's names?"

"I'm Christopher Robin," he answered, extending his hand. "And this is Harmony, uh, I forgot her last name."

"Hammerschmidt," she put in.

"I'm Ramón Alvarez." They shook hands. He was 18, a third generation Mexican-American born and raised in Oklahoma City. He was in Ellsburg, Nebraska, helping his uncle finish the interior of a building to be used as a hardware store. They were finished now and Ramón was preparing to return home.

"We'd sure appreciate that ride," Christopher put in.

"Aren't you forgetting something?" Harmony asked.

Christopher looked at her with a frown, then turned to Ramón. "Oh, I almost forgot. We have two other friends waiting back where we camped last night. Could they come too?"

Letting out a long stream of air, Ramón removed his hat and scratched his head. "There's four of you?"

Christopher nodded.

Ramón thought a moment, then put his hat back on. "Well, I guess so," he said a little hesitantly, unsure of just what he was letting himself in for.

"Oh, thank you!" Harmony was ecstatic. "We never thought we'd get out of this town!"

"Tain't nothin'. Like I said, I could use the company. It's a long drive."

"When you leaving?" Christopher asked.

"This afternoon."

"We'll have to go back to camp and get our friends. Where should we meet?"

After a moment's consideration Ramón said, "Tell me where y'all are camped and I'll come by."

"We're camped by a creek straight east of town."

"That must be Nichol's crick. Route 12 runs out that way. I'll tell ya what, at around 3:00 o'clock y'all meet me on route 12 where it crosses the crick. I'll be drivin' that blue Chevy over there." He pointed to a battered ragtop parked across the street. It was a big sedan, faded blue, dents on every side and older than the hills, the white convertible top threadbare and torn at the left rear corner, the rear plastic window yellowed and cracked.

"Great!" Christopher replied. "We'll be there." He and Ramón clasped hands once more before parting.

"And don't be late!" Ramón called after them, "I cain't wait for too long."

"We won't be!" Christopher yelled back as he and Harmony started up the street. Turning to her, he slapped his hands together, rubbing them briskly like he'd seen Quentin do the evening before. "Now, how about some lunch?"

"You took the words right out of my mouth," Harmony grinned.

At a convenience store they got a couple of turkey sandwiches and fruit juices, bagged two more sandwiches and juices for Quentin and Ol' Henry, and then had a little picnic in the city park beneath towering shade trees. Afterwards they stretched out on the cool green grass and made-out for a while, then set a quick pace for camp, the Nebraska sun hot on their backs.

*   *   *

"We gotta hit the road!" Christopher yelled as he and Harmony came crashing through the weeds and down the embankment.

"The road?" Quentin and Ol' Henry looked up drowsily from where they were lounging in the shade beneath a huge, old cottonwood.

"Yeah," Christopher nodded, "we got a ride all the way to Oklahoma City."

"You guys hungry?" Harmony asked, holding up the plastic lunch bag. "We brought you a couple of turkey sandwiches and some juice."

Grinning, Quentin immediately leapt to his feet, snatched the bag, and exclaimed, "Starved! Thanks, you guys."

"Hold on," Christopher interjected. "Wait and eat by the road so we don't miss this guy. He's supposed to pick us up at 3:00 o'clock where the highway crosses the creek and it's close to that right now."

Quentin nodded. "We can wait, but how'd you do it?" he asked as they started off following the creek south towards the highway.

"Well…" Christopher began with a glance at Harmony, "we just said a little of this and a little of that and the guy said he'd take us with him."

"Hah!" Harmony laughed. "You should've heard him. In

case you don't know it we're going down to see my sick dad—before he dies!"

Everyone burst out laughing, Christopher cautioning, "Now you guys know what to say."

"I hopes we don't get caught in no lie," Ol' Henry commented.

"Ah, it don't matter," Christopher retorted, "the guy seemed pretty cool."

Cool or not, it was unanimously agreed upon that they would take the ride. After all, they certainly didn't have to worry about this guy jumping *them.*

12

SEEDS OF TRUTH

Sitting on the concrete bridge abutment and bouncing her heels off the side, Harmony asked, "I wonder what's taking him so long?"

"He'll come," Christopher assured her.

Quentin and Ol' Henry said nothing. They were hungrily chomping down on turkey sandwiches and guzzling juice when the old blue car appeared in the distance. It disappeared as the road dipped. A moment later it reappeared much closer.

"It's him!" Harmony exclaimed, slipping off the abutment.

"I told you he'd come," Christopher said, harboring a secret fear that Ramón might pass them by when he saw the two black men waiting with them.

His fears proved to be unfounded, the dilapidated blue Chevy rolling to a stop with a complaining squeak from its worn out brakes. A hog-eatin' grin on his face, Ramón touched the brim of his big black Stetson and asked genially, "Y'all wouldn't be lookin' for a ride to Oklahoma City, would ya?"

All four nodded.

"Y'all look like you been standin' there for months," he said, still grinning, the car door groaning on dry hinges as he got out. "Let's put that big ol' suitcase in the trunk."

Quentin grabbed the suitcase, crossed the highway and met Ramón at the rear of the car. Ramón popped the trunk, tossed the suitcase in and slammed it. Before getting in, Christopher introduced everyone, then Ramón called out with his biggest smile, "All aboard that's goin' aboard!"

Ol' Henry rode in front, the other three in back, Harmony in the middle. With the big Stetson stored safely behind the rear seat, Ramón said, "Well, here we go." The car bumped onto the highway with various creaks and rattles and slowly accelerated. It reeked of burnt oil and gasoline. And at 60 mph the wind whistled through the many leaks around the windows, and the torn roof fabric at the left rear corner flapped incessantly.

"Y'all want a beer?" Ramón asked loudly to be heard above the wind. "We got 'bout 500 miles to cover. Might as well tip a beer or two." He turned to Ol' Henry and motioned towards the 12-pack on the seat between them. "Go ahead, bust that sucker open and pass 'er around."

Ol' Henry tore the carton open. "Quentin? Christopher?"

For a moment there was only silence, then Christopher called out, "I'll have one." Reaching behind Harmony, he playfully slapped Quentin on the back of the head, adding, "And so will Quentin."

"Break 'em out, Henry!" Ramón cried with a hoot and a holler and a slap of the knee, "Gonna have us some beer this afternoon!"

At first Quentin started to refuse, but hesitated at Christopher's urging, "C'mon, man, when's the last time you partied? And when'll you get another chance?"

Quentin at last gave in. "Okay." Ol' Henry and Harmony both declined.

As beer was passed around and tops popped, Ramón asked with a knowing grin, "Y'all get high?"

Quentin and Christopher both started chuckling conspiratorially, Christopher asking, "Does the Pope read the Bible?"

A beer in hand, Quentin was feeling a little more relaxed now. Safer. Ramón seemed like a nice guy, and the closeness of the car and his friends felt cozy and secure. When would he have another chance to really unwind?

Forty miles down the road and the three boys were feeling the first effects of their second beers and the light-headed, paranoid confusion of a marijuana high. Ol' Henry and Harmony had both declined the pot as well. "You guys are gonna drink yourselves to death," Harmony remarked as the boys finished up their second beers and Ramón, handing them back over his shoulder as he drove, passed around thirds.

"That reminds me," Ramón said, glancing at her in the rearview mirror, "where 'bouts in Oklahoma City does your father live?"

Quentin coughed. Ol' Henry cleared his throat and looked out the window. When Harmony didn't answer Ramón assumed the monotone of a robot and bleated, "Earth to Harmony, come in, Harmony," which started the boys laughing.

Harmony glowered at Christopher as if to say, *what do I do now?* After a moment she blurted, "I don't know where he lives. I've never been there before."

"Parents divorced, huh?"

"Yes." She hated lying.

"How y'all goin' to find him if you don't know where he lives? Oklahoma City is a big place."

"Look him up in the phone book, I guess."

"What if his number's not listed?"

"What if there's an atomic war?" she retorted.

"Whoooa!" Ramón said like he was trying to stop a horse, "I didn't mean to pry." Harmony had half a mind to tell him the truth and the heck with all of them, but she held her tongue.

"You got to excuse Harmony," Quentin interceded, "she just tired."

"I am not!"

"Here be the road we's lookin' for," Ol' Henry interrupted, pointing to the highway marker Ramón had earlier told everyone to watch out for.

Ramón slowed, pressing lightly on the squeaky brakes and narrowly avoiding hitting the corner dividing island when, tires squealing and debris flying, he made the right turn. "We're headed straight south now," he informed everyone, "and this two-lane blacktop will carry us all the way across Nebraska and halfway through Kansas."

"You're gonna take back roads all the way?" Christopher asked.

"Almost," Ramón answered. "It's a straight shot and less cops."

"We'd better make a pit-stop," Christopher intoned.

"I gotta go too," Quentin put in.

"Only three beers left, y'all," Ramón informed them, slowing and pulling onto the shoulder where he stopped beneath a roadside oak tree. Everyone got out with groans and stretches, the three boys immediately heading for the far side of the tree to relieve themselves.

Harmony and Ol' Henry turned their backs on the boys and stretched their legs along the shoulder. "Where be Oklahoma City, child?" Ol' Henry asked as they strolled.

"Somewhere in Oklahoma, I guess. But we're heading the right way, I know that."

"I hopes so."

Before they got back on the highway Ramón twisted up another joint, handed out the last of the beer and commented, "We'll get another twelver first place that comes up." He finished rolling up the illicit smoke, passed it to the boys in back and pulled out onto the highway.

The three boys were catching a good if silent buzz and all were reaching the bottoms of their last beers when Ramón spotted a welcome sight ahead; A gas station with a blue neon sign in its window advertising "COLD BEER." Ramón pulled in and stopped just beyond the pumps. He shut the engine off and twisted around in his seat. "It's y'all's turn to buy," he said.

"Harmony?" Christopher inquired.

"What?"

"You got the money."

Heaving a resentful sigh, Harmony dug out a $10 dollar bill and handed it to Ramón. "You guys think we should be wasting our money on beer?" she asked.

After Ramón was gone Christopher said, "Relax, by tomorrow or the day after we're all gonna be rich."

A minute later Ramón was back at the car window. "The dude carded me."

"Let me out, Henry," Quentin ordered.

Ramón handed him the $10 dollars. "A 12-pack oughta do it."

"Right." Quentin took the money and went inside.

He returned with the beer and they were off again, Ramón remarking over his shoulder, "That dude seemed like a major foreigner, didn't he?"

"Yeah, like he just went an' got off the boat," Quentin laughed, adding, "Probably an A-rab. I wonder what a clay-head's doin' pumpin' gas in the middle of Nebraska?"

They all started laughing until Ol' Henry sharply interjected, "Foreigner? What a foreigner? Just remember one thing, till all the peoples of the world recognize each other as brothers and sisters we is *all* foreigners."

No one said a word. The boys silently swigged their beer. Christopher, Quentin and Harmony were especially shocked. It was the first outburst from Henry Rathbone they'd ever heard. Attempting to lighten things a bit, Quentin asked, affecting Ol' Henry's own accent and phrasing, "What be eatin' at you, Mr. Henry?"

"Nothin', Mr. Quentin," he answered gruffly, "I just don't like that kind'a talk none. Puttin' down a man just 'cause a how God made 'em. I been livin' with that kind'a bull too long. Know what I mean?" Before Quentin could respond he went on. "An' it ruffles my feathers ta hear my own kind takin' part in the very thing they hate so much. I would'a thought you would know better."

Earlier Christopher had carried on at length, telling Harmony to "be cool" and smoke pot with them and berating her extensively when she repeatedly refused. Now Ol' Henry decided to give him a piece of his mind as well. "An' you, Christopher, tellin' Harmony she hast ta smoke pot to be cool. What you know 'bout bein' cool? She's a sight more cooler than you where I's from. If'n you wants to be cool you gots to be an individual, o' else you just a moron like everybody else."

The silence that ensued was complete, the only sound being the tires clicking off the expansion strips in the pavement, the whistle of the wind and the flapping of torn roof fabric. When Harmony realized he was finished she said softly, "Thank you, Henry."

"It be all right, child. I's just tellin' the truth. An' the funny thing 'bout the truth is, if'n ya follows it with your heart, an' with your mind also, ya learns to love it even when it be like sand in your mouth, 'cause without the truth you can't never gets to the light."

"What do you mean you love the truth even when it's like sand in your mouth?" Harmony asked.

"I mean when I gets to lookin' into my very own soul, darlin'."

"Oh."

Christopher crumpled his beer can, threw it on the floor and asked for another. Ramón automatically passed one back for Quentin too. By now the sun was a distant, yellow ball over their right shoulders, the sky crystal clear. It would be a fairly uneventful sunset, the daylight gradually fading to gray to black.

Inspired by Ol' Henry, Quentin's mind was churning with new thoughts that he immediately voiced. "When you said 'without the truth you can't get to the light,' you equating light with God, right?"

Ol' Henry smiled to himself. "That be right, Quentin."

"Uh-huh," Quentin nodded with understanding. "Then what do 'seek the truth and the truth shall set you free,' mean?"

Ol' Henry scratched his jaw thoughtfully. "Let me 'splains it this way. Listen. In each an' every one of us there be a seed a truth. That is, a knowledge a God. An' it may be just a wee bit different for each of us, but it all be leading to the same basic core a truth that be rulin' all, which is God. Trouble is, when we discover this here truth, the closer we gets to it the greater becomes our desire to resist it. To pretend it don't even exist. Why? 'Cause truth tells us what be really important instead a what we done made up in our own minds to be important. Finally, we start creatin' the truth instead a seekin' it. An' then we becomes the slave to a lie of our own makin'. A slave to the prince of darkness, Satan. So if'n you seeks the truth, it be the truth that will set you free, 'cause all truth leads to God, an' when you finds God, you'll find infinite strength, an' from strength comes power, an' from power one can forge the way of freedom in any land—or hold onto the freedom they got."

All four teenagers were listening with rapt attention. The man had a way of putting things that was inescapable. "Do that answer your question, Mr. Quentin?"

"Yes it do, Henry, thank you. But there is one thing I have to know."

Ol' Henry cocked an ear. "What?"

"Okay. Aside from its relationship to God as you describe it, how you definin' the word 'truth'?"

"The truth," Ol' Henry began, "is a total absence of dishonesty. Or, to puts it another way, the truth is openin' our very own hearts to total reality without allowin' ourselves to color it with our own desires or ambitions. Ya see, lies can be made up, but the truth stands alone. You surely can pretend it's not there. You can call it a liar. You can hide it so no one knows. Nevertheless, it is there. It can live with you an' it can live without you, but it most surely will live. An' everything outside of it will die, for the truth is the very trunk of the tree of life."

Quentin was startled by the strength of the man's convictions. Letting out a long stream of air, he sat back. "Where," he began slowly, his voice revealing hope, "where do I begin seekin' this truth?"

Ol' Henry paused a moment to clear his throat. "Begin at the bottom of your heart, Mr. Quentin, and work your way up from there. An' remember," he cautioned, "anything even just a wee bit less than the truth is a lie, an' a lie is 'bout as far from God as you can get."

Quentin was impressed. Who was this Henry Rathbone, anyway? He seemed to have an understanding of God that went far beyond any preacher he'd ever heard before. It was almost strange. With that in mind he asked another question. "The Bible say love God above all else. Love God with all your heart an' soul, right?"

Ol' Henry's head bobbed once in agreement.

"How do I love God? How do I love somethin' that ain't there? I mean, that I can't see or hear or feel. Somethin' that I can't touch or taste or smell? How do someone express love for someone who may only exist in his mind? I mean, it ain't as if I can shake God's hand an' ask if he'd like a cold one."

"God ain't so much worried 'bout us lovin' him as he is 'bout us lovin' each other," Ol' Henry answered solemnly, "'cause if'n we had love in our hearts for one another it would most surely be a reflection of our love for him. But to answer your question; love the truth, embrace the truth, an' you'll be lovin' God. It be that simple. But that be part a the problem, too. It be so simple people can't comprehend it; love without possession, love without jealousy or judgment. Love without fear of loss."

When he finished speaking it was quieter than a church on Monday. A northbound semi-truck thundered by, rocking the car on its squeaky springs. Darkness was closing in fast. "Better put your lights on," Christopher said quietly, his mind whirring with the many thoughts Ol' Henry had inspired.

Ramón clicked on the lights, which suddenly made it seem much darker outside.

For the last several minutes Christopher had been formulating his own question. The perfect question. The one that would defeat the old man. "I've got a question, Henry," the teenager began condescendingly. "God is perfect, right?"

"That be right, Christopher."

"And yet the most beautiful creature he ever made rebelled against him and screwed up the world. Satan, right? It seems to me creating Satan was a mistake."

"In the end Satan be a tool of God. But okay, for the sake of argument let's say Satan be a mistake."

"Okay," Christopher went on, "that proves right there it's all a lot of bull. How can a 'Perfect Being' make mistakes?"

Ol' Henry twisted around in his seat and looked at Christopher with knowing eyes. "Will ya listen whilst I answer?"

Christopher nodded, an inexplicable apprehension rising up from deep inside. His "seed of truth" had been sprung by the words of his own mouth. Now he could nurture it—or let it die.

"Okay," the old man began carefully. "God, he perfect in his love. In everything else he an artist. A creator. An' what does an artist do when he done made a mistake?" There wasn't a sound. "He erases it an' does it over till it be just right, thus," Ol' Henry snapped his fingers, "perfection!"

His final proclamation of "perfection" was lost when the front right tire blew out with a bang and a rumbling jar, the tires screeching as the Chevy swerved from side to side, Ramón fighting the wheel. The car finally slowed, the blown tire flopping like a dead fish as Ramón steered onto the shoulder and stopped. He was still clutching his half-full can of beer. "And I didn't spill a drop!" he proudly proclaimed, holding it aloft.

His four passengers burst out laughing, the tension of the moment relieved. "Thank God there wasn't any traffic around or we'd all be dead," Harmony said.

"Hope you got a spare tire," Quentin put in.

Ramón shook his head. "No way, José."

Everyone groaned.

"But I do have a jack. All we gotta do is take the wheel off, hitch into town and find a used tire to buy."

"Letch have another beer an' think on it," Christopher slurred, his tongue swollen with alcohol and pot from the last several hours of drinking and smoking. Ramón and Quentin were feeling pretty disoriented as well.

"Good idea," Ramón said cheerily, downing his beer and digging out three fresh ones for himself and his two drinking buddies. The pop and hiss of opening beer cans seemed to echo throughout the car as multiple tabs were pulled.

Ol' Henry's door squeaked open and with a shake of his head he got out of the car. "I's gonna stretch my legs for a spell."

"Me too," Harmony said and released the front seat-back, tilted it forward and climbed across Quentin to get out.

It was a clear, balmy night, the velvet-black sky dusted with billions of shimmering stars, the wind just a whisper through the tall prairie grass. Not 50 feet from where Ramón had stopped the car was a quadrangle of towering pine trees silhouetted against the sky. "Looky there," Ol' Henry pointed. "Feel like takin' a look-see what those trees is gathered around?"

"Okay."

They walked up the highway a short distance to a dirt driveway overgrown with prairie grass and tumble weeds. All that remained of the farmhouse the quad of trees had once sheltered from the howling winds of the plains was the foundation, filled in with dirt and a tangle of brambles and weeds.

"Leaves ya wonderin' why they left such a lovely spot, don't it?" Ol' Henry quietly said as they ambled up the driveway and took a seat on the foundation. "Seems a body could spend all its days here in peace."

"Yes it does," Harmony replied in a reverent whisper.

The quiet moment was shattered as the three boys, arm-in-arm, came swaying and stumbling up the overgrown drive boisterously singing *Those Ol' Cottonfields Back Home*, each trying to sing louder than the other. They staggered up to Harmony and the old man, serenading until a verse escaped them and their song, if you could call their wailing singing, fell apart. Then Quentin, at the center of the trio, dropped the 12-pack and kicked the feet out from under his two companions, which sent them sprawling on the grass. Ramón and Christopher wasted no time tackling Quentin in a mad free-for-all that had them tumbling across the grass in a tangle of legs and arms, curses and laughter.

Harmony and Ol' Henry watched in silence.

Trying to catch their breath through their laughter, the boys broke apart and leaned back on the heels of their hands. When they were breathing normally again and it had grown quiet Ramón, wondering what religion Ol' Henry was so ardently promoting, called with a note of sarcasm in his voice, "Hey Henry, if I wanna find God what religion should I join?"

Ol' Henry stared at him for a silent moment before answering, "God won't address no church or religion, only individuals."

"Then what church should I join?"

"Join the church of believers."

"Where's zat?"

"In yo' very own heart."

"I never been there before," Ramón laughed, "where's zat?"

"Think of it this a way," the old man began slowly. "If'n a man be standin' in a forest an' he be lost, an' can't admits to himself that he be lost, then he be lost. But if'n that same man be a standin' in that same forest an' he lost an' be willin' to admit it, he *still* be lost. But at least he knows there is somethin' to be found."

When Ol' Henry finished there was a moment of silence broken by Ramón announcing, "Time for another beer!" Taking one for himself, he passed the carton to his two drinking buddies. Harmony watched the three of them with disdain, looking down upon them from her perch on the foundation.

"I don't care if I do go to hell," Christopher giggled slovenly as he took another beer and wiped his chin with his sleeve, "all my friends'll be there!"

That broke Ramón up, the two boys laughing uproariously as Ramón pounded Christopher's back and declared, "Me too!" Quentin fell silent. Everything the old man said hadn't merely struck him as true, it was profound. "Besides, there ain't no hell," Ramón went on, still grinning, "'cause there ain't no way a person can burn forever, 'cause I never heard a no fireproof man!" Again this brought on howls of laughter from he and Christopher, both completely oblivious to the fact that Quentin was no longer participating.

"The burnin' won't be a the flesh," Ol' Henry said softly, "but of the eternal burnin' of your empty heart, filled with a terrible loneliness as you is cast into the dark, cold, bottomless pit."

"What bottomless pit?" Ramón challenged.

Ol' Henry motioned upwards with his head.

Both boys looked up. "All I see is stars," Christopher snickered.

"That be right, Christopher. An' beyond that is just about the biggest universe you ever saw. An' it be dark an' just goes on an' on forever an' ever. An' that universe gonna be about the biggest bottomless pit you ever saw, an' the lake a fire'll be your very own fiery soul, your heart cast in as it rushes away from the light forever an' ever an' you be in the dark an' all alone with your presence of mind an' everything you know until the judgment an' the second death. An' that what burnin' forever means."

Ramón and Christopher were too sodden with beer to comprehend much of what the old man said. At the moment everything was a joke. Quentin might have been in the same boat had he not been listening with such intense concentration. In his heart he was already asking God to show him the way of hope and faith.

Eyeing the old man, Ramón asked, "So ya really believe in God and all that religious bull, huh?" Ol' Henry responded with a short nod. "Then 'splain to me why God made all these weirdos that do all these terrible things like murdering children and stuff? Why'd he make them?"

"God didn't. Those characters is the fruit a man, a product of this culture. And ya see, if'n we all loved one another, deep down in our hearts everyday love like Jesus taught, then there wouldn't be any unsavory characters. But it be like this; What men do the sons of men gots to live with. But like pain, that only gonna last a little while, an' then the King gonna come back forever.

"But the madness that you be seein' all around you ain't God's doin', it's his leavin'. The spirit of God is withdrawin'. The spirit, it be flowin' out of this people an' leavin' this land like shadows on a cloudy day. Where be God in this land if'n he not in the hearts of the people?

"Oh, they be a pocket of people here an' there that's got him, but there be a whole lot more just usin' his name, if only because it be politically correct, or 'cause they be raisin' money for this or that. But the truth is, the world be in a mess, spiritually speakin', an' no amount of scientific wonder gonna separate mankind from the spiritual part of life mankind be needin' to get along in this world. Ya see, makin' life better for people ain't no longer a matter of makin' better machines. Now, the only way the people of this world is goin' to survive the scientific wonders of their own creation is gonna be through holdin' onto their spiritual nature—through recognizin' an' holdin' onto their relationship with God…" Ol' Henry stopped abruptly, got to his feet and walked off into the darkness.

"Where's he going?" Harmony asked, puzzled.

"To take a leak," Ramón replied.

"No he's not," Harmony said as she jumped to her feet and hurried after him.

"It seemed like he was going to say something else," Christopher commented curiously.

"I think," Quentin started slowly, staring straight ahead

with a frown of concentration, "he was goin' to say, 'but it's never goin' to happen.'"

"Meaning what?" Christopher wanted to know. In the time they'd spent together he'd developed as much of an affection for the old man as anyone, and his sudden departure had sharpened the focus of Christopher's fermented brain somewhat.

"Meanin' there ain't goin' to be any spiritual changes an' the world is gonna continue on its headlong plunge into warfare an' societal madness, like the bombin's, school shootin's, an' suicidal rampages goin' on all over the place, I guess."

"Looks like we're gonna be spendin' the night here," Ramón interjected. "Why don't we get the car and pull it up on the grass, Chris?"

Christopher nodded. "Okay."

The boys got to their feet and went for the car, leaving Quentin alone to ponder the fate of the world. But Quentin wasn't worrying about the world. He had found something new and much more exciting. For the first time in his life God was REAL! Taking in the vast evening sky, he reached for another beer and stood up and stretched. Heaven and Hell both straight up, huh? Sort of. He cracked the beer.

13

HITCHIN' A RIDE

Harmony and Ol' Henry were up for more than an hour before the boys. Harmony wanted to wake them, but Henry told her to let them sleep. They'd be suffering from last night's overindulgence soon enough.

Ramón was curled up on the front seat of the car. Quentin had taken the back. Harmony and Christopher had slept on the ground under one of Ol' Henry's blankets, the old man beside them with the other blanket. When she got up it hardly disturbed Christopher. Drawing the blanket tighter, he just rolled over on his side.

"They be wakin' up in just a bit now," Ol' Henry was saying, "burnin' a thirst an' their kidneys bustin' to be emptied."

"Thirsty? Why? They drank enough last night to sink a battleship."

"'Cause that what drinkin' do to you, darlin'. You saw how they was goin' to the bathroom so much last night? It draws all the water out an' dehydrates a man, body an' soul. They won't be worth two cents this mornin'. Probably won't get outta here till this afternoon."

Upon awakening and relieving himself behind a nearby tree, the first thing Ramón wanted was a beer. On the "hair of the dog" theory. His whole body ached and his head throbbed. A quick beer or two would ease the pain. Unable to remember if they had finished them off last night or not, his doubt was satisfied when he found the empty carton in the grass and gave it a swift kick.

The second thing Ramón wanted was water. Spotting the canteen Ol' Henry had left on the hood of the car, he snatched it up and guzzled thirstily, capped the canteen and boosted himself to a seat on the edge of the hood, feet dangling, head cradled in his hands.

With a sorrowful groan Quentin came alive. Not a word was exchanged with Ramón as he staggered from the car on wobbly legs, his mouth dry as a bag of cement. With shaky hands he grabbed the canteen and chugged water until it trickled from the corners of his mouth. Wiping his chin with his sleeve, he corked the vessel, left it on the hood and headed for the nearest tree.

Thoroughly relieved, Quentin returned to the car. Folding his arms across his chest, he rested his rear against the fender and crossed his legs at the ankles.

"I sure hate the thought of havin' to screw with this here tire," Ramón mumbled.

"Might as well go an' wake Christopher an' get started," Quentin replied through an extended yawn. "The day already half over."

Harmony and Ol' Henry were sitting on the overgrown foundation in the same place as the previous evening. Quentin smiled. For all he knew they'd been sitting there all night. His aching brain couldn't seem to remember too much about the night before. "We could get started, anyway," he said without looking at Ramón. "Maybe by then Chris'll wake up."

After a long pause Ramón slid off the hood and said without much enthusiasm, "Okay. Let's get the jack and stuff."

Being careful not to jar his tender brain, Quentin eased himself off the fender and went around to the trunk. The lid was already up. With seeming lead in their joints and lead in the seats of their pants they removed the bumper jack and various parts, threw them on the grass and stood there staring down at them as if they expected the parts to get up and walk to the front of the car. Rubbing the back of his neck, Ramón remarked, "I guess we tied-on a good one last night."

Quentin chuckled. "Guess we did. Been awhile since I went an' done that."

"Seems like I do it too often," Ramón intimated, "got to slow down."

"If you don't you gonna age fast," Quentin warned with a grin as he poked at the jack stand with the toe of his shoe. The poisons working their way out of his system, he was gradually starting to feel some relief as he became more awake and active.

"I don't see no gray hairs yet," Ramón said as he stooped and picked up the parts.

Quentin shrugged and grabbed the lug wrench. "You will," he warned again as they started for the front of the car.

Quentin elected to loosen the lug nuts while Ramón set up the jack. Getting down on his knees beside the tire, he fit the lug wrench to the first nut. Grunting with the effort, Quentin slowly twisted. His initial relief turned to dismay when the lug snapped off in his hands. "Damn thing just broke off."

"What?" Ramón came over for a closer look. "Well ya busted it ya buffalo fart!"

Quentin looked up in surprise. "*I* broke it?"

"It didn't bust itself!"

"I can't help it if your lugs are no good!" Quentin angrily shot back.

At his sharp retort Ramón laughed. "Take it easy, Hercules," he said, clapping him on the shoulder, "just try not to bust anymore. We need something to hold the wheel on."

Quentin let out a long stream of air and nodded. "Okay." On the next lug he revised his methods. Instead of muscling it he grabbed both sides of the crossbar and with a series of short, sharp, snapping motions, broke the nut loose. He turned it back and forth several times to clear the rust, then repeated the process on the remaining three lugs as Ramón began jacking.

"High enough yet?" Ramón asked.

"Higher."

"Well dig some of the sand out from under the wheel."

"Already did."

Ramón stopped jacking. "I'm almost to the top."

"Gotta get it higher."

Ramón cranked on it four more times. "That's it. Won't go any higher." The jack leg was sticking out from the bumper at a precarious angle.

Quentin got to his feet and changed places with Ramón, each examining the other's work. "Well hell!" Quentin exclaimed, "You not jackin' the car *up*, you jackin' the base *down* into the sand!"

Standing up and dusting off his jeans, Ramón said, "This ain't working. We gotta get this car up a little bit at least."

"What we need is a board under the base of the jack," Quentin said. Feeling a presence near, he turned.

Ol' Henry was standing there with a piece of board. "Be needin' this, Mr. Quentin?" he asked mildly.

Shaking his head, Quentin laughed. "You too much, Mr. Henry, too much."

"That be what my mamma used to say," he said with a grin and handed over the plank.

Quentin took it and tossed it nearby, cranked the jack down and got on his knees and dug the base out. After filling in the hole and smoothing it out he put the board in place and set the jack on it. The claw fit easily into the bumper slot and he jacked the car up.

"Good! Good!" Ramón called. In a matter of seconds the wheel was off. Looking at Quentin with a broad smile, he said, "Now for the fun part. Let's get sleepin' beauty over there outta the sack."

Quentin nodded with a grin, "Yeah."

They took two steps in Christopher's direction when, the blanket falling to his lap, he rolled over and sat up. "What're you guys doing?" he asked sleepily.

Ramón and Quentin froze in their tracks. "Gettin' the wheel

off," Quentin said drily, "wanna help?"

"Looks like you guys got it done," he said through a wide yawn. Getting to his feet and heading for the nearest tree, he called over his shoulder, "Where's the canteen, Henry?"

Looking up from the game of tic-tac-toe he and Harmony had drawn in the sand, the old man answered, "On the hood a the car."

Christopher found the canteen empty. "All out," he called, tossed it high into the air and caught it again.

"Take it with you an' fills it, then."

"Sure, Henry," he said, slinging it over his shoulder, "you guys ready?"

"I'm gonna go an' wait right here," Quentin said. "It'd be too hard gettin' a ride with three of us."

Christopher nodded. "Okay. Me and Ramón can do it."

"You carry the tire," Ramón put in, "since we took it off."

Unslinging the canteen, Christopher tossed it to him. "Okay." Standing the tire up, he said, "Let's go."

Harmony scrambled to her feet. "Aren't you forgetting something, Chris?" They exchanged a kiss. "How long will you be gone?"

Christopher shrugged, "You got me."

"Will you hurry back?"

"No. I'm gonna walk real slow everywhere I go."

Harmony gave him a swat on the butt. Christopher laughed and they kissed again. Then he asked for a dollar so he could get a soda, took it and the tire and said, "Let's go, Ramón."

The others watched the boys walk down to the highway and stick out their thumbs. "Chris, he didn't seem like he was even feelin' it at all this mornin'," Quentin remarked.

"Sometimes it gets ya an' sometimes it don't," Ol' Henry intimated, adding, "I'd bet ya a plug nickel he be feelin' it more than he lettin' it show."

It must have been their day. The second vehicle to happen by, an older, dusty, but well-kept pickup pulled over. A middle-aged farmer with close-cropped blond hair, a green John Deere cap on his head and a ready smile leaned forward on the steering wheel, looked across at the boys and pleasantly inquired, "Fellas had a blowout, eh?"

"Yes sir," Christopher said. "Could you give us a lift into town?"

"Shore 'nuff. Toss the tire in back and hop in."

The boys did as they were told, except that neither wanted to sit in the middle. For an embarrassingly long time they stood at the open door arguing.

"You get in."

"No, you get in," Christopher insisted.

"Go ahead, I was here first."

"I put the tire in."

"So?" Ramón looked at him.

"So you're smaller."

At last the farmer interjected, "You boys comin' or not?"

Ramón finally relented, got in the truck and slid to the center. Christopher followed and shut the door. They rode in silence into town where the farmer let them out.

Broken Bow, Kansas, had only one gas station. The proprietor, mid-fifties, graying hair in a crewcut, dirt and grease-stained coveralls bulging with a big potbelly, chomped on a huge cigar and watched from the doorway as the boys removed the blown tire from the pickup and approached. The gravy for yesterday's mashed potatoes had just arrived.

While Ramón did the talking, "Y'all wouldn't happen to have some used tires for sale, would ya?" Christopher dropped the tire at the man's feet and went straight to the drinking fountain.

Puffing on his cigar, the man nodded with a grunt. "Got some right good ones. What size you lookin' for?"

"H-78 14's," Ramón answered.

"How many?"

"Just one."

"Around the corner of the station house you'll find a whole mess of 'em. Pick yourself out one."

"Thanks," Ramón said.

After Christopher had his fill and wiped his mouth with a forearm, the boys headed for the side of the service station. When the boys were gone the proprietor put a hand to his lower backside, stooped, picked up the tire and brought it inside to dismount.

"Wow," Ramón exclaimed as they gazed upon the pile of tires. "We could come back tonight and get all the tires we need. It doesn't even look like they're locked up. Maybe we could get inside the station house and get some tools, too."

Christopher eyed him levelly. "You think so?"

"Sure."

But even as Christopher spoke something else was in the back of his mind. Something Henry had said the night before left him with the vaguely uncomfortable feeling that maybe he was wrong about God and maybe Harmony was right. He absently kicked at a bolt embedded in the asphalt. "Probably keeps dogs here at night, anyway," he said, keeping his eyes on the bolt he was trying to work loose.

Head cocked to one side, Ramón watched Christopher for several moments. "You ain't never stole nothin', have ya?"

Christopher stopped kicking and looked up. "Sure I have," he said defensively. "I've stole plenty of things."

"Like what," Ramón sneered, "a piece of gum?"

Christopher was taken completely by surprise at Ramón's attitude. The conversation reminded him of being 14 again. It was funny, though. He swiped stuff all the time. Why, all of a sudden, was he getting cold feet? "You see any good tires?" Christopher asked, changing the subject.

"Ya still ain't told me what ya stole."

"I've stolen lots of stuff," Christopher snapped, "ya think I keep track? Come to think of it, I stole this lighter just the other day." He proudly held up the Bic lighter he'd swiped from the kindly grocer in Greensprings, Iowa.

Now Ramón was embarrassed. He turned to the pile of old tires and searched with discerning eyes. "Here," he said, picking one out of the heap. "How's this one look?"

Christopher shrugged. "Looks okay to me. The tread's pretty good." He leaned closer and examined the tire as Ramón turned it. "No cracks in the sidewall," he said and straightened up. "Looks good."

"What should we give for it?"

Again Christopher shrugged. "I don't know. They're supposed to be real highway robbers out here in the middle of nowhere, aren't they?"

"We'll tell him it's for our spare, then he won't think he's got us over a barrel."

Christopher nodded. "Okay."

When they entered the garage, Ramón rolling the tire, the cigar puffing station owner was just finishing up removing the remnants of the old tire from the wheel. "This oughta make a fair spare, ya think?" Ramón asked and showed his choice.

Rolling his cigar to the center of his mouth and back to the corner again, the proprietor nodded with a grunt.

"How much?"

"Thirty bucks."

"Thirty bucks!" Ramón exclaimed indignantly.

"Uh, wait a minute," the man said, holding up a finger as he took a closer look at the tire. He straightened up. "My mistake. Thirty-*five* bucks. That's a Super Royal Steel Belted Whitewall. And look at the tread left on that tire, son. This ain't no charity organization, this is a business. Plus, it'll cost you for taking the old tire off and mounting the new one."

"How much?"

"Ten bucks. The whole thing comes to $45 bucks."

Ramón frowned. He wanted to give five or ten dollars for the tire and maybe five bucks to mount it. "Forty dollars," he stubbornly bargained, his jaw set.

"Sold!" the proprietor boomed and stuck his hand out.

Ramón took it glumly. "And that's it," he warned, "I'm not givin' you any more than $40 bucks. No tax, no this, no that."

The proprietor nodded solemnly. "That's it. No other charges."

"Okay. Put it on." Ramón rolled the tire at him. "Come on," he said to Christopher.

The two boys went out into the bright sunshine and sat down on the concrete apron that surrounded the front of the station house. "Sun's hot," Christopher commented.

"Sure is," Ramón replied. "But I think I just got took for that tire. What'd you think?"

Christopher raised a shoulder, "Who the heck knows these days, ya know?"

"Guess I'll go fill the canteen," Ramón said, got to his feet and went inside the station house. When he came out, the canteen's canvas jacket dripping water, he dug into his pocket for change and asked, "Want a soda?"

"Sure."

"What kind?"

"Grape."

Ramón turned to a vending machine near the door, fed it coins, got them each a soda and sat down again. After a long, satisfying drink he crossed his legs and rested his forearms on his knees. Eyeing the diner across the street, he said, "I sure am in need of some grub."

"Me too," Christopher agreed, "but we should wait on the others and all have lunch together."

Ramón nodded. "Yeah, I guess so."

Just then the station owner poked his head out of the garage. "Tire's ready."

While Ramón paid, Christopher stood the tire up, looked it over, and headed out the door rolling it along with one hand. Ramón caught up to him at the highway and immediately began hailing passing traffic.

Cars were few and far between and the wait grew long as vehicle after vehicle whooshed by. Just when the boys were beginning to give up hope a shiny new green Ford pickup stopped beside them. The kid at the wheel, a farmhand in his early twenties dressed in jeans, denim shirt, cowboy boots and a hat, drawled, "Got a flat out on the highway, huh?"

Ramón and Christopher nodded. "Between here and the next town someplace," Christopher put in.

"Come on, then, I guess I could give you a lift."

"Thanks," Ramón said, opening the door as Christopher threw the tire in back. When Christopher turned around Ramón was still standing at the open door. "Take turns, Chris." Unable to fault that logic, Christopher nodded and got in. Ramón followed and pulled the door shut.

"It's a pain in the butt gettin' stuck out on the highway in these parts, ain't it?" the young farmhand commented.

"Sure is," Christopher replied.

"Runnin' without a spare?"

"Yep."

"That'll teach ya."

"Yep."

A 15-minute run down the highway and they were back. "Thanks for the ride!" both boys called as they jumped out of the truck. Christopher grabbed the tire.

"Anytime," the kid smiled and drove off with a wave.

As the boys approached, Christopher rolling the tire along with one hand, Harmony looked up from a game of *Hangman* she and Quentin had drawn in the dust on the car's hood. "What took you guys so long?"

"I thought we made good time," Christopher replied and leaned the tire against the fender of the car.

Unslinging the canteen, Ramón put it on the hood and loudly announced, "Let's get this tire mounted and get going 'cause I, for one, am starvin'."

Mounting the wheel was a snap compared to dismounting it

and shortly the boys were getting to their feet and dusting off their pants. "How far to Oklahoma City, you figure?" Quentin asked.

"'Bout four hours or so, I guess," Ramón answered while stretching a kink out of his back.

Christopher was busy putting the jack in the trunk. Harmony and Ol' Henry were shaking out the blankets, folding them and putting them in the suitcase. Afterwards Ol' Henry sat on it and buckled the straps. When he was done, Christopher tossed it in the trunk, securely slammed the lid and sang out, "All set to go!"

Taking the same seats as before, everyone piled into the car. Ramón managed to coax the tired old engine to life. Sputtering oily smoke, the car rocked and creaked across uneven ground as Ramón guided it to the highway.

In Broken Bow, where the boys bought the tire, Ramón stopped at the diner. Everyone got burgers to go because no one wanted to take the time for a sit-down meal. Before ordering, though, Ramón went to the rest room. Christopher took that opportunity to voice an idea he'd had. "Why not just tell him what we're up to and offer him, say, $400 dollars to drive us straight to Jackson? He might jump at it."

Surprised, Harmony exclaimed, *"You're* the one that made up the big tale about my dying dad because you were so afraid he was going to get in on it!"

Christopher shrugged. "So? It's a good idea isn't it? Four hundred dollars between our four shares isn't much. And we'd have a ride right to where we're goin'."

Ol' Henry looked at him with a sawtoothed grin. "Could be the best idea you done had in the last two days."

Quentin shrugged. "Why not? Be a whole lot easier than hoppin' freights. An' faster an' safer, too."

"All he can do is turn us down," Christopher put in. "And who would turn down $400 dollars just to drive someone a few hundred miles?"

"If'n you young'ns wants to," Ol' Henry shrugged, "Okay."

When Ramón came out of the rest room his four passengers silently eyed him. At the looks on their faces he did a double take and suspiciously asked, "What're y'all plottin' now?"

Figuring they might as well get right down to it, Quentin said, "Chris'll tell ya after we get our food an' get back on the road."

Once on the highway, everyone munching burgers and fries, Christopher plunged right in. "How would you like to make $400 bucks, Ramón?"

"How?"

"Drive us to Jackson, Mississippi."

"Do I get paid in advance?"

"No. After we get there."

Ramón laughed. "Sure. What'd ya think I am, some fool tinhorn or somethin'?"

"Hold on a minute," Christopher interjected, "let me tell you the whole story." With Ol' Henry's occasional assistance he told the entire story about the house and the hidden money. "And so," he concluded, "as you can see there's a possibility we won't get the dough, but doesn't it sound like a good gamble?"

Ramón was silent for a moment before answering, "I have to go on down to Oklahoma City first no matter what. My folks are expecting me."

"That be okay," Ol' Henry assured him.

"I cain't take y'all home with me," Ramón cautioned, "ma would have a heart attack if I was to bring darkies... uh, I mean...."

"Don't matter none. We'll just finds us a place to hide out till you ready. Providin' that ain't too awful long, a course."

"A few hours at most," Ramón replied. "I'll just tell them I got a chance to make a little money."

"It be settled then," Ol' Henry said with finality.

14

BLACK AND WHITE

Just before they reached the outskirts of Oklahoma City, a fiery orange sun half-buried behind the western hills silhouetted against a crimson sky, Ramón clicked on the headlights. Cresting a rise in the plains, the distant lights of the city shimmering in the twilight haze were scattered before them like glittering diamonds in the red Oklahoma dirt. "There she is," Ramón sang out, "home!"

"That's Oklahoma City?" Harmony asked and leaned forward for a better view.

"Sure is."

"I didn't know it was so big."

"Biggest city in the state," Ramón informed her.

Waking from a doze, Ol' Henry asked, "We's there, huh?"

"We're there," Christopher affirmed it.

"Where're we gonna go an' get off?" Quentin asked.

"Anywhere y'all want," Ramón answered.

"Henry?"

"We'll see," the old man answered, exuding patience.

The two-lane highway soon intersected with a big, brilliantly illuminated four-lane interstate. Ramón drove up the southbound ramp and merged into traffic on the freeway that would carry them the last 20 miles into the city.

"It sure do feel good to be back in civilization," Quentin commented.

"It sure does," Christopher agreed. "Makes me a little homesick."

"Not me," Harmony cheerfully said.

"Looky there!" Ol' Henry pointed as a gleaming, vintage gold Eldorado with a set of longhorns on the hood cruised by.

"I didn't know they had skyscrapers here," Christopher said.

"Oh yeah. And they're building more," Ramón answered proudly.

Pointing to several steel-grid structures rising up faintly in the growing darkness, Harmony asked, "What're those towers out there?"

"Oil derricks," Quentin quickly answered. "The whole city been built on an oil field."

"Really?"

"Oil built this town," Ramón put in. "They even used to have an oil derrick on the capitol lawn till it run dry and was tore down in '86. They replaced it with some kind'a cowboy statue."

At Crossbuck Avenue Ramón exited east. At the bottom of the ramp they caught a red light. While waiting for it to change Ramón commented conversationally, "We're gonna be goin' through the black section of town now so keep your windows rolled up." The silence that followed Ramón's remark went unnoticed by him until, with a start, he remembered that two of his passengers were black. With an embarrassed laugh he added awkwardly, "This here's the worst area in Oklahoma City, y'all. Dudes get killed down here all the time."

For several seconds no one said anything. Then Ol' Henry and Quentin started chuckling, Quentin saying with an exaggeratedly "black" accent, "It be coo', bro, you can roll yo' window down. I'll jist tells 'em you wid us." At that everyone burst out laughing.

In fact once off the highway with its steady blast of 60-mile-an-hour wind, it was quite warm. A grinning Ramón cranked down his window. Ol' Henry did the same. The light changed and Ramón turned east.

Crossbuck Avenue, a major east-west artery of the city, was decorated with Burger Kings and Kmarts, clubs and bowling alleys, flea-bag hotels and seedy peep-show shacks, its confusion of glowing, blinking, multi-colored plastic neon lights somehow debilitating. And the fine, reddish Oklahoma dust seemed to tint everything.

Interspersed with the commercial districts were residential areas of rundown frame and brick homes. A little after 8:00 p.m. on a Friday night, the main social event appeared to be sitting on front stoops or porches and drinking. And it seemed almost every other corner supported a crowd of rough-looking teenagers gathered around dice or bottles or smoldering roll-your-owns. "I see what you mean, though," Christopher commented, "this area does look pretty rough. I bet even Quentin wouldn't want to walk around this neighborhood."

Everyone laughed, Quentin saying, "Hey, wouldn't bother me a bit. Blood's blood, man."

"Listen to him," Christopher chided, "they already got him sayin' 'man' after everything and we haven't been in the neighborhood three minutes."

Once again affecting his "black" accent, Quentin reached behind Harmony and gave Christopher a playful slap on the back of the head, saying, "You gotta be *coo'*, man!"

When the laughter subsided Ramón wisecracked, "I still wouldn't wanna breakdown here, even if Nelson Mandela was ridin' in back." As if in defiance of its owner's desires there was a sudden, loud clanking and thumping off the bottom of the car that the rear-seat passengers felt clear through their shoes.

"Leapin' lizards!" Ramón cried, immediately releasing the accelerator and slipping the transmission into neutral. "It sounds like it's going to explode!" He coasted to the curb and shut the engine down.

As luck would have it they came to a stop right where the neighborhood began changing from commercial to residential. The imposing stone structure they parked in front of was the last commercial building in the area, then the houses began.

On the west side of the building was an empty lot. Beside that was a massive stretch of broken, weed-infested asphalt that had once been the parking lot of a boarded-up "Bozo's Discount Store." To the east of the building were houses, and across the street, a row of clapboard homes shedding chalky white paint in huge, curling chips. On the front porch of the first house a group of folks sat in folding chairs, their small children playing in the reddish dirt in the tiny, fenced front yard.

Ramón let out a long stream of air. "Might as well get out and check the damages."

"I think I know what it is," Christopher said.

"So do I," Ramón put in grimly, the door groaning on dry hinges as he got out, looked under the car briefly, got back in and slammed the door.

"Broken U-joint," he and Christopher said in unison.

"What you goin' to do, Ramón?" Quentin asked.

Ramón shrugged. "Don't know."

"How far you live from here?"

"'Bout nine miles or so."

"Why don't you go an' hitchhike the rest of the way an' we'll stay here with the car?" Quentin offered.

Twisting around in his seat, Ramón looked at him. "Hitchhike? From here? You crazy?"

"Hey," Quentin shrugged, "it ain't so bad here, bro."

"Call for someone to pick you up," Christopher suggested.

"Or the bus," Ol' Henry put in and pointed to a westbound bus that hissed to a stop a block up the street and discharged a single passenger.

"That's it," Ramón said. "Should be an east-bounder along any minute, too." Turning to Quentin, he asked, "Will y'all walk me to the bus stop and wait till the bus comes?"

"Sure," Quentin answered immediately.

"I'll come too," Christopher said.

"Me too," Harmony volunteered. "I'm sick of sitting in this

car anyway."

"Well thanks, y'all," Ramón said. "Hand me my hat and let's go." Ol' Henry elected to wait in the car.

"It ain't so bad as you thinkin', Ramón," Quentin said as they walked the block to the bus stop. "Most people don't want trouble, they just want to go an' live their lives in peace like everybody else. Generally speakin', if you don't give 'em a hard time they ain't gonna bother you neither. All the gunplay you hear about is mostly gangs shootin' at each other over drugs an' turf, not random violence. It ain't even about racism."

Ramón shook his head. "Not in this neighborhood. Ya hear too many stories."

"That's just it, Ramón. Stories. Talk is cheap. Look, figure it this way, man. The last time a black walked through your neighborhood did the people jump off their porches and attack him?" When Ramón didn't immediately answer he repeated insistently, "Did they?"

"No."

"See?"

"But it has happened."

"Okay," Quentin conceded. "But it's usually just punks like you an' Chris," he grinned and gave them both the elbow.

"Too bad everybody can't be friends," Harmony said.

At the corner they stopped to wait for the bus. "Think it'll be hard getting U-joints?" Christopher asked.

"Could be," Ramón answered, "but probably not. I'll bet U-joints for this car are pretty standard."

When the bus hissed to a stop and its doors squeaked open the boys shook hands and sent Ramón off with a slap on the back and assurances that they'd be seeing him tomorrow. On the way back Christopher and Harmony walked hand-in-hand. At the car they found Ol' Henry sound asleep where he sat.

"Look to me like it's goin' to be a pretty uncomfortable night," Quentin said, taking a seat on the hood, which caused Ol' Henry to open one eye momentarily.

Christopher and Harmony hoisted themselves onto the hood beside Quentin. "It sure does," Christopher agreed. "Two in front and two in back's about the only way I can see."

Quentin couldn't argue with that. Too bad he'd be stuck beside an old man while Christopher got to sleep with a hot young babe. With thoughts of the girl he'd left behind, Quentin suddenly pushed off the hood and started up the sidewalk at a determined pace.

"Where're you going?" Christopher called after him.

"For a walk!" he hollered without turning or slowing. Quentin quickly became a distant, forlorn figure pounding the gritty sidewalk beneath the yellow haze of the street lamps, shoulders hunched against the bitterness he felt.

"Something's bugging him," Harmony said quietly, the warm spring night close around them.

"He'll get over it. Feel like getting in the car?"

"You read my mind," Harmony said through a yawn. Moments later they curled up like kittens on the backseat and were soon sound asleep.

Quentin got no farther in his walk than the bus stop. Across the street a westbound bus hissed to a stop and discharged four people; a young woman clutching a shopping bag to her head, seemingly trying to hide behind it, and three youngsters, two boys and a girl, all about ten or 11, Quentin guessed, who were taunting her with insults he couldn't quite make out. At last the young woman broke away and ran blindly across the street towards Quentin. The youngsters gave chase, encircling her like a pack of wild dogs as she made the curb.

The young woman, still hiding behind her shopping bag and oblivious to Quentin and everything else save her tormentors, turned every which way while crying out, "Get away from me! Leave me alone! I never did anything to you!"

The kids insolently brushed past Quentin as they surrounded her and hurtled insults. "Devil worshiper!" the boys cried. "That'll teach you to be molestin' retarded white boys, nigger!"

the little girl hollered.

With Quentin still not quite sure what was going on the little girl, a snot-nosed kid in a dirty red dress, turned to him and said, pointing a finger at her target, "That girl be damned by God himself! My Mamma said she was takin' little white boys that was retarded to bed with her. That why she got the leprosy."

"That ain't leprosy!" one of the boys retorted, "she turnin' white!" Then he reached up and tried snatching the bag away, taunting her with, "Let's see yo' face, Witch Woman!" Sobbing aloud, the young woman twisted away from his grasping hand.

In one swift motion Quentin stepped into the circle of taunting youths, grabbed the kid's arm, spun him around and twisted it up behind his back until he cried out. With a swift kick in the butt Quentin sent him on his way. He turned on the other two, who were staring at him in wide-eyed amazement. "Now get!" he snarled, jumping at them.

They scrambled away, the little girl calling over her shoulder, "Now you gonna start turnin' white, mister, now you gonna get it too!"

Bewildered, Quentin watched the kids run hootin' and hollerin' up the sidewalk. When he turned back the young woman was already half a block away and hurrying along with the bag still clutched to her face. Keeping his stride just short of a run, Quentin raced after her and caught up at the big, two-story stone building where Ramón's car was parked. At the side of the building steps ran up to a landing and a spacious, second floor apartment.

Still sobbing profusely, the young woman put her foot to the first step but stumbled, crying all the louder. Quentin gently caught her elbow, unnerved at her wailing but offering assistance. When he reached for the bag she still held clutched to her face the young woman shrieked bloody murder. Quentin winced and backed away with emphatic apologies when the building's front street-side door was thrown open with a bang and a tall, healthy black woman, a red bandanna tied about her head, charged out in a heated rage and began beating Quentin over the head with a huge, wood-handled straw broom.

Blocking with his arms, Quentin stumbled backwards as she bore in on him relentlessly. By now the commotion had drawn neighbors off their porches in swarms where they gathered in the street in a semicircle to watch.

Still groggy with sleep, Ol' Henry was just getting out of the car to see what all the excitement was about when the upstairs door was thrown open and a rather tall, muscular man of 57 came bounding down the stairs. He stopped beside his daughter momentarily and ordered, "Get upstairs, Molly!" Then turned his attention to the scene on the sidewalk.

By now Ol' Henry had managed to get the woman to stop beating Quentin, but she still brandished the broom like a club as if holding the both of them off for her very life. The big black man took one look at Quentin and Ol' Henry, then turned on his wife and sharply ordered, "Get upstairs, Clara!" The woman hesitated. "Clara," the man warned.

Turning to leave, Clara stopped short. "Go on, get out of here!" she shouted at the onlookers in the street, shaking her broom at them and moving suddenly in their direction as they collectively shrank back. "Go on," she bellowed again, "this ain't no zoo!"

"Get in the house, Clara!" her husband ordered harshly for the second time. Then he whirled on Ol' Henry. "This your boy?" he demanded, the deep creases of an angry frown marring his otherwise pleasant face.

"Sort of," Ol' Henry admitted.

"Well me an' you is gonna have a talk, sir," he said. And before anyone knew what was happening, least of all Ol' Henry, the man had him by the front of his coveralls, Ol' Henry's feet barely touching the ground as he dragged him through the building's front door. Then the door slammed shut with a bang.

Satisfied the action was over, the people in the street drifted back to their respective porches. Suddenly it was quiet,

Quentin standing alone on the sidewalk utterly baffled, his imagination running wild with visions of flashing red lights, sirens, screeching tires and burly cops tackling him. He caught Christopher and Harmony cautiously peeking over the edge of the front seat, went to the car, opened the squeaky door, got in and gently pulled it closed with a sound *click*.

"What the heck's going on?" Christopher whispered.

Breathing heavily, his stomach churning with fear, Quentin heaved a shaky sigh and answered, "You got me, Chris."

"Jeeze, Quentin, what were you trying to do, rape the chick on the sidewalk?"

"Knock it off," Quentin said tiredly. In no mood for humor, he was considering hitting the road just in case those people did call the cops. But he also had confidence in Ol' Henry's ability to iron things out. Harmony hadn't said a word since he'd returned to the car. "Harmony sleepin'?"

"No, just scared."

"I am not!"

"All right, that's enough!" Quentin snapped, his patience with the world in general having worn thin. "Let's just sit here quiet an' wait for Henry."

There wasn't another word from the backseat. Sliding behind the wheel, Quentin turned his back to the door and put his feet up. Being pumped with adrenaline was exhausting, but as he kept vigil on the building's front door it receded and his eyelids drooped low. Henry would be along, he kept telling himself. Any minute now. Any minute....

*   *   *

Maurice Sandwood seated Ol' Henry in a chair in a corner of his darkened shop and began a five minute tirade, pacing back and forth, occasionally raising a clenched fist to the ceiling and bringing it down again, his words coming in angry, staccato bursts like machine gun fire. Ol' Henry sat there politely and listened. "Do you people know what you're doin' to my daughter? You're killin' her, that's what! Just the same as if you took out a gun and shot her! You nearly done drove her to suicide, and I'm gonna put a stop to it even if I have to kill someone! Understand? The nerve of all these people pickin' on that little girl. For nothin'! She's suffered enough. They done drove her clear outta high school the year she's supposed to graduate! They wrecked her life is what they done, an' just 'cause a rare skin disease befall her. Could'a happened to anyone. But for the grace of God...." He heard his wife on the inside stairs and turned around.

Leaning over the railing, she ordered, "Maurice, stop it at once! We made a terrible mistake. Molly says that boy drove off some young'ns that was teasin' her. She said he was trying to help her up when I come outside. Now stop that cussin' and get up here, an' bring that nice man with you."

Bewildered, embarrassed, Maurice Sandwood turned to Ol' Henry apologetically and wordlessly held out his hands.

Ol' Henry rose to his feet and took Maurice's hands in his own. "It be all right," he said softly, "I understan' what you been goin' through."

Maurice smiled and blinked back the emotion welling up inside. "Come upstairs if you would," he offered, "I believe we got some explainin' to do."

"I be more than willin'," Ol' Henry replied with a smile. "Besides," he added on a lighter note, "I gots to use the bathroom."

Maurice laughed. "Hungry?" he asked as they mounted the stairs.

"Starvin'."

Over eggs, pork sausage and biscuits, washed down with a mug of steaming coffee, Ol' Henry listened to the Sandwood's story. About a year ago their daughter, then just starting her senior year in high school, had contracted an unusual and for the most part incurable skin disease known as "Vitiligo." The disease is characterized by a dropping out of pigment from certain areas of the skin, which then becomes completely white.

In the case of their daughter, Maurice went on to explain, it was isolated around her eyes, giving her a sort of "white mask" look. Ever since, the taunting, teasing and lurid, slanderous stories went 'round and 'round unceasingly, driving the poor girl out of school and to the brink of suicide. And their daughter, once a vivacious, popular student, had been reduced to a shy, trembling girl afraid of her own shadow.

By this time tears were welling up in Maurice Sandwood's eyes. Banging a defiant fist on the table, he declared, "And it better stop, too!" Then he quickly got up and disappeared into another part of the large, spacious apartment. Ol' Henry ate on in silence. After a minute Maurice returned with an apology for his outburst and sat back down.

Both the Sandwoods were rather large people. Not heavy, just big-boned and well-built. He of a lighter complexion, his wife darker. His pleasant, rugged face smiled easily, revealing two rows of sound, even teeth. At 57 he still had them all. His kinky black hair, a tinge of gray at the temples, was cut close.

Clara Sandwood, hair in a tight bun with a red bandanna tied about her head, was the serious one as revealed in her intent, smoldering eyes and the perpetual creases of thought engraved in her forehead. She had long, delicate fingers and was good on the piano. Naturally creative, though not a master of any single art like her husband, she had an eye for color and a sense of balance that tended to temper her more serious side, which left her with a rather sunny disposition.

Their own feelings vented, the Sandwoods asked Ol' Henry about himself and what brought him to the neighborhood. With Clara moving about the kitchen taking away dishes and keeping the men in coffee, her backless slippers slapping time with an almost deliberate rhythm, Ol' Henry told his story.

First he told about Quentin and what had happened to him. Then, how Harmony had run away from a foster home, and how Christopher had wrecked his father's prized car and felt he couldn't return home. The Sandwoods offered their sympathies. He failed to mention, not deliberately, that Christopher and Harmony were white. It just skipped his mind.

With the immediate chores done Clara poured herself a steaming cup and, folding one long leg under her, took a seat at the table. "You look like you gettin' a little old to be travelin' all over the country adoptin' wayward young'ns," she smiled.

Ol' Henry shrugged. "I got nothin' better to do."

"Where's your young'ns now?" Maurice asked on sudden thought.

Sipping coffee, Ol' Henry answered, "Down in the car sleepin' I hope."

Clara looked horrified. "You don't have anywhere to stay?"

"No, ma'am."

Clara looked at her husband expectantly. He gave an almost imperceptible nod of approval. "You march right down there and get those young'ns up here!" she ordered.

Ol' Henry looked sheepish. "It be all right, ma'am, they's used to it an' we'll get along jist fine."

"It is *not* all right," she stated, pointing a finger at the kitchen door that led to the outside stairs, "now march!"

"Yes, ma'am," Ol' Henry said with a grin and headed for the door.

15

HOUSEGUESTS

When the car door opened with a squeak Quentin jumped awake. "What's wrong?" he asked in wide-eyed fear.

"You really done it this time, Mr. Quentin."

"What'd I do?"

Seeing the look of stark fear in Quentin's eyes Ol' Henry quickly admitted, "I's just funnin'. But come on an' get outta that car 'cause we gots us a place to stay."

"Where?" It was Christopher.

"Never you minds where, just come on." He stepped back and held the door open as they tumbled out one by one.

Moments later the three teenagers were blinking and rubbing their eyes in the bright, fluorescent light of the Sandwood's kitchen. Christopher and Harmony weren't at all surprised that the Sandwoods were black, although the Sandwoods were certainly surprised to see that Christopher and Harmony were white. "Land sakes!" Clara exclaimed, one hand to the side of her face, "Where'd you get *these* children?"

"I told you," Ol' Henry began.

"Clara," Maurice intoned, "never mind all the yik-yak, get the food on the table. These young'ns is starving."

"Whew!" Clara said, pinching her nose closed, "these young'ns is in sore need of a bath is what they is." Turning back to the stove, she warned over her shoulder, "An' gettin' in the tub'll be next."

Still dazed by it all, Quentin, Christopher, and Harmony remained where they were as if their feet were glued to the floor.

"Belly up to the table, gang," Maurice said cheerily.

"Come on," Ol' Henry urged, guiding Harmony by the shoulders to the table, pulling out a chair and seating her. "You too, Chris," he gestured. Quentin followed suit.

Minutes later they were wolfing down the best scrambled eggs and ham they'd ever tasted and washing it down with tall glasses of cold milk. As they devoured their first servings Clara moved around the table heaping their plates again, her backless slippers slapping time. "More milk?" she asked Christopher.

"Yes, please."

She filled his and topped off Quentin's and Harmony's. "You'll be first in the shower," she said to Christopher.

He looked up with a frown.

"Don't look at me like that, boy," she warned.

Christopher lowered his eyes. "Yes, ma'am."

Maurice held his cup up. Clara got the pot off the stove, filled his, paused to top off Ol' Henry's, then turned to her husband. "Maurice?"

"Yes, dear?"

"See if you can find Quentin an old pair of jeans an' a shirt. Those clothes he's wearin' ain't no good. Lordy, they can't even be cleaned. No wonder he scared Molly right out of her socks."

With a chuckle Maurice assured her, "I do believe I have something he can use."

"Good. Now, what's this other boy's name?"

"Christopher," Ol' Henry answered.

"Get Christopher an old pair of your flannels, Maurice, for after his shower." To Christopher she said, "I'll be doin' the wash tomorrow."

Christopher nodded uncomprehendingly. This whirlwind of a woman wasn't looking for any discussion on the matter and Christopher wasn't about to offer any.

"I'll get something of Molly's for Harmony," Clara added

"Anything of Molly's gonna be way too big for that little wisp of a girl, Clara."

"We'll do the best we can."

"Yes, dear," Maurice said as he got up from the table and went for the flannels.

As soon as Christopher put the last forkful of food in his mouth Clara snatched the plate and ordered, "Come with me." With a last look at his companions Christopher got up and followed the big woman. In the hall she stopped briefly at the linen closet for a towel, then showed him to the bathroom. At the door she flicked on the lights and handed him the towel. "Everything you need's in here. Soap, shampoo, whatever. Just throw your clothes in the hall. Maurice will bring you some long johns."

"Thank you," Christopher said, respectfully bobbing his head once.

"An' don't be too long. There's three others behind you."

"No, ma'am."

"Well don't just stand there lookin' at me, git!"

"Yes ma'am," Christopher said, deciding at once that Clara Sandwood was the kind of woman who required plenty of "yes ma'ams" and "no ma'ams." He closed the door and turned around, his mouth dropping open in surprise. He'd never been in a bathroom quite so large or beautiful before. The toilet, sink and tub were of gleaming black porcelain, the fixtures of brushed gold-plate. The entire wall behind the sink and vanity was mirror, the opposite wall a mosaic of a buffalo in white, black, and pale-green tile.

Shaking off his awe, Christopher quickly undressed and threw his clothes out in the hall as instructed. When he stepped into the shower and turned it on he knew what heaven must be; a porcelain shower with an endless supply of hot water and plenty of soap. There must have been two inches of sweat-caked dirt on him. He had forgotten how good it felt to be clean. Not creek-clean, but shampoo and fluoridated water clean, the hot water pounding his neck and back so relaxing that he could only close his eyes and sigh with contentment—and hope he wasn't taking too long.

On her way back to the kitchen Clara stopped by her daughter's room. She tapped lightly on the door, opened it and stuck her head in. "Are you asleep, dear?"

Molly reached over and switched on the bedside lamp. "Who's here, Mamma?"

"That nice young man who helped you, and his friends. Now darlin', two of his friends is white, and one's a little girl. I thought maybe she could stay in here with you. Would that be okay?"

Molly nodded. "Sure, mamma."

"You think maybe you could fix her up with a shirt or something to sleep in?"

"Why sure, Mamma. But I don't understand...."

"That's all right, Molly, we'll talk about it in the morning, okay?"

"All right, Mamma."

"You're sweet, darlin'," her mother said with a smile. Pulling the door closed, she left and returned to the kitchen to fetch Harmony. "I'm going to put you in with my daughter," she explained as she led the girl down the hall. "She's going to fix you up with something to sleep in. So as soon as Christopher gets out of the shower you just go right in. Leave your clothes in the hall and I'll wash them for you tomorrow." At the door Harmony turned and thanked the woman. "That's all right, darlin', you just go an' make yourself real comfortable and don't worry none about nothin'. Now go on." Without another word Clara turned and disappeared down the hall.

Harmony knocked lightly on the door. "Come in," a tiny voice from inside responded. Harmony opened the door. Molly was in bed with the covers pulled up to her chin. "Hi," she said.

"Hi. I'm Harmony."

"I'm Molly. Come on in and close the door, Harmony."

Harmony did as she was told. After closing the door and turning around she stood there gawking. "This is all your own room?" she asked in awe.

In the middle of the floor was a thick oval rug of white, gold, and blue. Everything else was white lace and pink flowers, the king-size bed pearl-white with feathered gold trim and a matching dresser and makeup vanity with a huge, oval mirror. She also had her own television on a stand near the foot of the bed, and a stereo, the component parts stacked in a custom-fitted cabinet, as well as a phone on a nightstand at bedside. "It's beautiful!" Harmony gasped, "just beautiful!"

Molly smiled. "Thanks."

"It's all yours?"

Molly nodded.

"God, are you lucky!"

"Lucky? Hah!" Molly's laugh was a short, shrill note of contempt. "You think just because a person has *things* that makes them lucky?"

Harmony shrugged and said with a grin, "I can think of worse things happening to a person."

"Like this?" Molly asked cruelly, holding her head high and looking directly at Harmony for the first time. The expression on Harmony's face was honest puzzlement. "Well look!" the girl almost shouted, her voice rising.

Harmony was truly baffled. "At what?"

"Don't tell me you don't notice around my eyes?"

"That white stuff?"

"Yeah, that white stuff," Molly mimicked bitterly.

"T-That's not makeup?" Harmony stammered, her ears burning with embarrassment.

"No," the girl pouted, suddenly calm. "It's a skin disease. Don't worry," she added sardonically, "it's not contagious."

Harmony didn't know what to say. Actually, the girl had a delicate, soft face, lovely almond-shaped eyes and long lashes. Harmony hadn't even noticed the white around her eyes until Molly brought it up. Looking down at her shoes now, she said in a small voice, "I'm sorry."

"Well don't be. It's not your fault," Molly bluntly replied.

Throwing off the covers, she swung her long, shapely legs over the side and sat on the edge of the bed, an elbow on one knee supporting her chin in one hand. "Now let's see, we got to find somethin' for you to sleep in, right?"

Harmony nodded, embarrassed by her intrusion into this girl's life. "I still don't know what I'm doing here," she offered lamely. "Henry just came to the car and dragged us here."

"Well don't worry none about it," Molly said, adding with a light laugh, "what happened out on the sidewalk is sort of a long story. I'll tell you about it sometime."

"Okay," Harmony answered.

"Now let's see," Molly said once again and stood up. Clad only in panties, she moved about the room banging through drawers in search of something for Harmony to wear. At least as tall as Quentin, the girl literally towered over Harmony. And she had one heck of a figure, Harmony thought admiringly, discreetly eyeing the girl and her firm, exquisitely-shaped breasts which jutted up to perfect points, the nipples like little pink flowers that glowed against satin smooth, cocoa-brown skin.

Startling the poor girl, Molly abruptly turned from the bureau she was digging through and looked Harmony up and down. Harmony thought she'd been caught looking. "All my stuff's way too big for you," she said. "Think you can make do with a shirt? Shoot, any of mine'll be like a dress on you."

She was right. The dark blue T-shirt Harmony chose came down to her knees. "Okay?" Molly asked once Harmony was in the shirt.

Stooping over and gathering up her discarded clothes, Harmony said, "Perfect."

"Where you goin' with those?" Molly asked when her new roommate headed for the door.

"To the shower. Your mom told me to leave my stuff in the hall."

"Oh. Well, have a good shower. I'll wait for you."

"Thanks," Harmony smiled. Then, pulling the door closed

behind her, she turned and left.

She met Christopher as he was leaving the bathroom. "Wait till you see in there!" he exclaimed, letting out a long, low whistle, "what a john!"

Harmony giggled at the sight of him in long johns that were two sizes too big. Christopher felt silly as well. He had them rolled over at the waist three times and still had to hold them up in front with one hand. And the seat of the drawers hung halfway to the backs of his knees. "So. They're only to sleep in," he said defensively.

"You still look funny," she giggled again and threw her clothes in a heap on top of his.

"Look who's talking," he snickered, "I really like your T-shirt. A perfect fit."

"Why thank you," she said with a little curtsy.

He laughed and gave her a kiss. "I'd better get going before that lady comes after me. Jeeze, how would you like to have her for a mother?"

"I'd love it."

He looked at her like she was crazy. "Well, bye," he said at last, giving her a quick peck on the cheek before turning and padding down the hall towards the kitchen. Watching him go, she smiled and shook her head, then went into the bathroom and closed the door.

When Christopher wandered into the kitchen the four people at the table burst out laughing. "Maurice!" Clara exclaimed, "is that the best you could do?"

Her husband shrugged, "That's the smallest I got, honey."

Clara sighed. "Oh well, he's only got to sleep in them."

Christopher hardly heard the laughter. After his awakening in the bathroom he was looking the kitchen over with renewed appreciation. The solid oak cabinets were expensive, the handles and knobs of solid brass. The appliances, and the kitchen had them all, were black. There was a huge, double-door refrigerator with ice and water dispensers and a built-in dishwasher. A garbage compactor and a microwave oven. The stainless steel double-sink had an organic garbage disposal. Just off the kitchen was a fair-sized utility room with a washer and dryer, a pressing machine and a conventional ironing board.

Clara rose from the table and hooked a finger at Quentin. "Come on, I'll show you boys where you're sleeping. And as soon as Harmony's out of the shower you can take yours."

Clutching the clothes Maurice had given him, Quentin pushed his chair back and stood up. "Thanks, Mr. Sandwood."

Maurice waved him off. "Don't mention it, son. I appreciate you lookin' out for my daughter."

"It weren't nothin'," Quentin said modestly.

"Come on," Clara urged him along with a smile and started down the hall towards the living room.

"Night, boys," Ol' Henry said as they turned to go.

"Night, Henry," Quentin replied.

"Yeah, night, Henry." Still unsure of his host's name, Christopher expressed his good night to Maurice with an upward gesture of his head. Maurice gestured back. Then the boys followed Clara down the hall to the living room, pausing momentarily while she retrieved crisp, clean sheets from the hall closet.

The living room couch folded out into a huge double-bed. Tossing the sheets onto an easy chair, Clara pulled a heavy glass and chrome coffee table clear, then ordered Quentin to the opposite end of the couch and together they pulled the bed out.

"You boys'll sleep here," she instructed, grabbing the sheets off the chair and snapping them open with brisk efficiency. Then she moved about the bed tucking in the sides with quick, sharp motions. "There," she said with satisfaction. "Now don't worry none 'bout Mr. Rathbone, we have a place for him, too." The boys nodded. "And you," she pointed an accusing finger at Quentin, "don't even *think* about gettin' in this nice clean bed until you had your shower."

"No ma'am."

"Okay then, don't worry about a thing, just take your rest and we'll see you boys in the mornin'."

"Thanks, Mrs. Sandwood," Quentin said.

"Yeah, thanks," Christopher joined in.

"That's okay. Now sleep." It wasn't an offer, it was an order. About to leave, she stopped and turned. "The hall light'll be on in case you need to use the bathroom durin' the night."

The boys nodded again, Quentin calling out, "Thanks, ma'am," but she was already gone.

"Will you look at this place?" Christopher whispered, still clutching the front of his drawers as he sat down on the edge of the bed.

It was an expansive living room with soft, ankle-deep beige carpet. A glittering, cut-glass chandelier hung from the center of the beamed ceiling. In the far corner a round fireplace of shiny copper with a flat-black chimney was suspended from the ceiling by chains, blue and beige pit furniture gathered around it. Then there was the baby grand piano and two leather recliners facing a gigantic TV.

Near the entrance to this grand room stood a black marble statue of a nude African woman cradling a suckling baby boy. Examining it closely, Quentin remarked, "It sure do look authentic."

"What do you mean, 'authentic'?"

"I mean someone went an' carved it out of solid marble with a mallet and chisel instead of a fake poured from a mold. It must be worth thousands. It kind of looks like Mrs. Sandwood, don't it?"

Christopher nodded, whispering, "These people got money, don't they?"

"They got somethin' goin' for 'em, that'd be a sure bet."

"Wait till you see the john."

"What's the john like?"

"Big. And the toilet and everything is black with gold faucets and stuff."

Quentin nodded, his thoughts turning. "I don't know 'bout you," he intimated, scratching his jaw, "but I smell an artist in the house."

Christopher shrugged. "You got me."

"I think the downstairs, it's a shop of some kind or another."

"Like a gift shop or something?"

Quentin shook his head. "No. The front of the building don't look like no store or nothin'. I noticed an overhead door in front. I think it's some kind of shop where they make things like that copper fireplace over there."

"Could be. Do you think it's okay if we watch television?"

"Don't touch nothin'," Quentin warned. "That's all we need right now is for somethin' to go an' get broke."

"Would it be okay if we asked?"

"Go ahead."

Christopher chuckled under his breath. "No way, José. *You* ask."

"You the one that wants to watch it."

Christopher shook his head. "No way." He stood up and crossed to the glass and chrome coffee table and took a magazine from several that were arrayed in its center. "I'll just look at this, thanks."

Quentin grinned. "Enjoy your magazine. I'm gonna go see if Harmony's out of the shower yet."

"Okay." Christopher climbed into bed, tucked a pillow behind his head and sat flipping through the pictures.

*   *   *

After Harmony returned from the shower and got into bed she and Molly talked in the dark for over an hour. Molly told Harmony all about school and how horrible it had been. How her whole life had changed when she contracted Vitiligo around the eyes. Everyone had treated her like a leper and worse, the name-calling and cruel accusations founded on superstition and whatnot finally driving her to the very edge of suicide. At that point she had quit school.

Oh, she wasn't really shy she informed Harmony, but who wouldn't start avoiding people under the circumstances? The worst part was when her boyfriend dropped her. That was when she wound up in the hospital with a nervous breakdown. Now she spent most of her time alone in her room reading, playing the stereo, or watching TV. Sometimes she would go to a movie—alone. And that was about it. Her life story.

Harmony wanted to know what happened with Quentin. Molly told her how he gallantly stepped in when some neighborhood kids were taunting her, and all the rest of what happened. Afterwards Harmony told Molly about her mother abandoning her and dying a week later in a car crash, about her miserable three years with her uncle's family, and how she came to be on the road with Christopher and Quentin. Molly was fascinated by her story, saying it sounded like a movie. Before rolling over to sleep she assured Harmony the conversation would be resumed the following day.

*   *   *

When Ol' Henry finished telling the Sandwoods about Quentin's artistic inclinations and the figurine he had shaped out of clay in only minutes with his fingers and a penknife, Maurice Sandwood smiled. "You saw what it says on the front of my building, didn't you? What business I'm in?"

Ol' Henry shook his head. "No sir."

"It's carved in stone over the front entrance to the building; *Sandwood's Stone-Cutting And Statuary.*"

Ol' saw-toothed Henry smiled broadly. "No!"

Maurice nodded. "Yep." He sat back in his chair and looked up at the ceiling, rubbed the back of his neck and said half to himself, "Sure could use another pair of hands around here."

"More coffee, Henry?" Clara asked.

"No, thank you, ma'am. Else I won't never gets no sleep tonight."

"Which reminds me," Clara said, "the young'ns are probably 'bout done. You want to shower tonight or in the morning?"

"My bones is so weary I think I'd just like to wait till mornin' if'n it be okay."

"Of course. Just let me know whenever you're ready..." she hesitated, then turned to her husband when she said, "I was thinkin' of puttin' him in Samuel's room."

Maurice looked at her gravely.

"Well we got to open up that room some time," she stubbornly insisted. "We been too long livin' in the past."

An extended silence followed as husband and wife stared at one another. "Okay," Maurice suddenly relented, "I believe you're right, woman."

With moist eyes Clara said gently, "Now his memory can rest easy in your soul, Maurice."

"Yes, dear," he replied vacantly, his mind crowding with thoughts of long ago.

After a moment's quiet reflection Clara turned to Ol' Henry. "I'll put you up in our son's old room."

"You gots a son?"

"Had," Clara corrected. "He was in the Marines. Got killed durin' the last military action over in..." her hand fluttered off into the air, gesturing to some distant place, "wherever it was." She heaved a sigh. "He was only 19."

"I's sorry to hear it."

"Quentin sort of reminds me of him," Maurice said wistfully. "He was big like Quentin and strong as a bull, that boy was. He was going to come into the business when he got back. Loved it, he did, and had a real knack for it, too."

"'Specially throwin' them pots an' such," Clara interjected, adding with a giggle, "he could just about make that clay stand up and dance!"

"Clara!" her husband scolded, "let's not be tellin' no tales, now."

She looked at him sharply.

With a twinkle in his eye he added, "He might'a been able to make it walk, but dance? Never!"

The three of them had a good laugh over that. When their chuckles subsided Clara set her cup down. "If you're ready, Mr. Rathbone, I'll show you to your room."

"Yes, ma'am," Ol' Henry said, pushing his chair back as he got to his feet. "An' thank you both ever so much."

Maurice Sandwood smiled, saying softly, "Forget it. Quentin coming along just when he did could be the best thing that ever happened to our little girl."

"Enough," Clara interrupted. "Follow me, Henry." She turned and left the kitchen. With a nod to Maurice, Ol' Henry hurried after her.

There wasn't a speck of dust anywhere, for Clara dusted it thoroughly once a week. Yet, when she opened the door and flicked on the lights it was obvious the room wasn't used. And hadn't been in many years. Everything was too perfect. Too neat. On the mirrored dresser was a comb, a small bottle of cologne, and some gold cufflinks in a little blue velvet-lined pewter box whose lid stood open, each item in its proper place, never used, never moved, never touched. The many books in the bookcase were never opened, the stereo never played.

Clara crossed the room in three strides, drew the curtains aside and threw open the window. "Musty in here," she said. "Some nice fresh air will take care of that."

Ol' Henry watched from the door, afraid to step into the room and disturb its rigid perfectness. When Clara turned from the window and saw him still in the doorway she beckoned impatiently, "Come on, it's your room for tonight. And high time, too!" she added defiantly. When Ol' Henry remained hesitant she placed her hands on her hips and leaned forward slightly, inquiring, "You afraid of ghosts?"

Embarrassed, Ol' Henry took a step forward. "No, ma'am."

"Then get in here and in this chair and get those boots off!" she ordered and yanked the chair out from its place at the desk.

Without a word Ol' Henry crossed the room, sat in the chair and began undoing his bootlaces. At the door Clara stopped and turned, "Now you sleep easy, Mr. Rathbone, and we'll see you in the mornin'."

"Night, ma'am."

"Night." She closed the door and was gone.

It was just after midnight when Clara and Maurice finally climbed into their own soft, warm bed. Reaching up and switching off the bedside lamp, Maurice said, "Funny, isn't it?"

"What?"

"How much that young man resembles Samuel."

"Oh pshaw! It's only because that boy's about the same age Samuel was the last time you saw him."

"It's more than that, Clara. I'll bet you he could fit right into Samuel's clothes."

"Oh, Maurice," his wife sighed, "go to sleep, will you?"

16

ARTISTS-N-ARMS

The Sandwood's day usually began at 6:00 a.m. and Saturdays were no different. The first thing Clara did was put coffee on. The second thing, while her husband sat at the table sipping his first cup, was throw the kids' clothes into the washing machine. With the machine safely thumping and whirring away she grabbed a cup and joined him at the table. "How long you think they stayin'?" she asked.

"Don't know," Maurice answered through a yawn and a stretch. "Henry said their car broke down. I imagine till it's fixed."

"I've been doin' some thinkin' this morning," his wife intoned, "and that boy Quentin, what if... well, all that trouble he's mixed up in, he needs a place to stay till things blow over."

"We'll see," Maurice answered, sipping coffee, "if it comes to that."

"Ask him."

"We'll see."

"He could work with you in the shop. From what Henry said about his ability he could be a real...."

"Okay, okay, I'll ask him. But not until towards the end of their stay. In the meantime we may find he's less than we first expected."

"I don't think so," his wife intimated. "That boy, he the pick a the bunch he is."

"We'll see," he repeated for the third time. "Now don't go gettin' yourself all worked up about it. In the end he might not

218

want to stay anyway."

"He will," his wife said confidently, "he will." She got up, went to the utility room and transferred the laundry to the dryer. Her backless slippers slapping time, she returned to the kitchen. "What should I make for breakfast, Maurice?"

"French Toast."

"Ate up all the eggs last night, remember?"

"Toast and jam, then."

"I'm glad you said that 'cause I'm just about out of everything else till I get to the store."

"Pick up some toothbrushes for them young'ns when you're there."

"That's the first thing on my list."

When the clothes were dry she gave them a quick ironing. Christopher's clothes went to her husband. Quentin already had his. "Go get those boys up. I'll get the girls."

When Maurice got to the living room he found Quentin already up and dressed and closely examining the marble statue of the woman and child. "You like that?" Maurice asked from the doorway.

Startled, Quentin turned. "It's beautiful. Must'a cost plenty, too."

Maurice shook his head. "Did it myself. That's my wife and son."

"You done this yourself?" Quentin asked in amazement.

Maurice nodded. "That's my business, son."

"That what the shop is downstairs?"

"Yep. Course mostly I just do headstones an' stuff. And we make lots of pottery and different things for gift shops."

By now Christopher was awake. He sat up yawning and stretching. "What time is it?"

"Time for you to get up," Maurice answered and tossed him his clothes. "Here. They still warm from the iron."

"Thanks." Christopher threw the covers back and swung

out of bed. Pulling off Maurice's oversized flannels, he got into his shorts and warm, familiar jeans.

Maurice turned back to Quentin. "You ever carve in stone?"

"Just a little. I still got a ways to go. But I can sure work in clay and throw pots."

"We got a kiln that'll take a five-foot vase," Maurice informed him.

Quentin's eyes lit up. "Cool!"

"You boys make up your bed and come to the kitchen and we'll get a little something to eat, then I'll show you the shop if you want."

"I'd love to, Mr. Sandwood. I can't wait to get my hands in some clay."

"You'll be gettin' your hands dirty," Maurice assured him, "don't worry none about that. Hurry up now. Clara's already started breakfast."

Christopher and Quentin folded the bed away, pulled the coffee table back in place and headed for the kitchen.

*   *   *

Upon awakening the first thing Molly did was rouse Harmony and begin questioning her about Quentin. "What's he like?" she asked.

"I don't know," Harmony shrugged. "He rescued you from those kids didn't he?"

"He'd do that for anyone," Molly countered.

"That's true," Harmony admitted, "and that's what he's like."

When Clara opened the door and flicked on the lights she was surprised to find the girls sitting up in bed talking. "Why Molly," the big woman exclaimed, "I haven't seen you up this early in ages. I was expectin' to have to roll you girls right out of bed!" Holding Harmony's clothes out to her, she added, "Here you go."

Taking her things, Harmony said, "Thank you, Mrs.

Sandwood."

"That's okay, honey. Now you girls get outta that bed and get dressed or you gonna miss breakfast." Closing the door behind her, she headed for the kitchen wondering if she should awaken Henry when his bedroom door opened.

He stepped out with a cheery, "Good mornin', ma'am."

She smiled brightly. "Why good mornin' to you, Henry. You just in time for breakfast."

"Why thank you, ma'am," he said with a little bow. "I believes I will."

Upon reaching the kitchen Clara and Ol' Henry found Maurice, Quentin, and Christopher already at the table sipping coffee, Maurice and Quentin talking shop. "When I'm taking off the big pieces I hold the mallet up towards the top," the old master was explaining, Quentin's eyes intent upon him. "But when I'm doing detail I choke up on it, know what I mean?"

Quentin nodded.

When Clara and Ol' Henry came in Maurice looked up and beckoned to his elderly guest, "Come, sit down, Henry."

"Why thank you, Maurice," the old man grinned and took a seat at the table.

Setting a steaming cup of coffee before Ol' Henry, Clara said, "Guess I better start makin' the toast."

Molly and Harmony came in as the first of the toast popped up. They stopped just inside the room as the men at the table looked up. "Good mornin', sweetheart," Maurice said cheerily to his daughter.

"Mornin' papa," she replied with a shy smile. Embracing him from behind, she gave him a kiss on the cheek.

After everyone exchanged their good mornings Maurice said with a gesture towards Quentin, "This here the young man that saved you last night."

"I'm sorry if I went an' frightened you yesterday evening," Quentin said.

Almost hiding behind her father, Molly said haltingly,

obviously embarrassed over the whole thing, "I—I'm the one that's sorry. For acting like such a birdbrain. Thank you for defending me, Quentin." With growing confidence she added, "You were a perfect gentleman. And I told my mom that, too, once we were in the house."

"I understan'," Quentin replied easily. "Really. I'd stick up for you anytime."

"I know," Molly giggled, warming to the situation. "Harmony told me so."

"Harmony?" Quentin looked at her.

She grinned.

Setting the butter dish and jelly on the table, Clara said to Harmony, "Sit down, darlin'," then turned back to the toaster as six more slices popped up.

"Eat up, everyone," Clara said, placing the first stack of toast on the table, "there's more on the way." She was taken at her word. The first stack of toast was devoured before the second reached the table.

Once, when Harmony whispered something to Molly and both girls started giggling, Maurice interrupted with a stern, "We'll have none of that at the table."

"Oh, Papa!" Molly exclaimed, then promptly drew Harmony's head close and whispered in her ear.

With a defeated sigh Maurice shook his head. "Women!"

When the girls finished their whispering Quentin made a stab at conversation, directing his words to Molly, "You in college now or still in high school?"

At the question Molly's face fell.

"What...."

"Molly don't go to school," Maurice sharply interjected.

"Oh," Quentin said lamely. Then in a moment of inspiration he added with a grin, "Neither do I!"

Molly looked up with a smile.

More toast was brought to the table and passed around. To Quentin, Christopher, and Harmony two meals in a row was a luxury they'd had to do without for quite some time and eating breakfast was pure heaven. Ol' Henry had lived with the uncertainty of where his next meal was coming from for so long he was unaffected. When there was food he ate, when there wasn't he didn't. Simple.

As the others were finishing up, Clara finally sat down. Spreading strawberry jam on a piece of toast, she asked, "Everyone have enough?" There followed a chorus of "yes ma'ams" and "thank yous."

Maurice drained his cup and set it down for the last time. "I'd better get started," he said, "I got a whole lot to do today." Turning to Quentin and Christopher he said, "Maybe I can put you boys to work. Want to see the shop?"

Quentin and Christopher nodded, Quentin rather enthusiastically. He could hardly wait.

"I imagine Henry would like to use the shower," Clara said, "would you show him to the bathroom on your way?"

Shoving his chair back from the table, Ol' Henry volunteered, "I know where the shower be."

"We're off, then," Maurice said. "Come on, boys." He led them out of the kitchen to the inside stairs.

"Have you got clean clothes to change into?" Clara asked Ol' Henry.

"Yes ma'am," he answered. "They's down in the car. I'm off to get them now."

Clara nodded. "When you come back just help yourself to towels or whatever you need." Ol' Henry thanked her and left via the kitchen door to the landing and the outside stairs.

With the men gone Clara turned her attention to the girls still at the table. "In just a bit here I'm goin' out to do some shopping. While I'm gone I want you girls to clean the house. One of you vacuums while the other dusts. And I want a good job done. No cuttin' corners. Understand?"

Both girls nodded.

Everyone fed and the chores delegated, Clara sank back in

her chair and visibly relaxed. Another cup of coffee and she'd go get dressed to do the shopping.

*   *   *

The shop was a model of neat efficiency. The loading dock, where Maurice's brand new box-truck was parked, was at the east end. This was also where raw materials were stored, as well as finished products ready for shipping.

In the middle, under the stairs, was Maurice's business office. Towards the front center was the customer receiving area where walk-in trade was greeted. This "waiting room" was completely open to the rest of the shop, designated only by a square cut of navy-blue carpet and its furnishings; A brown leather sofa, coffee table, two matching easy chairs with end tables and brass floor lamps, all in a casual living room arrangement. Various works of art including beautifully glazed pottery of every size, shape and description adorned shelves, and sculptures from baroque to modern stood on pedestals throughout the room.

At the west end was the stone and clay-working area. Quentin's eyes lit up when he saw the electric potter's wheel and the kiln. Far bigger than any he'd seen at school, it was large enough to take a five-foot vase, just as Maurice had said. The tour completed, Maurice turned to Quentin. "What you think of my little operation here?"

"Way too cool!" Quentin exclaimed, gazing about the room. "I'd be lovin' havin' a shop like this."

"Would you know what to do with it if you had it?"

Boldly stepping up to the potter's wheel and sitting down, Quentin said, "Watch." On a small table to his right was a pitcher of water and a box of clay, its moisture protected by a plastic bag. With the pitcher of water Quentin thoroughly wet the wheel, opened the plastic bag, dug out clay with both hands and plopped it on the turntable. He worked it to remove any air pockets, then switched on the wheel. Expertly centering it on the disc, he shaped the clay into a thick slug. As his big hands lovingly enveloped the clay it magically began to rise out of his gentle grasp and flower into an exquisitely-shaped vase. "There," Quentin said, switching off the wheel and turning on his seat.

"That's great, Quentin," Christopher said in admiration. "I didn't know you could do stuff like that."

Maurice was impressed. Quentin's product looked perfect. "Very good, Quentin."

"I done a little with mallet and chisel too," Quentin said proudly. "But just a little," he added. "Like, I can carve flat letters, easy things like that. I'd be glad to help out while we're here if you want."

Maurice smiled. "I could sure use the help."

Getting to his feet and extending his hand, Quentin said, "You got it." They shook on it.

Afterwards, Maurice gestured with a wave of his hand and said, "You can start by painting, glazing and firing these pitchers I made yesterday."

Quentin nodded. "Any special color or design you lookin' for?"

"Use your imagination. And take your time. Quality is more important than quantity. Each one should be a work of art in itself."

"Each one will be," Quentin assured him confidently. "I'll get started right away."

"Good." Maurice turned to Christopher. "You want to earn your lunch, Chris?"

Pleased to be included, Christopher nodded.

"Follow me then." Leaving Quentin to his own devices, he turned and strode off across the shop.

At the loading and storage area he pointed out the stones he wanted moved to his work bench and informed Christopher that when he was done with that he could sweep the shop from one end to the other. Christopher nodded that he understood and set to the mundane chores.

Retreating to his office, Maurice donned his white smock, its pockets holding various sized chisels, returned to his work bench and went to work on a marble statue of a lion he was carving for a customer.

Several times while sweeping Christopher stopped to look out the small window in the overhead door. The car was still there, but Ramón was nowhere to be seen. Of course that wasn't surprising. It was only 8:00 o'clock in the morning. He heard the vacuum cleaner go on upstairs.

*   *   *

By the time Clara Sandwood returned from the grocery store the girls had the upstairs dusted and swept, scrubbed and vacuumed. Looking the house over, Clara was pleased. Then she promptly enlisted the girls to come down to the car and help carry up the groceries.

Over hamburgers and homemade french fries Maurice told his wife about the pitchers Quentin had painted and fired. Personally, he thought they were beautiful. But of course she would have to see for herself. When everyone was done eating, Clara handed out new toothbrushes to Ol' Henry and the kids.

It was then that Christopher got up from the table and looked out the window. Noticing Ramón and a companion down by the car, he called, "Ramón's here!" Everyone looked up except Quentin. His attention was directed exclusively at Molly. "C'mon, Harmony," Christopher said and started for the kitchen door and the side stairs.

Pushing her chair back, Harmony said, "Later, Moll. And thank you for lunch, Mrs. Sandwood," she added as she headed for the door in Christopher's wake.

"Let us know when the car gonna be ready," Clara hollered, but Harmony was already gone and thumping down the stairs.

"Hey, Ramón!" Christopher called, rounding the corner with Harmony hot on his heels.

Ramón looked up from where he and a companion were squatting on the sidewalk beside the car. "Hey Chris, Harmony." He stood up. "I was wonderin' what happened to y'all. Figured the old man and Quentin run off and by now y'all was just another statistic."

Christopher shook his head. "Nah. They're upstairs."

"Some people took us in last night," Harmony put in.

"Darkies?" Ramón squinted at the girl.

She nodded.

"Darkies took y'all in?" Ramón was clearly surprised.

"It's not so amazing," Harmony said, starting to get self-conscious about the way Ramón was going on about it.

Ramón shrugged. "Maybe not where y'all's from, but around here things are bad."

"Did you ever think that maybe things are so bad only in your own head?" Harmony pleasantly inquired.

Ramón bypassed the issue. It was starting to sound like last night. "This here's my brother Carlos, by the way. Carlos, this is Harmony."

"Hi, Carlos," Harmony said with a smile.

Carlos held up a hand. "Hi."

He introduced Christopher next. They slapped hands. The formalities done with, Christopher asked, "What all's wrong with the car, Ramón?"

"Just the U-joints, thank God."

"When do you think we'll be on the road again?"

"Ain't no tellin'," Ramón replied. To Carlos he said, "Let's get the tools and get this critter apart."

With a nod Carlos turned to his perfectly restored silver-blue '54 Chevy pickup parked behind Ramón's car, got out a tool box, set it on the street by the car and flipped open the lid.

Meanwhile Ramón slipped a piece of cardboard under the car and slid in after it on his back. Carlos, clutching the necessary wrenches, slid in beside Ramón and the boys went to work.

Christopher and Harmony stood on the sidewalk staring as

if they could see through the car to the work being done underneath. Christopher opened his mouth to speak but closed it again when a muffled curse from Ramón signaled trouble. Then Carlo's curses were heard. "Hand me the hammer, Chris," Ramón called from under the car.

Christopher got a hammer from the tool box and held it under the car until an unseen hand took it. Straightening up, he looked across the top of the car at Harmony and said with a grin, "I don't know about you but I feel like trying out my new toothbrush. Feels like fur's growing in my mouth."

With a laugh Harmony tossed her blonde hair back. "Feels like caterpillars are crawling around in there, huh?"

Christopher nodded. "All the bristles will probably wilt and die the first time I use it." To Ramón he called, "We're taking off, you guys. We're in the apartment upstairs of this building here. Let us know what's up, okay?"

"Okay," Ramón called back.

When Harmony and Christopher returned to the kitchen only Clara and Ol' Henry remained at the table sipping coffee. Clearing his throat, the old man set his cup down. "When the car gonna be ready?"

Christopher shrugged. "They're not sure."

Clara smiled. "Oh?"

"Yeah. I doubt it'll be ready today, though."

Clara almost said "good" but held her tongue, asking instead, "Aren't you kids gonna try out those new toothbrushes I bought you?" The toothbrushes were still on the table where they'd left them.

"We'd love to," Harmony answered.

"Yeah," Christopher chimed in as he reached for the toothbrushes, "we'll let you know how it turns out." Leaving Clara and Ol' Henry chuckling, he handed Harmony hers and headed down the hall to the bathroom.

Christopher was surprised when Harmony followed him in, stopped at the sink and elbowed for room as she began stripping the cellophane off her toothbrush. After observing her for a moment he asked with a frown, "Can't you wait your turn?"

"Wait my turn for what?"

Puzzled, Christopher looked at her. In his whole life he had never shared a bathroom with anyone. In the house he grew up in even brushing one's teeth was considered personal. Harmony, on the other hand, had never had a bathroom to herself. Brushing her teeth in front of someone was no more unsettling than tying her shoes. Had she known the cause of Christopher's concern she would have burst out laughing, which she did when Christopher told her.

"What?" she turned on him, brandishing her toothbrush and poking the air with her every word, "you want to brush your teeth alone?"

Christopher grabbed her wrist, arresting her poking, which was coming uncomfortably close to his face. "Yeah," he said defensively, "what's the big deal?"

Harmony laughed and pulled her wrist free. "No big deal. I just never heard of anyone being shy about brushing their teeth before, that's all."

For a long moment Christopher searched her smiling face, a grin slowly spreading across his own. "You want to brush our teeth together, huh?" With a diabolical snicker he grabbed the toothpaste, squeezed some onto his brush and turned on Harmony, jamming his toothbrush into her mouth with the declaration, "I know, let's brush each others' teeth!"

Clamping Christopher's toothbrush between her teeth, Harmony jerked her head back and yanked the handle from his grasp. Then, taking him completely by surprise, she lunged forward, shouldering him across the room where the backs of his knees caught the edge of the bathtub. Toppling backwards, he tore the shower curtain down as he crashed into the tub.

Harmony snatched the toothpaste and had her own toothbrush armed before Christopher's butt hit porcelain. As he struggled to get out of the tub, Harmony leapt on him and was about to jam her own toothbrush up his nose when Clara's voice boomed out from behind, "Is this the way honkeys brush their teeth!!?" The big-boned woman filled the doorway, hands on hips. "Now get out of there, the both of you," she angrily ordered, "an' hurry up!"

Harmony clumsily backed off Christopher, stood up and turned around. Feeling like a fool, she removed Christopher's toothbrush from her mouth and along with her own, set both on the sink. Christopher pulled himself out of the tub and stood up.

Clara surveyed the damage from where she stood, scowling at the sight of the torn shower curtain heaped in the bottom of the tub. After an unbearably long silence she commanded, "Look at me!"

Both raised their eyes but kept their heads bowed.

"You finish what you came in here to do, and I mean be quick about it, then get this bathroom cleaned up." Turning to leave, she stopped, her voice soft as velvet when she added, "I'll be waitin' in the kitchen."

"Now we did it," Harmony said the moment Clara was gone.

"Never mind," Christopher replied sullenly, "let's just get done in here and go take our medicine."

"What do you think she's going to do to us?" Harmony asked, squeezing toothpaste onto her brush.

Christopher shrugged. "We'll soon find out." Side by side they began brushing their teeth.

While Harmony straightened up the rest of the bathroom Christopher tried to see what he could do with the shower curtain, but it was hopeless. All the O-rings were torn clear through. At least the bar wasn't bent. That was lucky. "I guess we'll have to work it off," Christopher said, thinking it would be best to hang onto the money Harmony still had.

"If we don't get kicked out," Harmony put in.

They weren't surprised to find Clara Sandwood right where she said she would be, sitting at the kitchen table with Ol'

Henry, their empty coffee cups in front of them. They both looked up when the two teenagers entered. Ol' Henry did not look pleased.

"Sit down," Clara said, motioning to the vacant chairs around the table. When they were seated she continued. "I'm a little disappointed in the both of you, to say the least. How dare you come into my home and behave like a bunch of wild animals."

Christopher decided then and there the best way to handle the matter of the torn shower curtain was to be forthright about it. "The shower curtain's ruined, Mrs. Sandwood," he informed her, trying to look his humble best.

But Clara was having none of it. "I know," she said in clipped tones. "An' you both gonna pay for it, too."

Christopher raised his eyes to hers. "How?"

"With your two hands. An' I have a job that would be just perfect for both of you. Course if you want to go an' run off there ain't nothin' I can do about it. That's up to you."

When Christopher realized she was waiting for an answer he immediately said, "We'd be happy to work it off, Mrs. Sandwood."

"Yeah," Harmony put in. "We appreciate you letting us work it off."

Somewhat hesitantly Christopher asked, "What's the work you have for us?"

"Something I been lookin' forward to gettin' done for some time now. I want you to paint the outside kitchen stairs. When you get done with that I want you to paint the inside stairs."

They both nodded, Christopher assuring her, "We can do that."

"Good," she said conclusively. "We'll go to the paint store right now." Turning to Ol' Henry, she asked, "Would you like to come along for the ride, Henry?"

"Sure. I needs to rattle these ol' bones once in awhile else they get rusty."

"Well let's go," Clara said, rising from the table and herding them all out the kitchen door and down the stairs to the family Buick parked at the side of the building.

*   *   *

Maurice Sandwood listened to the delighted laughter of his daughter and smiled to himself. Quentin was showing off with the clay, spinning creatures out of the potter's wheel and generally entertaining Molly with his antics. What with her brother's death when she was but a child, and then coming down with Vitiligo, it had been years since he'd heard her laugh like that.

Funny, but his wife was right. It was the best thing that happened to them in a long time, Quentin coming along just when he did. A small miracle. His daughter at last saw a ray of sunshine in her otherwise gray world. And even if Quentin were only around for a day or two, Molly, once having seen the light of true affection shining in his dark eyes, might find a new confidence in her ability to be loved. Raising his eyes heavenward, Maurice took a moment to thank the Lord for the blessing. And maybe, just maybe, like Clara said, they could get Quentin to... Maurice decided not to think on. Or pray on. Time would tell. And the Lord knew his heart. If it was meant to be it would be. If not, well, he should just count his blessings then.

Maurice Sandwood laid his mallet and chisel on the workbench and approached his daughter and Quentin. "Okay, hotshot," he began good-naturedly, "let's see what you can do with stone."

Laughing, Quentin held up both hands dripping with clay and said, "Good. I can't wait to get out of this wet clay."

"Sure, Quentin," Maurice smiled, "I believe you."

Quentin grinned. "I'll clean up and be right with you, Mr. Sandwood."

"Maurice, Quentin. Call me Maurice."

"Okay, Maurice."

"And as for picking up, I'm sure Molly will be glad to put

everything away, won't you dear?"

Molly nodded. "Sure, Papa."

"Thanks, Molly," Quentin said as he crossed to the utility sink and rinsed off. Then he and Maurice were off to the stone-carving area. As with the potter's wheel Maurice was again pleasantly surprised at Quentin's keen handling of mallet and chisel. It was obvious that he was more than a little talented.

*   *   *

Returning from the paint store, Christopher sank way down in the backseat and pulled Harmony down with him as they passed Ramón and his brother working on the car. It was easier than answering a lot of questions which, undoubtedly, Ramón would ask if he saw them. And it would be embarrassing to have Ramón find out he and Harmony had to paint the stairs for the "darkies," as Ramón called them.

As for Ramón catching them in the act, Christopher already had an answer for that, too. They'd simply start by painting the inside stairs first—and take their sweet time about it. Hopefully the car would be fixed and they'd be on their way before it got as far as the outside stairs.

Being careful to pull up far enough so paint drops wouldn't fall on the car, Clara parked the Buick in the driveway at the side of the building. She had plans of her own. "We'll start right here," she said and popped the trunk lid.

"Why?" Christopher immediately asked. "I was thinking of doing the inside stairs first."

"Because," Ol' Henry answered for Clara, "the weather be real nice today. Tomorrow never knows, it might not be, an' you know what they say; make the hay while the sun be shinin'."

"You do have a way with words, Henry," Clara smiled. She turned to Christopher, whose long face made it obvious he was unhappy, and said in a voice without a hint of mercy, "What you standin' there for, boy? Grab them paint cans and let's get to work."

Christopher's gaze shifted to her, but the big woman's cold, unblinking stare made him drop his eyes and reach into the trunk for the paint cans and brushes. Harmony did likewise. It was plain to Christopher there was no arguing with this woman. She was going to have her way. Period.

Harmony didn't seem to mind at all. She was chattering away with Ol' Henry about what a beautiful day it was to paint outside and how she had never painted anything before and wouldn't it be fun? Ol' Henry just chuckled and nodded. He knew what was on Christopher's mind, too. That thought made him chuckle again.

Everything removed from the trunk, Clara slammed the lid and led the way, saying over her shoulder, "Let's go, everybody upstairs. An' bring all that stuff with you. We're goin' to start at the top."

"What's all this 'we're' crap?" Christopher muttered to Harmony as they started up the stairs behind Ol' Henry.

Harmony frowned. "Never mind. Just be glad we didn't get in trouble for wrecking that shower curtain."

"Huh! Trouble!" Christopher grumbled as he laboriously climbed the stairs lugging his two paint cans.

Clutching the plastic bag full of paint brushes, Harmony cheerfully exclaimed, "Well at least we've got brand new brushes!"

Christopher rolled his eyes and sighed. Women.

Clara waited at the top of the stairs, the kitchen door held open, and shooed them inside as they reached the landing. "Set all that stuff on the table," she ordered. "Now, the first thing you gonna do is sweep everything down real good," she instructed, handing Christopher the broom. He looked glummer than ever. "You can't leave any dirt, else the paint won't stick, okay?"

Eyes downcast, Christopher nodded.

"An' make sure your shoes is real clean before you begin. By the time you get done with that I'll have Harmony started." She paused, placing her hands on her hips. With absolutely no response from Christopher, she commanded sharply, "Look at me!" When he raised his eyes she continued quietly, "This is important. Paint as you go. Don't go paintin' the railing all the way down or anything, thinkin' you gonna come back up after-wards and do the stairs separate, understand?"

Christopher and Harmony nodded.

"Then let's get to it."

"Do a good job now, Mr. Christopher," Ol' Henry put in as the boy turned to go, "the sweepin' be an important part."

Christopher's fondness and respect for Ol' Henry had grown immeasurably since they first met. He turned and looked the man straight in the eye. "I will, Henry." And he did, too.

They worked side by side hour after hour, stooped beneath the blazing afternoon sun, drenched in sweat and experiencing their first work-induced backaches ever. At last Christopher straightened up with a mighty groan, stretched, then pulled his sweaty T-shirt off.

Carefully setting her brush on the edge of the paint can, Harmony stood up too, also stretching the ache out of her back. They were almost finished and so far Ramón hadn't come around. Christopher was glad of that.

"We're getting there," Harmony sighed, wishing she could take her sweaty shirt off too. Painting wasn't much fun any-more, her jolly cheerfulness having faded hours ago. Then, for no apparent reason she started giggling.

"What's so funny?" Christopher asked sourly.

"You've got paint on your nose."

"I do?" His eyes crossed momentarily as he felt his nose.

"Right on the end," she pointed, laughing at the look on his face.

He stopped feeling his nose and looked at her. "Well you've got some on your hair."

"I do?" she asked with concern, her grin turning to a frown as she tried to see, first over one shoulder, then the other.

"It's just a little," Christopher assured her. "C'mon, let's finish up. You can wash it out later. It's almost dinner time."

*   *   *

Maurice was impressed. Quentin's stone-cutting showed real potential. And he learned fast. Throughout the afternoon Maurice never had to explain anything twice. When he demonstrated a technique it seemed as if Quentin were able to adopt it as his own by merely watching. By late afternoon they had each rough-cut a stone, Maurice instructing as they worked. But now it was done and so was the day. Maurice laid his mallet and chisel down. He watched as Quentin carefully chiseled out the last letter of the stone he was working on, then asked, "Ready to call it a day?"

Quentin let out a long stream of air and set his own tools down. "You bet," he said, "I think my hands are gonna fall off."

"You did a good job, Quentin," Maurice said appreciatively.

"Thanks, Mr. Sandwood."

"Maurice," the master sculptor reminded him.

"Maurice," Quentin reiterated.

Digging a crumpled $20 from his pocket, Maurice extended it to Quentin.

"What's that for?"

"For the work you did today. I appreciate it."

Quentin shook his head. "You don't owe me nothin'. Heck, you've taken us all in an' fed us. If anything we owe you."

Insisting, Maurice shook his head. "You did a good day's work. This just a token of my appreciation." When Quentin started to protest again he interjected, "Besides, I want you to take my daughter out tonight an' you can't do that without money in your jeans."

"You want me to take Molly out?"

Maurice nodded. "Why not? I can tell she likes you." He stumbled a bit getting his next words out. "Do you... well... how do you feel about her?"

Quentin grinned. "She a doll. I'd love to go out with her."

"Then take the money an' ask her," Maurice warned, "'cause I ain't gonna offer again."

Quentin leaned forward and snatched the bill with his left hand and with a loud *smack* slapped his right into Maurice's and pumped the man's arm. "Thanks, Mr. Sandwood," he said gratefully.

"Maurice," he reminded him.

Quentin nodded. "Right. Maurice."

"Another thing," Maurice said as they mounted the stairs, "we got a closetful a clothes here that is just goin' to waste, an' I do believe you could fit right into them."

Quentin hesitated before admitting, "I wouldn't quite fill out your clothes, Maurice." At the moment he was wearing Maurice's old clothes and they were pretty breezy up and down the legs.

"I'm not talkin' about my old clothes," Maurice informed him as they gained the upper landing and pushed through the door into the hall. "I'm talkin' about my son's. He got a whole closetful. And it's mostly like new."

Quentin stopped and eyed Maurice seriously. "He wouldn't mind?"

Maurice smiled. "He won't mind."

"No?"

"He in heaven."

"Oh."

Quentin was wondering if it would be appropriate to ask what happened when Maurice, seemingly reading his mind, said simply, "The war."

"Oh." Which war? There had been so many in the last few years it was hard to keep track of all the "Police Actions," "Interventions," and "Peace Keeping Missions" since Vietnam, the Korean War, and Desert Storm. Quentin correctly surmised that "the war" was probably a sore spot with his host and said nothing except to thank him and accept the offer.

"Fine." Without another word Maurice turned and led the

way to his son's former bedroom, threw the closet doors open and stood aside with a sweeping gesture. "It's all yours, whatever you want."

Quentin's face lit up. The closet was chock-full of jeans and western shirts, mod suits, conservative suits and outlandish suits. He turned to Maurice Sandwood with heartfelt thanks.

Maurice put a hand on his shoulder. "I mean it, Quentin. You just go an' pick out whatever strikes your fancy."

"Thank you."

"There's no way they could'a found a better owner," Maurice smiled warmly. Then, closing the door behind him, he left the room.

Everything Quentin tried on fit like it was tailor-made for him. He grinned at himself in the mirror after settling on a conservative, charcoal-gray pinstriped suit with vest, matching tie and black loafers. Whatever pain he had experienced in the past didn't seem to matter anymore. He was living in the present—and happy as ever. The scent of the girl, her smile, her warmth, were intoxicating. He was high. He was going to her room to ask her out immediately.

In the hall he encountered a bedraggled Christopher and Harmony. Speckled with paint, they both stopped in their tracks and looked him up and down, Christopher letting out a long, low whistle and applauding. "What'd they make you, chief banana peeler?"

"Never mind him," Harmony interjected, "you look real nice, Quentin."

"Thanks. Seen Molly?"

"Kitchen," Harmony said over her shoulder as she and Christopher moved on towards the bathroom arguing over who would shower first. In the air-conditioned shop Quentin hadn't worked up a sweat all day.

When he stepped into the doorway he found Molly and her mother preparing dinner. Sensing his presence, Clara Sandwood turned from the stove where she was stirring gravy and said with a knowing smile, "Tryin' on somethin' for church tomorrow?" Maurice had already secretly informed his wife of the situation.

Molly looked up from setting the table and smiled radiantly. "You look great, Quentin. Where'd you get the fancy duds?"

Quentin wasn't sure whether to answer "your brother" or "your father," finally deciding it was her father who had given them to him since her brother wasn't around anymore. Before he could answer at all Molly added, "You have good taste."

"Thanks."

They stood gazing at one another for several seconds. When he didn't say anything she asked curiously, "Any particular reason you all dressed up?"

Quentin shifted uncomfortably. It wasn't that he was afraid of being turned down, he just didn't want to be turned down in front of anyone.

"Well?" Molly was waiting.

"I—I wanted to ask you something."

"What?"

"Could we go an' talk someplace else?"

Molly nodded, set aside what she was doing and followed him down the hall where they stopped and turned to one another. "Would you go out with me?" Quentin asked the moment their eyes locked.

Molly broke into a grin. "You want to go out with me?"

Quentin nodded.

Hesitating for just a moment, Molly replied, "I'd love to."

"Where should we go?"

"Wherever you want."

"We could do a movie. Or bowling."

"Bowling," Molly interjected. "I haven't been bowling in ages."

Just then Ol' Henry came down the hall. He stopped, took one look at Quentin and said, "My, my, looky here, must be a movie star!"

"Thanks, Henry," Quentin grinned sheepishly.

"You look real sharp, Mr. Quentin," Ol' Henry went on.

"Thanks," Quentin said again.

"Where're you young'ns goin', anyways?"

"Bowling."

When Maurice came plodding down the hall it was time to move on and the four of them filed into the kitchen and took their places at the table. Glancing over her shoulder, Clara remarked, "Land sakes! Y'all aren't hungry or nothin' are you? First time in my life I haven't had to call everyone to the dinner table. Only, where's my two painters?"

No one seemed to know. "I'll go an' get 'em," Quentin volunteered.

"Thank you, Quentin," Clara smiled.

Naturally Quentin found them in the john. "Hurry up you two, everyone waitin' on you."

"Harmony's trying to get paint out of her hair," Christopher said, holding up one side of her long, silky blonde hair so it wouldn't fall into the soapy water in the sink. They had decided to skip showering until after dinner.

"Let's see." Quentin leaned closer for a better look at the strands of hair Harmony held between her thumb and index fingers. "Oh, that ain't nothin'," he scoffed, "I wouldn't even worry 'bout that little bit. By the way," he asked on sudden thought, "how'd you two get stuck paintin'?"

Hunched over the sink and talking through her hair, Harmony said, "Chris."

"Harmony," Christopher just as quickly lay blame.

"In any case we tore the shower curtain down," Harmony admitted, "so now we're paying for it."

"Have you seen Ramón today?" Christopher changed the subject.

Quentin shook his head. "Nope. But the car still out front."

"Probably having trouble getting U-joints." Then, "So where'd you get the fancy threads?"

"Mr. Sandwood. He lettin' me borrow them from his son who got killed in the war."

"Which war?" It was Christopher.

"Which war?" Quentin looked at him for a moment, then answered flatly, "The Eskimo Rebellion of 1999."

"Oh."

"Taking Molly out?" Harmony interjected with a grin.

"Yeah. Now hurry up or Mrs. Sandwood gonna come after you herself."

Christopher knew exactly what that meant and nodded.

Quentin said, "Okay, see you two later," and left.

"Hurry up, Harmony, or I'm going without you," Christopher warned after Quentin was gone.

"Ratfink."

Ratfink or not, Christopher grabbed a towel and roughly started drying Harmony's hair. She pulled away from him. "I can do it myself." She took the towel and finished. A few quick strokes with a comb and she was done. "Let's go."

They didn't waste any time getting to the dinner table. Everyone was already seated when they took their places, Clara just setting out the standing rib roast, buttered peas, and steaming mashed potatoes and gravy. After she sat down they bowed their heads while Maurice said grace, then got busy as the serving dishes were passed around.

Scooping potatoes onto his plate, Christopher caught Quentin's eye and asked, "So, where're you and Molly going?"

"Bowling," Quentin answered, "an' no, you can't come," he was quick to add. Christopher was about to ask why when Harmony kicked him under the table.

With everyone's plates piled high conversation momentarily ceased, the only sound being the clinking of silverware as the feast was hungrily consumed. "Anyone for more meat?" Maurice asked when his own plate was empty. Only Molly and her mother declined. The last round finished off the roast and with every dish and vessel scraped clean everyone settled back with sighs of contentment.

"Thank you, Clara, for a most wonderful meal," Ol' Henry beamed from the opposite end of the table.

"Yeah, thanks," Christopher chimed in, "it was great."

The thanks-offering then made its way around the entire table, finally concluding with her husband. "A finer meal no woman ever made, Clara. The meat was cooked to perfection."

"Well thank you all," Clara said, beaming, "I'm glad everyone enjoyed it."

When she was done Quentin cleared his throat. "Uh, would it be okay if me an' Molly go now?"

Digging into his pants pocket, Maurice said, "Just a minute." Despite Maurice Sandwood's generous disposition Quentin was surprised when he held up the keys to the Buick and insisted that no daughter of his was going on a date in a bus. Quentin graciously accepted the keys.

As he and Molly started for the side door Clara stopped them in their tracks with a loud demand as to what time they'd be home. Quentin started to answer but Molly spoke over him, "Soon's we get back."

"You'll need a better answer than that, young lady," Clara warned.

"Midnight," she finally answered, having no intention of staying out later than that on a first date anyway.

"I guess we can live with that," Clara replied and sipped her after-dinner coffee.

"Thanks, Mamma," Molly said.

With a wave to the grinning peanut gallery at the table, Quentin and Molly said goodbye and were about to go out the kitchen door when Christopher shouted, "Hey, stop! I just painted those stairs!"

"Whew! That was close," Quentin said and closed the door. "Glad you caught me."

"So am I," Clara said, "so am I."

"Well, goodbye all," Quentin said again as he and Molly

went to the inside stairs and exited through the shop.

*   *   *

Once the table was cleared and the dishwasher was humming Maurice slapped a deck of cards on the table and called for everyone to gather around and play some gin.

"Sound good to me," Ol' Henry said, scooting his chair closer to the table, sweeping up the cards and shuffling.

"Do we have to?" Christopher asked.

"You don't have to do nothin', boy, 'cept die and pay taxes," Maurice quipped.

"And go to the bathroom," Harmony added.

At that everyone burst out laughing.

"You in?" Ol' Henry asked Christopher as he began dealing.

"Yeah."

He dealt seven cards to each, set the deck face-down in the center of the table, turned over the five of hearts and placed it face-up beside the deck. Maurice snapped up the five of hearts and discarded the seven of spades. Harmony drew a blind card and discarded the ace of spades. When Clara drew Harmony's discarded ace Christopher groaned, "I wanted that one."

"What you want an' what you get ain't always gonna be the same, honey," Clara intoned and discarded the queen of diamonds.

And so it went, 'round and 'round, until Harmony ended it by excitedly squealing, "GIN!" and laying down her winning hand with a triumphant flourish.

The others slapped their cards down. "Beginner's luck," Ol' Henry muttered as Maurice began tallying up points.

"Beginner's luck my eye," Harmony retorted, "me and my ma used to play gin all the time."

"Figures," Christopher put in sourly.

*   *   *

Being a Saturday night the bowling alley was doing a

booming business, yet they still managed to get a lane and were soon into it. His eyes constantly on Molly, Quentin hardly noticed he was throwing one of his best games ever. Her eyes constantly on Quentin, Molly hardly noticed she was throwing one of her best games ever. And if their coming together hadn't been predetermined from the beginning of time it would have been hard to convince them of that. Quentin was absolutely intoxicated with the girl. Molly felt relief. Safe. He made her feel wanted. Worthy. Desired. And she hadn't felt that way in a long time. Besides all of that, she thought he was great. His face. His smile. The way his voice sounded and his imposing physique. She liked the way he held her hand. And she was sure she would like the way he kissed, too.

*   *   *

The others slapped their cards down with disgust. "What's wrong, you guys quitting?" Harmony asked innocently.

"Might as well since you 'bout took most every hand," Clara grumbled.

"No use playing against a girl like you," Christopher put in, "you always win."

"I'd sure like ta go another round," Ol' Henry declared, "lady luck done set on her shoulder long enough."

"It isn't luck," Harmony stated flatly.

Maurice looked from Ol' Henry to Harmony. Raising his eyebrows, he leaned forward and said, "Well if it ain't the lady a luck then you cheatin'!"

Everyone laughed.

"Well if that's the case," Clara grinned, swept in the cards and began shuffling, "let's make do with another round."

Christopher looked bored. He'd rather get Harmony in Molly's room, put the stereo on low and make-out rather than sit there and lose another hand to the little cardshark. "I wonder when Quentin and Molly'll get back," he said, examining his cards. The words barely left his lips when they heard footsteps on the inside stairs. A moment later Molly and Quentin came in.

"Who's winning?" Quentin asked, somehow looking not unlike the cat who ate the canary.

"I am," Harmony replied.

"Then we'll just go an' let you continue," Quentin said as he and Molly turned and left the room. They were so high on each other they were on the verge of getting silly.

As soon as the lovebirds were gone Ol' Henry smacked his cards down and sat back cackling with laughter.

"What in the name of heaven's gotten into you?" Clara asked with a frown.

Still chuckling, Ol' Henry shook his head. "The look on that boy's face. He don't get that high on merrywanna!"

Christopher and Harmony burst out laughing. Maurice smiled. Clara shook her head, warning, "They best not be foolin' with no merrywanna."

"Oh hush up," Maurice admonished. "The only thing that girl high on is the young man that's escortin' her. And thank God for that. It's the happiest I seen her since I don't know when."

"Glory be for that," Clara agreed.

Christopher caught Harmony's eye. "Let's go see how their date went."

"Okay," Harmony said, sliding her chair back, "let's."

As soon as they were gone Clara looked at Ol' Henry with serious eyes. "Think he'd want to stay on if we asked him?"

With a saw-toothed grin Ol' Henry said, "Missus, I *knows* it!"

Getting up from the table, Maurice clapped him on the shoulder. "Good, Henry. I'm glad to hear that."

Summing up all their feelings in a single word, Clara said with finality, "Amen."

17

ON THE ROAD AGAIN

Christopher was totally unprepared for Sunday morning. At 6:00 o'clock Clara had them all out of bed and in a hurried rush to get ready for church. "But I don't go to church," Christopher informed her.

"Honey, in this house ever'body go to church 'ceptin' the dog, an' that's 'cause we don't got a dog," Clara informed him right back and briskly snatched the blankets off. Christopher immediately bounced out of bed and into his jeans. Quentin didn't wait for any encouragement and was out of bed in double-time. "Now get your butts to the kitchen. Breakfast is on the table," she said as she was leaving the room.

Pulling his T-shirt on over his head, Christopher scowled, "Church! I haven't been to church since I was a little kid."

"You still a little kid," Quentin grinned, adding with a philosophical shrug, "but so what? Goin' to church won't kill ya. When in Sandwood land do as the Sandwoods do." Christopher said nothing. Sitting on the edge of the bed, he began lacing up his boots. Quentin sat down next to him, shoes in hand. "Ya know, we pretty lucky to be stayin' here."

"Just because you found a girlfriend."

Putting a shoe on, Quentin asked, "So, what's wrong with that?"

"Nothing. But I got a feeling you're gonna be staying here."

"Why you say that?"

Christopher finished tying his boots, straightened up and

returned Quentin's gaze. "I don't know, I just have this feeling you're not coming with us when we leave."

"You don't have to worry none 'bout that, Chris," Quentin answered evenly, "I want my share a the money too."

"I don't care about the money, it wouldn't be the same without you around," Christopher replied.

Quentin stared at him for a moment, then threw an arm around his shoulders and pulled him close. "Thanks, Chris."

"I mean it," Christopher said, feeling oddly uncomfortable at being so emotional. As if he were doing something shameful.

As stealthy as a cat, Harmony silently appeared in the entrance. Casually leaning against the wall, feet crossed at the ankles, arms folded across her chest, she laughed aloud and jeered, "Kiss 'em! Kiss 'em!"

Startled and embarrassed, the boys quickly disengaged. Jumping to his feet, Christopher demanded, "What's *your* problem?"

Harmony laughed again and clapped her hands. She was dressed in her "road" clothes; jeans, rust-colored sweatshirt and tennis shoes. "Nothing," she answered, still grinning, "I've just never seen you guys so friendly before."

Christopher's face grew red as he stammered, "I was just... we were...."

"Yes, yes, go on," Harmony urged with a merciless snicker, "just what *were* you doing?"

Quentin and Christopher exchanged glances, then leapt to their feet, both enveloping Harmony in a hug and sweeping her out of the room.

*   *   *

The expanded Sandwood family got some surprised and curious looks from the all-black congregation when they entered the church, but no one was unkind. It was mere coincidence that the minister's prepared sermon dealt with reverse discrimination and returning hate for hate, concluding with the "turn the other cheek" routine.

Christopher didn't hear a word of it. He closed his ears immediately upon entering the church. After all, *he* wasn't religious. Harmony sank lower and lower in the pew as the minister spoke, embarrassed, as if the minister's subject had been chosen especially for them.

When the service concluded the assemblage exited through the rear doors where the minister greeted each family. When he came to the Sandwoods, Christopher and Harmony practically hiding behind Clara, the minister intoned confidentially, "New addition to the family, Maurice?"

"Cousins," Clara interjected loudly, "from the *other* side of the family!"

Every eyebrow within earshot raised, including the minister's. "Well, have a good week," he said, "and we'll see you next Sunday."

Clara and Maurice both smiled and thanked the minister, then guided their flock out the door and down the steps, Ol' Henry bringing up the rear. As they were getting in the car Maurice admonished his wife in hushed tones, "You shouldn't oughta lie to the minister, Clara."

Sliding across the seat, Clara said defensively, "It weren't no lie, it was a fib. I's just pullin' his leg a bit." Ol' Henry got in next to her and shut the door. Quentin, Molly, Christopher and Harmony squeezed in back. On returning home they found Ramón's brother's truck nosed up behind Ramón's car and two pairs of ankles sticking out from beneath the battered blue Chevy.

As soon as Maurice had the car parked Christopher and Harmony were out in a flash and bounding around the front of the building. They were getting antsy for the road and glad to see progress being made. Not so Quentin. He was content right where he was—with Molly. Following the others into the shop and up the stairs, Ol' Henry seemed unconcerned as well.

"When's it gonna be ready?" Christopher asked by way of

greeting.

"Chris?" came a muffled voice from under the car.

"Yeah. When's the car gonna be ready?"

"Just a minute."

Harmony and Christopher could hear Ramón and Carlos quietly discussing something, then some light tapping with a hammer, a curse, more tapping.

"It's almost done, I think," Christopher said quietly.

"How can you tell?" Harmony asked.

Christopher shrugged. "I can't. It just seems like it."

At last Ramón and Carlos struggled out from under the car, stood up and dusted themselves off. "Well, that last one went easy enough," Ramón grinned.

"Then the car's ready to go?" Harmony asked.

"Sure is. Y'all ready to head east and get that money?"

"You bet," Christopher answered, thinking of the stairs he and Harmony weren't going to have to paint.

*   *   *

Sitting at the kitchen table with Quentin and Maurice, Ol' Henry's uncanny perception told him their stay at the Sandwood's was coming to an end. Clara was busy preparing Sunday dinner while Molly had gone to change. Turning to his host, Ol' Henry said, "I do believes that ol' car gonna be ready this very afternoon, Maurice."

Maurice unclasped his hands, laid them palms-down on the table in front of him and took a deep breath. "Well..." He didn't know where to begin. He looked to Ol' Henry for support.

Wondering what was up, Quentin's gaze shifted from one to the other. Ol' Henry finally turned to Quentin. "How would you likes to stay here, Mr. Quentin?"

Quentin stared at him, then turned to Maurice, who smiled broadly and said, "You welcome to."

"B-But I'm a...."

"I know all about it, Quentin," Maurice assured him.

"Henry told us. I guess you got a pretty raw deal. But none a that matters with us. Shoot, you can take my son's old room. Fit right into his clothes, too. And you can work with me in the shop. With a new name an' a wallet full a ID's you'd be all set." With a shrug he added, "After enough time go by you could even get in touch with your family again."

"How much time would that be?"

Maurice shrugged, "Long as you want, I guess, but ideally speakin', one year at least. And besides," he added, "by then you'll be long forgotten by the law. They certainly won't be actively lookin' for you by then. An' the truth of the matter is, you probably never was an' still ain't exactly a top-priority case. But mostly it depend on how comfortable you feel with the situation. You might take a visit home even sooner if you wanted. But that's up to you."

"That's mighty generous of you, Mr. Sandwood."

"I told you, call me Maurice."

"Maurice," Quentin repeated, then turned to Ol' Henry. "What you think, Henry?"

With a shake of his head Ol' Henry said, "It gots to be what *you* think, Mr. Quentin, not what I think. But I'd give you a swat in the head if'n you didn't stay. You could do the work you love, an' you would most certainly be safe from the law. You gots a pretty girl…" he quietly concluded.

Quentin looked at both men and grinned. "I do believe I'd be crazy to turn you down."

Keeping her eyes on the chicken she was preparing for the frier, Clara smiled to herself.

*   *   *

When Molly strolled into the kitchen, the bright blue T-shirt and tight-fitting jeans she wore accentuating every hill and valley of her lithe young body, everyone stopped talking and looked up. "What's goin' on?" she asked suspiciously, eyeing the others around the table.

Turning from the stove, her mother said nonchalantly, "Quentin's goin' to be stayin' with us."

Molly's face lit up. "For good?"

"For good," her mother smiled.

With a tiny squeal Molly threw her arms around Quentin and kissed him on the cheek. "That's wonderful, Quentin!"

"Thanks," Quentin grinned.

"Heck," Molly said, shyly lifting a shoulder, "I was half-thinking 'bout goin' with when you left."

As the words left her lips Christopher and Harmony burst through the door. "Car's ready!" They both announced in unison.

To no one's surprise Clara told Harmony to take a seat and Christopher to turn around and fetch Ramón and his brother. Christopher returned pronto with Ramón and Carlos.

"Come in, come in," Clara said, gesturing to the boys in her hurried manner. Ramón and Carlos shuffled two more steps into the room. Clara smiled at the guarded looks on their faces and gestured to the places she had set for them. "Would you like to have dinner with us?" She was looking at Carlos when she spoke.

Ramón answered, "We already ate, ma'am."

Her eyes shifted to him. "Well, it won't be ready for more'n an hour."

"It be worth waitin' on," Ol' Henry grinned.

Ramón looked unsure. "What time y'all thinkin' of havin' dinner, ma'am?"

"Around 2:00 o'clock."

Ramón looked around the room. "If the others want to," he shrugged, "I don't care."

"Good," Clara said, announcing that anyone who wanted to could take one last shower and knew where it was, even offering Ramón and Carlos the use of it. Both declined, Carlos explaining that he wasn't going.

"I'd like to shower again!" Harmony declared.

"Well don't get in a heated rush about it," Clara answered, "you still gonna be here a few hours yet so hang tight, there's somethin' you gonna wanna hear." Harmony sat down next to Christopher and took his hand in her lap. "Anyways," Clara began, then stopped and turned to her husband. "Maurice, why don't you tell them?"

Maurice did a double-take. "What? Why me?" He turned to Quentin with a big grin and said, "Why don't you, Quentin?"

With a smile Quentin cleared his throat, looked around the table once, stopped on Harmony and Christopher and said levelly, "The Sandwoods have been kind enough to offer me a home here an' I decided to accept."

"You're staying here?" Christopher asked, his voice rising, "why?"

"Because, Chris. You know where I been. This is more than I could ever a hoped for. It's like a miracle. I got a chance now to make somethin' of myself doin' the kind of work I love. I'll be safe from the law, an' I'll even get to see my family again."

"Oh," Christopher said dejectedly and lowered his eyes. Suddenly his head popped up and his face brightened. "What about the money? You sure you wanna pass that up?"

"The money's not a sure thing, Chris. This is."

Christopher sighed. "I know."

Harmony opened her mouth to say something but closed it again. "We'll miss you," she said after a moment.

"I'll miss you guys, too."

"We'll miss you more," Harmony countered with a twinkle in her eye.

Quentin laughed but it quickly faded and he looked down at the table.

"It be the best thing, Mr. Quentin," Ol' Henry said quietly.

"I know. An' much thanks to you all," Quentin said, raising his eyes to Clara and Maurice.

"Don't you worry none about nothin', Quentin," Clara said reassuringly.

"We're glad to have you, Quentin," Maurice added, "I really need the help in my shop."

Molly slipped an arm around his shoulders and kissed him on the ear, whispering, "An' I need you most of all."

*   *   *

Strolling arm-in-arm and soaking up the warm sunshine on a lazy Sunday, it was just after noon when Quentin and Molly started their fourth lap around the block. And then it dawned on Quentin—there would be many, many such Sundays from now on. A whole summer full of Sundays. And spring Sundays. And fall and winter Sundays, too. The two of them didn't talk much. They would have plenty of time for that. Now they were both lost in a deep reflection on the past. All at once Quentin stopped and looked at her. "Let's go back."

"Why?"

"To spend some time with Christopher and Harmony. I don't think I'm ever gonna see those two again." Waxing philosophical he added, "It's kind'a funny how close we've all become in such a short time. An' you know the funniest thing of all?" He locked eyes with her.

"What?"

"After livin' on the road with them I come to realize white people no different than you or me." With a sigh he added, "Still, I suppose by the time a few months pass I won't even think about them no more. And yet, somehow I'll always remember them, too. An' Ol' Henry of course."

Molly grinned. "I know," she said, taking his face in her hands, "I was only with them two days and I don't think I'll ever forget them either." They exchanged a kiss. Then another for luck and started for home.

The kitchen was warm in spite of the air conditioning, the delicious aroma of frying chicken wafting through the air. "Glad to see you two made it back," Maurice said as Quentin and Molly came in.

Clara turned around, fork in hand. "Everybody smiling?"

"Everybody," Quentin and Molly grinned at her. "Where's Christopher and Harmony?"

*   *   *

The fried chicken dinner, complete with corn, mashed potatoes and gravy and coleslaw was stupendous and everybody said so. Aside from that it was a pretty quiet dinner except for Christopher making a lame joke about Quentin becoming a famous sculptor, but everyone managed a polite laugh.

When they'd had their fill and were sliding their chairs back Clara leaned across the table for the serving plate still piled high with golden-brown chicken. She'd deliberately made too much so her guests could take the leftovers for later. Now she turned to the task of packing it up for them.

Getting to his feet, Carlos said to his brother, "I think I'm gonna get on up to the house. Gonna stop by on your way out?"

Ramón shook his head. "Nah. I'm just gonna run them over to Mississippi, turn around and come right back. Whole thing shouldn't take more'n two days."

Carlos nodded. "Good enough. See you then." To the room at large he said, "Bye, y'all," and left.

After Carlos was gone Quentin, Christopher and Ramón turned to bantering about whether or not Ramón's car would make it to Mississippi. Discreetly nudging Ol' Henry with an elbow, Maurice got up from the table and disappeared down the hall. A moment later Ol' Henry followed. Once in the living room Maurice turned and without a word pressed a $20 dollar bill into Ol' Henry's hand.

Looking down at the $20, Ol' Henry exclaimed, "Well I'll be blessed! What this for?"

Maurice shrugged. "For anything you want." When Ol' Henry started to protest he quickly added, "For bringing us Quentin."

"I don't take no charity."

Maurice took a step back, held his hands up and said with a grin, "You might just as well take it now 'cause I'll slip it in your back pocket 'fore you get out of the house anyways."

Taking the $20, Ol' Henry smiled warmly. "Thanks, Maurice. You a kind an' generous man."

"Like I said, Henry, thanks for bringin' us Quentin. Molly needed that."

Ol' Henry stopped and looked at him. "I didn't *bring* you nobody. It just happened."

Maurice chuckled. "I know. But sometimes it seems like it didn't just happen." They looked at one another for a quiet moment before Maurice added confidentially, "Just between us, where you bringin' those other two young'ns?"

"I ain't bringin' them no place," Ol' Henry insisted. "Course they's pretty young to be out roamin' aimless. But maybe the road'll be gettin' pretty old by the time we gets ourselfs down to Mississippi. Course that young lady seemed pretty determined right from the start that she weren't goin' back. But maybe after we get that darn money we's after I'll talks 'em into hoppin' a bus back north with me." He sighed, concluding with a shrug, "I don't know."

*   *   *

The last thing Ol' Henry did before leaving the house was fill his canteen. And then they were all down on the sidewalk saying their final goodbyes. Christopher and Harmony thanked the Sandwoods first, Harmony embracing Molly, Clara, and Maurice in turn.

After shaking hands with Maurice, a timid embrace for Clara, and a handshake for Molly, Christopher turned to Quentin. They gripped hands for one long moment, Christopher saying levelly, "I wish you'd come with us."

Quentin slowly shook his head. "Can't, Chris. This is where I belong now."

Christopher nodded, "I know."

"See ya, bro."

"See ya." They slapped five.

"An' come back an' visit, will ya? Both of you?"

"Of course we will, Quentin, you can count on it." But even as the words left his lips Christopher somehow knew it would never come to pass.

Then Harmony jumped up so that Quentin caught her in his arms. They exchanged a kiss. "Bye, Quentin," she said, looking deeply into his dark eyes, "I'll never forget you."

"An' I won't forget you, neither," Quentin smiled and set her down. He turned to Ol' Henry.

The old man firmly took Quentin's hand in both of his. "Keep the faith, Mr. Quentin, an' always try an' find out what be right an' then sticks by it an' you'll do okay."

Holding the man's gaze, Quentin answered solemnly, "I will, Henry."

When everyone had shaken hands at least twice, and with Ramón standing somewhat impatiently at the driver's door, Christopher and Harmony tumbled in back. Ol' Henry settled in front, the doors were slammed shut and Ramón fired up the engine.

Puffing a cloud of gray smoke, the old blue Chevy with the tattered white ragtop limped away from the curb and out onto the boulevard, the Sandwoods and Quentin standing on the sidewalk waving goodbye until it was swallowed up in the Sunday afternoon traffic.

HARMONY'S ANGEL

18

BURGLARS AND BUNGLERS

At 6:00 o'clock that evening Christopher broke out the chicken. At first no one thought they were hungry, but after trying a little piece here or a bite there they suddenly found themselves ravenous. Blessing Clara Sandwood for her thoughtfulness, everyone dug in, the canteen passed around to wash it down.

Just the other side of Little Rock, Arkansas, Ramón announced he needed gas. Christopher told him to eat more beans, to which Ramón threateningly asked if that was a crack at his Mexican heritage. Everyone laughed at that, Ol' Henry remarking that maybe he'd been driving too long. Ramón admitted that maybe he had and guided the car into a gas station.

The moment the car stopped beside the pumps the doors were thrown open and everyone got out. After an extended stretch Christopher asked Harmony for money to buy a soda. She gave it to him and said, "Think I'll hit the ladies room."

"I'll walk with you," Ol' Henry volunteered.

Harmony stopped and looked at him. "Okay." As they started for the station house she asked, "What gives?"

"Listen careful," he began, his voice low and serious, "'cause tomorrow never knows." Harmony's ears perked up at his tone. "I decided just in case somethin' do happen to me I's gonna tell you how to gets to that darn money, okay?"

Harmony stopped and turned on him with a frown. "Nothing's going to happen to you," she stated flatly

"Never you mind," he said, wagging a finger at her. "If'n

257

somethin' did you guys couldn't get that money no way no how. Now that don't make no sense, do it?"

With a half-shake of her head Harmony said, "No, I guess not."

"Good. Now listen careful what I's gonna say. The house you lookin' for is on the southwest corner of Lee an' Maple streets. You got that? Big two-story house."

Harmony nodded.

"Okay. Say it a few times so's you'll remember. Big ol' two-story house on the southwest corner of Lee an' Maple streets. Say it."

"Big, two-story house on the corner of Lee and Maple streets," Harmony reiterated like a student to a teacher.

"Which corner? There be four of them," Ol' Henry said anxiously, agitated that she had already forgotten part of the instructions.

"The southwest corner."

"It be mighty important to remember everything I's tellin' you. Say it again." Once again Harmony repeated the instructions, this time leaving nothing out. Ol' Henry smiled. "Good. Now say it to yourself a couple more times whilst you usin' the can. Go on," he insisted, watching as she started for the rest room. Then he turned and headed back to the car. He found Christopher leaning against the fender sucking on a grape soda.

"Want some?" Christopher offered.

Ol' Henry dug in his pocket, fingered the $20 dollar bill and shook his head. "Think I'll gets one a my own, thank you." Then he turned and headed for the station house.

"Hey!" Christopher called, "Where'd you get money?"

Without turning or slowing his pace, Ol' Henry called back, "Off'a earth angel!" Puzzled by the old man's answer, Christopher shook his head, drained the can and tossed it in the trash.

Returning from paying for the gasoline, Ramón asked, "Where's everybody?"

Christopher shrugged, "Here and there."

Turning his back to the car and leaning against it, Ramón said, "We're 'bout halfway I figure."

"Easiest $400 bucks you ever made, huh?"

Ramón gave a short nod. "Sure will be—if I ever get it."

"If it's there you'll get it," Christopher assured him. "Henry don't cheat nobody."

"I ain't worryin' about him cheatin' me, I'm worryin' about what if the money ain't there?"

Christopher shrugged. "Can't do anything about that. If it isn't there it isn't there. But heck, you have to admit it's a good bet for you. I'd a done it if I was in your place."

"Who wouldn't?"

"Then quit worryin' and start hopin'."

"You're right," Ramón agreed. Noticing Ol' Henry and Harmony approaching, he called, "Y'all ready to hit the road?"

An hour southeast of Little Rock the alternator light started glowing its red warning. "Uh-oh, looks like trouble," Ramón said as they rolled into the small town of Alligator, Arkansas.

As if he had a place in mind and knew exactly how to get there Ramón turned left off the main highway and drove two blocks east to an old, three-story red-brick industrial building built around a courtyard with a tall, arched entrance. The bottom of the car scraped as he pulled into the drive and through the arch, rolled across the empty expanse of asphalt and nosed up to the far wall opposite the entrance. The courtyard served as a loading area for trucks, with a few parking spaces for company VIPs.

"This building looks pretty cool, don't it?" Ramón commented and killed the engine.

"What we stoppin' for?" Having dozed off, Ol' Henry was suddenly alert.

"Alternator light just came on," Ramón answered.

"But why are we stopping *here?*" Harmony interjected.

Ramón shrugged. "I just thought the buildin' looked sort'a cool, like it was built in the thirties or somethin'."

Peering up through the top of the windshield, Ol' Henry said, "Probably was. She an' old one all right."

"I like the way it's built around the parking lot with an archway to get in," Harmony commented.

"It's more like a loading dock than a parking lot, Harmony," Christopher informed her. To Ramón he said, "Well, let's pop the hood and take a look at this critter."

Ramón heaved a sigh. "Might as well." He pushed the squeaky door open and got out.

"Ought'a oil them hinges," Christopher remarked as he climbed out. Turning around, he held the seat forward for Harmony, "C'mon, I'll teach you about cars."

Harmony looked at him in surprise. "You will?" She was thrilled at this little token of interest that went beyond his natural drives. Scrambling out, she paused and turned back to Ol' Henry. "You getting out?"

He shook his head. "I'll just sets right here, thank you."

Had he sounded testy? Harmony shrugged it off.

By now Christopher and Ramón were under the hood muttering about belts, bolts and pulleys. "What's wrong?" she asked when they straightened up.

Christopher looked disgusted. "Nothin' that doesn't surprise me. Belt's so friggin' loose it's a miracle it didn't jump the pulley and bust."

"All we gotta do is tighten 'er up and we'll be on our way," Ramón said defensively.

Standing with hands on hips, Christopher retorted, "You got a wrench?"

"No," Ramón admitted.

Christopher rolled his eyes.

"I know!" Ramón exclaimed, snapping his fingers in a way that reminded Christopher of Quentin. Half turning, he pointed to the darkened building. "I'll bet we can find a whole boxful of wrenches in there."

"We'll just get the one we need," Christopher stated flatly, then stopped, surprised at himself. What was happening to him?

"Let's go," Ramón said, quickly deciding they could worry about the details later.

As the boys started towards the dock Harmony called after them, "I'm coming too!"

"Well c'mon, then," Christopher sighed and turned to wait.

Pulling the car door open a crack, Harmony told Ol' Henry they were going for a wrench and would be back in a minute. Ol' Henry nodded. "I'll be here, darlin'. Don't go gettin' in no trouble now."

"We won't," she assured him and pressed the door closed.

"No talkin'," Christopher warned when she caught up.

"I won't."

The three started across the lot with an adrenaline rush of excitement. Mounting the stairs, they found the steel roll-up door on the dock locked. So was the walk-in door beside it, naturally. "How're we gonna get in?" Harmony whispered.

"Shhh!" Christopher warned, "you're not supposed to talk."

"Sorry."

"Easy," Ramón answered. "Just punch a small hole in the corner of the glass above the handle and unlock the door."

Christopher looked doubtful. "I don't wanna damage the place, I just wanna borrow a wrench."

"Y'all got a better idea?" Ramón asked sharply. "Besides, one little hole in the glass ain't much damage."

"What if there's an alarm?" Harmony whispered.

"Shhh!" Christopher admonished again, "you're not supposed to talk." He turned to Ramón. "What if there's an alarm?"

"I don't think so," Ramón answered, sounding unsure nevertheless. "Who'd put an alarm on an old building like this?"

Christopher shrugged. "I don't know. I've never been a burglar before."

"Who'd even want to break into a building like this?" Ramón continued building his case.

"Depends on what's in the building," Harmony put in.

"You're not supposed to talk, Harmony," Ramón warned.

Christopher wasn't listening to either of them. He had found something interesting. Over the dock was a steel rain awning to protect workers and material. It would be easy to shinny up a support post to a second story window. "Right there," he pointed. "All we do is climb to the second story and get in at one of those windows. Probably isn't an alarm up there."

"If there's one at all," Ramón put in, "but I think you got the right idea, Chris."

"So do I," he quietly replied, stepped up to the post, shinnied up and at the eave, grabbed onto the roof and swung up on top. "C'mon, it's a cinch," he said.

Ramón was surprised at how effortlessly Harmony shinnied up and got on the roof. He followed and joined his friends at the window. "Just break out one pane, unlock the window and raise it," Ramón coached.

"I know," Christopher said and pulled out his pocketknife. Leaving the blade folded, he gripped it tightly and tapped the butt-end on the glass several times with increasing force until the pane cracked. He hit it again and the pane broke in two and shattered on the floor. Christopher reached in and released the latch. "Well, this is it," he said.

"Never mind the speeches, raise the window and let's get goin'."

Christopher pushed the window up. "C'mon, Harmony, I'll boost you through." Squatting, he shouldered her through the window. She landed flat-footed on the old wooden floor. It sent a booming echo throughout the dark, cavernous building, the broken glass crunching beneath her sneakers. "Easy!" Christopher whispered harshly, "you tryin' to wake up the whole neighborhood?"

"The more noise we make we gotta figure the less time we have," Ramón put in.

Unknown to them their time had already expired. The

moment they raised the window it had triggered a silent alarm.

Back in the car Ol' Henry was wondering where his young friends had run off to. Well, good time to take a leak. Getting out of the car, he flipped the door closed, went around to the front, faced the wall and unzipped his fly.

HARMONY'S ANGEL

19

UPTOWN ALLIGATOR ARKANSAS

Blind hate. Some children are born without eyes. Some without arms or legs. And some to parents without hearts. And they teach hate. Maybe because their parents taught them to hate. And so it goes. The heart shrivels, the soul dies.

Herman Muckbrane had frizzy, orange, Bozo the clown hair, a bulb of a nose smack in the middle of his face and bulging eyeballs that, when he talked, seemed to roll 'round and 'round behind lashed and browed slits that were his eyes. Rather than natural and spontaneous his facial expressions, and even his laugh, seemed practiced and rehearsed.

Indoctrinated into the Ku Klux Klan by his father when the boy was 14, Herman Muckbrane was groomed for his role from the beginning. Taught early that "feelings" were sissy, by the time he reached an age where he could even hope to understand, he didn't have any. His heart was hollow. His emotions stunted and dry.

Dutifully attending the local Baptist church did Herman no good for he changed the words of the Good Book to fit his calloused heart and justify his perverse hatred. Thus, he never had a chance at reality. He was blinded from within by a darkness that he himself kept alive and nurtured.

On his application for volunteer patrol officer he didn't put down that he was a member of the KKK. As a Klan member one of his duties was to aspire to positions of influence and power no matter how slight that position might be, for each was but a stepping stone. Who knew? Maybe he could be president of the

United States one day.

Herman Muckbrane thought it was beautiful. The shotgun. It was a Remington 870 pump-action with a polished walnut stock and a gold-plated front sight-bead. He had received it as a gift from his parents for his twenty-third birthday, and Herman cherished the weapon.

Though his best friend, Willy Laymhart, had never joined the Klan he did sign up for the volunteer police force with Herman. And Willy, a tall, lanky, easy-going lad whose black hair was shaved almost to the scalp in a marine cut, would have joined the Klan too, except that his parents were so violently opposed. Of course nobody told when, from time to time, Willy would sneak off to a Klan meeting. The others treated him as a recruit hopeful and constantly badgered him to sign up. But Willy, respecting his parent's wishes, never did.

He didn't care about joining anyway. He didn't hate anybody. Not the Chinese. Not the Catholics. Not the Mexicans nor the Jews. No, he didn't even hate blacks. He just wanted to see a killing. Out of curiosity. He knew there would be one eventually as they were always talking about lynching some poor soul or another. And he wanted to see the face of the condemned man as he took a bullet, or when they put the rope around his neck. Especially the face of an unjustly accused man. An innocent man. What would he look like? What would he say? Would he plead and cry? Would he struggle hopelessly? Would he pray?

When the boys joined the volunteer police force they had anticipated excitement and adventure. Of course that never materialized. They were promptly assigned such mundane chores as high school basketball games or dances, directing traffic during the fourth of July parade, or writing parking tickets and such. By the end of their first year as volunteer police they were thoroughly disillusioned. The only good thing about it was that they were allowed to carry sidearms. Guns. Just like real police. That and the fact that they could harass people they didn't like was the only thing that kept them in the program. So it goes.

Sunday evenings usually found Alligator, Arkansas about as dead and dry as a bag of buffalo chips, and Willy and Herman knew they weren't in for much excitement when they put their shotguns in the rack in the rear window and climbed into Herman's pickup, a 12-pack of beer on the seat between them. They headed up town first. Maybe there was something going on they didn't know about. If nothing else, maybe a few of the boys would want to go coon hunting.

Naturally they found Alligator deserted. After their third beer and their third pass around the town square Herman parked the truck, turned off the *Country Music Jams* they'd been listening to and switched on the police scanner. "Maybe there's some action a goin' on," he commented without much hope.

There was a quiet burst of static, the red points of light marking the channels winking in rapid sequence as the scanner searched for radio activity. It stopped searching, one red light glowing steadily. Herman held up a hand for silence as Willy started to say something. "Listen."

They only caught a portion of the message but it was enough. "Silent alarm burglary in progress at 13 north Macon."

"That's just 'round the corner a couple a blocks," Willy drawled.

"Ah know where it is," Herman said excitedly, firing up the engine and pulling away from the curb with squealing tires. "Our first real burglary, and it's ours!"

The truck screeched around the corner and roared up the street two blocks north to the warehouse. With dust flying and tires smoking, the truck exploded through the archway and skidded to a stop, its headlights brightly illuminating the faded blue Chevy nosed up to the far wall. An elderly black man was standing at the front right fender with his back to them. On the second floor the three youngsters heard the pickup screech into the courtyard and ran to the window.

Herman and Willy leapt from the truck brandishing their shotguns. With a quick pump of the action Herman rammed a slug into the chamber and shouldered the weapon. "Freeze!" he ordered, the command echoing off the dingy brick walls.

Startled, Ol' Henry nearly jumped out of his skin, but his steadily emptying bladder just wouldn't quit. Besides, whatever the trouble it could wait a few seconds until he finished.

"Put your hands up and turn around!" Herman bellowed.

Ol' Henry glanced over his shoulder. Blinded by the glare of their headlights, he couldn't see the shotguns or the young men holding them. "Gives this ol' man just a minute an' I be right withs you," he called as if he were responding to a request for a fourth player in a game of cards.

"The porch monkeys is out tonight," Willy Laymhart whispered, his heart quickening.

"An' a stupid one, too," Herman chuckled under his breath. Then, "Ah said put your hands in the air and turn around, *boy!* Three strikes an' you gonna be out!"

Ol' Henry almost made it, but in his haste caught himself in his zipper. Still, he couldn't just stick his hands in the air and turn around with his thing hanging out. And who did they think they were, anyway, talking to him like that? "Just a minute, now," he nervously called over his shoulder.

Thrice Herman had ordered the man to turn around and thrice the man had refused. What if he wheeled around firing a pistol? What if he were loading it right now? With a glance at Willy for approval, Herman closed an eye, sighted on the old man's back and pulled the trigger. The kick of the shotgun's blast resounded off the walls and echoed away into the night.

They say you don't feel it when you get shot. Ol' Henry never did. The shot caught him square in the back. Human meat mixed with quivering guts and chips of shattered bone blew out his stomach and clung to the brick wall before his very eyes as he stood there with his thing in his hand. It left a gaping hole in his midsection that a cold wind would've whistled through. As it was, he toppled forward, dead before he hit the pavement.

The three kids stared down from the window in open-mouthed disbelief. It was like a horrible nightmare turned real. Heart-wrenchingly, sickeningly *God-help-us-please-make-it-not-real,* real.

Christopher didn't even think about his next move. It came naturally like a reflex as he watched the girl's neck muscles turn to knots, her throat swelling to let loose an angry, wounded scream. In one swift motion he was behind her with a hand clamped tightly over her mouth.

But she wasn't giving in as easily as he thought. Fiercely jerking her head from side to side she tried to struggle free, her muffled cries getting dangerously louder as his hand slipped. Then she started biting. In the dark, Christopher wasn't aware he was standing just to the front and side of some floor-to-ceiling iron pipes. Desperately attempting to renew his grip on Harmony, he faked to the left, then flung her with all his might to the right, accidentally slamming her head smack into the iron pipes with a force that left them ringing.

Momentarily confused as to what had happened, Harmony slumping in his arms, Christopher struggled to hold her up but couldn't. Fear churning sick in the pit of his stomach, quietly sobbing for divine intervention, he sank to the floor cradling her in his arms.

Ramón watched for a moment, then crossed to them and tugged at Christopher's sleeve, pleading desperately, "C'mon, man! We better git, cops are comin'!" Of course neither realized the boys in the courtyard *were* cops. Or a variation there of.

As far as Ramón was concerned their only chance, if they could get out of the building at all, was to split up. After giving Christopher and Harmony as much time as possible to get away he could call the police and say his car had been stolen. Naturally Ol' Henry would be implicated and they'd all get away scot-free.

Feeling a tugging at his sleeve, dazed, Christopher looked around and finally focused on Ramón. "Huh?"

"C'mon, c'mon!" Ramón was pulling frantically now.

"Pick 'er up and let's get out of here before we get killed!"

That did it. That and Ramón's incessant tugging. Suddenly the fight, and the sensibilities that came with it, returned to him. Christopher gently and easily lifted the 98-pound girl and carried her like a small child, her head lolling on his shoulder.

They made their way carefully but quickly down a flight of stairs to the ground floor. Ramón simply unbolted the first street-side door they came to, opened it a crack and peeked out. Much to his relief the street was deserted, but several wailing sirens were approaching from somewhere—and fast. "Let's go!" Ramón whispered harshly as he threw the door open and stood aside for Christopher with his bundle of girl.

Christopher immediately sprinted for the cover of some houses across the street, ran through a backyard and leapt into a flood-control ditch that was five feet across and as many feet deep. Except for a tiny rivulet of greenish, scummy water at the bottom it was empty.

To avoid giving themselves away right off the bat Ramón carefully closed the door, then ran after his friends and leapt into the ditch too.

For several seconds they sat side by side in the slimy clay, their backs pressed against the wall, their hearts pounding as they struggled to catch their breath. As soon as he was able, Christopher shifted Harmony from his shoulder, cradled her and spoke in a low voice as he gently, almost strand by strand, removed the sweat-dampened hair from her face.

At his touch she groaned, tried to sit up, then fell limp again. Choking back tears, Christopher cursed himself and the purplish, golf ball-sized knot swelling up on her forehead.

Ramón touched his arm. "Easy, Chris. She'll be all right. Besides, it was an accident. If those boys had discovered us sure a shootin' they would've figured we'd seen them murder the old man and probably would've killed us too. You saved her life is what you done. And ours too."

Sniffling and rubbing his eyes with the heels of his hands,

Christopher whimpered, "I know."

Across the street several emergency vehicles screamed through the archway of the factory and screeched to a stop as their sirens popped off. The boys could clearly hear the hissing static and gaggle of voices from the emergency vehicle radios.

Ramón found it very unnerving still being so close to the action. While Christopher was uselessly trying to dry Harmony's sweaty face with the front of his equally damp and dirty T-shirt, Ramón got to his feet and started looking for an escape route out of the area.

He was pleased with what he saw. The chips had fallen in their favor again. The ditch ran behind the houses for as far as he could see. Farther down, the houses on the right gradually rose up on a hill until their properties no longer bordered the ditch. By the glowing points of yellow lights that marked the houses farthest away, he judged that the hill turned into a bluff. Between the base of the bluff and the ditch was at least a hundred yards of trees. Lots of trees. A forest. A blessing. "You ready?" he asked, turning to Christopher.

"Yeah." Cradling the girl, Christopher struggled to his feet, unwilling to hold her with only one arm even to help himself up for fear he might drop her and bang her head again.

They trudged up the ditch at a steady pace. A couple of times Christopher lost his footing and one boot would land in the brackish water with a splash. Then they'd freeze, ears and eyes straining, Christopher breathing hard, Ramón whispering for him to be more quiet.

The featherweight girl was beginning to feel like a ton of bricks. "You take her for awhile," Christopher rasped, wiping sweat from his brow and leaving a streak of dirt on his forehead. He was dying for a taste of cold water.

Ramón opened his mouth to reply when Harmony groaned, mumbled incoherently and made a feeble attempt at lifting her head. "C'mon, Harmony," Christopher pleaded, "speak to me, baby. Wake up. *Please*, Harmony!"

Mumbling a little louder, she seemed to be responding to Christopher's coaxing and tried lifting her head once more. But it lasted less than 30 seconds and with a sigh she slumped again.

"God, what if I really hurt her? What am I gonna do?" He looked at Ramón with pleading eyes, as if the young Mexican had all the answers. The thought that he might have seriously injured her was more than he could bear.

Touched by the depth of Christopher's anguish, Ramón held out his arms. "Here, let me carry her for awhile."

But Christopher had changed his mind. "No. I have to." Ignoring the ache in his back he hitched her up higher and they trudged on.

Following the curvature of the bluff the ditch made a long, sweeping turn to the right. As they started into the turn Ramón knew they'd be parting company soon. They were a safe distance away now. He slowed a little until Christopher was beside him. "Hey, Chris?"

"Yeah?"

"Think if y'all get to that money you could send me a little bit for my troubles? I don't mean the whole $400 we talked about. Just half, maybe."

Christopher's chuckle was low and pain-filled. "We're not ever going to get to that money now," he sighed, not really caring anymore.

"Why not?" Ramón was curious if not skeptical.

"'Cause the only one who knows where it's at is dead."

Ramón said nothing. Once around the curve with the lights of the nearest houses out of view he at last felt safe. He stopped, Christopher almost stumbling into him. "This is it," he said quietly.

"This is what?" Protectively cradling Harmony in both arms, sweating profusely, Christopher sank to his knees, then to a seat along the south wall.

Squatting beside him, Ramón answered evenly, "This is where we split up."

Christopher shifted Harmony to a different position, his muddled mind only partially perceiving Ramón's words. Shooing a mosquito with a wave of his hand, he asked, "Where're you going?"

"Listen," Ramón said with renewed urgency, "I'm goin' to get out on the highway somewhere towards the south side of town and tell the cops somebody stole my car. Naturally they'll blame the old man. Now, I ain't even gonna mention you an' Harmony, so y'all got nothin' to worry 'bout. Tomorrow or whenever, y'all just keep on followin' this here ditch and I'm sure it'll get ya to a main road. As for tonight, get on up in the woods. They go all the way to the bluff. Who knows, y'all might even find a little cave or somethin'. Heck, might even be safe to build a small, I said *small* fire just in the opening, if you found one. Got matches?"

Christopher felt his back pockets. "No."

"Here," Ramón handed him a book.

"Hey, Ramón?" Christopher asked, blinking sweat from his eyes and turning his dirt-streaked face up to look at him.

"What?" Ramón was getting anxious to leave. It was going to be hard enough explaining to the cops what took so long to report the stolen car, but he'd think of something.

"It was good knowing you," Christopher managed a weak smile and extended his hand.

Ramón grinned and grasped his hand momentarily. "Y'all take care. And don't go worryin' none 'bout my part. Cops'll never even know you were in this town."

Christopher gave a short nod. "Thanks. Sorry it turned out this way."

Ramón shook his head. "Wasn't your fault. Wasn't anyone's really." He took a moment to wipe sweat from his forehead. "Well, I better get goin' if my story's ta hold water."

Christopher nodded. "Good luck."

"You too," Ramón said sincerely, somehow feeling a certain kinship with this kid he'd only known for a few days. He turned to leave.

"Hey, Ramón?"

Christopher's voice stopped him dead in his tracks. He turned around. "What?"

"Think you could leave us a little money? Just to help us get out of here?"

Ramón hesitated, then reached for his wallet and pulled out a $20. "Think this'll do it?"

"Thanks," Christopher took the bill and stuffed it in his back pocket. "See ya."

"See ya," Ramón grinned his hog-eatin' grin and reached up to tip his hat, but it was back in the car.

20

WITCH WOMAN

Christopher remained in the ditch where Ramón left him. Being careful not to get Harmony's feet in the water he stretched her out on her back, shoulders in his lap, and cradled her head in his arms. Steadfastly trying to coax her to full consciousness he asked her questions about anything and everything. He asked about her uncle, about what she did last Christmas, and what the name of her best friend was. Nothing seemed to work until he slid his hand up under her sweatshirt and rubbed her stomach in a slow, circular motion. When she stirred he started talking louder and faster. "C'mon, Harmony. Time to get up. Wake up!"

The girl groaned. Christopher leaned over and kissed her gently, his hair falling in her face. With growing hope he watched her hand twitch, then slide up under her shirt in search of his. Christopher intercepted her, their fingers interlocking as he said in a loud voice, "Harmony, it's me! Chris!"

He smiled when her eyes fluttered open. He didn't notice how glazed and unseeing they were. She mumbled something that he couldn't make out. "Open your mouth when you talk, Harmony, I can't tell what you're saying."

She said two words.

He put his ear close to her mouth and said, "Again."

She twisted her head to the side as if to look across the ditch. He straightened up, expecting her to ask where they were. Instead, she struggled a moment trying to sit up, then slumped back into his lap, her eyes rolling around once in a manner that frightened him. Then her eyelids closed shut like two trapdoors.

"Wake up, baby! Please!" the boy cried, his voice quaking with fear, tears burning in his eyes. He squeezed her limp hand and scrunched her up closer to him. "Harmony!" he said sharply, "it's me, Chris!"

Again her eyes fluttered open as she struggled to speak, "Tired... Chris... sleep... head... aches...." She wobbled a moment, then curled up on the ground with her head in his lap and went back to sleep.

Thank God! Christopher thought to himself with relief, *at least she knows who I am!* For a solid hour he sat there gently stroking her hair and carefully listening to her every breath, which sometimes quickened and slowed. Now he would let her rest. That was all she needed he assured himself.

From time to time during that long night she would groan aloud with feverish whimperings. One time Christopher was able to make out Ol' Henry's name. Another time Quentin's. After awhile, though, his eyelids drooped, his own anguished mind finding refuge in the sweet unconsciousness of sleep.

*   *   *

When Christopher opened his eyes fear seized his heart by the throat and he sat up. Harmony was gone! Then, with a sigh of relief that left him weak he saw her sitting at the opposite side of the ditch, her back to the wall. She was staring slack-jawed into nothingness. He grimaced. In dawn's early light the purplish knot on her forehead looked worse than ever.

And he felt worse than ever. The damp mud and clay smeared on his face, clinging to his hair and ground into his clothes stank like dead fish. Yet somehow they'd made it through the night. That was something to be thankful for.

The ringing chorus of chattering birds that filled the forest and the huge, yellow sun not yet above the trees told him it was close to 6:00 a.m. For several minutes he sat watching her, afraid to speak, as if the sound of his voice might cause her eyes to close and her body to go limp again.

She never budged an inch the whole time but kept staring expressionless at some point beyond her muddied tennis shoes, the palms of her hands pressed flat to the ground on either side of her for support.

Without taking his eyes off her, Christopher eased himself to his feet. He paused, looking up and down the ditch and into the trees across the way, then slapped a mosquito on his neck.

His mouth a tight line, he crossed the ditch and knelt at Harmony's side. Her face was speckled with mud and dried sweat, her silky blonde hair a tangle of matted dirt. For the first time he realized, sick at heart, that she had more than a knot on her head. In fact her whole forehead was swollen.

He reached for her hand and was about to speak when she turned to him and croaked in a dry, cracked voice, "I had a terrible nightmare, Chris...." She stopped in mid-sentence, her voice trembling as she asked, "Where's Henry?"

Fearful of her reaction, Christopher said stonily, "it wasn't a nightmare, Harmony."

Harmony's gaze returned to the mud beyond her shoes. "I know," she said faintly, adding in a barely audible whisper, "I just thought maybe if I hoped hard enough it would change what happened—or God would."

Christopher impulsively started to reply that even God couldn't make dead men undead but shut his mouth before uttering a word. "How're you feeling?" he asked softly, gently squishing a mosquito on her shoulder with his thumb.

Heaving a sigh, she answered in a voice that revealed none of the pain she was in, "My skull feels like it's cracked in two."

Christopher averted his eyes. "I'm sorry, Harmony."

"You ought to be," she replied.

"Well I didn't do it on purpose," he said defensively.

"I know," she quietly admitted after a long pause. As bad as she felt, the worst was over. Aside from a nasty headache of bad-hangover caliber she was starting to feel pretty normal again.

"If you want maybe we could find a little cave at the base of the bluff and camp there for a day or two until you feel better. And I could hike into town and get some food and water and stuff. What'd you say? Want to?"

Harmony looked at him, half a grin creeping across her face. "Right now all I want are two aspirin and a giant glass of ice-cold water."

Christopher hesitated, anxious to please but not sure what to say next.

With two fingers Harmony gingerly explored the bump on her head. "You really nailed me."

"Sorry," Christopher began, then stopped. "I'm surprised you even remember."

"I remember everything," Harmony said, a certain coldness in her voice. "What're we going to do about those guys shooting Henry?"

Christopher sat down heavily beside her. "The police already know about it. What's there to do?"

"We saw them do it. We're witnesses. We can't just hike out of here like nothing happened. At least I can't." She rubbed her temples in an attempt to drive away the throbbing pain.

"If you want to stretch out and lay your head in my lap I'll rub your temples," Christopher offered.

"Thanks," Harmony said and took him up on the offer.

"Does that feel better?" he asked, rubbing the sides of her head and then more lightly across the top front.

She closed her eyes. "Mmmm, feels good. I feel so tired, though."

"You probably didn't sleep too good last night," Christopher suggested, not realizing she had suffered a mild concussion. For a while neither spoke. Then, half to himself he said, "If only there was some way to get that darn money maybe we could do something."

Suddenly remembering her conversation with Ol' Henry at

the gas station, Harmony asked, "Like what?"

"Like get on a bus back to Oklahoma City. Quentin and the Sandwoods would know what to do."

Harmony sat up. "All we have to do is go to the police."

"Harmony," Christopher began tediously, "use your brain. We were burglarizing that place last night. If we go to the cops we'll get busted for that. In the second place we're both runaways and you'll just get mailed back to your uncle's and I'll be sent home or to a reform school for stealing my dad's car. And in the third place it could take God only knows how long to bring the murderers to trial, if they've even been caught. (The police had already made sure that would never happen by putting a stolen—untraceable—pistol in Ol' Henry's dead hand the night before to cover their own asses.) And chances are you and me would be packed away and long gone anyway. So what good would it do? If you want to go back to Chicago just say so and we'll go, but do we have to get busted to do it? I mean, face it, Henry's dead and there's nothing we can do about it."

Harmony looked at him steadily. "And if we got the money what good would going to the Sandwood's do?"

Christopher looked disgusted. "What difference does it make? We're not going to get the money."

"Why not?"

Christopher glowered. "You know why."

"Except for one little thing."

"What?"

"Last night at the gas station Henry told me where the money is." And right there to refresh her own memory she recited Henry's instructions verbatim; "Big two-story house on the southwest corner of Lee and Maple streets."

Christopher hadn't been prepared for the recitation and cried out for her to repeat it, which she did. "Let's go there right now!" he said breathlessly as if he wanted them to leap to their feet and start at a full run for Jackson at that very moment.

"Hold on a minute. You said if we got the money we could

maybe do something. Like what?"

Christopher shrugged, his blood pressure dropping five points. "I told you. About the only thing we could do is catch a bus for Oklahoma City. Between Quentin and the Sandwoods they'd know what to do. And then we'd have the money to do it, see?"

Harmony thought for a moment. "I guess you're right. Seems like the only thing to do."

That settled, Christopher changed the subject. "Ramón gave me $20 bucks last night before he took off. How much you got left?"

"Oh, about ten bucks maybe."

"Good, that means we've got plenty of eating money at least. You want to stay here tonight or what?"

Wavering a little as she stood up, Harmony fought off dizziness. After a minute she said, "I'll be all right as long as I get some water and aspirin."

"You sure?" Christopher asked with concern, "staying here another day don't matter."

"It's okay. I just want to get out of this place altogether, Chris."

"You sure?"

"Let's go."

With a groan Christopher got to his feet, every muscle aching from the strain of carrying Harmony the previous night. "Let's keep following the ditch around."

"Okay," Harmony agreed, having no idea from which direction they had come the night before.

Divided by the trickle of scummy greenish water, they plodded through the ditch with flat-footed steps to avoid slipping on the slimy clay. As they came around the curve the ditch ran straight again for as far as they could see. Less than a quarter mile ahead was an overpass, a road from which to escape the miserable, fetid trench.

Once again houses cropped up on the left. And up ahead, on

the right, the sheer sides of the bluff gave way to slopes. Fine, expensive homes of redwood or cedar, stone or brick dotted the hillside, their huge backyards of clipped grass separated from the ditch by groves of trees which served as a buffer.

"Looks like we're on the classy side of town," Christopher commented.

"Hope they got aspirin," Harmony said, her teeth on edge from the pain.

"That's gonna be the first thing we do, Harmony," Christopher assured her.

At the overpass they kept hiking until they were directly beneath it and out of sight. Overhead they could hear the tires of countless car thudding over the ribbed asphalt as locals hurried to work on this sunshiny Monday morning. Feeling safe in the shadow of the bridge, they planned to tidy up a bit.

The attempt was hopeless. Harmony could barely get her fingers into her hair let alone through it. And when she tried to wipe the dirt from her face all she did was smear it around. The clay and mud ground into her clothes was damp. It was like trying to beat oil out of them. In exasperation she abruptly stopped slapping her jeans. Finished with her vigorous and extended efforts, she didn't look any different than before. Or smell any different, either. Stinky.

Christopher started laughing at her frustration. "If you could see your face you wouldn't be worried about your jeans!"

"Hah! Look who's talking. You think you look any better?"

"At least I wiped my face off!" Christopher declared.

Harmony's head fell back with a burst of laughter. It was so absurd, him standing there with his dirt-smeared face pointing an accusing finger at her.

"What's so funny?" Christopher demanded.

"You should wipe the dirt off your own face before laughing at someone else for having dirt on theirs."

Christopher's fingers went to his face. "You mean I still got...."

With a broad smile Harmony slowly nodded. Christopher started laughing then and swept her into his arms. After an intense kiss he held her at arm's length and asked, "You still got a headache?"

"Wish you hadn't asked that."

"Why?"

"It just came back. Guess I forgot about it laughing at you."

"Glad I'm good for something," he grinned.

"You're good for a lot. You got us out of last night, didn't you?"

"C'mon, let's go get cleaned up and get some aspirin," he said, his love for her welling up inside all over again. Then, hand in hand, he led her from the shadow of the overpass into bright sunshine. Already he could tell it was going to be a warm day. At the side of the ditch he squatted and interlocked his fingers to form a cradle with his hands. Harmony put a foot in and he easily boosted her over the side and clambered out after her.

The climb up the embankment to the road went fairly easy. Christopher sent Harmony up first so he could catch her in case she slipped. Gaining the blacktop, they immediately turned their backs on the traffic to hide their extremely muddied condition and looked out over the putrid ditch they had just escaped from. With a furtive glance over his shoulder that revealed nothing but trees and houses and more trees and houses, Christopher said conclusively, "Well at least we're on a main road."

"What should we do?"

Christopher shrugged. "Let's just fake like we're normal and walk into town."

Slipping an arm around her shoulders as they started off, Christopher turned to the problem of getting cleaned up. A self-service car wash might work but a nice sandy creek would be better. In this part of the country there must be hundreds of them, he figured. And they could take their clothes off and clean them in the creek bed and have a nice, leisurely bath to boot. But first, aspirin for Harmony. And food. As for answering any curious inquiries as to why they were covered with mud he'd simply laugh and act like a kid and say they'd gotten into a mud fight. That'd work like a charm.

Harmony thought the creek idea was good, too. And then she asked where the aspirin store was. As they crested the hill her question was answered. At the bottom was the main drag of downtown Alligator, Arkansas. And right on the corner, a drugstore. In a jovial mood now that they had a plan, they started down the hill at a fast clip, their soles slapping the pavement. Harmony was feeling better just anticipating the aspirin—and the ice-cold water that would go with it, her thirst so acute it was almost painful.

"What do you say after we get some aspirin, instead of eating in town we pick up something to take out to the creek and have us a little picnic?" Christopher asked.

"Okay," she said, adding, "I can't wait to see Quentin again."

"Me too," Christopher agreed wholeheartedly. "After we get the money," he hastened to add. The thought of having a place to go to was comfort enough, besides the fact of having someone to tell their terrible story to. The Sandwoods would know what to do for sure.

"Do you remember the Sandwood's address?" Harmony suddenly asked.

"I'll find it," Christopher answered confidently.

"How?"

"Because I remember where they live, that's how."

The corner entrance to the drugstore was recessed, forming a little concrete porch with rounded steps that curved to the sides of the peeling clapboard building. A little bell tinkled when they pushed the door open and walked in, Christopher's boots clumping heavily on the bare wooden floor. Closing the door behind them, Harmony's eye fell upon the soda fountain. "Look," she said and tugged at his sleeve.

"Let's get aspirin first."

"I'm all for that," she agreed.

A white-haired woman that didn't look a day over 99, her bones showing through her skinny arms and wrists, her pink, scaly-white face hanging on her like the skin of a dead chicken, sat stoop-shouldered on a little wooden stool behind the counter. The dour look on her face reminded Christopher it was Monday, but before he could open his mouth to speak she squawked like a parrot in a cage, "You're dirty." Stooped over, head thrust forward, the woman's upturned eyeballs peered at him suspiciously through thick eyeglasses. Then her neck extended like a turtle's as she peered over the counter and asked, "Ya got shoes on?" Emitting a satisfied grunt, her neck withdrew between her shoulder blades.

Christopher was baffled. He wasn't sure how to respond. What did she want? "We're dirty because...."

"'Cause you don't take baths," she exclaimed, fanning the air in front of her nose. "Whew! I can smell you from here!"

Christopher's frustration was beginning to mount and with it his anger. Standing a foot away from him Harmony could feel it like radiation and quickly interjected, "We'd just like some aspirin, ma'am."

Cackling like the wicked witch of the east the old buzzard sniffled, wiped her nose with a forefinger and in a voice that told Christopher they were in for a long one said, "There was a killin' in town last night."

Christopher cut her off immediately with, "Do you have aspirin, ma'am?"

"Sure we got aspirin."

Christopher waited expectantly for several seconds. Finally, unable to keep the edge from his voice he asked, "Where?"

For a moment it seemed she was refusing to answer. Then, "Don't ya wanna hear 'bout the shootin'? They kilt a nigger last night."

Christopher and Harmony both adamantly shook their heads in tight-lipped silence.

"Middle row," she at last gave in.

Christopher turned and clumped down the aisle, took a bottle of pills off the shelf, returned and set it on the counter. When she made no move to ring up the sale he dug the crumpled $20 from his pocket and tossed it on the counter. With a sigh he waited. And waited.

"Anything else?"

Christopher was about to say "No" when he remembered the soda fountain. "Yeah, could we have a couple of cokes?"

"Soda fountain's closed. Come back at 10:00."

"We just want two cokes, ma'am."

"Soda fountain's closed."

"Okay, water then."

"Soda fountain's closed."

Christopher stared at her for a moment. "Well all right then!" he concluded sharply, his anger plain. He waited expectantly, tapping his fingers on the counter, the crumpled bill between them. Finally he snapped, "What's wrong now? Don't you take American money at this store?"

The woman snatched the bill, mashed down a key and declared with a squawk, "You got a sass mouth, boy. Don't you got no Jesus learnin'? All a my young'ns do, praise the Lord!" She handed him his change, shorting him a buck for sassing her, and slammed the drawer. "Now git! And don't come back till you got the Lord right here!" she pounded her chest just above her heart. "Else you'll burn in hell!" she shouted after them as they hurried out the door.

"Whew!" Christopher exclaimed once they were on the sidewalk. "That old lady was a real witch woman."

"How do you like *her* telling *us* about Jesus!" Harmony spouted indignantly.

"Forget it. She's just a crazy old lady." Motioning with his head towards the convenience store across the street he said, "C'mon, we'll get water over there."

The store, with ten gas pumps on two islands out front was

a modern, white-painted steel building with gigantic, mirrored plateglass windows. It wasn't exactly bustling with business. One car was at the pumps fueling. The only other customer was a woman picking up a loaf of bread and a gallon of milk. The young man behind the counter, no more than 22, looked up from the "How To Use Jesus To Improve Your Financial Position" pamphlet he was reading and smiled as Christopher pulled the door open for Harmony. "Hi," he said at once.

"Hi," Christopher and Harmony both responded.

"How'd y'all get so full of mud?"

"Just had a mud fight!" Christopher declared with a grin.

The clerk's glance shifted from Christopher to Harmony and back again. "Oh. Cool." Then, "What're you kids lookin' for in here?"

Holding up the asprin bottle, Harmony replied, "We're going to buy some stuff in a minute, but I need some water to take a couple of aspirin."

"Whyn't ya'll get water at the drugstore? They got a fountain there."

Christopher stood arms at his sides, unconsciously clenching and unclenching his fists. "The fountain's closed," he said evenly, about ready to jump over the counter and beat the clerk to a pulp if he said one smart word.

The clerk noticed. "Oh. Well, sure. The sink's in the back right through that door there," he pointed.

With a "thanks" Christopher and Harmony headed for the door at the rear. In the back room they found the janitor's sink in a little alcove off to the left. Harmony turned the cold water on, let it run for a second, took a long, satisfying drink, popped two aspirin, a third for luck, and drank again. And again. And didn't stop until Christopher pulled her off with declarations that it was his turn, the gushing ice-cold water suddenly driving him with an overpowering urge to slake his dry, hot thirst. Gulping thirstily, now he knew what heaven was; ice-cold water. He drank until bloated. Then, after they both had seconds he turned the water on warm and stepped back. "Go ahead."

She looked at him suspiciously.

"Ladies first," he added with a gesture towards the sink.

Harmony grinned. "You better watch it, you're getting soft," she said and stepped up to the sink. Cautiously testing the water first, she soaked her head under the warm stream for three solid minutes, rubbing and scratching at her scalp until it was tender, yet she could still feel grit. At last she pulled her head out and flung her hair back with a jerk of her head that unwittingly splashed Christopher from head to toe. After washing her face and arms with the available bar soap she stepped back from the basin. "Your turn."

Just as Christopher stuck his head under the stream the door opened. "What's takin' so long?" the clerk demanded.

"We're almost done," Harmony assured him.

"Well hurry up, Ah cain't have y'all in here the whole day. If my boss came back right now Ah'd be in trouble."

Harmony nodded. "Okay. We'll be right out."

"Well hurry up," the clerk said again before pulling his head out and closing the door.

It only took Christopher a minute. After seeing Harmony's hair and feeling his own he knew it was hopeless. He quickly washed up, shut off the water, flung off the excess dripping from his head and then he and Harmony were back in the brightly-lit store. The clerk looked up from his pamphlet briefly as they closed the door behind them, then resumed reading.

"What should we get?" Christopher asked, scanning the shelves immediately before them.

"Shampoo," Harmony said without hesitation.

Putting an arm around her shoulders and pulling her close, he said with a grin, "I was thinking the same thing."

"We usually are," she smiled back.

"Headache gone?"

"It seems like the aspirin's working," she admitted.

Examining her forehead with narrowed eyes, he said,

"Looks like the swelling's gone down some, too."

Harmony reached up and felt her forehead with the palm of her hand. "Feels big as ever to me."

"No, it's gone down some," he assured her, "I'd bet my life on it." Harmony could sense the great relief he felt. It came out of him like a sigh. He gingerly touched the knot, which had changed from purple to blue, and asked, "Does that hurt?"

At the slight pressure a remnant of the previous pain returned in a small wave that quickly receded. "Yes!" she cried, afraid the terrible headache would return. "Don't touch it!"

"Sorry."

"That's okay. It's just that when you touched it the headache started coming back like before."

"I won't touch it again," he promised.

"All right. What should we get to eat?"

Christopher shrugged. "What do you want?"

"Pizza!"

Christopher laughed. There she was, acting like a little kid again. "We can't make pizza. You think they got an oven down by the creek?"

"What then?"

"How about sardines in mustard sauce with crackers?"

"Yuck!"

"You never had them before," Christopher protested.

"They're little fishes in a can!" Harmony shot back.

Christopher sighed. "Okay. How about if we get some lunch meat, bread, chips, and something to drink?"

Harmony thought a moment. "I sort'a feel like something cooked."

"Well we don't have any way of cooking anything."

"All right," she grudgingly gave in, "let's go pick out some lunch meat."

At the counter they laid down a packet of Ham, cheese, a loaf of bread, four sodas, chips and a tube of green shampoo. While the clerk counted out his change Christopher asked about the nearest creek. "Just follow the highway here southeast out of town," he explained. "There's a real nice one just about ten, 15 miles down the road."

"Thanks," Christopher said, grabbed the groceries and headed out the door with Harmony in tow.

HARMONY'S ANGEL

21

TIMBUKTU

"Should we just walk it or hitchhike?" Harmony asked as they reached the edge of the highway.

"Both," Christopher answered. "Being strangers in town I think we'd draw the cops pretty quick just standing here."

They followed the highway southeast out of town, hoofing it along the gravel shoulder, Christopher carefully scrutinizing the horizon for cops each time he stuck his thumb out. They weren't having much luck. Car after car whooshed by, the occupants rubber-necking the two teenagers as if they were creatures from outer space or something. They trudged on.

"I wonder why nobody's stopping?" Harmony asked.

"It's Monday."

"Oh."

In silence they walked on. After awhile Christopher grew tired of turning and peering at each passing car and decided to give up hitching for a bit. Maybe it would change their luck.

Whether that decision had anything to do with changing their luck he entirely forgot to wonder, but after he quit hitch-hiking, the very next car to go by, a battered faded-to-pastel-yellow Ford careened onto the shoulder and skidded to a stop in a shower of gravel and swirling dust. They heard the transmission clunk as the car was reversed, and took to the weeds at the edge of the shoulder as it weaved backwards and stopped beside them. The driver, a pint-sized kid of 16, a stoned smile on his face, said through the open window, "Y'all look like you could use a ride."

"Sure could."

"Where y'all goin'?"

"To a creek up the road. Know where I'm talking about?"

The kid nodded. "Sure do. That's not too far. What's goin' on up at the crick?"

"Nothin', I hope," Christopher shrugged. "Me and my girl-friend just want to clean up and rest a bit."

"Y'all had a rough one last night, huh?" the kid grinned.

"Yeah, rough."

"Well get on in here and I'll take y'all up to the crick."

"Thanks." Tossing the groceries in back, Christopher got in front. Sitting half on his lap, Harmony squeezed in too.

Turning up the radio, the kid glanced in his rearview mirror and pulled onto the blacktop. As the car laboriously accelerated up the highway heavy metal rock music erupted from twin speakers on the rear deck. "Buffcat," the kid introduced himself once they were under way.

"What!?" Christopher shouted above the music.

"I said…."

"Turn down the music!" Harmony yelled, "I can't hear!"

Buffcat lowered the volume. "Sorry. I always kick up the jams when I'm cruisin'." Then, "I said my name's Buffcat."

Christopher and Harmony both looked at him. "Buffcat?"

The kid nodded.

"How'd you get a name like that?"

"The black guys at work gave me the name," he explained, "'cause I kin wax an' buff a car faster than anybody they ever seen. That's what I do, work at the Ford dealer gettin' the new cars ready for the customer 'fore he comes and picks it up." After a moment he added, "What's y'all's names?"

"I'm Chris, and this is Harmony."

"Well howdy to ya. Say, y'all get high?" he asked with a wink and a telltale grin.

Christopher and Harmony exchanged glances. "I do, sometimes," Christopher answered.

"I don't," Harmony replied.

Noticing her swollen forehead and the blue knot on it Buffcat remarked, "Looks like you got a heck of a bruise there."

Harmony motioned towards Christopher and was about to say something when Christopher nudged her. Thinking fast she answered, "Uh, fell down last night."

Buffcat let out a long, low whistle. "Must'a been a mean fall." Then, peering closely at her, "You don't get high?"

She shook her head. "Never have and don't want to start now," she answered flatly.

His glance shifted to Christopher. "It's good smoke, man, wanna get high?"

Christopher looked doubtful, then shook his head. "Nah, I got some serious thinkin' to do today. Better pass."

"It's really good smoke, man. I just had a bowl a little while ago," he insisted.

Again Christopher shook his head. "Nah, better not. Might need my brain today."

"I know what you mean there, man. I started smokin' when I was 12. Been smokin' ever since." He laughed, "Sometimes I plum forget how to tie my own shoes!" He laughed again before asking, "Smoke much?"

Christopher shook his head. "Nah, not much."

"'Member when they used to say it wasn't addicting? Hah! What bull. I tried to quit once. Made it a whole three days. Who would've thought…" His voice trailed off. Then, "Say, you wanna buy a little for tonight, man? It's really good smoke."

"We don't have much money," Christopher answered.

"Sell you an eighth. Twenty bucks. I need the money for gas. It's really good, too," he said earnestly.

Christopher laughed, mimicking Buffcat with, "What kind of smoke is it, man? Really good smoke?" At that Harmony started laughing too.

Mistaking Christopher's miming for interest in the deal, Buffcat's speech quickened with urgency. "Yeah. *Really* good.

The best. Want an eighth?"

"I told you, we don't have the money." Christopher was beginning to get irritated with the insistent little stonehead.

Buffcat looked at him like he didn't believe a word of it. "Y'all don't have $20 bucks between ya?"

"That's all we got. Period."

"Oh well," he sighed, head tilted back as he peered over the top of the steering wheel, "just thought I'd ask." They rode in silence then until Buffcat pointed out the creek and steered onto the shoulder. "See y'all later." With a grin he added, "Ya sure y'all don't want...."

"No," Christopher cut him off. "But thanks for the ride, Buffcat."

"Sure. Have a good trip, wherever y'all is goin'."

Harmony got out and stood aside for Christopher. "We will," he said and grabbed the groceries. Flipping the door closed, he stood back and gave Buffcat a wave. "See ya."

With an upward gesture of his head Buffcat said, "See ya," put the car in gear, pulled out onto the highway and was gone.

The sun, bright in a crisp blue sky dotted with puffy white clouds, was already warm on their backs. It reminded Harmony of summers past, her favorite season since it was when she got to be outside most and could get away from the little tyrants she had lived with for the past three years.

But it was the smell of warm asphalt mingled with the exhaust of the occasional car whizzing by that spurred the memories, not the clean country air. Nor the trees on the hillside across the highway, their branches lush with green leaves. Nor the purple, red, and yellow wild flowers that grew along the pasture fence. No. It wasn't the scent of fresh-mown hay nor the air abuzz with honey bees, either, but the smell of burnt fuel and hot asphalt, the smells of the city, that brought her home—within her mind, at least. But home was an ugly thought she pushed away with a prayer to God thanking him for such a lovely day.

Christopher went to the bridge abutment and looked down at the clear water sparkling in the sunshine, the sandy bottom ribbed with little ridges. Already he could feel its soft grittiness against his bare feet, the water swirling around his legs. Coming up quietly from behind, Harmony rested her head against his shoulder.

Without moving he whispered, "Isn't it beautiful?"

"Mmmm, must've been made by God."

Afraid of getting her started on one of her "God" discourses Christopher ignored the remark. Harmony knew what his silence meant but she just sighed and kissed his cheek, confident that, given time, somehow she'd be able to make him see the truth of God and the way of faith.

"That way looks best," Christopher said, turning his gaze to the hills 100 yards north of the highway where the creek wound lazily from a deep ravine that cut like a gash through the lush, green, rolling landscape.

"Let's go," she said happily, "I can hardly wait."

After pausing for traffic they ran across the highway. Holding hands, they slipped and slid down a gravelly footpath in the shadow of the bridge. At the bottom the trail followed the creek bank. To the right it ran under the bridge towards the lowlands and grazing cattle. To the left it followed the creek into the hills. Without hesitation they turned left.

At the mouth of the ravine they stopped and gazed in awe. Unable to see around the next bend, the sheer rocky white, sunbleached walls on every side formed a grotto. Sunshine streaming in on bars of light played on the broken, stratified stone, highlighting the rust-red, orange-amber and golden-yellow watermarks that streaked its sides. "Oh Chris, it's beautiful!" Harmony whispered.

Christopher nodded. "Never seen anything like it myself. C'mon, let's keep following the trail."

Christopher held her hand as they made their way single-file along the narrow path, the right edge of which made a sharp, three-foot drop to the water. On the left a wall of rock went straight up. They followed the trail around a 50-ton boulder the size of a small house and entered another somewhat more shadowy "room" where the path ended in a little flat area of cool, hard-packed dirt. Christopher spotted a fishhook embedded in the mud, and on a flat rock that protruded from the wall about four feet up someone had left a beer can. "Let's sit down," he said and let go of Harmony's hand. Setting the groceries aside, he took a seat on the edge, feet dangling over the water. "C'mon."

She sat down next to him. "Is this where we're gonna do it?"

Christopher shook his head. "Nah. It's not sunny here and it's too close to the road. A lot of people come down here."

"But it looks like this is the end of the trail."

"So? We'll just take our shoes off and walk up the creek. It'll feel good." He paused. "By the way, how's your head doing? The aspirin work?"

"Yeah. My head's still a little tender but the ache's gone."

Drawing her close with an arm about the shoulders, he kissed her lightly. "Good."

She grinned. "The feeling's mutual. You ready to eat? I'm starved."

"Me too, but why don't we find a nice, sunny spot where we'll be alone? We won't have to go far." When she hesitated he urged, "C'mon, it'll be fun."

"All right."

Christopher immediately began untying his boots. Harmony undid her shoes as well. Then they rolled up their jeans. Taking his boots and the bag of groceries in one hand, Christopher slid over the edge and splashed into the knee-deep water.

"Your pants got wet!" Harmony called.

"So? We're gonna wash our clothes anyway."

Laughing, she asked, "Then why did we roll up our jeans?"

"'Cause it'll make it easier to walk through the water."

"Is it cold?"

"Not at all. Feels great, come on in." He positioned himself directly beneath her and held up a hand. "C'mon."

Taking her sneakers in hand, Harmony slid off the edge into Christopher's arms but came down a little quicker than expected. He fell backwards, splashing into the water on his butt. Harmony landed on her knees astride his lap, he holding his boots and the groceries high. It had happened so quickly both were stunned to silence, then they burst out laughing, Harmony chiding, "You clumsy ox! You got rubber legs or what?"

Grinning, Christopher threw his arms around her and they kissed. When they parted his grin changed to a mischievous smile as he softly said, "Just stay right where you are."

With a smile like sunshine Harmony asked, "Why?"

Ignoring the question, he kissed her again. "You like that?" he asked, his breathing quickening.

Perceiving the subtle changes in him, Harmony smiled to herself and decided to tease him a little bit—like until he couldn't stand it anymore.

Searching her face, Christopher asked, "What're you thinking about?"

Harmony shrugged. "You. How much I love you."

"A lot?"

"Yeah. A lot. How much do you love me?"

She squirmed in his lap a little which made Christopher pause before answering, "A lot. A real lot."

She kissed him once, then more passionately. To her surprise she discovered that although she may have been teasing him *she* was getting aroused. "Let's go," she suddenly stood up and held out her hand.

He sat there for a moment looking up at her, his head still spinning, then took her hand and let her pull him to his feet. "At least the water's warm, huh?"

She nodded. "It's perfect."

He held out an elbow. "To Oz?"

She giggled and slipped an arm through. "To Oz." And unconcerned about getting wet they sloshed up the middle of the meandering creek in search of the perfect spot, the sunlight sparkling off the water, the sand squishy-soft and gritty against their bare feet.

Feeling more comfortable and confident than ever with the love they shared they forgot about time and place. They could have been anywhere. The moon. Timbuktu. It wouldn't have mattered.

Once, they caught a deer off guard. The startled animal looked up and froze. Then, in an instant it was gone, bounding up the creek with graceful, splashing leaps.

"I never saw a deer before!" Harmony exclaimed, "except at the zoo."

"Me neither."

The sides of the ravine were no longer sheer, rocky walls but steeply sloping, heavily forested hillsides lush with greenery. Around the next bend was a sharp jag in the creek with a deep pool. A sand deposit on the far side formed a sunny miniature beach.

At last Christopher had found the perfect spot. They stopped in the middle of the creek and silently surveyed the area. Not wanting to disturb the wildlife that croaked and chirruped, chittered and sang all around them, Harmony almost whispered, "It's beautiful, Chris."

"It sure is," he agreed just as quietly. "We can have lunch over there on that sandbar if you want."

"I want," she affirmed, immediately wading for the beach via the long route around the deep pool. With the faintest hint of a smile Christopher followed.

By now they were both wet clear up to their necks, but the air was still and it was getting downright hot as the sun headed for the noonday sky. After setting his boots and the groceries down Christopher peeled off his shirt. It felt good to get the sopping thing off. Then he plopped down in the sand next to Harmony, who was already on her knees getting out the ham, cheese and bread.

"I feel like I haven't eaten in a year," she said, glancing over her shoulder and taking in his bare-chested body.

"Me too. You going to make one for both of us?"

"Of course." She already had one made and handed it to him, then quickly put one together for herself.

"Thanks, Harmony," Christopher said, consuming half the sandwich in one bite. He popped the rest in and with a full mouth asked for another.

"Make it yourself or wait till I'm done," she answered, sinking her teeth into her own sandwich. "And hand me a pop."

Christopher grabbed a soda, popped the top and handed it to her, then reached for the flattened-out bag the meat, cheese, and bread were on and pulled it to him. As hungry as she was she couldn't manage to down a sandwich in two bites and Christopher was too hungry to wait.

He did eat his second sandwich slower, though. This time in four bites, finishing up just as Harmony began fixing her second. And they both kept right on eating until there was nothing left but a few slices of bread. They wisely held the other two cans of soda in reserve and lay back on the warm sand, their full stomachs and the sunshine making them sleepy.

For over an hour they lay there side by side drifting in and out of sleep. Once, when something in her sleep scared her Harmony jerked upright, but when she saw Christopher beside her she lay back down again, closer this time so that they touched, and fell back asleep.

Christopher had a dream that neither roused him nor caused him fear. Rather, he smiled. An old man with a head and shoulders like a mountain told him to marry his daughter. A daughter of the kingdom. At first Christopher was apprehensive, but when the girl came down from the mountain, her beautiful golden hair flowing out from behind and eyes as blue as the sky, it was love at first sight. And then he realized the girl was Harmony.

His dream burst like a bubble and he sat up rubbing his eyes. "Were you ever in the mountains, Harmony?" he mumbled without even looking to see if she were awake.

Lying very still with her eyes closed she answered, "That's a strange question. What made you ask that?"

"I don't know," he replied with a shrug, the dream lost somewhere in the recesses of his mind.

Harmony heaved a sigh and sat up. "How long you think we been out?" she asked.

Christopher leaned back on one elbow, his head almost in her lap. "I don't know," he said through a yawn. "Maybe an hour or so." And then he did rest his head in her lap.

"We've still got to bathe and wash our clothes," she said.

"I know."

"And wash our hair."

"You especially. It's so beautiful when it's clean."

"Thanks, Chris."

"I mean it."

"You really like it, huh?" Harmony was beginning to wake up now.

"I love it." So was Christopher, though he remained where he was with his head in her lap.

She leaned over and kissed his forehead. "I love you," she whispered.

"I love you, too." And after a pause, "Hey, Harmony?"

"What?" she asked, ever wary of his "Hey Harmony" questions.

"You wanna go skinny dipping?"

"No," she answered immediately.

"Why not? It'll be easier to wash our clothes that way. And it's no big deal. I won't stare at you." He sat up then and lightly massaged the back of her neck. "C'mon, it'll be fun."

Harmony shrugged, eyes downcast as she grudgingly

agreed. "Okay, I guess."

After a moment he stood up. "Well, let's do it then."

She glanced up at him once, blushing, then looked away.

"What's wrong, Harmony?"

She was still looking down at her lap when she stammered, "It's just that I, uh… my…."

"What?" Christopher's voice rose with impatience.

"It's my… my…."

"Jeeze! Will ya spit it out!"

"My breasts are too small!" she blurted.

At the spontaneous burst of laughter from Christopher she looked up with a frown. "Silly girl," he said, dropping to his knees and engulfing her in a bear hug that pulled her over on top of him. He kissed her face a couple of times until she was smiling. "What makes you think your breasts are too small?"

"They just are," she pouted.

"Not from what I've seen."

"You've never seen them."

"I felt them that time, remember? They seemed perfectly normal to me."

"They did?" she asked, her blue eyes intent upon him.

"Sure," he answered, still holding her close. "You wanna look like Tits Lonnegan or what?"

"No, but…."

"Well shut up, then. I love you. That's all that counts."

"It is?"

"Isn't it?"

She grinned and kissed him. When they parted he asked, "Can I wash your hair?"

Harmony smiled and touched his cheek affectionately. "If I can wash yours."

"It's a deal. You ready?"

"Yeah. But one thing," she cautioned.

"What?"

"You have to turn around while I get undressed and get in

the water."

Christopher laughed. "Ya nut. Why do all that? We'll just undress in the water, wash our clothes first and hang 'em on a tree branch to dry."

"*You* can hang them on a tree branch to dry. *I'm* staying in the water."

Getting up, Christopher readily agreed. "Okay." He held his hand out and pulled her to her feet. As they waded into the water he whooped, "This is gonna be fun!"

Harmony stopped abruptly and yanked him around so they were nose to nose. "Uh, just how much fun did you have in mind?"

Looking at her with a straight face he held up a hand and with a forefinger and thumb measured about an inch of air. "This much," he answered evenly.

They both laughed, Christopher throwing an arm around her waist and pulling her close as they started into the water. To their delight the deepest part of the pool came up to their necks.

"It feels pretty good, don't it?" Harmony asked.

"It'll feel a lot better after we get out of these clothes," Christopher replied. "And a whole lot easier to move around."

Struggling out of her jeans and pulling her sopping wet sweatshirt off over her head, Harmony said, "Let's do it, then."

Christopher was out of his jeans and shorts and at her side in an instant, his eyes roving over every inch of her youthful, taut body through the crystal-clear water.

Harmony grinned. "Feels kind of funny being naked, don't it?" she said and slipped her panties off.

"Yeah," Christopher chuckled. Straight-up hard, he wrapped his legs around her middle and treaded water.

"EEEK!" she squealed. "Get that thing away from me!"

Christopher burst out laughing. "It don't bite," he said as he released her and stood up.

"I told you, not till we're married."

Rolling his eyes, Christopher exclaimed, "You're not gonna

get pregnant from it touching your side, knot-head!" Then, in light of the knot on her forehead they both burst out laughing.

"Just don't get so close," she said as their laughter subsided, "because then one thing leads to another, know what I mean?"

Christopher nodded, saying disgustedly, "Yeah. I know what you mean." He stuck his head underwater for a second and came up flinging his hair back. "But so what if you got pregnant," he continued, "you think I'd dump you 'cause of that? Heck no. I'd marry you."

Harmony heaved a sigh and shook her head. "You just don't get it, do you?"

Christopher shrugged. "What's there to get? What more can I do then marry you if you get pregnant?"

"Don't you see?" Harmony asked emphatically, "Doing it *is* getting married. That's what marriage is, uniting as one. When you do it you've done it. You're married in the eyes of God. Doing it is the real ceremony of marriage, sort of. That's what Henry said."

"So what does Henry know?" Christopher shot back, adding, "and if that's the ceremony of marriage then what about the church and the preacher and all of that?"

"That's just the outside stuff, Chris. But it's what's inside that counts. Like, look at it this way; what if a girl married a guy for his money but didn't love him. And they did everything proper. Went to church, had a license from the state and all. And then there was another couple that united in love but never went to church and never got a state license. Which marriage is God gonna look more favorable on? Huh?" She paused before continuing in a quieter tone, "You see, that's why we can't do it. Because to you it's only a marriage if a baby comes but to me it becomes a marriage when we do it. And then we have to stay together forever."

"I don't see what God has to do with it!" Christopher snapped.

"What does God have to do with it? The spiritual part of a

person comes from God, dummy. To deny God is like... like denying your right arm or something."

"But why do you *need* a God, Harmony?"

Harmony shook her head in exasperation. "It's not a *need*. It just is. It's reality. You have to accept that."

"Well I wish there was some proof is all."

With a sigh of defeat Harmony said, "Let's wash our clothes." There would be no proof. Of that she was sure. As she understood it God was not into proving himself to people, he was into people proving themselves to *him*.

Turning to the task at hand, Harmony scoured her jeans against themselves with a little shampoo. Christopher did the same but scooped up sand from the bottom and sprinkled it between the folds. Harmony saw what he was doing and tried it herself. "It works great!" she said, congratulating him on his brilliance.

"I can't help it I'm smart," he replied with a grin.

Harmony did the same with her sweatshirt, but on Christopher's T-shirt nothing seemed to work. It came out a streaked yellowish. He squeezed the water out and held it up. "It looks awful," Harmony said, wrinkling her nose.

Christopher shrugged. "It's the best I can do. That's it."

"So? We'll get you a new shirt soon as we get the money."

"Wish I hadn't lost my jacket."

"Left it in Ramón's car, huh?"

"Yeah." After the socks and underwear were done Christopher turned to Harmony, his clothes in his arms. "Here, give me your stuff and I'll hang it on a tree to dry."

"Thanks," she said, piling her stuff on top of his.

"Now don't look," he said over his shoulder as he started for the bank.

"I won't," she promised, never taking her eyes off him as he emerged from the water. Already slightly aroused from simply being naked, watching Christopher's lean, well-muscled body quickened her breathing and caused her face to flush. He glanced over his shoulder once and though she quickly turned her head, he'd caught her looking. Good. Maybe she'd like what she saw.

Whistling a little tune, he picked out a big old tree with a lot of thick, low branches and took his sweet time about hanging the stuff up. Socks, panties, bra, sweatshirt, jeans. Then his own clothes. "Don't forget to bring the shampoo!" Harmony called. When he boldly turned around she dived beneath the surface, swam to the deepest part of the pool and popped up in a spray of water, her back to him.

Christopher grabbed the shampoo, splashed into the water and dived in. Bursting to the surface, he held the green tube aloft and called, "Over here, Harmony!"

"You ready?"

"Yeah."

She turned and swam over to him. Her feet found bottom and she stood up in water that came to her navel, her petite breasts shyly shielded from the light of day with both arms.

Christopher laughed, "You afraid they'll get sunburned?"

"No," Harmony answered defensively.

"Well don't be so worried about it. I'm not someone you just met, ya know. I'm your boyfriend. You don't have to hide from me. I mean, they're part of you. That's how God made you, what's the big deal?"

Harmony's face reddened. "I know all that. And if we were married it probably wouldn't bother me at all. But, well, I guess I'm just the modest type."

Christopher smiled and patted the side of her head affectionately. "Okay. Let's go where we can sit down. That way you can dip your head back in the water to rinse. We're going to have to wash it at least twice so we might as well be comfortable."

She nodded. "Okay." They waded in until they could sit with their shoulders just above water. Harmony sat down first.

Releasing a stilted, shaky sigh, Christopher slid down

behind her up close like they were on a toboggan. Hard as a rock
and about ready to boil over, for a moment it was almost too
much, but after a few seconds he relaxed and regained his composure. "Ready?" he asked.

"Yeah." She tilted her head back, guided by his hands, and
thoroughly soaked her hair. Afterwards he applied shampoo and
worked it in with his fingers.

"Feel good?" he asked, massaging her scalp.

"Sure does."

He paused. "Hey Harmony?"

"What?" she asked, ever suspicious of his "Hey Harmony"
questions.

"I know what you were saying before about marriage and
everything and I think you're right." He was working the area
behind her ears and down her neck.

"So?"

"So I'm ready to marry you. I mean, why not? I love you.
If we're going to spend the rest of our lives together why wait?
What's too young? I don't know and I don't care. The only thing
I know is I want you."

"Hah!" Harmony's laugh was a short burst of contempt.
"And what about after we get the money and you go home to
buy your dad a new car or whatever? Huh? What then? Marriage isn't just for a day, Chris, it's forever. And that's the only
kind of marriage I want."

He was massaging the top and sides again and being careful to wipe the lather from her forehead so it wouldn't get in her
eyes. "That's what I'm talking about, Harmony, forever. And
when we get home I'll just tell my folks you're my wife. If they
don't like it, well, they can lump it or leave it. Here, tilt your
head back and let's rinse." She leaned back into the water while
he gently rinsed her hair. "It's coming out beautiful," he remarked, "but we'd better do it once more." She sat up and he applied more shampoo from the green plastic tube floating in the
water at his side.

After a moment's reflection Harmony said with quiet seriousness, "I love you too, Chris, and I'd love to marry you, but are you sure you want to get married now? We're only 16. What about the rest of our lives? We'll never have anything decent because you won't be able to get a good job. Are you sure you're ready to spend the rest of your life working in gas stations or factories? Because that might be all we got coming. But if you go home and go back to school who knows all the different things you could learn to do?"

Christopher was silent for a moment as he continued massaging the rich lather through her hair. "Yeah. And if I do that what happens to you?"

Harmony shrugged, no longer shielding her breasts, her shyness forgotten as the novelty of being naked wore off. "I don't know," she sighed. "I'd hate to go back to my uncle's." Then on sudden thought, "Maybe the Sandwoods would let me stay with them."

"See?" Christopher implored, "If I just go home I'll never see you again. And you don't have anywhere else to go anyway. The Sandwoods won't let you stay forever and you know it. Besides, could you really leave me that easily? Just wave goodbye and that's it? Well maybe you could leave me so easily, but baby, I couldn't just walk away from you, married or not. I mean, all we got in this world is each other, Harmony, and if I have to work in a warehouse or whatever then I will, 'cause what's important is being with you. That's all I care about. Now, tomorrow, next week, next year, next century, next world. It'll be you and me and whatever happens happens. As long as we stick together we'll figure something out. We always do don't we?"

At that Harmony raised herself off the bottom with her hands, turned herself about and settled down astride his thighs. Looking intently into his blue eyes she asked, "Do you really mean that, Chris? I mean, serious *serious* mean it?"

Christopher kissed her face. "What else can I say,

Harmony? I want you to be my wife. Now and forever. Will you marry me?"

Grinning, she nodded. "Yeah, I think I could handle that."

"Good." He took her in his arms then, kissing her deeply as he rolled her over and shoved off the bottom with his feet. They glided to the bank where her head came to rest in the sand, her arms wrapped warmly about him. "Uh, wait a minute," she said, interrupting a kiss, "are you sure you're not just doing this? I mean, you'll call me your wife from now until we die?"

Christopher looked hurt. "I told you, Harmony...."

"But I don't have a ring."

"My words are a ring," he answered evenly, looking deep into her shining blue eyes. And one day he'd discover how easy it is to keep one's word when it's spoken with conviction from the heart.

For a moment Harmony just looked at him, then broke into a sunny smile. "That's a good one, Chris."

He grinned and kissed her again. "I know."

"Wait a minute," she said as he started to get amorous again. "What?"

"What if I get pregnant? Then what?"

Christopher's brow furrowed momentarily before he answered matter-of-factly, "If it's a boy, I get to name him. If it's a girl, you do. Okay?"

Grinning from ear to ear, Harmony nodded. "You're too much, Chris." Then, swelling with a love for him that she had never quite experienced before, she threw a leg over his back and rolled *him* over, their laughter echoing up the ravine as they wrestled about. And there in the sunshine of an Arkansas creek under a blue sky in the springtime of their youth, he took her forever.

22

HALOS AND HALF-WITS

In the fading light of late afternoon, their souls taller than their shadows, Christopher and Harmony sat on the sand and drank their last sodas. Just to be on the safe side Harmony popped a couple more aspirin, though her headache seemed to be gone. The food, the nap, and the swim in the cool water had helped enormously. To Christopher's great relief her forehead had gone down entirely. All that remained was the knot, its color fading from blue to an angry red.

By the time they made their way out of the ravine the sun was below the amber, gold-tinged clouds floating in a crimson sky. Underwear excepted, they had avoided dressing until they made the trailhead. Thus their clothes were fresh, clean and comfortably dry after airing out in the sun all day. And though a little wild-looking from being uncombed, their hair was soft and clean, their faces fresh-scrubbed and rosy-cheeked.

Hand in hand they followed the path through the tall grass beside the creek and up along the bridge to the highway, their voices soft like the gently flowing water as they discussed their uncertain future. Crossing the blacktop, its surface still warm from the hot day, they stood on the shoulder beside the eastbound lane. Having slept on and off for hours throughout the afternoon they were both feeling feisty and ready for just about anything. "If we hitchhike through the night we should get to Jackson sometime in the morning or early afternoon," Christopher said.

"Maybe we'll get a ride straight through," Harmony replied

hopefully as a big Cadillac blew by.

"That," Christopher intimated, "would be a miracle. I just hope we get a ride before dark," he added, "otherwise it's gonna be rough."

"We will," Harmony said confidently. "I have this feeling. And whenever I get these hunches I'm usually right." She shrugged, "Don't ask me why."

"Okay," he grinned, "I won't. But I sure hope you're right."

She was. The very next car, a sleek, new, metallic-green turbo-charged Pontiac glided to a stop beside them, its driver not bothering to pull off the pavement. With the whir of tiny gears the passenger side window electrically slid down and a 30-ish looking, clean-shaven man with short, neatly combed cinnamon-colored hair leaned across the seat and asked with a southern drawl, "Y'all are goin' where, now?"

"Jackson, Mississippi," Christopher answered promptly, wondering why the man had stopped in the middle of the highway. It was dangerous. Even as he stood talking a car rushed up from behind. Slowing abruptly, the driver angrily leaned on his horn as he swerved dangerously close around the Pontiac and was gone, blasting up the highway with impatience.

"It must've been God's will," the man muttered.

"What's that?" Christopher moved closer to the window, one hand on the roof of the car.

"Uh, nothing. Y'all say you're goin' to Jackson, Mississippi, huh?"

"Yep." It was Harmony. "And we sure could use a ride."

"Well, seein' as you must have the same God as me, otherwise *he* wouldn't have guided me here, hop in."

At the word "God" Christopher hesitated. "Uh, what'd you say?"

The man sighed and with a smile shook his head. "Ah said that's just where Ah'm goin'. Jackson. Come on."

When Christopher didn't move Harmony elbowed him. What was he waiting for, an engraved invitation? Uneasy about accepting the ride, at Harmony's nudge Christopher said, "Thanks, mister," opened the door and stood aside for Harmony. He followed her into the back and soundly shut the door. To Christopher's utter amazement instead of putting the car in gear and taking off the man twisted around in his seat, stuck his hand out and introduced himself. Ignoring the man's hand and the name that went with it, Christopher snapped, "Aren't you worried about getting rear-ended?"

Laughing lightly, the man tossed his head back. As if dealing with the absurdly simple question of a small child, he answered easily, "Of course not," turned around, put the car in gear and slowly accelerated, the car seemingly gathering speed inch by inch. "Gets better gas mileage that way," he mistakenly believed and gave Christopher a wink. Christopher just stared at the man in disbelief. The guy was dumber than a box of rocks.

"Why?" Harmony inquired.

"Huh?" the man looked at her in the rearview mirror, lost, reality having momentarily escaped him.

"I was asking why you weren't afraid of getting rear-ended back there."

"Oh." A smile crept across his face. "Well, that's easy. Haven't y'all ever heard of Jesus Christ before?"

Putting his head in his hands, Christopher groaned.

Harmony answered simply, "Yes."

"Hmmm, Ah thought y'all might have."

"So?"

"So then ya know the answer. You know," he insisted. "When ya take Jesus into your heart, put on the armor of righteousness, like the Bible says, y'all are safe. God will protect you."

Harmony looked perplexed. "What does that have to do with stopping in the middle of the highway?"

The man sighed and shook his head again. "Don't you see?" he asked emphatically. "Once you put on the armor of Jesus Christ he'll protect you. Nothing can hurt you 'cause you're in the hands of God. It's like... it's like, well, we all know it's silly when you see a drawin' of a saint or somethin' with a halo over his head. Naturally that don't happen, but that gives y'all the idea. When you take Jesus into your heart you're sort of covered by an invisible force-field. And when Ah get in my car, the car being an extension of me, it, that is the force-field, or armor of God, even surrounds my whole car, protectin' it and all the people in it. See?" Before she could respond he went on in the same breath, a broad smile on his face, "Ya'll might say since Jesus is all around this car right now, you might say y'all are ridin' with God!"

Oh brother, Harmony thought to herself.

Christopher lifted his head from his hands and cleared his throat. "Could I ask a question?"

Reminding Harmony of Peter Perish, the man assured him, "Y'all can ask any questions you like. God has an answer for everything."

"Okay, God," Christopher began with heavy sarcasm but was cut off by the man's heated protests.

"No, no, no," he laughed, "Ah'm not claimin' to *be* God! Ah just said *he's* in me and therefore *he's* in the car!"

"All around the car," Harmony corrected.

"Not *God,* silly," the man was getting agitated. "His shield is all around the car."

"Anyway," Christopher continued insistently, "why didn't you just pull onto the shoulder out of traffic?"

"Because Ah didn't want the gravel dingin' up my brand new car. Ah always say you can judge a man by what condition his car's in. Ah mean what true Christian would let his car fall into disrepair? And if a person don't have sense enough to look after his car chances are that person is cavortin' with the devil. Y'all see?"

In the silence that followed his ranting Harmony quietly asked one more question. "But if a car had crashed into you while you were sitting on the highway someone might have been injured or killed. What about the people in the other car?"

The man shrugged. "That's not my problem. If they hain't found the Lord yet what can Ah do? Ah spend half my life tryin' to tell people 'bout Jesus, but what good does it do? They usually end up makin' fun of me. But Ah ain't worried about it. They'll get what they got comin' sure as God's in heaven. And if God wills that they crash into my car and die, well, that just makes me an instrument of God's judgment, see? So that's why y'all got to take Jesus into your heart before it's too late. Course," he chuckled, "y'all are safe with me, but you got to think about a few hours from now when y'all will be leavin' this sanctuary of holiness. And that reminds me," he breathlessly went on, "Ah didn't get y'all's names."

Startled to notice it was dark out and the headlights were on, Christopher was suddenly left with the eery feeling that an hour had just slipped by in a matter of minutes. Where had he been? "Chris," he answered the man's question. "And this is my wife, Harmony."

At that Harmony beamed, threw her arms around him and kissed him repeatedly. It was the first time he had introduced her as his wife and her heart leapt with joy for it had come out of his own mouth without any prompting from her. When he'd said he would take her as his wife he'd meant it. It was in his heart. And now she knew it.

"What was that for?" Christopher looked at her.

"Nothing," she said lightly and settled back with a contented smile. It was the best feeling in the world. Her man was true.

"Hey now, none of that," their host cautioned. "This is a Christian car."

Christopher frowned. "Christians don't kiss their wives?"

The man took a deep breath and said sternly, "First of all, y'all shouldn't tell lies. Second of all, Ah don't like bein' taken for a fool. Y'all are just a couple of kids. Ain't no way you're married and y'all know it and Ah know it and if y'all are gonna start gettin' perverted in my car Ah'll have to kick ya out." He paused a moment. "How old are y'all, anyway?"

"Sixteen," they answered in unison.

"See? Y'all can't get married at 16 without your parent's permission. It's against the law. And Ah'm sure y'all's parents wouldn't give you permission at your age. Y'all are hardly in high school for heaven's sake!"

"We're married," Harmony said firmly.

The man shook his head. He'd pin their ears back real quick. "Okay," he began, speaking rapidly, "what church did y'all get married in? Huh? Huh?"

"An Arkansas creek," Christopher replied.

"The Arkansas Creek Church?" the man frowned. "Never heard of that one before. What was the minister's name?"

"God," Harmony quipped, stifling a snicker.

"Oh, that's very funny!" the man caustically retorted, "but if y'all is married, what state did you get your license in?"

"A state of excitement!" Christopher blurted as he and Harmony burst out laughing.

Their host didn't join in. He frowned. "Y'all think you're real funny, don't ya? Y'all shouldn't go around tellin' people you're married. It's lyin'. And to say that God presided is blasphemous!"

"We're not lying," Harmony stubbornly insisted, remembering what Ol' Henry had told her, "marriage is an affair of the heart and has nothing to do with churches or government licenses. Those things are just the outside part, but what counts is what's on the inside."

The man let out a long, low whistle. "Boy, are y'all in trouble. Do you really believe you're married just 'cause y'all make up your minds to be? 'Cause if you do y'all are goin' to hell."

Neither Christopher nor Harmony replied. The man was obviously a nut. Christopher wanted to ask why the shield of God surrounding his car would protect him in a collision yet couldn't keep the gravel off when he drove onto the shoulder, but he kept his mouth shut. Tight.

For 20 minutes they rode in silence. In a one-horse town called Clawfoot they stopped for gas. As the driver wheeled the car up to the pumps he said with forced casualness, "By the way, Ah never did tell y'all my name." He switched off the ignition and twisted around in his seat. "It's Don Newitt," he said, extending his hand to Christopher. "What's your name again?"

Christopher briefly touched the man's hand. "Christopher. And this is my wife...."

"Don't say 'wife,'" Don Newitt interjected.

Christopher, his hand on the door handle, looked at the man hard, his mind churning with a dozen different replies, but Harmony pressed her hand into his and drew off the heat of his anger. His temperature down by ten degrees he shrugged. "Okay, I won't." Then, a wide grin splitting his face, he snickered, "This is my *spouse*," pushed the door open and climbed out, his hand never leaving Harmony's as he drew her along.

Don Newitt quickly opened his own door, got out and called over the roof, "Well what's her name?"

Halfway to the station house, Christopher stopped and turned. "Who?"

"Your, uh, girlfriend."

Grinning, Christopher called back, "I don't have a girlfriend," then he and Harmony turned and continued to the station house.

Don Newitt banged a fist off the roof of the car. Somehow he was going to save these two kids. They were too young and innocent to spend the rest of their lives living in sin. It was up to him to save their souls for Jesus. Heaving a sigh, he went to the rear of the car, fit the nozzle and started the gas pump. For a moment he stood staring at the tumbling digits, squeezing his chin with a thumb and forefinger as he pondered his next move. When he turned and headed for the station house he still didn't know what that would be.

Pulling the plateglass door open, Don Newitt stopped and

frowned, one foot holding the heavy door ajar. Rock music filled the whole building. And it was loud. Louder than he would have liked to hear gospel music. And the attendant behind the counter, a pimply-faced kid with bright blue eyes and long, auburn hair, a black bandanna tied about his head, was definitely a drug user. Of that he had no doubt. One look at him, one earful of the Satanic rock music, and it was obvious. The place was a bastion of evil.

He glanced around with careful, discerning eyes. The owner was probably a sinner too. Otherwise, why hire a devil-worshipping, drug-popping kid? He smiled. Now was his chance to strike a blow for good. He pushed the door open and went in.

"Hi," the kid behind the counter said.

Don stared him down with narrowed, angry eyes.

The kid became uncomfortable under Don's hard gaze. Scratching his head, he looked up at the ceiling.

His discomfort didn't go unnoticed by Don. It was Don Newitt's glowing goodness, the power of Jesus, that was making the lad uncomfortable. Don knew it. His mere presence set the forces of Satan quaking in their boots. He knew it was true because he'd seen many evil people react just the same way towards him. With the shield of God he was invincible and other people unconsciously sensed it and got scared.

"Pump stopped," the kid's voice snapped Don back to reality.

"How much?"

"Go shut the pump off and hang it up first."

Don took the boy's request to be an affront to his honesty. With a snarl he crossed the linoleum-tiled floor in three brisk strides.

Snatching up a heavy wrench, the kid bounded off his stool and backed into a shelf-lined wall behind the counter. At that moment Christopher stepped out of the rest room. For several moments he stood there trying to make sense of what was happening. Don was leaning across the counter as if beckoning to a small, caged animal, his prey backed to the wall, wrench held high. "Hey!" the kid shouted at Christopher in a panicky voice, "is this guy crazy or what?"

With a laugh Christopher started towards the counter. "No, man, he's a Christian." It was as much Christopher's manner, long hair, and the way he was dressed as what he'd said that relieved the kid. He lowered the wrench but remained safely out of reach of the grasping hands of Don Newitt. Christopher turned to Don, hands on hips, and asked bluntly, "What *are* you doing?"

Don looked at him and straightened up. "Tryin' to scare the demons out of him."

"The dickens is more like it," the kid intoned.

"If y'all would shut off that music it would help," Don went on like some kind of therapist. "It's the music. Y'all are enslaved to Satan by the music." Christopher and the kid were grinning at each other by then, sharing a common bond that required no definition. The door to the ladies room squeaked open and Harmony stepped out. "You don't want to shut off the music, then?" Don was asking.

"No," the kid answered firmly. "What's wrong with rock music? Never mind," he quickly added, "I don't want to know."

"You don't want to know," Don griped in a whiny voice, moving his head back and forth like it was loose on its hinges. "Fine. Burn in hell for all Ah care!" He turned abruptly and went outside to shut off the pump.

"He a friend of yours?" the kid asked with a grin as soon as Don was gone.

"Don't know him from Adam," Christopher chuckled, "he just picked us up hitchhiking."

"Sure is a weird one."

"Yeah. All them Christians are alike."

The kid laughed. "No they ain't. I'm a Christian."

"So am I," Harmony offered.

Christopher looked at the kid with surprise. *"You?"*

The kid nodded.

"You don't look weird to me."

"That's 'cause I ain't."

"You don't have to be weird to be a Christian," Harmony put in.

"I don't know," Christopher was doubtful. "Did ya ever see those guys on TV?"

"There's con artists in every business," the kid replied easily. "Don't mean God's a chump."

"You're starting to sound like my wife," Christopher intoned.

"You two are married?"

"Yep. Got married this afternoon." Christopher slipped an arm around Harmony's waist and pulled her close.

"Uh-huh," the kid smiled knowingly. "Pretty lady."

Just then the door flew open and Don stepped heavily to the counter. "How much?" When the kid turned to read the meter Don Newitt quickly glanced at Christopher and Harmony, but they were looking at each other. In the wink of an eye he swept up three candy bars from the display case on the counter and slipped them into his sport coat pocket. Another blow to the Satanic forces, and by God he had delivered it! Another star for his heavenly crown.

"That'll be $25 bucks even," the kid said, swiveling on his stool.

"Why don't you make it $24 and Ah'll donate the twenty-fifth to the church for y'all?"

"Twenty-five bucks, mister," the kid stated flatly.

"Come on," Don Newitt urged, "Ah'm just tryin' to help. Could go easier for you come judgment day."

"Yeah, and if you pay what you owe it could go easier for you," the kid replied evenly.

Don laughed. "Hah! Ah don't have to worry about it goin' easy for me, buster, Ah got Jesus Christ right here in my heart and that's all Ah got to worry about."

"Yeah. Sure. Twenty-five bucks."

Don grudgingly slapped a $20 and a five on the counter. "Ah was only thinking of y'all—and the church."

The kid snatched the money, put it in the cash drawer and slammed it shut. "You can take your church and shove it up your bloomers, pal."

Don Newitt's eyes blazed. "You'll go to hell for such arrogance to God!"

"You ain't God."

"No, but Ah got him in my heart," Don retorted defiantly, "and that's just as good!" Looking around, he suddenly noticed Christopher and Harmony were gone. "Gotta go, see ya," he said, suddenly heading for the door.

"How far to Jackson?" Christopher asked as Don wheeled out of the gas station and pulled onto the highway.

"About five hours," Don replied with a glance in the rearview mirror. "Y'all aren't touchin', are you?"

"No, Don," Came the dry reply from the back.

There was a passing silence, then, "Say, y'all wouldn't want to contribute for gas would you?"

"Don't have any money, Don," Christopher lied, deciding to hold onto his seven bucks and Harmony's ten.

"Y'all wouldn't lie to me, would you?" Don asked suspiciously.

"No."

"It's a sin not to have any money, did y'all know that?"

"No, I didn't. What part of the Bible is that in?"

"All parts."

"Oh. Say, Don?"

"What?"

"You workin'?"

"Of course Ah'm workin'!" he retorted indignantly. "It's a sin not to work."

"Even if you don't have a job?"

"It's a sin not to have a job."

"Oh. What kind of work do you do?"

"Ah'm an electrical engineer. Ah work for the phone company. When somethin' breaks down in the system Ah go there and fix it. Course on the side Ah witness for the Lord and whatnot, which this job is perfect for because Ah meet a lot of people which gives me a lot of opportunity to serve the Lord. But Ah'd like to get out of the business and into somethin' where Ah kin serve the Lord full-time, know what Ah mean?"

"Yeah. Hey, Don?"

"What?"

"Would the Lord mind if we nap for awhile?"

"Oh no, not at all, go ahead."

"Thanks."

"Don't mention it."

Rushing down the smooth blacktop like a whisper, the new Pontiac was quiet, the two in back settling down for a leisurely ride as they comfortably tucked arms behind heads and stretched out, Christopher's feet on Harmony's side of the car and vice-versa despite the illicit touching where their legs crossed.

Both drifted in and out of sleep for hours, sometimes awakening to the fiery oratory of a preacher on the radio begging for money, other times to gospel music, and still other times to Don Newitt having a very one-sided conversation with God.

Of course neither of the backseat snoozers said a word. They'd heard enough for one day, though they were pleased to have had the unbelievable good fortune of getting a ride so quickly. And right to their destination no less. Harmony had silently thanked God for the blessing. Christopher had silently thanked lady luck. God he was still a little leery of, and the likes of Don Newitt's brand of Christianity didn't help much.

Once, they were both awakened by Don Newitt's soft inquiry. "Chris? Chris? Y'all awake?" He still hadn't gotten Harmony's name yet.

"Yeah," Christopher admitted with a heavy sigh.

"Good, 'cause there's somethin' Ah want y'all to do for me before we part company, and we haven't much farther to go."

"What?" Christopher wearily asked. He could guess what was coming next.

"Ah want y'all to make a commitment right now. A commitment to take Jesus into y'all's heart tonight. Because if you do it'll change your whole life. Y'all will never get sick again. Y'all will never have to worry about hunger or poverty or anything because the Lord looks after his own."

"I'm not worried about hunger or poverty now," Christopher interjected.

"Yes you are!" Don sharply retorted. "You don't know where your next meal is comin' from!"

"No, I don't," Christopher agreed, "and I'm not worried about it, either."

"Well y'all should be," Don replied in clipped tones, "'cause if ya don't have the Lord in your heart y'all's in serious trouble. Y'all's in the grip of Satan."

"I'm not in the grip of anyone, pal."

"How about you, little girl?" he looked at Harmony in the rearview mirror. "Would you like to accept Christ into your heart tonight?"

"What makes you so sure I don't already have Christ in my heart?" she asked flatly.

Don Newitt was silent for a moment before answering, "Because Ah can tell. Ah can feel the resistance every time Ah mention the Lord's name. One thing Ah have to tell y'all, once a body accepts Christ it gives you the power to discern the truth, which means you can tell when people are lyin' and when they're not. Right now, to be honest, Ah can tell you're lyin'. But Ah only want to ask one question; Why? Why resist the Lord? If you only ask he'll free up your sick heart and make you whole again. Doesn't it make sense? Ah mean, what have y'all got to lose?"

"First of all, mister, my heart is not sick!" Harmony snapped resentfully, "and second of all, I am *not* lying!"

"You're the one that's sick, mister!" Christopher blurted. "The only God you follow is some fantasy inside your warped little brain, 'cause you sure as heck aren't following the God of the Bible. That much I know."

Holding the wheel in a white-knuckled grip a red-faced Don Newitt began spluttering in rage, almost choking on words he couldn't quite get out. Christopher and Harmony weren't paying any attention to him anyway. They were looking at each other. "How on earth would you know *that?*" she asked incredulously, "you've never so much as cracked the cover of a Bible and you know it."

Christopher shrugged. "I know. But if what's in that book is the garbage he's talking the book never would have survived for over 2,000 years." Grinning, Harmony rolled onto her knees on the seat, flung her arms around him and kissed him.

"Hey!" Don Newitt barked, glaring in the mirror, "Ah told y'all, this ain't a whoremobile. Y'all start whoremongerin' one more time and you are gonna find yourselves standin' out on the highway right quick."

Harmony complied immediately. They were so close it would be stupid to get kicked out now. Yet she couldn't help insisting, "We're married. How can a newly married couple whoremonger?"

"Yeah," Don said curtly with short, quick nods, "well y'all are gonna find out, little lady, come the judgment day. And then Ah'm gonna be a laughin' at y'all when you get booted out of the Kingdom of God. Then y'all will know the wrath and judgment of God. Then Ah'll be able to say 'Ah told you so,' but y'all won't even want to look at me because you'll be so ashamed. And Ah'll just laugh...."

The tirade went on for more than 40 minutes, Don Newitt totally unaware that the targets of his relentless ranting had long since fallen asleep. It wasn't until the lights of Jackson were twinkling all around him in the thick, early morning darkness that he noticed. There was no response to his declaration of arrival. He said it again, louder. "Hey, we're there!" He was watching them in the rearview mirror as they stirred. "How long y'all been sleepin'?" he asked, hurt that they had fallen asleep in the middle of his sermon.

"We're in Jackson?" Harmony asked, suddenly wide awake.

"Yep."

"What time is it?" Christopher asked through an extended yawn.

"Four-thirty. Boy, ya missed one of the best sermons Ah ever gave. If y'all had listened you'd probably have Jesus in your hearts this very minute. Y'all want to confess the name of the Lord right now?"

Ignoring Don and turning to Harmony, Christopher asked, "What corner is that house on?"

"Lee and Maple streets."

"Will you take us there, Don?"

"Why not? Ah'll be a Good Samaritan. God remembers little things like that." At 4:30 a.m. theirs was about the only car on the mammoth multi-lane freeway that circumvented downtown Jackson. "What's at the corner of Lee and Maple streets?" Don asked, changing lanes and exiting the freeway.

"Just a place we want to go to," Christopher replied.

"Ah got a pretty good idea where that's at. It's over towards the rough side of town."

Christopher nodded. "Cool."

They coasted down the off-ramp and stopped. For a moment Don seemed indecisive. Then, heaving a sigh, he turned left and slowly accelerated up the deserted street. At a traffic light he slowed the car and peered up at the street sign. "This is it," he said and turned right. "Hey, look at all the flashing lights." But they had already seen the myriad of flashing red lights and were leaning over the front seat for a better look.

Within a block of the main event they encountered a squad

car closing off the street, a bored officer leaning against the hood. Don stopped the car at the intersection. At the far end of the block were several firefighting vehicles. Christopher had been watching for Lee street since they'd pulled onto Maple and knew they hadn't passed it yet. But they had to be close. "Thanks for the ride, Don," Christopher said and suddenly popped open his door. "C'mon, Harmony." But as one foot hit the pavement Don stopped him.

"Where y'all goin'?"

"We're there, Don. We appreciate the ride, but it's time for us to go."

"Ah got lots of time. Mind if Ah hang around with y'all for awhile?"

Christopher looked at him like he was nuts. "No way. We've got business to take care of. But thanks for the ride. Let's go, Harmony."

Without another word Christopher got out of the car, flipped the door closed, walked around the back and intercepted Harmony getting out on the other side. Taking her by the hand, he headed straight for the police officer lounging against the hood of the squad car blocking the street.

HARMONY'S ANGEL

23

WHERE ANGELS GO

"Could you tell me where Lee street is, sir?" Christopher asked.

Straightening up, the officer cleared his throat and replied, "Just yonder a block, but y'all ain't walkin' up this here street."

"No sir," Christopher replied with a half-shake of his head.

"Then move on, boy, don't need anymore folks hangin' around here than necessary."

Christopher started to turn away, Harmony in hand, when he stopped. "Uh, sir, could you tell me which corner here is the southwest corner?"

The officer responded with a nod towards the corner to his immediate right. "Now git."

"Yes, sir." Christopher and Harmony started down the cross street. One block south and they'd cut west again.

The neighborhood of tall, pillared and once stately homes dating from the twenties and thirties rose up ghostly out of the mists of the gray dawn. In the gathering light, peeling, chalky-white paint, sagging front porches, missing rails and broken concrete steps became apparent.

Over the years the original owners had died off or fled the encroachment of the city and one by one the fine homes deteriorated, many converted to low-income apartments. Yet somehow the neighborhood had acquired a quaintness of its own, its venerable oak and black walnut trees towering over narrow, bumpy streets, offering cool shade from the scorching southern sun that would soon be rising, while a myriad of nesting warblers filled the cool air with the chatter of their early morning song.

Christopher and Harmony strolled halfway down the block, dodged behind some houses and walked between the backyards towards Lee street. "I just know it's the house with the money that's on fire," Christopher fretted in a whisper.

"I wouldn't worry about it," Harmony said confidently. "God wouldn't do that to us. He knows we need the money to get back to Oklahoma City and catch up with the guys who murdered Henry."

Disgusted right up to his earlobes with God-talk, Christopher sighed tiredly. "Harmony, God doesn't have anything to do with it. You think he goes around putting out house fires?"

"No, silly, I just don't think he'd let it happen is all."

"Yeah, right," Christopher retorted sarcastically. "God's going to protect an abandoned house with some hidden money but he'll let a houseful of little kids burn up. Is that what you're telling me?"

Harmony blushed. "No."

"Well it sure sounds like it to me," he frowned, marshalling his thoughts. "Ya see, that's why this God business don't make sense to me. For this very reason here. Every day before your very eyes you see on TV where innocent children are burned alive in house fires. And then a Christian like you, or whatever it is you are, comes along and believes in light of everything that God would save an old house full of moldy money. If that don't seem crazy to you then you got a screw loose."

"You don't understand, Chris," Harmony began lamely.

"Shhhh!" he silenced her, "we're too close now." They hid behind the garage of the last house at the end of the row. "Cross your fingers," Christopher whispered.

"I'm not superstitious," Harmony whispered back, silently praying on the matter and fully confident that God would not let "their" house full of money, moldy or otherwise, burn up.

"Let's go," Christopher said and slid along the wall to the

corner of the sagging garage. When he felt her beside him he poked his head around the corner and gazed across the street.

It was definitely the old house on the southwest corner that was surrounded by fire trucks. Yellow rubber-coated, helmeted firemen stood with legs apart guiding high-pressure streams of water on the bright orange flames shooting from various windows to lick greedily at the peeling sides of the ancient residence. Christopher cursed under his breath. A stunned Harmony stood there staring in open-mouthed disbelief.

"Probably wasn't any darn money in that old house anyway," Christopher declared. "That old man was just connin' us because he didn't wanna be left alone."

As if in defense of Ol' Henry the sidewall of the big, two-story house suddenly buckled just below the eave, spewing a score of dollar bills into the air where they fluttered like so many leaves, carried up and away into the sky by the intense heat and smoke. And throughout the morning more than a few kids would be thinking it was *their* lucky day.

Christopher sank to his haunches, eyes never leaving the house. He couldn't believe it. There *had* been money in the house. He almost wished he hadn't found out.

Harmony sank down beside him. Sitting on her heels, she started laughing. "See? He was telling the truth all along."

"Yeah. Lot of good that does us," Christopher sulked. "God, if we'd just gotten here," he shrugged his shoulders, "maybe two hours earlier...."

"Ah," Harmony waved him off, "it wouldn't have mattered. We'd have waited till daylight to go in and lost out anyway."

They sat down then, their backs to the garage wall, legs stretched out, ankles crossed, not caring at this point if they got spotted by the cops. With a start Christopher suddenly realized it was daylight. Somewhere to the east a fiery orange sun was peeking over the horizon. A new day. "What happened to your God?" he asked contemptuously. "I thought he wasn't going to let the house burn up?"

Harmony looked at him coldly, hurt at his needling. "Okay. I was wrong, so drop it."

"Let's go," he said, suddenly getting to his feet.

In a flash Harmony was beside him. "Where?"

He shrugged and headed for Lee street. They took the sidewalk. Who would bother them? They were leaving the scene, not trying to get to it. When they walked past the officer blocking the other end of the street he never even batted an eye. Couple of kids.

For a long time they walked at a steady pace, neither speaking. There wasn't much to talk about. Where they were going hadn't been discussed. Christopher still had seven dollars in his pocket. Harmony, a ten. Once, when they passed a dingy downtown diner advertising two eggs and toast for two bucks Christopher asked Harmony if she'd like to eat but she declined. Neither was very hungry, their minds still churning with the thought that the money *had* been there. And it really would have been theirs. If only they hadn't spent the afternoon in that darn creek. If only they'd gotten to the house just one single lousy rotten day sooner.

In her mind Harmony was asking where her God was. Why would he let that house catch on fire and not the one next to it? Or why couldn't it catch on fire after they were on their way back to Oklahoma City? Or why couldn't they have arrived a day sooner? And then to have actually seen the money! It sure seemed cruel to her. It made her wonder. Maybe Chris was right. Maybe this God thing she carried around in her head was just a fantasy....

They didn't know how long they'd been walking. They didn't know how they got where they were or what time it was. All they knew was that it was oppressively hot and humid and they were walking through a freight yard, the smell of diesel fuel and creosote heavy in the air, the vibration and rumble of locomotive engines rising and falling, air mechanisms hissing.

Christopher asked a passing railroad worker which way

north was. The worker said they were headed that way. Christopher called out his thanks and he and Harmony kept hiking, but the exchange sparked something in Harmony. "Where're we going?" she asked.

"Back," Christopher snapped without slowing his pace.

"Back where?"

"Back to Chicago," Christopher answered sourly, "where do you think?"

Harmony stopped with hands on hips and shouted at the top of her lungs, "Hey!"

Christopher stopped and turned around. "What?"

"I thought we were going back to Oklahoma to get Quentin and the Sandwoods to help us?"

"Harmony, the man is dead," Christopher's voice rose angrily. "He's dead and there's nothing we can do about it, so just forget it!"

Harmony's determined stance wilted. She looked down at her shoes, a single tear rolling down her cheek. "So that's it, then?" she said in a choked voice, "there's no money so you're just going home and leaving me here?"

"Harmony," Christopher sighed, "what's with you? I'm not *leaving* you. I can't leave you. Don't you remember? We're married. Now stop acting stupid and c'mon."

Brushing a tear away, she looked up and smiled. "You meant it. You really meant it."

"Of course I meant it, now c'mon." He draped an arm around her shoulders as she joined him.

Almost as soon as they started walking she stopped. "Wait."

"What now?" He dropped his arm from her shoulders.

"We're actually going to your house now?"

Christopher nodded. "Yeah."

"Aren't you worried about what your dad's gonna say about the car?"

Christopher shrugged. "I'm gonna have to face the music someday. Might as well be now. Besides, I've had enough of roaming around aimlessly. I need to work or something."

"And you actually think your parents are just gonna let me move right in, huh?"

Again Christopher shrugged. "I don't know. They might not even let *me* move back in. But it doesn't really matter. If worse comes to worse we can get jobs and stay at a homeless shelter until we save enough to get our own place."

Harmony threw her arms around him and kissed him. "Thanks, Chris," she said softly, their noses touching. "I think I know what it is to be loved now."

Christopher smiled and quietly said, "You better know what it is to be loved now 'cause I love you and love you and love you. And I'm gonna tell everyone you're my wife and you will be 'cause you are." Surprising himself, almost haltingly, he added, "And evenings after dinner you can teach me about God and the Bible, 'cause I think you're right, Harmony. About God, I mean. I may not understand, but I'm willing to try. At least I'm hoping you're right. I'm hoping there's a God, and when you stop to think about it, isn't hope the beginning of faith?" He stopped suddenly and looked at her oddly. "Did that sound funny?"

"It sounded beautiful, Chris," she replied quietly, pulling his head down to hers and kissing him again. "And you're right. Hoping that God is real *is* the beginning of faith."

*   *   *

It was a relatively small freight yard and before they knew it the yard was behind them and they were crunching through gravel between twin sets of gleaming steel rails, a tangle of thick jungle-like foliage walling them in on both sides for as far as they could see.

Noontime came and went and Christopher's relentless pace was beginning to cause Harmony to wonder if he wasn't planning on walking all the way to Chicago. They hadn't exchanged a word since leaving the freight yard over an hour ago. Now

Harmony wished she had taken him up on the breakfast offer. She was starting to get lightheaded from hunger. And what she wouldn't give for an ice-cold Coke, the scorching noonday sun seemingly squeezing every drop of water out of her. She was about to grab his sleeve and say something when he abruptly stopped. "Look!" he pointed.

Harmony stood on tiptoe to peer over the wall of foliage. "What?"

"Can't you see that Kentucky Fried Chicken sign over there?"

"Oh. Yeah. You want to go there?" It was over a quarter mile away, its red-and-white-striped roof rising above suburbia like a beacon.

"Yeah," Christopher said and plunged down the embankment intent on crashing right through the wall of growth. He didn't get very far. He didn't even get entirely off the embankment before he was entangled up to his waist in the sinewy tentacles of a thicket of thorny plants, his own forward momentum dragging him to his knees where he came nose to nose with a huge banana spider. He slowly backed away, then turned and frantically ripped himself free and scrambled back up the embankment. "There's a giant black-and-yellow spider down there!" he breathlessly exclaimed, the sweat dripping from his face. "There's no way we're gonna get through that jungle, either."

But Harmony wasn't looking at him. Her eyes were focused past him and up the tracks.

Half turning, he followed her gaze. "Where'd he come from?" Christopher asked curiously.

"I don't know. I just now noticed him."

"He's probably just traveling like we are, only going the other way."

"Looks like he's carrying something," Harmony said, squinting.

"So what?"

Harmony shrugged. "So nothing. I'm dying for a cold drink and something to eat, though."

"We will. Promise. Next road-crossing we'll find something, even if it's just a drink off a garden hose, okay?"

She grinned. "Okay."

Christopher took her hand and they continued on their way, always keeping half an eye on the approaching stranger. As he got closer Harmony remarked, "Look, he's carrying that suitcase up under his arm just like Henry used to do."

"So what? How're you supposed to carry a suitcase with a broken handle?"

When they were no more than 40 feet apart Harmony pointed out that the man sort of walked like Henry, but even as she spoke her eyes were on his gray-tinged head and her heart started beating faster.

Christopher noticed. "Look," he warned, "you ought'a get your mind off'a that old man. It's starting to effect your brain. Henry's dead and gone so you might as well forget him." But Harmony stopped dead in her tracks and yanked her hand free. Christopher stopped and turned towards her with a frown. "Harmony?"

No more than 15 feet away, the stranger stopped too. Christopher's eyes traveled to the elderly black man. With a terrible start he realized it was Henry Rathbone! But Henry was dead. He'd seen it with his own two eyes. And then the man dropped his suitcase and opened his arms wide.

"Henry!" Harmony cried and took off like a shot, pounding the gravel as she covered the 15 feet in a record-breaking dash and leapt into his arms.

Christopher stood there dumbfounded. Who was going crazy, him or Harmony? It had to be one of them. Taking long strides, Christopher approached the two, his narrowed eyes taking in every inch of the old black man with ever growing wonder. By God it *was* Henry Rathbone! Christopher stopped and looked the man up and down, mouth agape, his whole body trembling. "But Henry you're dead!" Christopher blurted, "I saw you get blown all over the wall! You're dead!"

Ol' Henry's head fell back as he roared with laughter. Grinning from ear to ear and shaking his head, he said, "How many times an' ways you gots to be told, young'n? They ain't no death. Least ways for those of us that gots favor with God."

"B-But I saw you get blown to pieces with my own two eyes! I saw it!"

Again the old man laughed. "Now look, I done told ya all about this an' that, the rest you just gonna hast to learn from Harmony here 'cause I gots to be on my way. But 'fore I go I just want to remind you 'bout the most important thing in this here life."

Utterly baffled, Christopher reiterated, "The most important thing in life?"

"Tell us, Henry, tell us!" Harmony shouted excitedly, almost jumping up and down like a little kid wanting ice cream.

Christopher just stood there numbly. It was like waking up in the middle of a dream and finding out it was real. All at once he turned on the old man and poked a finger at his chest. "Never mind the most important thing in this here life. I want to know how you got out of the hospital and down here so fast, that's what I want to know." And with that he reached out and ripped the old man's shirt open. What he saw made his eyes bug out. "There's no scars!"

Ol' Henry looked him square in the eye and answered evenly, "Ain't no scars an' I ain't been to no hospital." He paused. "Now you wants to know where I been?"

Christopher nodded numbly.

"I been wheelin' across the sky, gettin' myself higher than the metal birds that breathes fire, an' waitin' for the word from God's kid, that what I been doin'. An' that be all you gots to do. Just find some thread a the truth an' follow it to the one that be holdin' all the strings."

The old man's voice was like a distant echo in the recesses

of Christopher's mind. *God's kid!?*

"An' don't be goin' to no man that gots a book in his grub-by hands an' askin' him to show you the way, 'cause there be only one book you need, an' it be best if'n ya read that with yourself an' yo' friends. Otherwise, just raise them ol' baby blues a yours to the sky an' ask the kid, 'cause the truth, well, sometimes it's just one a those things you gots to find out for yourself."

"What truth are you talking about?" Christopher almost shouted, feeling lightheaded, his own voice sounding somehow odd and disembodied to him.

Grabbing Christopher by the shoulders, Harmony spun him around so they were nose to nose. "God, Chris, God's the truth! Doesn't that make sense? Like Henry told you a long time ago, God's the source of all..." Stopping in mid-sentence, Harmony angrily frowned. "Well ask him yourself," she said, "he's only told you about a dozen times!" But when they turned around, the old man was gone.

Other Dreams, the 2nd novel by Nicholas Ifkovits....

Randy "Taterhead" Ellis is a simple soul who raises chickens and sells the eggs in a small rural Illinois town. When three adolescents, attempting to cover up a minor misdeed of their own, have him arrested on false charges of sexual impropriety the community is outraged. Released by the courts, his business destroyed, property vandalized, the young man attempts to rebuild his shattered life, but the incensed community, feeling the legal system was too lenient in its resolution of the case, begins plotting its revenge....

A spine-tingling suspense drama, *Other Dreams* is about an American community gone mad with the dark, sadistic ravings of the witch-hunter. It's about the victims. It could be about you. Remember, sometimes dreams really do come true. Watch out which ones come true for you.

About The Author

A graduate of Northern Illinois University with a B.A. in media communications, Nicholas Ifkovits is a member of the Golden Key National Honor Society in recognition of scholastic achievement, and recipient of the Outstanding Scholar Award presented by the Department of Communication Studies, NIU.

For his volunteer work with incarcerated youth he received a Certificate of Recognition from the Illinois Youth Center, Illinois Department of Corrections, and has seen his share of the darker side of the human psyche, including close encounters with serial killers Larry Eyler and John Wayne Gacy.

Other Dreams (ISBN 0-9651700-3-9) is available at bookstores everywhere.

> **Strange Change,** the 4th novel by Nicholas Ifkovits....

What were *your* adolescent fantasies? And what if you could have acted upon them? **Strange Change** will return you to that twilight time between childhood and adulthood in an erotic fantasy about a young man who discovers he has the incredible power to become anything he can imagine himself to be. And what he wants to be is in the girl's locker room at school at shower time.

As a result, Trenton Letreque experiences in a most bizarre and twisted way a brutal crime which profoundly and forever changes him within, while leaving him with his extraordinary powers to change himself without. Now, facing a terrible dilemma of his own making, he embarks on a new career as a budding super hero by night, devoted student by day. But are his amazing powers of transformation a blessing, or the curse of a lifetime?

About The Author

Nicholas Ifkovits was born in Chicago where he was raised until the age of nine, when the family moved into the shadow of O'Hare Airport in the western suburbs. A university graduate with a B.A. in media communications, he worked briefly as a videographer for a network affiliate in Rock Island, Illinois, before achieving success as a writer with his first three novels, **Cloud Drops,** *Other Dreams,* and **Harmony's Angel.** His various novels and screenplays don't fall neatly into one genre, but cover a broad spectrum, from romance/adventure to suspense to fantasy. Get them all and see

> **Strange Change** (ISBN 0-9651700-1-2) is available at bookstores everywhere.